The Ascent

Also by Stefan Hertmans in English translation

War and Turpentine
The Convert

The Ascent

Stefan Hertmans

Translated from the Dutch by
David McKay

PANTHEON BOOKS

NEW YORK

All rights reserved. Published in the United States by Pantheon Books,
a division of Penguin Random House LLC, New York, and distributed in Canada
by Penguin Random House Canada Limited, Toronto. Originally published in the
Netherlands as *De opgang* by De Bezige Bij, Amsterdam, in 2020. Copyright © 2020
by Stefan Hertmans. This translation originally published in hardcover in Great
Britain by Harvill Secker, an imprint of Vintage Publishing, a division
of Penguin Random House Ltd., London, in 2022.

Pantheon Books and colophon are registered
trademarks of Penguin Random House LLC.

**☐ FLANDERS
LITERATURE**

This book was published with the support of
Flanders Literature (www.flandersliterature.be).

Images from the Verhulst family archive, the Tinel family archive and
the author's private collection are used by permission of the families and
Aletta Verhulst, and the author. The photograph of the knobs for the Ghent
Radio Rediffusion Service on page 84 is used by permission of Laurent Stevens; the
photograph of the exhibition *Schaffendes Volk* in Düsseldorf on page 100 is used
by permission of Arkivi; Anselm Kiefer's *Innenraum* (Interior), 1981, on page 156
is used by permission of the Atelier Anselm Kiefer, copyright © Anselm Kiefer;
and the street scene on page 358 is used by permission of
Collection Archives Ghent (SCMS_FO_6584).

Library of Congress Cataloging-in-Publication Data
Names: Hertmans, Stefan, author. McKay, David, [date] translator.
Title: The ascent: a house can have many secrets / Stefan Hertmans;
translated from the Dutch by David McKay.
Other titles: Opgang. English
Description: First American edition. New York: Pantheon Books, 2023
Identifiers: LCCN 2022037766 (print). LCCN 2022037767 (ebook).
ISBN 9780593316467 (hardcover). ISBN 9780593316474 (ebook).
Subjects: LCGFT: Novels.
Classification: LCC PT6466.18.E76 O6413 2022 (print) |
LCC PT6466.18.E76 (ebook) | DDC 839.313/64—dc23/eng/20220808
LC record available at https://lccn.loc.gov/2022037766
LC ebook record available at https://lccn.loc.gov/2022037767

www.pantheonbooks.com

Jacket photograph © David Baker
Jacket design by Jenny Carrow
Original concept by Penguin Random House UK

Printed in the United States of America
First American Edition
2 4 6 8 9 7 5 3 1

Can you see the animal running, always in the same way?

—Alessandro Baricco, *The Barbarians*, translated by Stephen Sartarelli

The Ascent

In the first year of the new millennium, a book came into my hands from which I learned that for twenty years I had lived in the house of a former SS man. Not that I hadn't received any signals; even the notary, the day I visited the house with him, had mentioned the previous occupants in passing, but at the time my thoughts were elsewhere. And maybe I repressed the knowledge, saturated as I had been for years with the harrowing poems of Paul Celan, the testimonies of Primo Levi, the countless books and documentaries that leave you speechless, the inability of a whole generation to describe the unthinkable. Now I saw my intimate memories invaded by a reality I could scarcely imagine, but could push away no longer. It was as if phantoms haunted the rooms I'd known so well; I had questions for them, but they walked straight through me. There was nothing I was so loath to do as write about the kind of person who now began wandering the corridors of my life like a ghost.

I recalled the day I noticed the house for the first time. It must have been in the late summer of 1979. I was walking through a dusty city park bordered by a row of old houses; through the gaps between the fence posts I glimpsed the backyards. Winding through the rusty rails of one of these fences were the thick, near-black branches of a wisteria. A few late clusters of flowers hung low, sprinkled with dust, but their fragrance touched a deep place, taking me back to the overgrown garden of my childhood; curious, I stopped for a better look through the fence. What I saw was a small, neglected urban garden where a slender maple shot up among nondescript clutter; a coal shed with a little leftover firewood under a layer of black dust; some sixteen feet away, the broken window of a rundown annex; and next to that a porch with a high arched window offering a view of the interior, all the way to the other side. I stared straight through the dark, empty rooms. The front windows gleamed with vague light from afar.

A strange excitement ran through me; I walked out of the park and made a U-turn onto a small, dark street in an old part of town. There I found it: a large town house with a pockmarked front, into which moisture had eaten its way over time. With its high windows and flaking front door, the building had known better days; it was obvious it had been vacant for some years. In one window hung a sign, FOR SALE, wrinkled from the damp. It began to drizzle as it can only drizzle in old cities; the copper flap of the mail slot gave a brief, gloomy rattle in a gust of wind.

The district is called Patershol, named after the narrow canal that gave access to the monastery in the Middle Ages, through which the *paters*, the monks, would bring in stocks of food and, as the story goes, smuggle whores inside. The area once belonged to the Counts of Flanders; this historic district is next to a twelfth-century fortress and was for centuries the home of the city's leading dynasties and the haute bourgeoisie. With the rise of the proletariat in the nineteenth century, many stately buildings were replaced with working-class housing. Poverty set in, and over the years the district developed a bad reputation. The narrow alleyways and cul-de-sacs fell into decay until the student revolt of the late 1960s, when bohemian artists settled there. The house I was looking at was on the northeastern edge of the district, on a side street called Drongenhof, not far from where the slow, dark Leie River—the Belgian section of the Lys—flows past the damp old houses.

The crucial decisions in my life have rarely been calculated. Time after time, I've found myself in a kind of dream state, as if an invisible hand is prodding me forward, or as if I've become the pure fool of legend, strolling forth to meet my fate like a headless chicken. I pulled a notepad out of my worn peacoat and jotted down the telephone number. The building was owned by a French-speaking family, the De Potters. That same day, I called Mr. De Potter, a lawyer in the distinguished profession of civil-law notary, who represented the family and was also acting as the real estate agent for the house. We planned my visit for two days later. The family was eager to get several buildings off their hands as soon as possible, before a planned revaluation that would increase their property taxes.

During my viewing of the house, I saw the mildew and damp, the stale water in the flooded cellar, and here and there a moldering piece of furniture, but also the high stairwell, the beautiful brown and pink marble of the fireplace in the front room, the lustrous black Ardennes stone in the long hallway, fringed with gray-veined Carrara marble, the large upstairs rooms with their broad floorboards—the powerful pull of an unknown life.

We went from cellar to attic, an ascent that took more than two hours because Mr. De Potter had to draw up a detailed report on the state of the building, in my presence and with my approval. In the attic, I saw a length of rope dangling from a dusty beam; a few tiles were missing from the high peaked roof. You could see the gray city sky; somewhere I heard the flapping of pigeons' wings.

I have always had a weakness for the odor of damp and decay in old houses. As a child, born not long after the war, I must have walked hand in hand with my mother past houses damaged in bombings, so maybe to me the smell of wet stone and mildew is something like Proust's famous madeleine. When you're a child and still free of memory, even the stench of decay is a source of happiness.

3

I bought the property on impulse, for a sum that would not even buy me a midsize car today. Since I was not wealthy, I borrowed the money interest-free from my father, promising to repay him in monthly installments as soon as I could. In those days, many buyers paid cash; I can still see my father's spotless hands counting out his carefully saved bills onto the notary's calfskin desk blotter.

⁓

The book was entitled *Zoon van een »foute« Vlaming* (Son of a "Bad" Fleming). Everyone knew what *fout* (bad) meant in this context; he had sided with the German occupiers in the war. The first time I saw the austere cover, I was struck by the unconventional "German" quotation marks. The author, Adriaan Verhulst, was a former history professor—in fact, I'd been one of his students myself. He'd earned a dazzling academic reputation, chaired the boards of cultural organizations and the public broadcasting company, written countless scholarly articles, and become well known for both his broad-mindedness and his strict, stubborn personality. Toward the end of his life, he published his difficult confession. When I came to his recollection of the house where he'd spent his childhood, and he mentioned that I was the current resident, I stared in disbelief at the book in my hands. I had just sold that house in the working-class district of Ghent. I decided to go and see Verhulst, but before we could arrange a meeting, he died. I ran up against riddles and silence.

Fine, I thought, then I won't tell the story of an SS man; there are plenty of those already. I'll tell the story of a house and the people who lived there. But even so, it took me years to piece together the story that follows. The few surviving eyewitnesses, who are very old now, recounted their memories to me in detail, as far as they were able. Later, after I had trawled through all my documents and notes, I understood that, oddly enough, the meticulous historian Adriaan Verhulst had never asked to view the records of his father's trial. Nothing was stopping him from facing up to the truth, but he chose not to. If he'd decided otherwise, his portrait of his father might have been less forgiving.

I

And that led me to put off asking questions.

—Dante, *Paradiso*, Canto III

1

On July 10, 1898, Adriaan's father, Willem Verhulst, was born in Berchem, a stone's throw from Antwerp, the city where after many wanderings he died in 1975—barely four years before I bought the house in Ghent where he'd lived for decades.

In a peculiar autobiographical fragment entitled "Wil's Childhood," probably written in prison, he describes it as an omen that he almost came into the world on July 11, when the Flemish commemorate the Battle of the Golden Spurs. In that clash, which took place in 1302 and has been elevated by nationalists into a foundational myth, a few Flemish militias—aided, please note, by French-speaking Walloon soldiers—defeated the army of the French king Philip IV on the Groeningekouter, a field near Kortrijk.

Willem grew up in a large family with nine children: four boys and five girls. He was the youngest and, from birth, his mother's favorite. His father had a diamond-cutting business on Boomgaardstraat, between Berchem and the old Antwerp military hospital, not far from Koning Albertpark. Now, a century after Willem was born, it is an ordinary street with some fairly young trees where a few men, dressed in the Orthodox Jewish manner, are unloading a large truck at the entrance to an underground warehouse. Not many houses have depots at the back; who knows, I think as I walk down the street, maybe this is the house where the diamond cutter once lived. I ask one of the men next to the truck whether this is a warehouse for kosher food; the man asks me why I want to know. I could tell him I'm looking for the childhood home of an SS man, but decide it's better to keep my mouth shut.

Boomgaardstraat means "Orchard Street," and I pass a nursing home for the elderly whose name—Ten Gaarde, "In the Garden"—harks back to that same Arcadian past. The old inn where Willem's father often had one too many is still standing. A coachman is said to have lived in this neighborhood; the smell of horse droppings must have lingered in the streets. I've seen an old etching of a romantic farmhouse here: pollard willows and snow, a thick thatched roof, fields—a scene from a bygone age. These days, a slow, never-ending procession of cars shuffles past, as drab as the souls in Dante's hell.

In the annex behind the house, Willem's sister Caroline, known as Carlo, ran a "dance school for salon dancing." On the table next to the gramophone, the shellac records lay waiting in their thin brown sleeves, each stamped with an image in blue ink. It was all very modern for those days. Sometimes all you could hear was the shuffle of feet across the sand-strewn pine of the floorboards, and the young woman's rhythmic exhortations; toward the end of the lesson, after the music had played for the last time, the children fluttered in and ran back and forth between the couples in black.

One of them was young Willem.

It must have been on one such evening in spring that the four-year-old boy collapsed to the ground. He groaned, rolled his eyes, and made sharp gestures that turned into violent convulsions. He foamed at the mouth; his sisters screamed and called out to their mother, who ran over, saw the boy thrashing, tried to cushion his head, which was banging against the floor, and stuck a finger in his mouth so he wouldn't bite off his tongue. The child was retching and hiccuping; his eyes seemed to bulge out of their sockets. His mother, who knew about febrile convulsions, sent one of the girls to fetch a cloth soaked in cold water and kept the boy in her grip until his spasms subsided. He slowly returned to his senses,

10

babbling and whimpering. His mother picked him up and carried him into the house, where she laid him on the sofa. He fell into a deep sleep; when he awoke, hours later, he was given warm milk and bread with plum jam. He tried to drink but spilled half the cup and started crying again. Half an hour later, he wanted to use the toilet but walked into the door frame. More crying, and then the words "I can't see anymore." His mother ran over, examined him carefully, and saw that his eyes were staring into nothing. She murmured a quick prayer, helped him up onto the wooden board of the latrine in the backyard, and placed her hand on his leg as he relieved himself there. Everything will be fine, my sweet little Wimpie, she told him. Then she carried him to the sofa again, where he fell back to sleep until dusk. By then his father was home; he waved his hand in front of his son's eyes when the boy woke up. One eye followed; the other did not. Maybe that other eye will recover by tomorrow, his father said. He can see out of his right eye, anyway.

But the other eye did not recover. In the months that followed, the boy walked into everything; his head was constantly covered with bumps and scratches, and his knees were often scraped. When he hurried, he fell down the stairs; he misjudged distances and tripped over curbs and doorsteps; he walked into a large crate of potatoes with a protruding nail, which tore open the flesh of his left thigh. Neighbor children teased him by walking a step or two ahead and trying to confuse him, while chanting in chorus, "Here comes little Willem, his blind eye will kill him."

"In any case," he would later write with brazen irony, "what I should have seen, I did not see; but I also saw many things I'd have been better off not seeing, and pretending I hadn't seen a thing was often useful in later life, a habit that was difficult to break."

2

Willem is sitting under the glass canopy behind the house, playing with garnet pebbles and knucklebones. Inside, one of his sisters is playing the piano, the same ditty over and over again. He hears his father singing, *Je crois en toi, Maître de la nature / Semant partout la vie et la fécondité,* a hymn to the Lord's creative power and the fruitfulness of the earth still well known in France as "The Peasant's Creed." His father makes a mockery of the lines paying homage to the Divine, systematically changing "God" to "Beast": "Almighty Beast, who made Creation . . ." The music booms through the house until his mother calls out, Enough of that! The diamond cutter, a devout Darwinist, wants to protect his children from what he calls the "madness of religion." He quotes Voltaire from memory and calls priests "blackshirts" and "coal porters."

Willem has panic attacks when his mother is not around, and won't go to sleep until he has checked underneath his bed. He doesn't want to sit on the board in the outhouse anymore; the foul-smelling black hole fills him with terror. Shadows cast by candlelight make him tremble, and creaky doors send a shudder through him. When lightning flashes, he creeps into a corner, certain a demon is coming for his second eye. His sisters pamper him; sometimes one of them will let him join her in bed— about which he writes, "From then on, women comforted me, even though I was very shy—though some women strenuously deny that."

He becomes a little scamp, although with a sweet nature. At least once a week he is sent to bed without dinner. "So I would slink off to bed as soon as I'd misbehaved to avoid worse punishment." Until the age of six he wears a dress, as is customary in those days for reasons of hygiene, and he plays with dolls. He later recalls tearing them open in search of their internal organs. He also keeps trying to "fix their eyes," so the living room is strewn with eyeless, abandoned dolls.

Even in old age, he could still remember in detail how his mother came into his bedroom one day with two doctors. He even had a perfect recollection of their names: Dr. Van Rechtesteen and Dr. Bayence. He must have been about six years old.

Van Rechtesteen mutters all sorts of incomprehensible things to Willem's mother and then looks around the room. She points at the bedside table. The doctor takes one of Willem's picture books and tears off the thick front cover. Don't, Willem protests, it's my favorite book. The doctor, making shushing sounds, comes toward him, rolls the hard cover into a funnel, holds it over Willem's eye and pours a liquid through it. Willem loses consciousness.

When he awakes, he is lying in bed blindfolded, with thick bandages around his head that smell like disinfectant. He feels a piercing pain throughout his skull and then, groping, finds his mother's hand. He tries to tear off the bandages; his mother has to calm the panicking child. The doctor forbids them to remove the bandages by any means; the stain on the cloth, a vague rust color, almost makes his mother gag. She keeps watch by his bed for weeks, helping him with his bedpan, washing and dressing him, talking to him and reading him stories. He is given food in liquid form and remains in bed, blind, for more than two months. Whenever one of his sisters takes over for an hour or two, he reaches for his mother's hand and, finding her gone, throws a desperate tantrum until she returns.

When the doctor removes the bandages, the treated eye is still shrouded in a thin haze of milky fluid. He uses a small pair of tweezers to remove a few scabs, while the boy whimpers. Then he covers the eye with a smaller bandage and gives Little Wim a pair of dark glasses. *Tranquille, mon gars*, the doctor says soothingly, settle down, everything will be fine. Willem's good eye gradually adjusts to the light. The next day, the doctor returns, removes the bandage, places one hand over Willem's good eye, and asks, What am I holding? The child had seen the bunch of grapes on the table next to the doctor's hand: A bunch of grapes, he cries. Too bad—the doctor is holding a pair of scissors. The one eye is still blind, he tells Wim's mother. We'll have to start from scratch. The child panics; not again, he screeches, not again. He kicks, swings his head back and forth, refuses to calm down. His mother takes him onto her lap, it's all right, she says, hush now.

There will be no second operation; mothers walk a tightrope between perseverance and pity.

⌐

A year later comes his first day of school; the boy is timid and wanders aimlessly around the building, going through the wrong door into the office of the janitor, who promptly whacks him on the head. Blood runs out of his ear, he flees the school, a gendarme finds him and brings him back. An hour later, he is seated at his desk, sniveling and pressing a wad of cotton to his ear.

I loved chestnut trees in blossom, he writes in the exercise book, the twirling helicopters that fell from the maples in the autumn, and hissing streetlights in the mist; I stole fat yellow pears from the orchard and hid my spoils behind the rabbit hutch.

At the age of ten he got into his first fights at his Antwerp school. It was strictly segregated into two sections, one with a mixture of Dutch and

French for the Flemish children and another that was completely Francophone. Even the playground had a dividing line to keep the rowdies on either side away from each other. The Flemish children were objects of contempt, he writes, taunted and jeered at by the bourgeois boys and called all sorts of filthy names in French. We, the sons of the common people, struck back; I could not put up with that kind of humiliation. I have always felt compassion, he adds, for the road workers, the tram conductors and the coachmen. When I ran away from school and stole candy, I would share it with workingmen. With indulgent irony, he writes that "Little Man Wil," as he calls his younger self, never reached the age of reason, "whether because of his holy simplicity of spirit, or the foolishness that you could read all over his impish little face."

3

The diamond cutter has taken to drink. He is wasting away in the gloom of his workshop, but Wim's mother is an enterprising woman. For a long while now, she has been buying small plots of land in the city and selling them at a profit, and the small fortune she has amassed is out of her husband's reach. She uses it to have a large house built on a property with room both for a diamond-cutting workshop and for Carlo's dance school—a house with at least ninety-two rooms, Willem wrote a half-century later. He probably meant twenty-nine, but who's counting, and oh, the size of that gym and that dance studio. At the evening lessons, little Wil is allowed to help the bourgeois girls practice their dance steps. He is a real charmer: a boy with a black eyepatch twirling around the studio with the grace of a ballerina, now and then winning everyone's heart by stumbling, recovering, and continuing to dance.

The fighting at school becomes dramatic, each clash more violent than the last. Now and then, a boy hides a broken bottle or a stick behind his back. Often one of them is so badly hurt he has to be carried off by male nurses. Willem fails algebra, because his grasp of French—the language of instruction—is too weak. He becomes moody and cocky, standing up in class to demand that they be taught in Dutch. Flanders the Lion, he shouts, before charging like a bull at the well-dressed boy who was making fun of him. The school threatens to expel him. His reports get worse and worse; he tosses them into the gutter, steals a blank report from the main office and fills it in with excellent grades himself, until his father, suspicious of the chicken scrawl Wil blames on "the new teacher," discovers the deception. Wil receives a beating that will remain fresh in his memory decades later.

He runs away from school and roams around for a few days, wandering the orchard with a nail on a stick for reaching the low-hanging fruit. He stands at the gates of the girls' school with a bunch of wildflowers, but a nun grabs him by the ear and drags him down the street until he cries. He tries to look up the girls' dresses: "They said that it could blind you, that it was as dangerous as lightning . . ." In his old age, he will think back with a sigh on Mariëtte and Tilly and Eveline, who speak French and wear lace panties, glimpsed with his one good eye.

In the winter he goes with his father at six-thirty in the morning to light the stoves in the workshop and the dance studio. The workmen need coffee, then he has to shine all the dancing shoes. Sometimes, if a dancer is a bit of a clothes horse, he substitutes rabbit droppings for the shoe polish. He enjoys playing tricks on people. I looked like a model boy, he writes, I could act as if butter wouldn't melt in my mouth, I had a terrific childhood.

⁓

Then comes the real lightning bolt. He is thirteen years old when, to everyone's shock, his mother dies. The circumstances are unclear; Willem breaks off his narrative of his childhood with the news of her premature death, without going into detail. "I wander wistfully among the graves in the cemetery, in search of my life"—that's more or less his closing sentence.

It is thanks to one of his children that I, so many decades later, get my hands on a copy of this peculiar memoir. The front cover of the exercise book is illustrated with a picture of an athlete; above that, in both of Belgium's national languages, is the slogan "Behave like a true sportsman."

My eyes keep wandering to the runner's shadow, which looks like a boxer.

At the bottom, ironically enough, is the company name, "Cahiers de Belgique."

4

He wants to be a farmer, or a gardener, something like that—he's not sure why those occupations in particular—as long as he doesn't have to be a diamond cutter with a scratchy throat. His world-weary father sends him to the School of Gardening and Agriculture in Melle, near Ghent. At the time, precious little teaching or learning is going on there. The war is in full swing; in German-occupied Belgium, it is the period of the Von Bissing University.

Moritz Ferdinand Freiherr von Bissing, the general who governed occupied Belgium and an admirer of Rilke and Goethe, founded a Dutch-language university in Ghent in 1916, in complete disregard of Belgian law. This new institution, the Flemish Academy, opened a rift in the academic world. *Flamenpolitik*, the German policy of supporting the Flemish Movement, was seen as a provocation by the Patriot camp, whose priorities were national unity and the primacy of French. But the flamingants, supporters of the Flemish Movement, saw the new institution as a response to their legitimate demand for a university in their own language. There were demonstrations in the Ghent city center; some Flemish professors participated because they refused to collaborate with the occupiers. They carried French signs with slogans demanding their own Dutch-language academy: "*L'université de Gand français!*" Most of them resigned from the Flemish Academy and were replaced by ideologues. The situation could hardly have been any more divisive.

In those days, the Antwerp diamond cutter's son is playing truant and wandering the streets of Ghent. He visits student clubs sympathetic to the flamingants and joins the notorious Groeninger Guard, a fast-growing activist group. Their charismatic leader is August Borms, who addresses the organization on February 11, 1917. Even at this early date, the Guard's objectives are to create an official division between Flanders and Wallonia and to "drive out the fransquillons," the French-speaking elite in Flanders. Borms is an inspiring speaker: "We demand that the power in our hands now be exercised to remove elements that are undesirable on Flemish territory and therefore, in general mental and moral terms, can be nothing but unwholesome . . . Away with all the fransquillons! . . . Send anyone who still objects across the border! . . . Away with all who oppose us!"

Willem is one of the crowd of overexcited young men roaring and chanting along. He sits in pubs until late at night and chases girls, hot for the dreaded lightning under their skirts.

One spring day, Willem is taking the tram as he often does. The Germans carry out frequent, aggressive sweeps; the mood is tense, and everyone is nervous. Willem gets up and goes to the open rear balcony for a smoke. In the buttonhole of his jacket, he is wearing an emblem then popular in the Flemish Movement: a Belgian cockade with a Flemish lion in the middle. An elderly gentleman notices the cockade, flies into a rage, tears it off Willem's jacket and cries, *Maintenant c'est fini tout cela!* Enough of all that now! The bourgeois man's aggression sets off something deep inside the carefree boy. Before his eyes he sees the fights in primary school, he hears the humiliating French-language insults echo through his head, and for a moment he comes close to losing all control. He is on the verge of punching the man but, just in time, unclenches his young fists and jumps recklessly off the moving tram, landing on the stony street and twisting his ankle.

Later, he will often describe this as the moment he begins to loathe the Belgian state. Around the same time, he learns that his elder brother Edward has died at the front, but that seems far away to him. Willem himself has been declared unfit for military service because of that blind eye. What could those French-speaking officers on the Yser do with a Flemish cyclops like me, he whispers into a girl's ear with a soft chuckle.

⌒

By this time he is a lanky young man, almost six feet tall, with long black hair. In the one blurry photo that has survived, he looks more like a Neil Young born before his time than an early twentieth-century Flemish activist. The patch he wears over one eye gives him an air of mystery that appeals to girls with intellectual ambitions and intimidates his friends a little. When he enters a pub, everyone looks up. He becomes fascinated with films; in a small cinema, he watches a decomposing print of Alfred

Machin's anti-war classic *Maudite soit la guerre*. A week later, he sees a German propaganda film about the noble duty to wage war and comes out confused; the much-discussed film about the Battle of the Somme is not yet being shown in Ghent, but he hears stories about it. He has no more than a vague notion of what is going on at that moment in the trenches of Flanders and northern France; not much gets through to him. He is pelted from all sides with contradictory opinions; he hears someone call the newspapers "the lying press." Well then, no more papers, he decides; there's plenty of wisdom to be gleaned on the streets.

The Allies are mired as deep in the blood-soaked clay as the occupying forces; the catastrophe of Passchendaele is unfolding. In late August, the name Langemark keeps coming up again and again in conversation. Why Langemark, what happened in Langemark in 1914, where is that, Langemark, is it near Kortemark? he asks with a laugh. You shouldn't drink so much, a girlfriend says, putting her arm around his shoulders. When he meets other students, he is reserved and often timid at first, but once he gets going, he tangles himself up in muddled theories and bangs his fist on the table. He sees a newspaper article about the October Revolution; everyone is talking about Mensheviks and Bolsheviks. He hears about plans, said to have been made back in 1912, to found a "purely Flemish Party," the Vlaams Blok or Flemish Bloc. The Western world is collapsing, he hears someone say, a university student wearing a funny cap. Edmond Vandermeulen is a middle-class youth who joins Willem for a couple of nights of carousing, a man he'll run into again later, though he has no way of knowing that. By dawn, Willem is shouting Flemish nationalist slogans after his departing friend. Then he finds himself a dark corner in the last grubby wartime pub, which is serving gin made from rotten potato peels and fodder beets, wicked stuff that gives him a splitting headache for days.

His teachers at the agricultural school see little of him; he prefers to wander the city, debating the Flemish struggle until deep into the night with his companions from the Groeninger Guard. When he has a hangover, he sometimes sits in the botanical garden and daydreams. The controversy surrounding the Dutch-language university leads to a steep drop in enrollment at the agricultural school as well. Teachers fail to show up, class times become irregular. His motivation suffers; he goes on wandering the city at night, uncertain what to do with himself. He finds work in a café for a couple of weeks. I'm a friend of August Borms, he boasts. That helps when you're looking for a job.

From some meeting hall, he steals a signed photograph of his hero. I later found this photo, torn and yellowed, the frame and glass broken, when I cleared out the house in Drongenhof, but it didn't catch my attention then, and I threw it into the dumpster parked in front of the door, with the rest of the garbage.

5

When his father finds out that his son has been frittering away his time, he contacts the horticultural school in Vilvoorde. He tells Willem he has to leave Ghent and register at this new institution; in the middle of the war, he must abandon his city of Flemish heroes and start over in a northern suburb of Brussels. He finds a room above a bakery just outside the town center. Vilvoorde is still a rural place in those days; a horse-drawn tram runs to the school. The Advanced Institute for Horticulture is still there today. You can see it from the train on the way from Brussels to Antwerp, a large brick building with white limestone lintels and a large grassy field like that of an English public school. Willem is happy there, without the pressure of all those nights of carousing with his friends in Ghent.

His new lodgings entitle him to a quarter-loaf of bread every morning from the bakery, a considerable perk in those times of poverty and rationing. Whenever he comes downstairs from his attic room and leaves through the side door, he sees the baker's wife at the counter. He is drawn to her; he joins the hungry people in the soup line and regularly brings her a portion of the thin, unappetizing stuff, which she gratefully accepts. He makes her laugh, he flirts with her, and one day he asks her out, stroking her inner arm and saying, See you tonight?

Elsa Meissner—a sensible woman tired of her uneventful life, with a husband who leaves their bed every night to work and then sleeps until late afternoon every day—is overwhelmed. To her own amazement, she creeps up to Willem's attic room that night. Intimate scenes, suppressed sighs and hasty fumbling in his fourth-floor garret, while below in the cellar, the baker is kneading dough eked out with poor-quality potato starch. Elsa is thirty, Willem not quite twenty. She is of German Jewish descent, tall and thin, with dark red hair and freckled arms. In bed, she tells Willem she's cold; he throws his arms around her and says, Aw, you have goosebumps, playing the clown because he can't resist the melancholy note in her laugh. Toward morning, she creeps back down to her marital bedroom, flushed and giddy, and slips into her own bed just before her husband comes up from the cellar, exhausted. It is twilight, the steps creak, the baker lies beside his wife and snores. She waves away Willem, who stands smiling and naked in the doorway: You're out of your mind, go back to your room.

The romance proves to be more than a brief escapade; their nocturnal lovemaking becomes less intense but slower, deeper. They cling to each other for hours, with occasional gasps as if surfacing for air. While she lies in his arms, his voice is a soft rumble in her ear, telling her of his political ideals, describing his secret meetings in Brussels. He has made friends with the future collaborator and Flemish nationalist leader Hendrik Elias, now barely sixteen years old, through the local chapter of the Groeninger Guard, and no longer makes much of an effort to hide his Greater Germanic sympathies. When Germany capitulates and the Belgian state starts tracking down collaborators to put them on trial, he is an object of suspicion, because he went around boasting about being a personal acquaintance of August Borms and a radical activist and declaring that Belgium was headed for collapse. What do you have to flee from? Elsa says with a laugh. Your own big mouth? He confesses that for some time he's been the secretary of the Flemish Propaganda Office in Vilvoorde and he fears arrest. Elsa stares up at the ceiling, stunned.

The rumors swell that activists are being arrested and put on trial. The poet Wies Moens is accused of collaboration and sedition. The net is closing. We have to run for it, Willem says, we have to go to the Netherlands; I don't want to be picked up by the goddamn Belgicists. He is nervous and irritable, determined not to fall into their hands. Elsa sees him standing there, takes a deep breath, and says, I'll come with you. Leaving her baker behind at his kneading board, she steps out onto the deserted street with her lover. Half a mile further on, a few traveling companions are waiting for them. There she goes—an adulterous Jewish woman on a romantic escape with a group of jittery flamingants. They have to cross the border as soon as they can; in the Netherlands, they will be safe.

They cycle to Antwerp, a group of twelve young people, and spend the night on the floor of his sister Carlo's dance school. Another of his sisters, a committed suffragette who is sympathetic to the Flemish Movement, gives them food for their journey and some extra clothes. She says to Elsa in German, I hope that being with you will calm my brother down a little, please try to wear him out. Elsa's only reply is a wistful smile. At first light they ride off, pedaling against the north wind, crossing the border near the Kalmthout woods and collapsing on the roadside in relief just past the boundary marker. Willem is overjoyed; he dances and cries out, *Belgicist buggers!* The others worry about what will become of them.

———

It's not clear how or why, but they wind up in The Hague.

Willem's time in Ghent has turned him into a cinephile; he can talk for hours about movies, directors, and the opportunities cinema provides for propaganda that could liberate his people from the yoke of their Francophone oppressors. Expressionism! he cries. Jakob van Hoddis! he shouts. The floodwaters are rising! The hats will fly off pointy bourgeois heads! The railway trains will tumble from the bridges!

The drunkards of The Hague split their sides laughing at this likeable clown.

He's a smooth talker, good at winning people over. He also has initiative and a nose for opportunity. He meets a man who ran a small wartime cinema and gains permission to select and screen one movie a week there, with an introductory talk for the few moviegoers who turn up. He gives lectures on Belgium, because the Dutch don't know the first thing about it. You had a nonaggression pact with Emperor Wilhelm from 1908 onward, he snarls, while we bled and suffered because of our French bourgeoisie—you left us in the lurch. He quotes the opening lines of *The Spanish Brabanter*, a canonical play by the Dutch Golden Age poet Bredero, as evidence that Antwerp is superior to Amsterdam. The skeptical moviegoers shake their heads; afterward, some of them press a few guilders into the hands of the "sweet Flemish boy." He makes sure he always has just enough money for him and Elsa to get by. He teaches her to smoke and drink; they sometimes dance in working-class pubs until late at night. She loves the smell of his sweat and laughs in his arms, and in bed she begs him for more. You've finally made a woman of me, she says, standing at the window of their rented back room in the twilight, and he says, Before I knew you, I wasn't even a man. They are infatuated with each other.

When asked whether he's glad his country was liberated, he replies, Flanders is still far from liberated, just you wait. His southern accent seems to thicken as he says, Our time will come. His friends in The Hague don't know what to think, and he argues with Elsa, who tells him he should learn to keep his mouth shut.

Sometime in 1919, he meets Richard De Cneudt, a Flemish activist and poet in exile who lives in Rotterdam and gives regular lectures. During the war years, De Cneudt was an energetic advocate of Dutch-language education in Flanders, fighting within the Brussels school system for the correct application of language laws and gradually becoming more radical after he realized that the authorities in the Belgian capital showed arrogant disregard for the legislation. He became a supporter—a champion, even—of the *Flamenpolitik* of the German occupiers and a member of the Council of Flanders, an organization that strove toward a unilateral declaration of independence from Belgium. He crossed over to the wrong side of the law, and was convicted of collaboration after the war. He escaped to the Netherlands, where he became a first-rate French teacher. The defender of Flemish culture and the young zealot soon become good friends. They talk to each other about movies and books.

Oh, I almost forgot: Richard De Cneudt's poems. My God. While clearing out the house in Drongenhof, I threw them into that same dumpster in front of the house. At least fifteen copies. Yes, they'd been damaged by the leaky skylight; they were worn and ripped and full of stains. His style was sometimes sentimental, sometimes jingoistic. But all the same, it was poetry.

You flutter gracefully through my house
The way a dream-sound softly soughs,
a May-time whisper,
and meanwhile, in my shy, scared fashion,
pining away with tender passion,
breathless, I listen . . .

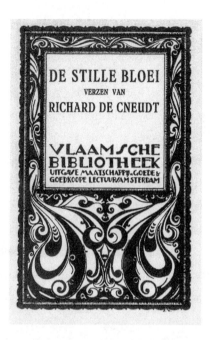

An acquaintance of Elsa puts them in touch with a Protestant group: idealists trying to find housing for the many Belgian refugees, often without much insight into why they fled. Everyone seems to be talking about a pacifist and Christian idealist named Kees Boeke, who has recently returned from England; his convictions are shared by Willem and Elsa's new friends, who introduce them to the pastor Hilbrandt Boschma, the author of countless brochures in the series Light and Love.

One topic that Boschma discusses with the young Belgian is the link between the Christian message and idealistic communism. Willem, who has not forgotten his father's mockery of religion in any form, is at first thrown into even greater confusion; one day, out of the blue, he announces that he intends to become a Protestant. He has heard about Frederik van Eeden's utopian commune, Walden, and wonders if it still exists, and if

29

he could become a gardener there. This leads to a series of open-hearted conversations with Kees Boeke. As the two men meet more and more frequently, Boeke becomes intrigued with the young Fleming. Meanwhile, to the distress of his new friends, Willem goes on thundering about "blowing up Belgium—death to all fransquillons!" One evening, when the conversation grows heated, he protests that his ideology is really Christian-anarcho-communist, but that he also intends to remain a republican and a Flemish nationalist. This cocktail sets off new debates among the members of the Light and Love group.

And yes, the photograph below was also lying in the cluttered attic when I bought the house. It shows Kees Boeke's baker, who delivered door-to-door, with the young Princess Beatrix, later Queen of the Netherlands, seated on the back of his scooter. Taken in 1946 or thereabouts, it's even signed by Boeke.

It may have been sent by post in the late 1940s.

"For my faraway Flemish friend."

He had no way of knowing that by then Willem was behind bars.

A few months later, Willem proposes to Elsa. They have only a few guests at the ceremony, which takes place before her first marriage is officially dissolved. Not long afterwards—it must have been sometime in 1922—Elsa develops severe cramps and a fever. She is told to stay in bed. When the pain grows worse, Willem, who is watching over her, sends for the doctor. Elsa's symptoms are vague but troubling; he can tell that much from the doctor's pensive silence as he examines her. Sometimes she has a brief recovery but then returns to bed and remains there for days. The costs of her medical care send Willem in search of additional income. A few members of Light and Love take in Elsa and care for her. Willem cycles far and wide in the hope of finding work. Sometimes he is gone for days; when he returns, he finds his wife much thinner and bedridden.

We have no idea how, step by small step, he ended up so far from The Hague, but at some point he must have met a family from Oud-Zevenaar, near Arnhem, in the east of the Netherlands. It's quite possible the flamboyant Boschma referred Willem to a fellow pastor: Adriaan Johannes Wartena.

6

1925. A new name crops up in conversation: that of the man who tried to overthrow the Weimar Republic from a beer hall in Munich in the putsch of November 1923. His militias wear armbands with an insignia from the Hindu religion. They salute by extending their arms. Someone claims this was the custom of the ancient Roman guards. Nonsense, someone else replies, it's all made up, nothing but theatrics, and poor theatrics at that. Their public appearances are steeped in raw violence and intimidation; at the same time, there is something exciting about it all, something new and unprecedented. Expressionism in word and act! The floodwaters are rising! The weather vanes are squeaking in the wind!

The new leader's speeches are often only half-comprehensible through the hysterical rise and fall of his voice. An electric energy surges through the loudspeakers in the yellowish glow of the radios. The loudmouth was sentenced to five years in prison for his failed coup, but was a free man again after less than nine months in prison. His detention did not diminish his restless energy. Quite the opposite: he dictated a book to a fellow prisoner on what he calls "his struggle."

Now he's resumed his screeching, as loud as ever. This fast-rising political whirlwind provokes fear and fascination: contradictory reports, sensational headlines and blaring newspaper vendors; bar fights and scuffles on the steps of theaters. Pastor Boschma tries to reassure the group, telling them it will all blow over. But politics seeps into personal life, and even the most intimate conversations become tangled up with the daily news. No one is safe from the general feeling that everything is interconnected. Not much later, the first windows are smashed in

Germany; the old Hindu symbol is everywhere; fistfights turn into roundups, arguments into organized violence; a new order emerges. Society splits into two camps, for and against, and betrayals within families threaten to tear them apart. In the quiet village of Oud-Zevenaar, the Wartenas have quickly made up a bed for their new arrival, the invalid married to Wim, that nice young man from Belgium who has such stirring conversations with the pastor about life and religion. Wim has gone to The Hague to fetch Elsa. He doesn't have the money for the train, so he borrows a horse and cart from the pastor's in-laws in Arnhem. The return journey, through the woods and fields of the Dutch heartland, leaves Elsa utterly exhausted. They spend the night in a small inn in Zeist, where Elsa lies awake half the night moaning in pain. The next day, Willem decides to take a detour through the forest near Woudenberg so that he can show his ailing wife the famous pyramid there, a monument to the Battle of Austerlitz. Look, Elsa! Napoleon! Heroic courage and Moravian nights! But she has grown so weak that she does not listen and barely opens her eyes.

Adriaan Wartena, aged fifty-two, has been a pastor in Zevenaar for more than twenty years. Three years ago, he and his wife Maria ten Bosch celebrated their silver anniversary. The two of them are caring for Elsa with the help of a young woman from the neighborhood. A doctor diagnoses her with cervical cancer. Looking after her is anything but an easy task; the vaginal bleeding and internal inflammation are appalling, and the cancer appears to have spread. Elsa is in unbearable pain, has lost control of her bladder, eats almost nothing, and sometimes loses consciousness for hours on end. She receives injections of novocaine and iodine, which relieve the pain for a couple of hours and allow her to sleep. At night, the rest of the household can hear her moaning in the front room; Willem usually sits at her bedside until almost morning.

During the day, he works as a gardener for the Von Gimborns, who own an ink factory in Zevenaar—a job arranged for him by Wartena. He rakes leaves, trims trees and bushes, neatens the borders, chops and saws wood, and earns next to nothing. He rents a small, damp room near the Catholic church, barely large enough for a chair and a cot. Elsa remains in the pastor's house. Her daily care has now been entrusted to a young neighbor, Miss Harmina, the daughter of a gentleman farmer who has served as an elder of the local Protestant congregation. When Willem comes by after supper, he sometimes finds Miss Harmina still at his wife's bedside, praying. Good evening, Harmina, he says, staring at the floor, and she says, May God be with you, your wife is dying. He sits beside her; she recites Psalm 23, her own version.

E'en though I pass through darkest death,
fear's clutches cannot hold me,
for Thou art ever by my side,
Thy presence will enfold me.

She reaches out with one hand to smooth the crumpled sheets just as Willem is doing the same, cautiously, trying not to wake the sleeping woman. Their hands touch. Hers, smoothing in the opposite direction, slides over his unexpectedly; startled, they pull away, but for an instant he feels his mother's hand again, from those months when he lay blind in bed with nothing but her touch. For one bone-chilling minute he can't see a thing; he feels his way back into his seat, but his vision will not return, he gasps for air. What's wrong, the young woman asks, and he says something incomprehensible in that strange dialect of his, he tugs at the patch in front of his blind eye, his hand shakes, the young woman springs to her feet.

Willem, for God's sake, what's wrong?

I can't see a thing.

He gropes for her hand.

The woman lays her hand on his.

He slowly settles down. Already, vague outlines are re-emerging, as if he is returning from the underworld and has to adjust to the dim light in the front room. Because he is still panting, she holds on to his hand. He's afraid to meet her eyes; she's bewildered by the childish helplessness of this large, striking man. They remain seated like that for a while, too shy to withdraw their hands. Outside, a cart bumps down the street with a barrel of liquid manure; the clattering fades into the distance, the woman in bed makes a rattling sound in her uneasy sleep. Once he's caught his breath again, he looks the young woman in the face with that strange single eye of his. How much emotion can one eye express? He tries to smile, but what she sees is a grimace, a grin. Something cuts through her, fear and dream interlaced; she looks from Elsa to him. It's late, she says, I have to go home. He stands up with her, stumbles over one leg of the bed, and almost falls on top of his sick wife. Harmina flees the room, leaving him behind alone, with dusk shifting into shapelessness and the rasp of that terrible breathing from the bed.

7

The man I hope to get to know is slowly coming into focus.

He walks through the village as evening falls, a disheveled loner from Belgium with an older Jewish wife who is deathly ill. In Oud-Zevenaar, the rumors spread. Sometimes a lace curtain is pulled aside for a moment; a door opens, just a crack. Can you imagine, he looked at me with that weird face of his, what would you do, gracious, what a freak. Farmer Wijers's girl had better watch out for herself, sitting there all day beside that Jewess's sickbed, shouldn't she be helping out on the farm, Pastor Wartena is much too kind for his own good, what can you do with a fellow like that, have you seen that one eye staring, it's enough to give you shivers, can't they stay down there in their monkey country, we've got troubles of our own up here, God help us, and will you look at that, what do you know, there's that featherhead Mientje walking side by side with that man, deep in conversation, what's going on there, nothing good, I expect, right you are.

Mientje, as everyone calls Harmina, cannot erase the image from her memory: Willem trembling, stuttering, groping desperately for her hand, and for a few moments, blind. He has shaken her, and her tender feelings for this strange character are new to her—frustrating, even. She has always kept men at a distance, never letting herself get mixed up with them. In any case, she certainly shouldn't be thinking about married men; that's intolerable. Still, she is already twenty-eight years old, a bright, sensitive woman with a strong character. Four years ago, when Pastor Wartena celebrated his silver anniversary, she made a speech that won the admiration of everyone in the Reformed community. Then she presented the pastor and his wife with a dinner service, a gift from the local business associations, to vigorous applause from all the guests. Pastor Wartena remarked, My goodness, Mientje, you'd make an excellent pastor yourself.

But anyway, she has to hop into the old cart every day to work in the fields, and on Sundays they go out for a ride in the good chaise. Why would you throw your life away?

She has been taking English lessons in secret from the village schoolteacher, at her own request. In her reverence for Pastor Wartena's idealism, Mientje has taken it into her head that she really should become a pastor herself; she hopes to enroll at a university and earn the required degree. The villagers gossip. Doesn't she have a boyfriend, then, with all her fancy talk? It's high time.

No, a life of hard work on a farm, there in the remote Liemers region, is the last thing she wants. She reads pamphlets about women's emancipation and suffragettes. When clumsy farm boys make eyes at her, she feels repelled. What is she supposed to do, then? She isn't sure. She fills her days by helping the pastor, who always has plenty to do—if not for his peace movement Church and Life, then for the Protestant Teetotallers Union or the building society, or else he's organizing lectures to promote Protestant education or helping some poor devil who's fallen on hard times. She also visits the sick and runs errands for indigent old villagers, hurrying hither and thither as her parents look on in disbelief. On weekends, she takes singing lessons; she wants to learn to lead the psalm-singing at church. But her elderly music teacher talks to her about Bach, Buxtehude and Heinrich Schütz, and teaches her to read music. He gives her a present: the score of the aria "Ombra mai fu" from Handel's opera *Xerxes*. Her father works himself up into a temper; with all that nonsense going on, how does she expect to build a good life for herself?

How can she help it if one day she goes to pick up a box of brochures at the Von Gimborn house and sees Willem standing in the garden with a rake, and notices him looking her way, or if he comes up to her and asks if she'd like to walk with him along the dyke that evening. How can she help it if on that walk he puts his arm around her shoulders and they go on together like that in silence, both too shaken and racked with guilt to say a word.

Elsa is doing poorly. It would be a terrible tangle for her to die in the Netherlands. Willem has been in touch with his sisters; Carlo and Suzanne tell him they're willing to take Elsa in when she arrives, but she'll have to go on to the hospital without delay. She'll receive better care in Antwerp than in Arnhem.

It is the last evening he sees Mientje before returning to Belgium with

Elsa. He's heard he no longer runs any risk of prosecution, if he ever really did. Their goodbyes are awkward and confusing; they part in silence, she with a deep feeling of guilt, he with a thrill of forbidden excitement.

~

Now he is sitting at Elsa's deathbed in Antwerp.

He watches the delirious woman waste away, sees her skinny hand claw at the felt blanket, thinks of Mientje's hand on the sheet, thinks of his mother's hand, sits in gloomy silence, looks on as she gasps out her last breath, carefully slides the wedding ring off her cold finger and puts it on his own. On the eleventh of July, of all days—the Flemish day of celebration, one day after his twenty-eighth birthday—Elsa Meissner dies. She is buried in the Berchem cemetery; Willem is the only mourner. Her humble grave is a mound with a wooden cross; she was no longer an observant Jew, and a cross was cheapest.

Willem leaves a geranium on the fresh soil; within three days, the rain has flattened it.

He will wear Elsa's ring for the rest of his life.

Ninety-three years after that day, I am holding her death announcement, which informs me that Elsa was born in New York on April 8, 1887. On a visit to New York not long afterward, I leaf through the phone book. There are so many Meissners that trying to track down her relatives that way would be like looking for a needle in a haystack. I consult the Genealogy Institute at the Center for Jewish History. They inform me in writing that Elsa Meissner is not listed in their databases. How she ever ended up married to a baker in Vilvoorde—not to mention fleeing from there with a Flemish boy who, in the Second World War, would become a Jew hunter for the *Waffen-SS*—cannot be determined, it seems.

« En aldaar zal geen nacht zijn, en zij zullen geen kaars noch licht der zon van noode hebben , want de Heere God verlicht ze, en zij zullen als Koningen heerschen in alle eeuwigheid. »
OPENBARING 22-5.

Mijnheer WILLEM VERHULST

zijn Broeders, Zusters, Behuwd-Zusters en Broeders

melden U met innige droefheid het smartelijk verlies dat hen treft door het afsterven van zijne teergeliefde echtgenoote en hunne beminde behuwd-zuster

Mevrouw Elsa VERHULST geb. MEISSNER

geboren te New York (V. S. N. A.) op 8 April 1887 en overleden te Berchem, op 11 Juli 1926, na eene lange en pijnlijke ziekte.

De teraardebestelling op de begraafplaats te Berchem, heeft in allen eenvoud plaats gehad.

Berchem, 14 Juli 1926.
Groote Steenweg, 3.

Drukk A Bastlaens.

Edm Bastlaens-Ruys Begraf Tel 660 00

8

Now that he's back in Berchem, he soon finds a job. His brother-in-law Oscar Schamp arranges for him to work at MEGA, a shop selling electrical goods, domestic appliances and lighting equipment. It specializes in bulk orders for small businesses and wealthy customers who own several properties. Equipped with a company car, he "takes to the road," becoming a "traveling light salesman," as he says with a laugh. It gives him a euphoric sense of freedom; every morning, he loads his wares into the back seat and rattles halfway across the country and back, enjoying the chance conversations, working hard to make sure everyone likes him, and smoking cigarettes the way he's seen in movies. After a while, he can afford to visit an eye doctor. It's never become clear to me what condition his blind eye was in. In later years, he will always wear glasses with one matte lens, and those who see him remove his glasses for a moment will observe a "cloudy" eye in which the pupil is barely visible. Even in the good eye, his vision is weak; he tells anyone who will listen that it's because of the hardships "in the war." The optician has glasses custom-made for Mr. Willem Verhulst, sales representative/*commis-voyageur*—that's right, he has impressive business cards now too.

Barely two months after Elsa's meager funeral, he drives to Oud-Zevenaar. He parks the car near the Catholic church and walks to the Von Gimborn house, where everyone is a little surprised to see him. Well, well, how nice of you to drop by, Willem, such terrible news about your wife, still so young, our condolences, my boy. He hardly seems to listen, even though he's the one who came to "say hello"; he is restless, making a show of smoking flat, yellowish cigarettes. He visits the pastor, who gives him a heartfelt welcome. The pastor's wife brews East Frisian tea: such stories, so terrible, what a life, and how wonderful that you've found a profession, there you are, my lad, and oh, look, here's Mientje Wijers paying an unexpected visit.

The shock is visible on both their faces; that doesn't escape the elderly couple. Mientje stammers that she can come back later and is halfway out of the door again, but the pastor's wife stops her: Now, Mien, won't you stay for a cup of tea with us? She can't help thinking there's something comical about the thick lenses of Willem's new glasses; to be honest, she preferred him with the eyepatch, like a pirate. She tries to keep herself from giggling but bursts into foolish laughter, is mortified, and hiccups, pressing her hand to her pursed lips.

Behind the Wijerses' lovely rustic house is a large barn with an old millstone in front of it. Willem told her he would wait for her there after nightfall. He is already standing there when she comes outside. As she starts to say hello, he throws his arms around her. Let's go for another stroll, he says. I don't know . . . Her voice is unsteady, and seeing her confusion, he blurts out, Mientje, will you marry me? Will I *what*? she says, and he says, I'm asking you to marry me . . . his southern accent growing thicker by the second. But Wim, she says, why are you talking like that, so vulgar, what's wrong, you're acting so strange, no, don't, not out on the street here, any moment now my father will see us, your wife's body is still practically warm, what are you thinking, let go of me, I don't know . . . She flees into the house; after hanging around by the millstone a little while longer, he returns to his car and drives the whole one hundred and twenty-five miles in the dark back to Berchem, arriving home in the middle of the night. The next day he oversleeps and gets a talking-to from "Nuncle Schamp."

He starts to write her letters—ungainly epistles, riddled with crossings-out and solecisms, but she's so tickled by his naive scribbles that every time she reads them she bursts into laughter; she just can't help herself. She doesn't reply—she's a sensible girl—but she does hold on to the letters, like a nest egg. She asks the postman to leave the letters for her in the hole in the millstone next to the barn: she'll find them there. The old postman gives her a pondering look and says, So you're letting someone get his hooks into you after all, are you, Mien? I'd watch out for that fellow. But he dutifully leaves the love letters that follow in the hole in the millstone, with a small rock over the opening so that old Wijers won't see them.

Two months later, there's Willem again, at a time announced in advance in one of his letters. It's dusk, she comes out of the house, you can hear the cattle in the shed, a farmer cycles by, calls out, how do you do, Mien, then sees that weird Belgian standing by the barn. There, where the old millstone is sinking into the earth, Willem takes her by the hand and proposes to her again. He clasps her hand and says, This way I'll be able to see you all the time. She smiles and is silent; she looks into that one eye of his, shrugs, laughs again and says nothing, but it's a nothing that means consent, that much is clear to him.

When old Wijers hears from his daughter that she intends to marry "that Belgian ding-a-ling," less than six months after the death of his Jewish wife, he bursts out in Old Testament wrath. His fists pound, his voice bellows, and her mother starts screeching too, in the vain hope that it will calm her husband down. Mientje flees outside with her hands over her ears.

Now, at last, she writes Willem a letter, telling him he should forget her. But the ding-a-ling from Antwerp will not let up. He keeps writing, odd missives packed with stupid jokes and puns, then stories about his job. They can live in Berchem, he tells her; he makes enough money, and Antwerp is the most beautiful city in the Low Countries, Bredero said so. Come spring, he returns to Oud-Zevenaar and waits for her once again at the millstone; this time, he has asked her if he can go inside and speak to the farmer. Mien dreads the meeting. Her father has never been much for conversation, let alone for changing his mind or seeing shades of gray. The old man is all set to give that Fleming a hefty piece of his mind, but when tall, long-haired Willem enters, all cleaned up with stylish new spectacles on his snout, greets old Wijers with a courtly air and even plants a theatrical kiss on Mrs. Wijers's hand, something happens: an energy surges into the room that changes everything, just like that, simple, that's how things go, look at his daughter over there, biting her nails like a girl of sixteen, oh, Mien, are you out of your senses. But ah well, it's obvious really, nothing to be done, the foolish thing is smitten, high time someone took her off the street before any other accidents happen, you know how it is, God almighty, Harmen, yes, Harmen would have been the name of his first son, Harmen Wijers, a son to be proud of, a gentleman farmer like himself, but then came that . . . baby girl, that daughter of his, and in his pigheadedness he said to his wife, By God, if Harmen wasn't meant to be, then we'll call this one Harmina, our almost-son, and now she's turned out twice as stubborn as a boy, the Lord wounds but He seldom heals, the way he sees it. Christ, that farmer is as gruff and surly as any character in a dog-eared rural novel; his starry-eyed daughter has pearls of sweat on her downy upper lip; the suitor, rattling away in his Antwerp accent, has seen too many movies and is much too sly and congenial to start a fight or make a good old-fashioned biblical scene; and now Farmer Wijers sees a conciliatory smile on his wife's face—women, they're all alike—and Christ, after half an hour the farmer agrees to the match with a wordless nod, or no, not agrees, he'll never agree, not if his life depends on it. He admits defeat, that's all, he gives up, on this whole absurd situation, he steps outside and slams the door behind him. Surrender doesn't take a lot of words. And anyway, he has animals to feed.

A month later the gentleman farmer, in his best suit, visits what he calls the "tawdry" city of Antwerp to "apprise himself of the circumstances" under which his daughter will live. There he is offered tawdry biscuits with his tea and many other tawdry treats he doesn't care for. He bites his tongue when Willem serves white wine with the food: German *waain*, he says in that Flemish accent of his, only German *waain*, none of that French slop in this house, I'm sure you understand. He's the only one laughing; the others stare down at their blue-rimmed plates. The old man drinks nothing but water and tea. He suffers through the afternoon and walks back with his wife to the grand concourse of Antwerp's Central Station, wondering what that pompous palace is good for when all that really matters is catching your train. Tawdry Belgians. He is stoic as he boards the evening train, but he curses his luck when a technical failure leaves them stranded somewhere near Utrecht and he has to book a room for the night in that sinful city.

—

Before the year of 1927 is out, Willem Verhulst marries Harmina Margaretha Wijers. Willem has his hair cut short and buys a smart black suit for his wedding day. The photograph shows the triumphant Willem surrounded by a large group, with his wife, five years older, next to him, dressed in a tasteful, serious-minded ensemble, and to her left, on the far right in the photo, the scowling farmer, still infuriated that his daughter is marrying the Belgian ding-a-ling.

The new couple moves into a house in Berchem, just a few minutes' walk from Boomgaardstraat, where Willem grew up.

9

Four months later. Not far from the Wijers family farm is a "natural pool," a pond called De Breuly. It's become a recreation area, also known as the "drowned village." According to legend, the dyke once broke and a whole village was inundated; on Christmas night, the eldest locals said, you could still hear the church bells ringing underwater. Willem walks there with Mientje one Sunday after visiting his in-laws. It's almost sunset; low-flying swallows and swarms of mosquitoes dance over the water. He takes something out from underneath his jacket.

What is that, Willem . . .

He shows her a pistol. Mientje stares open-mouthed at the gun in his hand.

Where did you get that horrid thing, Willem, throw it away.

My thoughts exactly, he says, and he flings the weapon into the water, sending the moorhens flapping into the air with shrill squawks.

Willem, what on earth is going on? You must tell me. Where did that thing come from? You know I hate weapons—

Oh, well, he says, I once agreed to take out Cardinal Mercier, a Flemish-hating fransquillon papist. Someone gave me that gun and promised to pay me after I killed him. But I kept thinking about what Kees Boeke always says, and now that Mercier's dead anyway . . .

And to top it all off he starts crying. Mientje stares at him, speechless.

Then she throws her arms around him.

Without a word, they walk back to the farm.

I visited Oud-Zevenaar myself recently, because one of Willem and Mientje's elderly daughters had told me about the place. The weather was bleak, and as I crossed Willem and Mientje's dyke, looking out over the endless pastures and fields that stretched into the distance, the prosaic buildings scattered here and there, I was overcome by a great sense of loss. I stood staring at the millstone by the barn, as if it were covering up all the baffling behavior that Willem had left me with. Now there's another stone on top of it, an angular one in several colors. It's not clear why it's covering up the hole in the millstone; maybe someone once twisted his ankle there.

Now there's a shop in the barn where you can buy organically grown fruits and vegetables; a few people are standing around, talking about the weather, which is much too mild for the time of year. Next to that is the lovely farmhouse where Harmina grew up. I look for the wisteria I've heard about, but of course it's long gone. What is a wisteria's life-span? A man passes the barn, throws me a suspicious look and notices my car's Belgian license plate; I decide to turn back. First, a final awkward moment of hovering over the millstone; a cold, wet wind is blowing over the polders. I try to send a series of photographs to the cloud, check whether there's Wi-Fi in the area; on the screen appears a single network, named—believe it or not—HANDS OFF. I start the car and drive slowly, for the sake of the cyclists pedaling against the wind on the well-maintained paths, until I reach the intersection, where my GPS knows the way back to my complicated homeland.

10

Less than six months after they set up house in Berchem, Willem lets her know for the first time that he is too far from home to return that evening. The message is delivered to the house in the form of a telegram, which she holds in her trembling hands.

A telegram? . . . For me? . . . Is something . . .

The postman taps the brim of his cap and is gone.

"Spending night in Lokeren. Visited August Borms in prison."

It happens a second time less than a month later.

"Spending night in Langemark. Gave a friend of Borms a ride home."

Lokeren? Langemark? She stares up into the darkness.

When he arrives home the next evening, he's too tired for conversation—he needs to catch up on sleep. No, Mien, it's nothing, please don't wear me down even more now, I have so much to handle already. After Mientje retreats to the kitchen like a whipped dog, he collapses into an armchair and smokes two cigarettes. She comes back into the room.

I can't take this, Willem. What's the matter? What's going on with that Borms person?

A bored expression. Barely suppressed impatience.

That's no business for a woman, he says.

The woman, who is a good deal more intelligent than the man who uttered those words, is taken aback. After a long silence, she returns to the kitchen.

Half an hour later, when she enters the living room again, he's gone to bed.

A week later, to her astonishment, he announces he's rented an apartment for her, not far from the Antwerp city park: You'll feel more comfortable there when I don't sleep at home. You need to get used to city life, a country girl like you. Her indignation, her protest—he sits through it all with a long-suffering look, waiting for her to finish shouting, then goes to bed, he's dead tired, he tells her, and the way women go on, all their emotional nonsense and fuss about nothing, when I see you in a state like that, I'm more certain than ever you'll be better off there. The next day, he has her clothes, shoes, underwear and personal effects moved out of the house. The day after that, while he's away, someone comes to pick her up, a small, subservient man with atrocious breath: It's not far, Madame Verhulst, you'll see, it's more comfortable than this place. The apartment is sparsely furnished. She finds herself in an unfamiliar room, she hears traffic noise drifting in, she sees bags filled with her belongings, she sees the grim buildings across the street; there's a violin on the windowsill, why is there a violin on the windowsill? . . . In her head, a few wires snap. Why should she stand for this? Willem has gone to Germany for a few days, the man tells her. He'll be back next week and contact her then. Contact her! O language, innocent mask of betrayal, hear me Lord, Thou hast promised me comfort in time of need, I, Thy most humble servant, how have I offended Thee? That preposterous word! He'll *contact* her—her *husband*?!

Beside herself, she walks to Oscar Schamp's office at MEGA and demands an explanation. What is Wim doing in Germany, Uncle Oscar? Oscar, a polite middle-class man, looks at her in surprise, takes a deep breath, and tells her he didn't know about the trip. His hands lie folded on the desk in front of him. Willem makes contacts of his own on the company's behalf, he says. Have a little patience, Mien, don't get hysterical, it will all be fine.

There is no record of how the woman from Oud-Zevenaar handled this shock, but ninety years later, when I speak to her eldest daughter, Letta, she seems as outraged as if it had happened yesterday. The sheer gall, she hisses, the things that man was up to—what makes a person tick, you're better off not knowing.

———

Willem often needs to visit West Flanders—he is a *commis-voyageur*, after all—but Oscar Schamp understands that the uncomfortable stalemate around the apartment must be resolved somehow. He offers Willem a job as "sales representative and chief warehouse manager" at the recently opened MEGA branch in Ghent. The company rents a large property for them—a home, a shop and warehouses—in Oudburg, a street by the Leie near Patershol. In those days it's a popular commercial area, crowded with shoppers. The year is 1929, Mientje has just become pregnant. The company organizes the move. The two of them drive to Ghent with a few suitcases in the back seat. The building turns out to be immense, with a large courtyard, outbuildings and storehouses. What are the two of us supposed to do with this labyrinth? Mien asks. We will fill it up with our children, Willem replies, and he runs his hand over her belly.

In a double portrait photograph taken a year later, the two of them are looking harmoniously in the same direction—he with gentle irony, she with a thoughtful, slightly tense expression. The vague background leaves it unclear whether the photo was taken in the house in Oudburg or in a studio.

11

Their son Adriaan, named after the much-admired Pastor Wartena, is the eldest child, born on November 9, 1929. Harmina is already thirty-six years old, Willem thirty-one. After giving birth at home, Mientje shows the child to his father. He takes him from her and can see at once that the boy has a misshapen foot, turned sharply inward. He doesn't dare mention it, and it takes a few more days before he can acknowledge even to himself that their firstborn child will have a lifelong limp.

It is the year of the Great Crash, but not for Willem. The recent death of his father has left him with a share of the inheritance—probably a substantial sum, in view of the diamond workshop and his mother's properties. He uses it to buy a scenic plot of land near the fashionable golf course in Sint-Martens-Latem, near Ghent. In that wealthy, picturesque town, known simply as Latem, he becomes acquainted with Albert Servaes, the Flemish expressionist painter and later collaborator who will flee to Switzerland after the war. He also meets other artists and intellectuals there, but remains an outsider. He makes plans to have a house built on the plot he's purchased, but nothing ever comes of this. The property in Oudburg, which includes the MEGA warehouses, turns out to be more convenient.

One day he lingers after a reception at Ghent's city hall for another drink, talking and laughing with a few of the other guests. On an antique cabinet by the grand staircase, an eighteenth-century book from the land registry is on display: an attractive showpiece, illuminated and leather bound. He is alone in the room; he looks around, swallows, sees the old maps and drawings, and leafs through the book a little more. Feeling a strange excitement in the pit of his stomach, he glances around again, slips it under his jacket and walks out of the building. He looks around; no one has seen him. In a lime tree next to the church, a magpie sits as if in a Bruegel etching. He takes the book home with him and exhibits it on the sideboard in the front room. When Mientje asks him where he got it, he replies triumphantly, It's a token of gratitude for all my accomplishments.

Years later, the antiquarian book remains on display on the sideboard, not only in Oudburg but also in Drongenhof in the war years, when high-ranking Germans crowd the living room. It must be some time in the late 1950s when his son Adriaan, a history professor by then, discovers the value of the rare Flemish *landboek* and investigates how it found its way to their house. To his surprise, he is told that this legacy from his father is on record as missing or stolen. Adriaan returns the book, shamefacedly and apologizes to the city.

One Sunday, the young family goes walking along the Leie. They sometimes run into Servaes and talk politics; Willem's firm opinions have won him the respect of the famous painter. He invites the young couple to his home for dinner; standing in his studio amid the smells of turpentine, linen canvas and linseed oil, they feel out of place and wonder what to say to an artist. Servaes presents Willem with an etching or small painting, which he lays on the rack under the baby carriage. It may later have been lost; when I ask, no one in the family knows a thing about it.

In 1931 a girl is born, their eldest daughter, Aletta, nicknamed Letta. A second daughter follows in 1934, named Suzanne, after her suffragette aunt in Antwerp, Suzy for short. I have spoken many times to these two daughters, now dauntless women in their eighties. Letta, in particular, remembers happy days in the house in Oudburg. Suzy was too young and has distanced herself more from her father's past.

When they were small, the large courtyard and the capacious warehouses were the kind of playground most children could only dream of. Their father, still a cinephile in his spare time, sometimes screened a few movies under a lean-to in the courtyard with a rented projector. Letta remembers jerky, disjointed scenes from a Laurel and Hardy film, her father laughing at their funny faces. Adriaan notes in his memoir that a Jewish family came to ask for help early in the war; he heard they asked Willem to drive them to Paris. But Oscar Schamp had instructed Willem to stay at the MEGA, for fear that otherwise the "rabble" from the Patershol district would plunder it.

To think that he was worried about looting, even that early on, Letta says, as she pours me another cup of coffee. Who knows—maybe MEGA had already become a front for underground activities, and for gathering intelligence about "enemies of the *Volk*" through a network of door-to-door salesmen.

12

Mientje's life in Oudburg is not always easy. She has to adjust to the Ghent dialect, which is difficult to follow, and her days are filled with taking and passing on orders. The whole headache of bookkeeping has fallen to her; sometimes she makes mistakes because the dialect is too thick, and then Willem scolds her. In Ghent, a *duuze* of light bulbs is a box, but a *duust* is a thousand, and you can't always hear the difference clearly on the telephone; oh, forgive me, Wim, I'm doing my best. In financial terms, they are much more comfortable, but the children can sometimes overhear their tense conversations late at night, in the drawing room downstairs or the bedroom upstairs. Their father often goes away for days at a time. When he returns, he's usually cheerful, with little presents for everyone, and he does his best to lift Mientje's melancholy mood with jokes and quips, which seldom elicit a smile. As she walks past the gray houses of pre-war Oudburg with her children, a few neighbors give her sympathetic nods, but most of them avoid being drawn into conversation with the Dutchwoman, either because they can hardly understand her accent or because they know they can't reply in the same "proper Dutch." She accidentally calls St. Bavo, of the nearby abbey, St. Batavo, and is ridiculed for it: why can't that woman "talk normal"?

All this feels a little abstract to Mien, who often just shrugs it off. By this point she's joined the Protestant congregation of the church in Brabantdam, just across town, a community of people she cares for. On the façade of the church is an acronym that appeals to her: SPQG, *Senatus Populusque Gandavensis*. The Senate and People of Ghent. Later, in the middle of heated arguments with Willem, she will often bring it up: Does your work benefit your city's people, Willem?

Soon she will start volunteering there on Sundays, bringing fresh flowers, helping to organize the services, placing all the psalters in neat rows on the rear pews or singing in the choir. Psalm 91 is dearest to her heart: The Lord is my refuge and my fortress, she sings, in Him will I trust.

Gand — Le Temple protestant.

No 195 — Héliotypie De Graeve, Gand.

In spite of all this, their years in Oudburg are among the best of their lives. He drives all over Belgium—God only knows where he goes or where he sleeps, but he seems happy. She is absorbed by her family duties. Seeing the courtyard and warehouses overrun with children, she is at peace and grateful for what she has. In her free time, she writes adaptations of psalms.

When Letta turns five, Willem writes her a letter for her birthday.

My dear little girl,

As this chapter of your life comes to a close, your father has something he'd like to tell you, and always remember it!

Your name is <u>Aletta</u>—after your dear grandmother Aletta Wijers on your mother's side—stay true to this family tree by practicing Christian humility and love.

You are also named <u>Wilma</u>—not Wilhelmina, as Ghent's stupid city father insisted, but Wilma as in Wilma Vermaat of Beekbergen, the Netherlands—the greatest Christian authoress. You already own so many of her books, try to understand them as you read because she was a noble woman—with a heart of gold, full of nobility.

Lastly, you are named <u>Sonja</u>—my favorite name from Dostoyevsky's book—Crime and Punishment. Wherever your life takes you, my dear girl, whatever happens to you in this world of sorrows . . . stay just as honest—just as pure—just as noble as this girl dragged down by society—better that than a dishonest, impure, ignoble "respectable" lady . . . because the murderer on the Cross went to Heaven with Jesus, and so did this girl Sonja—no thanks to the many "respectable" ladies and priests who closed their hearts to God.

Stay true to God,

Ghent, 16–4–36   *Your father, Willem Verhulst*

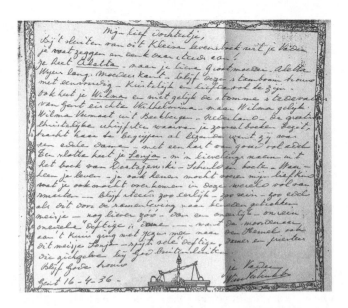

Willem met the writer Wilma Vermaat in Kees Boeke's circle, when he was with Elsa and talking about Frederik van Eeden's commune, Walden. He had the greatest esteem for Vermaat's work, which explores how people can bear the burden of disaster and suffering. Like Willem, she had lost her mother at an early age; the two of them spoke regularly. Wilma, twenty-five years older than Willem, must have meant a great deal to a man who was so susceptible to mother figures. He gave a number of her novels to Letta: *Mother Stieneke*, *The Bright Night*, *The Tree of the Cross* and *Resurrection*. Wilma's question—why must people suffer?—moved Willem deeply. "Where it all comes from, I don't know," she once wrote, "but this much is certain: what I write has to do with the long years of illness in my past, and with life as I experienced it after that, with all the sadness and all the suffering there is in the world."

When Mientje reads the letter to Letta, she can't help crying. Oh, Pappie, she says, it's so beautiful, and how do you suppose Wilma's doing these days, we haven't heard a thing since we came to live in Ghent. That night they make love again—it's been a long, long time.

13

1938. She has to hear it from a neighbor: two nights a week, her husband is screening movies in a private cinema for an audience of "Germanic nationalists," as the man says with a sneer, adding that he doesn't know what sort of movies they are, because "you'd have to be a member of that partickler club, Madammeke Verhulst." When she asks Willem about it, he says it's all unimportant, just documentation for work. What work is that, Wim, she asks, surely not your job at MEGA, and he says, Don't you have enough to keep you busy here, Mother, without sticking your nose into other people's work?

Mother. Our Mammie. Moeke. Almost never Mien, Harmina or Mientje, let alone a pet name or something sweet. "Go ask Mammie, Letta." "I don't know, Adri, Mama will tell you." "Mother, stop nagging, please, I'm bone weary, my God."

On other days, he is the life of the party, coaxing her to come and dance with him to the German tunes blasting from the gramophone—a gift from someone, he won't say who. The noise hurts her ears, sounds more like military marches than ditties for dancing. Give me the psalms any day, she thinks; those are the songs that comfort me in my hour of need.

Right, if you're so curious about the fine movies we show, then let's watch together, Mien, what d'you say? One Sunday they go to the pictures, a private screening in a backroom cinema, men in black uniforms in the audience, watching a movie about the Olympic Games in Berlin two years earlier, *Fest der Schönheit*, Festival of Beauty, apparently made by a woman, just imagine, an ode to the physical strength of the new age.

The idyllic start—sunlight in water, syrupy music in the background—briefly touches her, but the music soon shifts to a martial tempo, as near-identical young men rise up one by one like robots, and she already knows she does not want to see this. She doesn't care for the displays of power and the forced smiles at the camera. She hates the smell of sweat in the room and the sniggers at the close-ups of girl gymnasts. She fumbles nervously with her purse; Willem glances over in slight irritation. What's the matter now? he hisses in her ear. Aren't you the one who wanted to see the movie? She chokes back her discomfort. Reeling from an hour and a half of blaring music and maddening scenes of gymnasts and athletes who didn't even look like people but puppets to her, she returns afterward to her house in Oudburg, and thinks of the origin of the name, *die oude Burg*, the old Fortress, a mighty Fortress is our God. She feeds her children, leaves Willem alone with his never-ending paperwork and his strange pursuits, and holes herself up in her room, where she reads psalms and, for the first time, writes a letter to her parents, telling them she loves them and misses the spring wind over the fields of Oud-Zevenaar, oh those spring days when she cycled along the dyke alone.

They rarely visit Oud-Zevenaar. Life is too full, traveling is hard with three children, Willem never feels like driving that far on a Sunday, and as for the old gentleman farmer, he hates the journey no less—taking the train all that way just to see that ding-a-ling seated in glory at his table in Ghent.

One day—this is sometime in early 1939—the doorbell rings, long and insistent, it's eight in the evening, who could this be disturbing him now, no rest for the weary, fine, fine, I'm coming. A little disgruntled, he opens the door and says, almost aggressively, Well, what's this all about, then? A well-dressed couple timidly ask if they can come in for a moment. He glances at the woman with some trace of intimacy and lets them through the porte cochere into the courtyard. The man rattles off their story in German, explaining that he and his wife are Hungarian Jews afraid of being arrested. Hevesy is their name; they have a hunted look. Someone has told them that Willem can help them get their hands on an *Ausweis*, what they need is an *Ausweis*, and fast, is that possible, if you please, gracious *Herr*. With an expression of vague boredom, he listens, nods, exchanges a look with the comely, nervous woman in her dusty fur coat, sees the slight quiver of her lower lip, weighs his options, and says, Right. Come in. They sit down at the table in the front room in the dim light of a shaded lamp; out of his pocket the man pulls gold and jewels. Spreading everything out on the table, he says, Will you take us to Paris in exchange for this jewelry, *bitte schön*?

Das geht nicht, Willem says, impossible, I can't just drive off to Paris anytime I please, what do you think would happen at the border? He slides the jewels back toward the man; the woman begins to cry. Willem, please, she says. Her husband looks at her, bewildered, does she know this man . . . ? The woman sobs, Willem lowers his eyes, coughs, rises, and escorts them back into the hallway.

Come to my headquarters tomorrow, he says, I'll fix up your papers so you can travel. Then get out of Ghent, quick as you can, you hear me? *Haben Sie das richtig verstanden?* The man nods, the woman's eyes seek out Willem's but find him staring at the ground, unmoved. He shows the couple to the door, shuts the porte cochere, and sighs.

In the back of the hallway, Mientje has been listening at an open door. It dizzies her, everything she doesn't understand and must make sense of. Willem, she says, pinching him hard on the arm, what do you mean, your headquarters? What are you up to that I'm not supposed to know about? He turns to her, meets her eyes, sighs, and puts his arms around her. You don't have to worry, Mien, he says, everything will be fine, it will only get better.

Sure, sure, Letta tells me, Hevesy, that Jewish man Hevesy, he helped him, that's true. But why? What exactly was going on with that lady? Don't ask me, we were children, we were happy there. But I hear tell that he and Madame Hevesy went skating in the winter, in the water-meadows around the outlying district of Drongen. When my mother interrogated him about it, he said she was "just a friend, nothing more." But ach, I know my father . . .

And no, I have no idea what became of those people later.

14

1940. The first days of May: bushes in blossom in the city's small gardens. The first Belgian soldiers are retreating through the Ghent city center, exhausted, edgy and covered with dust. Soon afterward, Messerschmitts roar over the streets. Parachutists open their flimsy balloons in midair and drift down onto the rooftops, causing a commotion; above Sluizeken Square, a German soldier's parachute becomes tangled in the wiring of a tall telephone pole; he struggles to free himself. A few Belgian soldiers run over, one is about to shoot, another stops him; there are German troops everywhere by this time; from one moment to the next, the horror sinks in. The soldier is dangling against the cloud-dotted sky like a dark angel, his parachute dragging over the paving stones. He cuts himself free above a gaggle of onlookers; he leaps to the ground; the Belgian soldiers handcuff him and lead him away. The onlookers have seen their first enemy; a woman presses her hand to her mouth when she sees his clear blue eyes; the older people remember the last war. One of them mutters, The bastards are back. Adri, who has been watching open-mouthed, totters home and shouts, Pappie! Mammie! They're coming! They're coming!

Quiet descends on Sluizeken Square once more, but peace is gone and will not soon return.

⁓

Belgian deserters turn up regularly at the porte cochère of the MEGA, in panic and out of breath, begging for civilian clothes and tossing their uniforms into the waters of the Leie behind the warehouses. Willem helps them. You're doing the right thing, he tells them, off with those rags, you go on home, there's no point in resisting. He gives the youngest a friendly slap on the shoulder.

How do all those men find their way to our house, Pappie? What are you up to these days?

Motorcycles thunder through Oudburg; their rumble makes the old walls shiver. The children go outside and see a column of German soldiers passing by. They sit bolt upright on their motorcycles; in the sidecars are soldiers with rifles at the ready. The soldiers in their large goggles are terrifying; they look like giant insects in a nightmare. Seated behind the rider on the first motorcycle is a Ghent police officer, waving a white flag.

Then they hear someone shout, *Bastards!*

From an upper window come the dry bursts of three gunshots, which must have been fired on nearby Veerdamstraat; the first motorcycle stops short; the Ghent police officer jumps off, shouting and limping, and falls to the pavement stones, clutching his leg. The whole column comes to a halt; the soldiers spring from the sidecars; rifles click, bystanders scream and shout, whoever is still out on the street dives for the shelter of a doorway. Fucking hell, shouts a man who lunges into the MEGA, the fat is in the fire.

Mientje calls the children indoors in a shaky voice; even Willem appears to be panicking. He slams the porte cochere shut and bolts it, yelling at them to go downstairs right away.

The cellars of the MEGA, Adri recalls in his memoir, were often flooded; on the other side of the rear wall was the Leie. It was damp and chilly there; next to the stairs there were always boots in a neat row for the children. They put them on in a hurry, giggling. Faint light enters; a silence stretches on for minutes; they can hear themselves breathing. Then a loud roar swells above them. A moment later, they hear the siren go off over the streets, a slow, plaintive wail that rises and falls, from the far side of the city, under the mound in Citadelpark, where men deep down in concrete cellars are now furiously turning the crank—the Verhulst children know that, their father told them.

I believe they're going to bomb the station, he rumbles.

Everything shakes; one enormous thud follows another. Mientje grabs Willem's arm, without saying a word, and gives him a look that does not escape Adri, a look that raises the hair on the boy's neck and arms, much worse than the ominous noises, and his mother, caught in the act, looks away as his father pats her reassuringly on the shoulder.

—◡

We have to start hoarding, Mien says after they re-emerge, in a few days there will be nothing left to buy in the city. That afternoon Willem drives to a farm near Ghent. He is an old friend of the farmer, Vlerick, who comes from Drongen and in his spare time is also an electrician and a regular customer at the MEGA. He's sure to let Willem stock up on potatoes, milk and flour, and maybe even a piece of pork belly. It's a sunny day; Willem drives with the windows down, juddering through the streets and out of the city; he already has a radio, a rarity in those days. He hears the news, then a snatch of a German speech he only half makes out; he doesn't feel like listening carefully, what does it matter, more marching music, rum-pum-pa-pum, something in him is cheerful and full of energy; how lovely the pastures and meadows are, he thinks, and then the lush banks of the Leie, the poplars arrayed in the warm breeze, my dearest Flanders, how I adore you; he gradually reaches the open fields and, turning onto the unpaved road to the farm, runs into a Belgian checkpoint. The soldiers see an oddball with thick glasses, his windows open and his black hair blowing in the wind; they hear the martial music from the radio—one cocks his rifle and aims. Willem's hands shoot into the air, his heart pounds in his throat, he feels like flooring the gas pedal and running straight over the soldier in front of his bumper; they let him through with a nod; he arrives at the farm. Farmer Vlerick isn't there; his wife accompanies Willem to the barn and the cellar.

Yes, Mr. Verhulst, she says with red cheeks and a wide smile when they resurface half an hour later, strange times ahead—here, have a few loaves of bread with all that, but don't spread it around, because we don't really have enough to sell, but we know you, don't we, and here's another half a kilogram of butter, and give our regards to your lady wife, my husband will drop by soon, one good visit deserves another. I know just what you mean, dear woman, he says, you can count on me. He runs his hand over her rear with a broad grin, and she gives him a conspiratorial wink.

He loads the three full burlap bags into his car and drives back down the dirt road. When he reaches the crossroads, the soldiers are gone without a trace. Peewits, starlings and larks are swooping over the fields, the fruit trees are in blossom; he recalls his days as a young scamp running through the fields with a stick in search of low-hanging fruit, and he laughs.

When he arrives back home, there is a German truck at the MEGA entrance with its engine running; three officers are demanding all the radios in stock. Willem takes them into his office and shuts the door. The meeting takes less than a quarter of an hour; when they come out again, the officer closest to Willem makes a little bow. Mientje hears him say, *Das ist alles in Ordnung, Herr Verhulst, keine Sorgen und bis bald.* All sorts of supplies from the warehouse are loaded onto the truck. Willem meets Mientje's quizzical expression with a wink; his mind is on the farmer's wife.

15

In late May, as the German troops advance through the streets of Ghent, Mientje is rushing from Brabantdam to Oudburg. She sees the uniforms, the officers and soldiers clicking their heels, the lines of cars and trucks, and the arms thrust out when a superior officer passes. The few civilians still out on the streets are hurrying on, not looking up. In Hoogpoort, she is stopped by a young nitwit in uniform, who rifles through her grocery bag. With a German salute, he sends her on her way.

Belgium has capitulated. King Leopold III is led away as a prisoner of war; some decry him as a traitor, others honor him as a hero. A few Junkers fly low overhead, the roar of their powerful engines making the houses tremble; the children can no longer go to school. For several months now, the house in Oudburg has been strewn with German newspapers.

Shouldn't we move to Arnhem, Wim? Wouldn't that be safer for the children?

Mientje stumbles upon her forgotten musical scores, hums an aria, and demands in a heated tone that Adri resume his violin lessons, even though she knows he hates his old music teacher. International politics scares her; she is invited to speak about nonviolence in the church in Brabantdam, and her chosen topic is Jacob wrestling with the angel. The talk is followed by a few psalms. With renewed courage, she returns home, where Adri tells her Pappie had to leave on an unexpected trip to Germany in an awful hurry.

In Adri's memoir, he describes the day an open-top German car filled with *Luftwaffe* soldiers drove into the MEGA courtyard. "They asked us to fix the car radio. The head of the MEGA radio repair service, Mr. Ballière, was sent for. I later heard from Mother that Mr. Ballière, who was fiercely anti-German, had sabotaged the car radio instead of repairing it." Ballière tinkered with this and fiddled with that as the four soldiers looked on with impatience; in the end, they had no choice but to leave with their radio in an even more hopeless condition—to Willem's profound embarrassment. He could not risk his reputation with the German forces.

Many stories circulate in Ghent about the resistance, and much of the covert, wordless resistance has never made it into the history books, but Adri witnessed this spectacle in the courtyard with his own two eyes and may not have realized then what was going on. It was probably only much later, when his mother told him the whole story, that he understood what a risk the electrician had taken. He even speculates, in his memoir, that the man may have ended his life in some concentration camp, but reading his account of the incident, I can't help but wonder what gave him that idea. Did Ballière disappear soon afterward? And if he did, who might have turned him in, since the Germans themselves seemed unaware of the sabotage? Only one person could have done it: Adri's father, Willem, who was on such good terms with the German authorities.

That conclusion must have presented itself to Adri—an emeritus professor of history, hunched over his humiliating manuscript, the son of a "bad" father—but he did not write it down.

Incipit tragoedia. A political family tragedy.

How many signs does a person need, Willem, before he understands that his own life choices matter? She asks the question without expecting an answer, she once read Marcus Aurelius, her husband is tired, as he so often is these days, for a long time she hoped the psalms mattered to him too, now she's not so sure. He has just informed her that they will be moving to a nearby house in Patershol, Veerdamstraat, less than a quarter of a mile away.

But why, Willem, and who will pay for it? Why don't you keep working for your Nuncle Schamp? Aren't you happy in this house? And he, shaking his head, says, Don't worry, Mien, everything will be fine. She doesn't understand, the children don't want to go, and neither does she, she doesn't know why she dreads the move—the wind wails around the roof—why it shakes her so to see Willem's clouded eye in bed at night.

She learns that his new salary is enormous. The news shocks her, and again, she protests: The Lord does not tell us to live in undeserved abundance, we have no need for that much, Wim, we can trust in God's grace like the birds of the air and the lilies of the field, where is all that money coming from, please be careful, my darling husband, our children, you know what I mean, why won't you look at me when I'm speaking to you. He shrugs and smiles his sweetest smile. She lays her hand on his neck.

There are soldiers in Oudburg. Just after midnight they pass the house with their boots and booming voices, their fearsome stupidity, the rhythm of their deranged chicken hearts. He's amused by them, they're nothing but mischievous boys in uniform, after all, Mien. But all those uniforms make her skin crawl. How can you sleep side by side when your dreams lead each of you down your own dark road? The night is a beast. The children give off innocence with every breath that moistens their lips as they babble nonsense in their sleep. What does war do to us, dear Pastor Wartena? Why is my beloved a stranger in my bed? Why does the back I've so often caressed seem to have become three times as broad? Hey, ding-a-ling, don't I even get a good-night kiss anymore?

*

It is August, the end of the dusty month, the month of regret and last blossoms. The city is empty and alert and full of threat; over it looms a silence, a scarcity that makes everyone wary; sometimes, just after rain, it smells of gun smoke and late stock flowers. Where can I let my imagination go, she prays, O Lord, I do not want myself to. I hope I will not. I think he and I. What is wrong with him and what will I. I'm scared the children can't, I don't know, you understand, I mean. Forgive me my distrust. I will write a prayer for Thee in Thine infinite mercy, Almighty One. A ceaseless psalm. It is early morning, next week we will move and I don't want to. People shouting everywhere and civilians ducking for cover. The billing and cooing of the turtledoves on the roof is like the love song of falcons. Or don't falcons have one.

II

. . . and now the long, dark corridor lay open.

—Raymond Brulez, *Mijn woningen* (My homes)

1

It is October 1979.

The moon and the sun, simultaneous and pale in the cool, clarified air, seem to be waiting to see which will prevail, above a provincial city shambling toward morning's end; this instant of indecision gives rise, here and there, to clots of vehicles, clouds of exhaust fumes, aberrations in the flow of traffic, honking and hullabaloo, bicyclists ringing their bells and pedestrians cursing; as gusts of mild wind and moments of sun alternate with scudding clouds, balls of bluish smog swirl through the Grauwpoort city gate and over Sluizeken Square, like tumbleweeds through the Utah or Arizona deserts; in Oudburg, a truck with a fat red hood growls backward through the current of pedestrians to an open black portal; at the fish market next to Gravensteen Castle, a filleting knife flashes through the air and plunges behind the gills of a large cod, which thrashes and tries to escape the pretty vendor; a woman, still wearing curlers in her hair and no makeup, shuffles into a local shop, mindlessly grabs a bottle of water, a pack of cigarettes and a newspaper; the Tunisian grocer in Oudburg wraps yesterday's news around a kohlrabi, a red pepper and a bunch of radishes. The traffic cop dreams of the sticky colors of videos full of boylove and a large bag of paprika-flavored chips; a girl reads Walt Whitman in bed while softly stroking herself, "I sing the body electric"; in an attic room, a boy of sixteen is noodling on a saxophone, while six miles away his father races down the wrong side of the highway to his death; thin mist, late in the morning, enchanting in its lack of any discernible meaning; the city drifts in its own dream, in the hectic writhing of its many phantoms. On the wall of an alley is a message in large white letters: WRITERS DECIDE WHAT LASTS. At the corner butcher shop is a man with a bag made from a strip of old carpet, and deep inside it the empty bottles jangle; that last piece of horse sausage to begin with, then a morsel of tripe and a smidgen of liver, some fatty intestine and brains, and a dab of creamy pâté. *There y'are, Mister Arnold, comes to seventy-six francs.*

I stand waiting at the door for Mr. De Potter, the notary. It's a cloudy day; I'm cold in my thin army jacket, purchased in the Stock Américain in Vrijdagmarkt and decorated with a peace sign I drew myself in felt-tip pen. I've pulled my long locks back into a ponytail—"Almost Cut My Hair." You want to make a good impression on the old-fashioned notary when you're buying a house.

Turbulent times in Patershol. Most of the houses have started to fall apart since the flight from the city began in the mid-sixties. Anyone who can afford it trades in their damp old house and sunless city courtyard for a brick box outside of town, with a lawn and conifers out front: *Villa Bonanza.* The Flemish cities are losing the people with the most purchasing power; the left-behinds have just enough to make rent. Students and artists are squatting in the vacant monastery, filling the whitewashed cells with their Oriental rugs, their foxy ladies and their guitars; they build fires in the courtyards. When they're stoned, they sing protest songs: "If I had a hammer, I'd hammer in the morning." They organize happenings and be-ins because the city is trying to kick them out. One of their processions is drumming and dancing by as I wait at the door of the house; they're demanding the right to live in the monastery. They have a sense of humor—a thing their bureaucratic opponents know nothing about. "Buildinista Liberation Front," I read, a tongue-in-cheek reference to the Nicaraguan Revolution; cheering, drumming and dancing, the motley parade passes down the street and around the corner. Here comes Mr.

De Potter, shaking his head. He says hello with a look on his face as if he fears I've just stepped out of the procession myself.

⁓

Veerdamstraat's old French name was Rue du Bac, a name that summons images of one of the liveliest streets in the Saint-Germain neighborhood of Paris. That name was extirpated once and for all during the German occupation. Florimond Grammens, a well-known politician and activist in the Flemish nationalist party, painted over the street sign himself for the Flemish cause; this must have been in 1938. When the Verhulst family moved in, the house was the property of Mr. Henri De Potter, a Francophone Ghent trial lawyer. The street had not been called Veerdamstraat for many years, and in 1942, in the middle of the war, the city authorities officially adopted the name Drongenhof, which had been in popular use for centuries. This street name harked back to the Iconoclastic Fury, when Protestants rose up and destroyed Catholic religious images; in the late sixteenth century some Norbertine monks, fleeing the destructive rage of the Calvinists, abandoned their abbey in nearby Drongen and sought refuge in Ghent. The homes assigned to them were known as the "Drongen houses."

Ever since the Middle Ages, Ghent's working-class areas had been crisscrossed by canals and waterways, but in the twentieth century most of them were filled in: the old arm of the Leie known as the Lieveke, the Plotersgracht and the Tichelrei. Now, in 1979, the ground remains unstable in some places because the work on the canals was slipshod. Some houses are on insecure foundations, the soil in their small gardens is black and poor, and the pavement is full of bumps and potholes. There is frequent subsidence: sudden gaps and sinkholes that reek of sewage. The tram shakes the windows and floors as it races by; heavy trucks have caused cracks in the walls. The cast-iron manhole covers amid the bumpy pavement stones bear the word "Osnabrück." Osnabrück, I think to myself, the name of a German city I've never seen.

The house in Drongenhof faces a small city park where the waters of the Lieveke still flowed when the war began. The rusted gate has long been impossible to open, and these days there's no rowboat tied up at the doorstep. The rats creep all over, unhindered, making nests in the coal shed, among the garbage, eating the scraps the locals throw into the bushes for stray cats.

⁓

The front of the tall house was once, perhaps more than fifty years ago, carefully painted. Now all that remains is a sandy substance, eroded by the weather. No more is left of the window moldings than vague, pimpled swells of cracked plasterwork, and under the roof gutter, which tips threateningly because a few brackets have rusted away, the moisture has eaten into the house and made the paint blister. Some of the plaster has crumbled away completely, revealing the dark, hard, handmade Scheldesteen brick, its indomitable texture saturated with damp. At the level of the raised ground floor, there are neoclassical cornices in the plasterwork, or at least that's what the notary calls the horizontal moldings. But below that, at street level, are thick, ridged slabs of blue-gray Belgian limestone sprayed with now-illegible graffiti. The fine paint dust has settled deep in the porous stone and can probably never be scrubbed out of it. Outside the front door, by the threshold, is an antique boot-scraper recessed into a limestone slab, with a horseshoe-shaped frame and a protruding edge on which visitors can scrape their soles clean, an essential item in the days when the streets were filled with horse droppings.

The doorbell, an ivory knob shot through with thin blue veins, was once surrounded by a metal plate measuring six by eight inches, but the plate is gone, and the bell now dangles in a small vacuum, a hollow where the brick crumbled away long ago; you can see the electrical wiring behind it, like delicate internal anatomy. There is at least one other obstacle to entering the house: an enormous butterfly bush, growing exuberantly from the gap in the wall of the step-gabled house next door. As if feeding on the brick, which has softened to the consistency of pound cake, it must have flung one woody braid out through the crack, a tendril that swelled into a hard, knotted branch and then flared out into twigs like floral fireworks. A few late peacock butterflies and red admirals flutter around it.

The notary has a little trouble picking out the right key from his impressive collection and then stands fiddling with the uncooperative keyhole for a while before he grunts, in a slight French accent, "Should have known. The lock is upside down," and, with an impatient twist of his plump fingers, forces the click. The door won't open right away; it scrapes, sluggish and rasping, over the first row of tiles, where it has already left deep, fanlike grooves in the stone. "After you," says Mr. De Potter, as he steps inside ahead of me.

The warm October breeze blows in with us, but just two steps into the house, we feel a damp draft from its depths, like a wintry counterattack surging out of the cellar, resisting our plans to disturb the yearslong stasis. "Hmm," the notary rumbles, "what a draft. Another house with the windows left open so that everything can rot. Speculation, dear sir, is the bane of the real estate sector, take it from me." He turns to me with a look of mild irritation, his heavy, graying eyebrows shooting upward for an instant. Finding me still in the doorway, framed by daylight, staring wide-eyed at him, he coughs and writes, "Statement of Condition upon Viewing," in a calligraphic hand on a sheet of paper attached for this very purpose to a clipboard, which he holds in front of his broad chest with decorum. His pen scratches with the same aristocratic gravitas; apart from that, the room is silent.

De Potter launches into an ode to the solid construction of the building, accompanied by expansive gestures. "You see, sir," he says with all the aplomb of a professional man from a distinguished old Francophone family, "this house is built like a church"—his voice caresses the Dutch words, transforming stark *k*'s into eloquent *q*'s—"and even now, stripped almost bare, it is more or less timeless; the outer walls are almost twenty inches thick, and the spruce floorboards are nearly a foot wide and more than an inch thick, still the original *pitch pine*"—he stretches the sounds of the English loanwords, making "pitch" sound like "peachy"—"from one hundred and fifty years ago. And that is excluding the time that the wood took to grow. Let us simply say it is older than the country we live in."

80

Plastered ceilings with stucco around the edges; blobby patches from successive layers of paint that form an abstract fresco, a composition cracked and split by relentless moisture; vague drawings on the wallpaper made by stains, in which the childlike eye of the gaping would-be buyer imagines antique forms, a centaur wielding a sword, Homer's unknown face—one stain looks just like the head of a satyr. Electrical wires wind along the wall like a bundle of spindly snakes in cloth jackets, dangling in midair against the half-decayed wallpaper, creeping through the Bakelite sockets like spider legs, diving under a decades-old blanket of hazardous, spark-spitting, hard-crusted dust, darting out in unexpected places, plunging into the depths of old brick beside a doorjamb, and issuing into a porcelain switch, where the hydra permits a brief caress by the notary's hand, but to no avail: we remain in half darkness.

2

In the first autumn of the occupation, when Willem Verhulst rang the doorbell of the tall house, it was opened by the maid, Cordula. Her employer, Mr. De Paepe, was the retired principal of a Catholic school. No other facts are to be found about this earlier tenant, who lived in the house in the 1930s, nor is there any record of where he went when the Germans ordered him to leave at once. The monthly rent paid by Willem Verhulst to the De Potter family was abnormally high: 1,500 Belgian francs, at a time when the average worker earned not much more than 500 francs a month. Once these terms were settled, the Francophone De Potters appear to have made no further trouble about their new tenant.

A memory of the move comes back to Suzy, Willem's younger daughter, at the age of eighty-five: I had to hold on to a cart full of apples. The cart tipped over, and I was hanging on to the handle with my feet in midair. I was six years old.

The image is like an old photograph: a child at the start of the war, dangling from the handle of a pushcart with her feet nearly a foot off the ground, somewhere along the quarter of a mile between a familiar and an unfamiliar house, in the narrow streets of a working-class district, accompanied by a father who perhaps had not yet worn a German uniform—the sources do not make it clear.

The children's first impressions of their new abode were largely disappointing. It seemed cold and dark to them, and even though it was a middle-class home with three floors plus an attic and a cellar, the tall house seemed quite small when compared to their spacious rooms and warehouses in Oudburg. "We didn't feel at all comfortable there,"

Willem's daughter Letta would write in her memoir half a century later. "One of the minor improvements was the sink, which was not outdoors in the courtyard like the one in Oudburg but indoors in the annex. The wastewater ran straight from the sink into the Lieveke."

When I visited the property with the notary, there were only a couple of copper faucets for the entire house; I tried to imagine what the family had done in the harsh wartime winters without hot water or any bathroom fixtures to speak of.

The German occupation weighed heavily on Ghent. Many officials were turned out of their offices and replaced with people willing to collaborate with the *Verwaltung*, the city's military administration, which the occupying regime had installed in haste and by force. When Mientje wouldn't stop asking, Willem confessed that he was in the Germans' good books and had been offered a new job, partly on his brother-in-law's recommendation: an appointment, with immediate effect, as director of the famous Ghent rediffusion service, organized by the local authorities in the 1930s for the city's music lovers. Mientje and Willem had had a radio receiver at the MEGA, and another was soon to be installed in the house in Drongenhof; Willem told her it was "essential for doing my work."

The pre-war rediffusion service had been progressive and socially engaged, part of a political program of cultural uplift. A wired network relayed music from a center on Stoppelbergstraat to the listeners' living rooms. Customers had a small, dark brown Bakelite box mounted on the wall, usually with a large, crude knob that had a few settings; they could choose between "light" and "heavy" music, terms I sometimes heard my grandfather use in the 1960s, and a "spoken channel." I still remember seeing the Bakelite boxes on the walls of a home in a blue-collar neighborhood where I played with my cousins on summer days. Helmut Zacharias and his miraculous violin, "Ich küsse Ihre Hand, Madame," the nasal sound of the built-in loudspeaker is as vivid as if I'd heard it yesterday. The previous director of the rediffusion service, one Mr. De Vinck, had "fled as a result of the German occupation," as one of Willem's daughters told me.

A study of collaboration in Ghent tells the story in somewhat less innocent terms: "Soon after the eighteen-day campaign, on July 15, 1940, the Ghent radio rediffusion installations were occupied by the Germans. The former board members were denied entry to the premises. The German authorities appointed their own staff." Willem's predecessor had simply been booted out by the occupiers, who needed the medium of radio for their propaganda—a word that, ironically enough, includes the proud city's old Latin name of Ganda. They set about broadcasting marching music, Flemish choirs and blustering speeches. Ghent's rediffusion service had a new name, Radio Flanders. Willem was thrilled.

3

Once Suzy's feet are touching the ground again, Adri pushes the apple cart to the door of the house on Veerdamstraat and parks it in the middle of the sidewalk, so that the children, each taking an iron pail from the cart, can carry the apples down to the cellar. Willem fumbles with the key; Mientje, out of breath, sets the heavy bags of clothing down on the ground while she waits to go inside. She sees the copper plate of the mailbox on the massive door, bearing the word "Letters" in ornamental script; it rattles in a passing gust of wind. The weather is mild, with white clouds in a watery blue sky; here and there the breeze carries a whiff of brown coal, or of food simmering on a stove. The city is quiet and wary under the occupation.

Then the hallway opens before them. Mientje sees the black tiles and high stairwell, feels a damp draft wind up toward them from the depths of the house. Something in her shivers and knows that their carefree Oudburg days are behind them. She says to her husband, whose one good eye is twinkling as he looks around: How marvelous, Willem, what a beautiful house.

She lugs the bags of clothing to the middle of the hallway, sets them down there, and follows Adri and his bucket of apples to the rear of the house, where the stairs to the cellar gape like a dark maw. The beech steps are already well worn; Adri finds a porcelain switch, a dim bulb winks on. Cripes, Mama, he says, the cellar is flooded. It's from the canal behind the house, Mientje says, the water is coming straight through the walls. We'll pump out the cellar once we're all settled in.

Standing a few steps above her son Adri, she realizes how tall he is for an eleven-year-old, she sees the stubbly hair on the back of his neck and a warm current sweeps through her body. Come on, she says, it's all right, we'll take the apples up to the attic. As her son runs back up the steps and past her to the ground floor, while the two girls skip down the hallway and Willem's footsteps thump hollowly on the wood floor of the front room, she stands and stares at the shallow layer of murky water on the dull red tiles.

She pictures the old cellar of her childhood home, which was divided into two parts: a front cellar where jars of preserved vegetables were kept, and a rear cellar for their coal supply. The coal could be thrown straight into the cellar from outside through a trapdoor with beveled edges: glittering eggs of compacted carbon for the stove in the kitchen, and anthracite for the stove in the living room. Men who seemed to her like giants, black with coal dust, in helmets that made them look as if they'd come from the depths of the mines, brought the fuel in rough burlap bags; to pick up a bag, they stood with their backs to the horse-drawn cart, slung it over one shoulder in a supple motion, and carried it, back bent, to the cellar's mouth; for an instant, their load resembled a hunchback's deformity or a misshapen child; with a twist of the arm, they swung it off their shoulder and over the open trapdoor, grabbed it mid-fall, and deftly upended it so that it emptied its contents directly into the narrow opening; then they flung the scrap of burlap, surprisingly thin and limp now, over one arm, folded it in two, tossed it neatly onto the stack, and started all over, with bowed backs and pearled sweat like molten glass sparkling on their foreheads, turning their backs to the cart for their next load; the whites of their eyes gleamed ferociously, and they seemed to see nothing but the route to the trapdoor and back . . .

Letta comes to see what is keeping her mother, who, startled out of her reverie, hurries upstairs to the front room, where Willem, leaning on the mantelpiece with one elbow, points out the brown-and-rose marble: Look, what a beautiful mantel, Mien, it's a lovely house we're moving into, don't you think? Her smile is a little forced; she dislikes the damp place with its smell of sewage. Yes, Wim, lovely, she says, I'm happy you're so pleased. Framed in the light of the tall windows, he seems bigger than he really is. What goes on in her husband's mind she can only guess. He is wearing that sly smile of his and shoots a triumphant look through the lenses of his glasses; we're rich, Mien, we're rich, he said the day before yesterday, after making it clear to her that his monthly salary would be more than princely. Not until weeks later will she learn it is 15,000 francs a month, a figure that will shock her: what will we do with all that, she will ask him, what do they expect of you for that sort of pay, most people in this neighborhood can't afford the salt in their soup. But for now he is keeping the figure secret; in the months and years that follow, he will occasionally slip her a roll of cash, making her heart leap up because she can once again afford treats for the children, have a fresh supply of coal delivered to the shed in the backyard, and fix up the house.

⌣

Almost forty years later, Mr. De Potter and I find the same flooded cellar, the same old doors. The lawyer, wheezing his way ahead of me, is uncertain whether to entrust his weight to the rickety old beech stairs; judging by the many holes in the wood, they must be full of deathwatch beetles and old house borers. The sour smell of stagnant water rises to our nostrils; go ahead and look around for yourself down there, he says with a cough.

I go halfway down the steps and find little to reassure me. A few pipes, rusted through and broken, protrude from the low ceiling. In the gloom at the far end, the scant daylight trickling onto the wet red tiles through a ventilation grate reveals puddles of muddy water. The fine brick vaulting of the ceiling is being eaten away by mold. The attractive niches in the rear wall, intended for storing wine, have a huge drainpipe running through them; clinging to it here and there are drops of brown fluid. My God, I think, the sewage pipe is leaking. The elegant racks in the niches are ruined. On the opposite wall, dusty old boards have been mounted with rusty wire. On these shelves are a few abandoned jars filled with nails, a layer of dried-up paint, or a crust of oil. Everything that happened here, the people who took shelter from the bombing—I will not learn about them until much later.

I return upstairs and say to Mr. De Potter, Nice house, but it needs a lot of work; the brick in the cellar is rotting. Ah, well, he says, *Neurospora sitophila*, stands to reason you'll have to do something about that, my good man, there are excellent products these days, no problem whatsoever. The Lieveke used to run just behind the house, he adds, that's a branch of the Leie, filled after the war as you may be aware, apparently the Germans sank a boat there in 1944, but in any case, you know what they say: water always finds a way.

⁓

The front room was sizeable. On the left, the windows offered a view of old Drongenhof Chapel, which had gone unused for decades; its steep roof was the stomping ground of cooing pigeons. From the front room, you could see its high walls, which cast an angular shadow on the wet paveing stones. Above the narrow arch of a front window, the date 1607 in glazed brick was still faintly legible, and there were a few Masonic symbols on the left wall, under the Gothic windows. Mientje once found the large gate open and looked inside—again and again, she found herself drawn irresistibly to religion in all its aspects. Sometimes she heard singing in the churches of Ghent and stepped inside, even though all the spectacle—the statues of saints, the decorated pulpits— seemed frivolous to her, and she felt vague shame in retrospect about her curiosity. She noticed that in the vacant chapel there were old gravestones set into the floor, and that the tiles were damaged, sometimes shattered or even missing. Dust motes drifting against the sunlight, a few pigeons in befouled niches. She shook her head in silence. Such neglect would be unthinkable in a Protestant church, she reflected. From so close by, the sloping roof seemed somehow menacing, like a permanent scowl on the face of the sky. The Lord will help us, the Lord is good, she chanted in her mind, and to Willem she said, Oh, yes, Wim, just lovely, we'll have a lovely time here.

4

I turn back to the interior and now notice, for the first time, the marble mantelpiece. "A thing of beauty, you must admit," De Potter says, "pure authentic marble from Comblanchien..." He invests the words with great significance, as if I, the young potential buyer, have an encyclopedia of marble varieties in my head, but later, much later, I will drive past the quarries of Comblanchien countless times, somewhere in the heart of France, near the Burgundian town of Beaune and its vineyards with their smell of gravel and cat piss. It rains often; the huge quarries are damp and look more brown than pink. "Technically, it's not marble," the notary says. "Comblanchien is a hard, durable variety of limestone, prized because it resembles Italian marble but is quite a bit cheaper—so you can see, *mon cher*, that the people who lived here dreamed of a better life." He doesn't even say it with irony, but with a mild nostalgia. "Ah, well. They were perfectly respectable people, mind, and yet, how shall I put it—a war turns everything upside down, and before you know it, you're on the wrong side, if you know what I mean . . . When I was a child, I saw a bust on the mantel here, sir, of, well, you know who, Herr Dolf, if you take my meaning, not even a stone bust but common lime plaster."

A bust of . . . ? Here, in this house? But which people were those? Did you know them personally, Mr. Notary? Oh, yes, he says, with a nod, I knew them well, sir. He gives a guarded sniff. Not bad people, not that, or rather, except for the father, well, really, he wasn't a bad man either, but lost, wandering, blind, that's the worst you can say, though he caused my dear departed pater no end of trouble . . . but his charming Dutch wife and the children, they were decent people . . . Ah, well, what does it all matter now, the children have flown the nest, the eldest son is now a learned professor at the university here, you see how it goes, the house has stood empty for years, it was a long time ago, after all, dear sir.

It is incomprehensible to me, now, that I allowed everything I could then have learned, or at least suspected, to slip away without a second thought.

The Verhulst family settles in—the furniture is delivered to the new house that same day. A couple of the movers try to strike up a conversation with Willem, their voices full of admiration. He responds in a curt, bossy tone, to Mientje's surprise; she's not used to that, coming from Wim, her good-natured, enthusiastic husband, ever the charmer. He dispatches the children to the third floor to explore their rooms, which are much too big for them. He issues commands and points his finger: put that wardrobe there, the large table with lion's-paw feet in the middle room, those six kitchen chairs in the annex; whenever Mientje tries to say anything, he makes a shushing gesture, as if he cannot bear the thought of the workmen seeing her chime in. Later that day, to her astonishment, three black leather couches are delivered. For the front room, Mien, he says, the new city authorities have sent them. We'll have to start entertaining important guests, and that will be our salon. His one clear eye fixes her with a strange look; she turns away. Something is pounding in her throat; she goes upstairs, where two men are assembling the conjugal bed, and then to the upper floor where the girls have unpacked their dolls from the boxes of clothes and objects wrapped in old sheets. Letta and Suzy will share the large bedroom in the front of the third floor; Adri will sleep in the room at the back. He has already placed his violin in a corner of the room and is looking out over the sludgy Lieveke at the small quay on the far side, the decrepit Café Roosje, the few seagulls wheeling over the old roofs; his schoolbooks are stacked up and waiting to be shelved on the simple racks. This will be a good place for me to study, he says. He goes to his mother and flings his arms around her shoulders.

Willem sits by himself in the front room that night, while Mien sets up the upstairs rooms and makes the beds. He has some files to review, he says; she notices he takes along a glass of schnapps. He comes to bed late; the next morning he gets up exceptionally early, dresses, and says to his surprised wife: I'll grab breakfast at the office, see you tonight. The large door shuts behind him with a dull bang; Mien will have to get used to the sound. Even the heavy porte cochere in Oudburg was lighter. She calls out to the children to come; they wash themselves in an iron tub in the annex while she makes their sandwiches—we will want for nothing, Willem has assured her, everything will be fine, we are in the Lord's hands.

Two days later, it begins: a young *Obersturmführer* stops by in the evening to see Willem, the two of them sit in the easy chairs that have just been delivered, the double door of the front room is shut, Mientje stands at the door and listens. She hears her husband, in a German peppered with Flemish words, asking about the plans to redevelop the city center—how could this man, her shopkeeper from MEGA, her sweet rascal, always ready to charm her with some ridiculous joke, how could he have gotten himself tangled up in something as weighty as the construction of new city streets? The German officer quietly explains that the plans for broad boulevards straight through the city will never get off the ground—*keine Hausmannisierung, Heer Hülst.* The *Verwaltung* will never allow the destruction of one of the most beautiful *deutschen Städten.*

. . . That SS man, calling Ghent a German city! And her husband muttering in approval . . . Cigar smoke drifts through the gap under the door, and now she hears the German voice saying he is counting on Willem to go on coordinating the *vertrauensvolle Zusammenarbeit mit den Flamen,* the trusting collaboration with the Flemish, in his perceptive and *unempathisch* manner. *Unempathisch.* She swallows, hurries back to the simple kitchen in the annex, the children ask her who that man is, she tells them she doesn't know. When Adri asks her if after dinner she'd like to sing while he plays violin, she snaps that she's far too busy, dries her hands on her apron, and says, Go on, children, go to your rooms, I'll be up soon to say good night.

5

A few months after they move into the house, the doorbell rings. There's a workman at the door, who says to Mientje: Ma'am, here is your husband's order. He walks back to his handcart, picks up an unfinished wooden crate, and asks if he can set it down in the hallway. She sees a label with the name Verhulst, and a German stamp. The man doesn't stop long to chat: that's right, he says, for your husband, and you know, ma'am, some wives don't pronounce it *husband*—they say *has-been*. He leers at Mientje, taps his hand against his cap, grabs his cart by the handle and leaves the way he came. Her heart pounds in her throat; she keeps her distance from the crate in the hallway; Willem will explain that evening.

But Willem does not return home until after midnight, long after everyone has gone to bed. She hears him fumbling in the kitchen, perhaps eating some of the dinner, now cold, that she left for him; then she hears him tiptoeing up the stairs, the boards of the bedroom floor creaking under his feet; he slides into bed beside her, lies with his back to her, and breathes so softly she can hardly tell if he's alive.

After a hurried breakfast the next day, he's about to leave again, he seems nervous and rushed; when she asks what the crate is all about, he mumbles that she'll see soon enough. That afternoon the crate is opened by an assistant from the rediffusion service sent to Drongenhof expressly for that purpose. The contents make her head spin. The man places—at your husband's request, ma'am—a large bust of the Führer on the elegant Comblanchien mantelpiece, gives her a meaningful look, and says, Your husband's orders, ma'am, and I wish you the best of luck. He gives a vague

Nazi salute and bows. She lets him out without a word, returns to the front room; she stands, her hands wringing her apron, and stares in astonishment at that unpainted plaster-of-Paris head, the dead expression in the empty eyes; for less than three seconds, oh, a flame of revulsion shoots through her, quickly combusting into turmoil and fear; the children will be home soon, I have to close the door, I don't want them to see this, I still have groceries to buy for tonight—she walks to the annex, something tugs at the corner of her mouth, she stands staring at the dark waterway, through the bars of the old fence she sees a few ducks bobbing, life seems almost normal, still, may fate preserve us, the Lord knows all, she mumbles, the Lord will save us, amen. She tips coal into the stove, it's cold, the chimney doesn't draw well, the bitter smoke makes her cough, she wonders how her parents are doing in Oud-Zevenaar, she wants to take the children to see them for a couple of days as soon as she can, but what can she tell them about her own life, and can you even cross the border these days, maybe Willem can still arrange that kind of thing for her.

It's not clear exactly when Willem began wearing an SS uniform, but when I speak to Letta, she passes on a memory: her mother couldn't stand him wearing it around the house. So a clean, freshly ironed ordinary civilian suit awaited her husband on a rack in the front room upon his return from his unexplained appointments; whenever Papa came home, he could take off his boots and the uniform she detested, put on his ordinary clothes, leave the uniform in the front room and face his family as an ordinary civilian. From that moment on, Mientje forbade the children to enter the front room. Children, that is the death room, she would say, maybe because she had seen the death's head on his

96

uniform, and Willem, who would always remain a jolly joker, would take his playful revenge just before dinner by shouting *Heil Hitler!*, clicking his heels together and performing the well-known salute, after which he would sit down beside his startled children while his embarrassed wife bowed her head and thanked the Lord for the food on their plates.

—

Sunday's remains glide away into the drowsy darkness of the empty streets; as the evening draws to an end, the silence returns. There is only the reassuring rattle of the tram rolling past, through the Grauwpoort city gate, on its way to Gravensteen Castle, making the floorboards vibrate throughout the house; Mien lies awake in the darkness. Deep in the narrow alley below, she can hear a voice calling out to a child to come inside, a door slamming across the street, muffling the voices. After that a few tipsy soldiers passing; then nothing more until, after twenty minutes or so, the steel of the tram wheels glides over the rails right on time again, reassuring, now in the other direction. The wheels seem to carry her thoughts with them, to summon a longing to stroll along the route of the tram rails, toward the outskirts of the city and the harbor, to the turning basin for the barges—a vast black bowl of dirty water going around in circles, hesitating before it surrenders to the current of the factory-lined canal. The call of the outskirts, roused by the tram slipping past, makes her long to get up again, to go out into silence, to pass the junk shops on the edge of town with their cluttered window displays, to walk the ever-emptier streets until she reaches the wooden warehouses where the wind bites deeper and the smell of the stacked goods fills the lonely *flâneuse* with a yearning for boats, for leaving without looking back.

But instead she lies still, afraid to wake the sleeping Willem. She can see, out of reach, the notebooks she recently bought, in which she plans to keep a diary. She will continue the habit, with rare interruptions, until a few days before her death. They are gripping testimonies, which will later find their way to my desk.

⁓

It's Suzy's birthday, her gift is a bunch of flowers, we're celebrating with our friends the Vandermeulens and the Welvaerts, Pappie is at the table too, thank goodness, but at the explicit request of both the birthday girl and myself, we will not be discussing politics. After dinner Pappie, out of the blue, calls for his pajamas, his towel, his shaving things and so on, and Suzy remarks with a laugh, "Bring his swimming trunks too, Mama. He's going to Tielt." We are left behind, at a loss for words. Tomorrow I may go to Brabantdam, on the far side of the city center, if it please the Lord.

6

My most distant memories, Adriaan writes, go back to the 1930s; every summer I spent my vacation with my maternal grandparents in Oud-Zevenaar, near Arnhem, in far-off Gelderland. The journey, sometimes with the whole family, was long; Mama would fill a cloth bag with sandwiches, and we children would carry a small iron kettle filled with milk. We left early in the morning, usually walking to Sint-Pieters Station, sometimes catching the first tram, because it was a long way from Oudburg. We took the express from Ghent to Bruges, then the slow train to Breskens; after that, we caught the ferry to Vlissingen; I remember the salty wind over the gray water during the crossing. In Vlissingen, we boarded yet another train: a long, slow trip—Middelburg, Goes, Bergen op Zoom, Roosendaal, Dordrecht, Gorinchem, Wageningen, Arnhem. And from there we walked for hours more to the quaint house in Oud-Zevenaar with the big tall barn next to it. We children helped our Dutch grandfather, Farmer Wijers, on his farm there—"jobs like gathering the fallen ears of wheat, or 'gleaning', as they say in that area."

Adri ate milk porridge with the farmhands before bed; at the table, he heard half-mumbled conversations about the Dutch prime minister, Hendrikus Colijn, or about a neighbor who had scandalized the village by joining the Dutch fascists. He thought of his father and kept his mouth shut.

⁓

I remember, Letta tells me, that my parents went on "an excursion to Düsseldorf." What we children didn't realize until much later was that they had visited the Nazi propaganda exhibition *Schaffendes Volk*—that must have been in 1937, I was a girl of six, Adri was seven.

The exhibition in Düsseldorf was part of a growing culture of German resentment with its roots in the First World War. In the preceding years, a Nazi Party member had campaigned for an artistic platform in honor of Albert Leo Schlageter, a German volunteer in a paramilitary *Freikorps*, originally from Baden. In 1923, his acts of espionage and sabotage against the French occupiers of the Ruhr led to his execution at their hands on Golzheimer Heath near Düsseldorf. The Nazi Party made him the focal point of a cult of victimhood, even naming a new district of the city Schlageterstadt. The exhibition *Schaffendes Volk* (A Productive People) was organized around the new district and drew more than six million visitors with its futuristic style. The architecture looked utterly revolutionary by the standards of the day. Descriptions and photographs of the event remind me of my own impressions of the Brussels World's Fair of 1958, which I visited as a child with my grandfather.

In that summer of 1937, Willem must already have been in contact

with German organizations; Mientje probably resigned herself to accompanying him to the exhibition, even though she wouldn't have cared for the bombastic tone, the militant atmosphere and the relentless idolizers of political hysteria.

Mientje knew, of course, that Willem—who had been a flamingant activist in the First World War and then a supporter of the Front Party, which grew out of the Flemish Movement—had been part of the increasingly radical, "German-friendly" Flemish National Union Party. Despite all her efforts to talk him out of it, he had put himself forward in 1936 as a candidate for the Union's provincial council. In 1937 he broke with the organization; when Mientje asked him why he kept ranting about the same people he'd once revered, he replied, "Because they're a bunch of Catholic stick-in-the-muds, that's why." A friend of the family, Mr. De Pestel, told her a different story: "Your husband flew off the handle because there were supporters of the Walloon leader Léon Degrelle at the meeting." Degrelle was just as sympathetic as the Union to the Nazis, but not to the Flemish nationalist cause. "There was also friction because Willem said the Union wasn't radical enough; he started shouting that the goal of an independent Flanders wasn't ambitious enough. No, we had to become part of the new Greater Germanic Reich, because we, the Western Germanics, had a heroic role to play." De Pestel looked at her with a kind of apology in his eyes, and then added, "Don't tell anyone you heard it from me, Madame Verhulst. I'm not the only one who's scared of him."

Mientje, one evening: I can't make sense of it anymore, Willem, the people you spend your time with . . . Remember what Kees Boeke used to say, and Pastor Wartena? No one can ever hide from the face of God. They'd disapprove of what you're doing now. And he says, Mother, please, concentrate on the children, that's enough to keep you busy. He walks up the stairs to his second-floor library. She can hear him lock the door behind him.

7

At school, the absurd language policies in the Flemish educational system become part of Adri's daily life. Even his mother, Mientje, who as a Dutch farmer's daughter is burdened with an extremely logical mind, protests about the fact that her children have to stand and sing French songs without even having the words explained to them. Her protests lead to a stern lecture from the school administrators. A few years later, at a school where Flemish *is* spoken, Adri is called a "cheesehead" because of the northern accent he has picked up from his mother, and taunted because, with his misshapen foot and thick-soled right shoe, he's no good at soccer; he limps away through the school's front gate and goes to his violin lesson. His teachers have little sympathy for him, because he won't donate to the Red Cross and says, as his father instructed him, that his family only gives to the *Flemish* Cross, upon which his teacher asks if poverty and disease are now reserved for the Flemish. His imperturbable father has also forbidden Adri to stand for the Belgian national anthem—let alone sing along. On account of incidents like these, Mientje is summoned to school again for a talking-to from the principal, who has had enough of their son's outpourings of *Deutschfreundlichkeit*. Mientje argues and explains, she protests and bargains, she listens and despairs and says thank you, sir, thank you, sir, to the man who, with unmasked irritation, walks her to the door.

The poet Richard De Cneudt, a cousin and old friend from the years when Willem was still with Elsa, now visits the house in Drongenhof sometimes. Under the blank stare of the plaster-of-Paris leader in the death room, they reminisce. As the evening goes on and the gin is poured, the conversation grows more impassioned; sometimes they speak German, because not everything is for the children's ears; to liberate Flanders at long last from the grip of its elite, from the Jewish Bolsheviks and the French-speaking Freemasons, violence will be inevitable, Willem proclaims. The parliamentary route is hopeless in this goddamn country. You can hear him say it through the just-open door to the middle room; later that evening, Mientje snaps at him, saying she's worried the Evil One has possessed him. Come, children, time for bed, the evening's done.

Later, Adri writes, I heard my father and my uncle Richard talking about the extreme wing of the activist movement: the *Duits-Vlaamse Arbeidsgemeenschap* (German-Flemish Working Group), the notorious *DeVlag*, a cover for the SS.

Letta still vaguely remembers the lavish festivities when the Flemish poet published his collection *Mijn hart verlangt* (My heart desires) in 1942; a celebration was organized to which Mientje and Willem both contributed, with enthusiasm and unity of purpose: a banquet in the Gothic guildhall of Sint-Jorishof, under the tower of the Belfort with its proud Ghent dragon on the tip, directly opposite the Pacificatiezaal, the chamber of the city hall where once, in 1576, William the Silent had tried to forge a religious peace for the Netherlands. An evening of wassails and speeches, of poetry and rhetoric, of another toast and many *Heil Hitler*s and outstretched arms everywhere. Flemish idealists, here and there a black or *feldgrau* uniform, it's a mild September day in the middle of the war.

⁓

Adri had learned a few of Richard De Cneudt's poems by heart, Letta tells me; he delivered them with great ceremony and a pinched voice, sending his sisters into hysterics.

Ever you grant to me your curious beauty,
my city, recognizing me, your bard.
City of my song, fount of my life, O city
to which my yearning heart turns, near or far,

city of towers, and the Belfry, and ashen nights
swirling with menace round your venerable fort;
city of dark canals with secret depths,
enwreathed by flowers of every hue and sort,

city that mocks me in ever crueler ways,
yet each time gives me valor to rise above,
city of my fondest joys and finest days,
where I, aglow with pride, first fell in love . . .

In the house in Drongenhof, the three children grow up in the same rooms that, years later, I will make my own. They do not know why their father sometimes sits staring, tense and gloomy, in the half darkness of the annex, while Mientje hurries in and out, preparing dinner. Adri will leave all this unmentioned in the memoir he writes as an emeritus professor; there he claims, probably with more heartache than his words reveal, that all he can remember from the days of rising fascism is the sound of the boots of Flemish Dinaso militants pounding the streets of Ghent.

As for me, Letta tells me, I used to catch the rats that climbed out of the Lieveke into our backyard. I would put the rat trap out at night, and by morning I'd have another of those greasy creatures behind bars. Then my mother would say, Lettie, you take care of that, I can't stand the thought.

But I was scared too, every time, and I pitied them; no other eyes can glitter like a rat's, it's as if they're staring straight through you. I would take the trap, with the thing inside it squeaking, and dunk it, eyes closed, into the water of the rain barrel. It would put up a real fight; it sometimes took several minutes before the desperate squirming and struggling stopped.

The squeaking still rings in my ears, she says; whenever I dared to open my eyes for a second, I could see the creature's nose pressed against the bars, mercy me, after seventy years I still can see it, just imagine how that was for a child.

8

Now, with a slightly theatrical gesture, De Potter threw open the double doors that separated the front room from the middle room. It was the dreariest part of the house—a design flaw, really, of the kind found so often in this type of bourgeois architecture: the middle room received no direct light. Somewhere in his book *The House of Life*, the Italian author Mario Praz writes that children who grow up in a house with dark middle rooms will never stop longing for a light somewhere off in the distance, for transcendence; they grow up with the promise of paradise on the horizon, they will go on yearning for the promised land.

This shadowy room was dominated by a shade of stale dark brown that clung to everything like a melanoma, from the years when the house had not been heated in the winter. Not only the doors but also the broad wooden floorboards had been painted this sombre brown color, then worn by countless footsteps, dented here and there by a fallen object, or maybe a woman's sharp heel, the metal tip of a nineteenth-century walking stick, a pair of scissors or a coal shovel; the ceiling, with its plaster decorations, was smeared with the same gloom-inducing shade, which descended to more than a yard below the cornice and thus resembled an overturned box lowered onto the room like a snuffer, the decaying paint now covered with a pathos of fine cracks. Meanwhile, the thin particle board paneling along the walls had begun to come loose, revealing holes in the plaster.

And because even the notary was somewhat taken aback by the state of the place, he decided it was time for another encouraging remark, something about the fine ornamentation and how a fresh new color would bring it out. "Ah, well," he said, "it's not as bad as it looks, sir, you can sand down those broad boards until they're just like new . . ." With these words, he stamped one of his brightly polished shoes on the floor, making a hollow thud that resonated in the crawl space below. A few floorboards were creaky; one made a loud, wretched groan, an almost animal noise, as eerie to me as if the house itself had screamed upon awakening from an enchanted slumber. In the wail of that creaky plank, nailed into place in the days when the country was first becoming a nation, I could hear something like a beginning, a scream of birth; it was a red pine board, probably from a trunk that had sprouted when Austria was still horse-trading with France: the Southern Netherlands for Venice. This silent witness, with its loud, grim cry, made me feel welcomed, initiated and intrigued, drawn into the dance of the things all around me that I did not yet understand. Yes, I said, this house could use a little work. And De Potter gave me a slightly crooked grin, as if to say, If it were in better condition, you couldn't afford it, my lad.

In the middle of this gloomy middle room was a wheelbarrow with a few scoops of sand and gravel in it, and in one of the walls someone had hacked a rough opening, with a candle inside that had dripped onto the wallpaper below. Elsewhere, in a dark corner, lay a piece of cardboard with a few rags on it. Apparently a homeless person sometimes slept here, perhaps creeping in through the back door, which had come off its hinges. The room was dominated by a blackened fireplace made of gray-veined Ardennes marble, decorated with a few shells carved in white Carrara. Not much was left of the plaster on the ceiling other than formless clods still vaguely reminiscent of fruit ornaments; the round paunch of a small Bacchus looked more like a drowned rat's gut than a wine god's belly. In the left corner stood a table with lions' feet; the top was littered with old newspapers, as if the last resident had left the house in a tearing hurry. On the ground were a few pieces of cardboard with leftover food stuck to them. Next to the fireplace were soot stains and even a burned patch. The notary, who again felt the need to say something encouraging, declared that this could become the coziest room in the house.

I don't know if the Verhulst family ever ate there; maybe only when they had important guests. The kitchen was in the annex, and rushing back and forth with warm dishes, plates and silverware was not really convenient; Mientje would have had to go by way of either the hallway, which was always chilly, or the porch. That would have meant opening and shutting three doors—not so practical with your hands full, especially not on cold days in a house that lacked central heating and was too big to keep warm any other way. I was seized by ambivalence: on the one hand, I felt somehow sheltered, as if this room were a cocoon I could hide away in, far from the outside world—it was quieter here, the traffic in nearby Sluizeken Square was almost inaudible, merely a dull, vague rumble; on the other hand, the room was somehow asphyxiating, as if you might run out of air—it was the kind of room in which distinguished middle-class families used to place a large mirror over the mantelpiece, and in which they had dusky, otherworldly eyes, like the people in Léon Spilliaert paintings. It was the most liminal of places, a limbo from which you could move in all directions; a transition and a refuge. It occurred to me that maybe I should cover the walls with bookcases up to the ceiling, listen to music here, shut my eyes, and let the whole hectic whirl of thoughts slow down for a while.

It was almost afternoon; in the distance, above the rooftops, the skies opened for a moment; a watery light-blue gap formed in the clouds. I could vaguely feel the ground trembling; the tram was rattling through nearby Grauwpoort toward Lange Steenstraat; people would be getting on and off at the turn just before the medieval castle.

9

One day around noon Mientje hears repeated honking on the street; she opens the door, and there is Willem in his Nazi uniform in a big car, beaming; he asks her with pride if she'll go on a drive through the city with him; he is overjoyed and overexcited. His delight makes her uneasy; noticing the childish look in his eyes, she says, Just watch out, Wim, you've had a few accidents already with that blind eye of yours. He barely hears her; come on, wife of mine, get in, he says, we're going for a spin. He's still getting the hang of shifting gears; the large black vehicle sputters several feet forward, bucks like a stubborn goat, and whoops, they're off—past the narrowed eyes of neighbors and pedestrians, past the tranquil, foul-smelling canals, past the German flags flying over medieval Gravensteen Castle, past the restaurants in Korenmarkt Square, where customers at outdoor cafés look up or nudge each other. Look, driving that car, it's Willem, you know, used to work at the MEGA in Oudburg, they say his wife's from Holland, thinks he's quite something these days, doesn't he, right y'are, watch out for that man, he reported my nuncle to the Germans. Then they drive through the better neighborhoods, along Kouter, past the opera house where Flemish nationalist pennants with all-black lions now wave side by side with swastikas, and up Kortrijkses-teenweg to Sint-Pieters Station, headed toward Latem. What do you say, Mien, he coaxes, let's just pop over to Latem, to the Leie, all right? And she says, But Wim, I still have the house to clean, I'm sitting here in my apron, I want to stop by the church in Brabantdam, I promised. They drive down the old avenues leading out of the city; at some stage they reach a German military checkpoint; when Willem shows his papers the soldier clicks his heels, returns the passport immediately and gives the familiar salute that Mientje despises.

After Willem drops her off at home and drives back to work, she picks up her Bible and reads a few psalms. Then she goes to the Protestant church in Brabantdam, where Pastor Pichal, seeing her consternation, gives her a probing look. I have to pray for my husband, she says, I have to plead for mercy for him, may the Lord help us, the Lord is good, the Lord knoweth our troubles. She recites Deuteronomy 24:5 from memory:

> When a man hath taken a new wife, he shall not go out to war, neither shall he be charged with any business: but he shall be free at home one year, and shall cheer up his wife which he hath taken.

Willem loves books, especially about history; a package arrives weekly, delivered to their home by courier. A surprising number of these books are in French and bear the stamp of the École des Hautes Études in Korenlei, a French-language school for adults established in 1923, when the university in Ghent opened a Dutch-language division alongside the French-language one. A new gramophone also arrives for the front room, on which he plays music for his visitors; he cannot get enough of the overture to *Der Rosenkavalier*.

He announces to Mientje that they will soon be invited to performances at the city's opera house—the old Théâtre Royal is now Flemish, thanks to the generous contributions of Willem's patrons and the new, flamingant administration; the Germans have lavished financial support on the new opera company. She learns that Willem knows the new business manager, who has visited their home a few times already to discuss the repertoire for the next few months, a pay raise for the singers and musicians, and the new possibilities for cultural life in the city. The German benefactors have made their policy clear: the emphasis must be on works that suit the nature of the Flemish *Volk*. No more French experiments, but plenty of Wagner, or Weber's *Freischütz*. Mascagni's *Cavalleria rusticana* is still acceptable, and Beethoven's *Fidelio* is a must; a musical education, to give their long-downtrodden Germanic brethren renewed pride in their cultural heritage.

In every respect, Willem has transformed into a new man. Sometimes Mientje feels a warm glow when she sees how contented and self-confident her husband has become; but sometimes she lies awake at night wondering why he hasn't come home, what he's up to this time, until, close to dawn, she hears the soft scrape of the heavy front door across the tiles as it opens and shuts, and she falls into a heavy, gloomy sleep, waking up with a start an hour later because she has to get the children out of bed.

Although Willem rakes in a remarkably generous salary for his activities and drives around in a fancy car—in fact, he often has a chauffeur—there are frequent shortages of healthy food. In Adri's memoir, he recalls how the people of Ghent went hungry in the early years of the war. Food was purchased with ration coupons, the bread was poor in quality, butter and vegetables were scarce and expensive, meat was a privilege of farmers and the wealthy; city children suffered from malnutrition. It may seem surprising that Willem, with his connections, could not obtain better food for his children, but the reason was ideological: he forbade his family to buy food on the black market, because it could endanger his position, and besides, it was against his principles. "Ration bread," Adri writes, "was very dark, and as it had not fully risen, it had a mushy layer of sticky flour and yeast at the bottom." On the other hand, their father sometimes brought home ham, butter, cheese, milk and bread for his family. But what did Willem himself eat during office hours in the headquarters of the occupying regime? His answers were always vague.

10

It is an evening in the spring of 1942; the air pressure is dropping and the weather is mild; in the streets, the air has warmed up, and at Café Roosje on Sluizenkaai, four soldiers tumble out of the door and shuffle down the footpath, making slurred conversation, to the passageway where the working girls are waiting; a few moorhens splash in the mud of the vile Lieveke, a child throws pebbles at them. Through the gaps in the fence behind Willem's house, a passer-by could have seen Letta and Suzy at work with plants and a spade.

Only a couple of hours have passed since the incident. Mientje, while dusting, had removed the hated head from the mantelpiece in the front room, taken it to the attic and draped an old cloth over it. You stay right there for a while, Mr. Ugly, she mumbled. But Willem had a meeting planned in his home that very evening; when he discovered the bust was missing, he flew off the handle at her, forgetting he was still in uniform; he worked himself up and turned red in the face, truly ranting by this point; in a flash, Mientje saw not her husband standing there but a screeching SS officer with a death's head on his cap. Again, she felt that flame of fear and horror, making her whole self tremble. Calm down, Pappie, she said, don't shout like that, think of the children. Willem snorted and yelled to Adri to fetch the bust at once and put it back where it was.

Now Willem Verhulst is seated in full military regalia in the front room—the death room, as Mientje still calls it, to his great aggravation. He is deep in conversation with his fellow SS officer George Balliu and a German officer. Seated proudly next to the bust of Hitler with a glass of Riesling and a Dutch cigar, Willem says, Yes, *Sturmscharführer*, magnificent, isn't it, a striking likeness of our great leader, a masterpiece by a great Flemish artist, do you share my love of the fine arts? I knew the great Albert Servaes personally, oh, yes, those artists of ours, Truth and Beauty, that's the only way to elevate our people to new heights of culture. What's that? They call Bruegel *ein deutscher Künstler*? Oh, and we always thought Beethoven was an Antwerp artist, ha ha, and soon it will be your turn for an audience with *Obersturmführer* Jungclaus, before he is transferred to Brussels, a great honor for this country, the way I see it. Two cultured gentlemen chatting by the fire where decades later I will stare into the flames and kiss the woman I love.

All that hot air—Mientje doesn't want to hear it. Her heart is still pounding from the incident; arguing leaves her nauseated for hours. She has shut the tall double doors to the middle room and asks Adri if they can make music together again. No, she isn't teasing, not at all; that afternoon, when she was in the attic, she found the old sheet music that her teacher in Oud-Zevenaar had given her so many years ago; she stood there holding it in her hands, surprised at first, then moved; she hummed a few bars, standing there in the attic, and later that day, when Adri came home from school, she asked if he would play the melody. Now, after running through it once or twice, Adri can play it almost faultlessly, though even more slowly than normal; Mientje feels herself settle down, light enters her heart, light and a voice that wells up out of her, softly singing "Ombra mai fu," even if she does have a lump in her throat and an unsteady pitch. At one point she falters, because memory overwhelms her. She swallows her emotion. Once more, she says, like a child recovering her enthusiasm, once more, Adri, and no mistakes this time.

Just as Adri is playing the opening bars, they hear a thunderous bang from the front room. It's obvious a pistol has gone off; Adri almost drops his violin in shock, Mientje stares at him open-mouthed, they hear fumbling and murmuring, Mama, what's going on in there, Adri says. Mientje goes to the door, cautiously turns the hexagonal wooden doorknob, and opens it, just a crack. Willem is with his back to her, on his knees by the fireplace, the *Sturmscharführer* and Balliu looking on open-mouthed. Then she sees the shards on the floor, the pedestal knocked over by the impact, the whole bust of the Führer has been blown to smithereens. Balliu sees the woman's head at the door, oh dear, he says, your husband has had a spot of bad luck, ma'am, he was cleaning his revolver with an old cloth and a little turpentine and I was just saying to him, stop fooling with that weapon, Willem, you shouldn't hold it like that, I said to him, surely it's not loaded, my friend, watch out with that turpentine, it makes the gun slippery, I told him, and now just look what happened, look what happened . . . Mientje stares speechless, gasps for air, and then says, as calmly as she can, Could have done worse, Willem, could have done worse.

He turns slowly and gapes at her. Sometimes, like now, he is still a clumsy boy. His good eye, staring, looks as motionless and dead as the other, but helpless, God, she hasn't seen him so helpless in years; it's broken, he mumbles, turning back to the shards, his hand groping for support at the brown and rose Comblanchien marble. Mientje shuts the door again; everything's fine, she says to Adri, who has been waiting in dread in the gathering darkness of the middle room, absolutely fine, a sign from God, let's start over, da capo, from the beginning, all right? One, two, hup . . . And the half-lit room fills once more with the melody of the immortal "Largo":

Tender and beautiful fronds
of my beloved plane tree
may Fate smile upon you.
May thunder, lightning and storms
never disturb your dear peace

114

and may the howling winds
never defile you.
Never was the shadow
of any plant
dearer, lovelier
or sweeter.

Letta has taken the crumbling sheet music out of her desk drawer and spent the whole afternoon reminiscing. Here, look, she says, would you like to hold the score for a moment, my mother never got rid of it, I found it in Drongenhof after she died, lying next to her bed by her diaries.

She holds out her little treasure to me with shaky hands, and for several minutes, neither of us speaks a blessed word.

11

Look, Letta says, this is a Symphonion, we had it in the house in Drongenhof in the war years. She winds the antique-looking device with a large key on the side, and thin carillon sounds fill her entrance hall. I am visiting the energetic old lady in Edegem, near Antwerp. For hours she has been regaling me with spirited, warmhearted stories about the house where I passed twenty years of my life and where she spent her childhood and the war years.

The Symphonion, "Automate à Musique," was on the wall of the middle room, and the children could summon up its music whenever they wished—I picture days in the middle of the war, the house engulfed in the roar of raw reality, but inside, like the voices of untimely angels, a current of sound babbling on, too fast almost to hear the harmonies; the case is decorated with three golden stars and an antique lyre—a Christian symbol and a Dionysian instrument. The sound moves me; Letta's eyes glitter. She has lifted a finger crooked with gout, like a signal to a child to keep quiet and listen.

Her well-kept house is full of light and old-fashioned hospitality. She has a life of teaching behind her—physical education, exercise, persistence—but also of devotion to her family. She is even a kind of feminist in her way. She tells me about the suffragettes in the war years and the unconventional woman known as Aunt Mée—but I won't learn more about her until later. It's not hard for Letta to talk about her days in the house in Patershol, but I notice dark gaps in the story, places where her monologue makes a dignified detour or rests for a moment in silence. The Symphonion slows to a halt in the middle of a melody, like a bird dying in your hand; her bony fingers wind the mechanism again, and the sound is like music in a Viennese ballroom, a faint, faraway echo as if through a long-ago snowstorm; under the embellished glass panel, the metal disc turns slow circles.

Symphonion, hurdy-gurdy, music box, waltzes, a folk song—it's chilly in the hallway on winter days, the doors stick, it takes a firm push to shut them, and even then the wind keens through every crack and cranny; the cellar is icy cold and damp like the deepest recesses of Dante's underworld.

Come back whenever you like, Letta tells me. She gives me the treasures of her past to take with me: her mother Mientje's diary, her own life story, and a notebook with a runner on the cover and a title in her father's handwriting: "Wil's Childhood." She can hardly wait to see what will become of her father's story once she is no longer its keeper. She waves as I drive off, and on the way home I keep hearing the creak of the key winding the spring of the Symphonion, like windup birds in an old cage, mechanical creatures that fall silent in a jingle of metal wings because the end of a love affair is in sight and the young woman whose delicate hand wound the mechanism for her young man already knows in silence that she will leave him—that the mechanism of her emotions is lost forever to her lover, who is listening in desperation and moving in for one last, awkward embrace. But that's not how it sounds to Letta's ears; her hand is still leafing through notebooks and photos, long after I'm home again and asking myself, How can I explain to my readers that it was my very ignorance that brought this emotion, years after everything had vanished? *Sym-phonein*, the word simply means "together-sound," to make a sound together whose complex whole transcends the sum of its parts.

The next day, as I go through the transcript of an interview by a doctoral researcher who recorded Letta's memories, I realize how difficult it remains for her to face the cold facts—she describes the brutal SS takeover of the rediffusion service as "a better job offered to my father by the city administration, after the previous director had fled because of the German occupation." This innocent formulation is like a thin membrane stretched over raw flesh. No, the whole thing hardly holds together anymore; all that's left is the vague dying fall of scraping metal in that fine wooden case, something like model trains on a rusty track.

12

But what kind of work does Papa have to do, then, whines the youngest, Suzy. Papa has to write reports, says Adri, he has to report on the situation among the people. What kind of reports, then, says Suzy, and what kind of people? I don't know, Adri says, bad people, I think, because Papa's a confidential agent, that's what I've heard. Oh, so the good people have so much confidence in Papa that they let him punish the bad ones. Yes, obviously, says Adri, what did you think? Pajamas on, children, says Mientje, enough talking, off to bed and keep quiet and go to sleep, or Father Christmas will never come.

⁓

Willem is busier and busier all the time; sometimes he's away all night and tells her there was a special "operation" and he slept at work afterwards, on a bed the janitor installed for him. Then Mientje hears him say, I have to go to Diksmuide tonight, there's a meeting there early tomorrow morning, I'll find a place to sleep somewhere in the area. She keeps her thoughts to herself.

I picture him working until late in the evening at the heavy lion's-paw table in the middle room. And as the years went by, the demands on him mount; a "confidential agent" (a *Vertrauensmann* or *V-Mann*) is an informer and a manhunter. Willem has to report on anyone he and his staff feel is out of line—Anglophiles, Freemasons, Jews, socialists, enemies of the *Volk*, fransquillons, resisters, Bolshevists, and even, at the occupiers' insistence, on the Boy Scout movement, with its irksome pacifist philosophy. He has to keep an eye on a suspect billiards club on Sleepstraat, and on the fanatical Belgicists from the First World War—you can't let them out of your sight, with their talk of the unity of the Belgian nation and their books by Jean Jaurès and Romain Rolland. Yes, there is an impressive volume of paperwork involved in guarding the immaculate soul of the *Volk*.

By this time, Adri's father occupies a large office in the former École des Hautes Études, or at least that's what Adri has heard at school; Willem doesn't share that kind of information with his family—they have lives of their own, he says. Sometimes he is summoned to Brussels by *Obersturmführer* Jungclaus himself—*zur Betreuung der flämischen SS*, in support of the Flemish SS, as Jungclaus so eloquently puts it. After he returns, with a grin on his face, he and his German associates Siekmann and Erstling polish off the expensive Grauburgunder or *Eiswein* he's received from someone or other in recognition of his outstanding work. They are often joined by his buddy Richard P., whose code name in the espionage service is apparently Adolf; Willem prefers to call him Rijkhart, the Flemish version of his French-sounding name. Good old Rijkhart will later be convicted of attempting to sell the entire Belgian Congo to Germany. Those fellows love to while away the evening by the fire in Drongenhof. Dear me, what a happy home, and that in the middle of the war, you're a lucky devil, Mr. Verhulst, but I'd be careful if I were in your shoes, especially in all the dark little alleys around here, you know how easy it is for a person to stumble from a dark staircase in the night, if you take my meaning. Another glass, yes, don't mind if I do.

A week later, Willem brings Adri a present. He arrives home with it around six o'clock in the evening and calls his son into the front room. For you, my son, so that you can become the pride of your people. The object is inside a brown envelope. Adri reaches for it; in the envelope is a case, which he opens with care to find a large dagger inscribed with

Gothic letters: "*Meine Ehre heißt Treue.*" Adri stands with the dagger in his hand, not knowing what to think; he is a thirteen-year-old boy, he likes running in the woods around Ghent, carving the ends of sticks to a sharp point; he likes knives, he already has ten, of various kinds and sizes, but this thing is big and heavy—thank you, Papa, he stammers. He lays the gift in its case beside his plate at dinnertime, and his father gives him a warm, encouraging nod; his mother keeps narrowing her eyes at the thing; Suzy asks what the gift was. That's a secret, Willem hastens to say, big boys have secrets, and Suzy dutifully finishes her plate. After Willem goes up to his study, Mientje asks in a commanding tone if she can see that beautiful gift for a moment. She opens the case, takes out the SS dagger and gasps; could it be that Adri even hears his devout mother curse under her breath? She looks at him as if stung by a wasp, hesitates for a moment, and then pulls the back door open—Adri shouts *Mama, no!*—strides across the backyard and, with one great swing of her arm, throws the dagger and case through a gap in the fence, into the dark waters of the Lieveke. Adri looks on, red in the face, tears coming to his eyes; she puts her hands on his shoulders. Come here, she says, my silly boy. He pushes away her arms with a sullen frown and creeps up the stairs past the second-floor study so that his father won't hear him, to his room, where he sits on his bed, wipes off his tears and watches darkness descend on the roofs around Sluizeken Square.

The bustling École des Hautes Études in Korenlei was now home to a new and radical wing of the Flemish Movement, founded by Willem himself: the *Comité voor Dietsche Actie*, or Dietsch Action Committee. In that political moment, the ideologically laden word "Dietsch" signaled a commitment both to close collaboration with the Nazi occupiers and to the unity of the Dutch-speaking peoples, ideally in a kind of Greater Netherlands. Willem's office was the library on the second floor, at a remove from the ruckus at ground level, where you could hardly hear yourself think. Things got especially rough when Mr. Gaston Delbeke dropped in—it was no joke to him, interrogating enemies of the *Volk*. Gaston was a roughneck who usually had a few drinks before the interrogation; you could hear the roaring in the cellars, and the wailing and the sobbing and the cursing and the beating, much more than a person cared to know about. One afternoon, Willem, on his way to a promising lunch with the *Obersturmführer*, saw one of them stumbling out onto the street, a resistance member, fat Marcel from that den of degenerates in Patershol, his swollen face black and blue, his jaw out of joint, his left leg dragging behind him a little, a large stain in his trousers, that fellow was bawling like a baby, hardly able to walk anymore, a painful sight. For Willem's sensitive nature, this was a little too much, hard to take, bad for his heart; he preferred to sharpen his pencils, keep his fingernails clean, produce his neat lists, smoke fine Dutch cigars—Willem II, an excellent brand—and, in the evening, ask the children if they were working hard at school: Aren't you a good girl, Lettie, keep at it, and is your violin playing still going so well, Adri?

122

13

We crossed the narrow, sunless backyard to the annex, which was on the left. This bare structure was in the worst condition of all. The windows were opaque with dust, the walls looked waterlogged, and the flat roof was nearing collapse. The strips of asphalt roof sealant, which the notary called *terre-papier*, a local French corruption of "tar paper" were as leaky as a sieve; the ceiling had been damaged by rot and seepage; a few beams were broken and sticking out of the plaster, which was still mixed with strands of horsehair, a practice from the old days. The kitchen had been here in the days of the Verhulst family; the many student boarders must have joined them at the table in the years just after the war, when Mientje's husband was in prison and she had to take in lodgers to provide for her family.

I stared dumbstruck at the decay, which had been industriously eating away at the whole structure in silence for years, as if rotting goes faster when no living creature remains to disturb the air. There was hardly space for a counter. A zinc tub formed one last vague reminder of human activity. The narrow chimney in the left corner had a gaping, shapeless maw of soot where a pipe had broken off long ago; maybe Mientje had cooked on a Leuven stove, the kind I remember from childhood, with a round cast-iron firepot supporting and heating the cooktop. You could still see the remnants of the rudimentary sink and the hole in the ground through which the wastewater had flowed into the now-filled canal; where it led these days was anyone's guess—maybe to subterranean mud streams from which the tall birches took deep drafts. Next to the hole in the floor, a huge fern was growing. I looked around in a mix of astonishment and excitement, already understanding in some corner of myself that I could not resist buying this house. Notary De Potter jotted down a few notes on his Statement of Condition, his pen seeming to falter as if feeling faint in the musty air. From above us, through the weathered old asphalt on the partly collapsed flat roof, came the cries of three geese flying through the gray air toward the harbor. A fire engine raced through the intersection at Sluizeken Square; in the scruffy little park, a stray dog was chasing a pet cat, which fled hissing up the trunk of a birch tree. The air pressure seemed to be rising, vague, chilly clouds in watery blue; yellow leaves drifted over the gloomy annex of the neighboring house with the stepped gable, which was also quietly collapsing—just a few millimeters a year, but that's more than enough.

A rat shot into a heap of crumbled brick in the shed by the fence, where a pile of mildewed firewood was decomposing under an intricate festoon of dusty spiderwebs. The wood gave off the damp scent of mold and toadstools. In the midst of this decay, a slender maple tree was shooting up in the backyard. The stinging nettles around it were motionless in the gray city air, which seemed vaguely full of smells from outside the city (Brussels sprout cuttings, the fragrance of wet grass, pigsties) blended with impressions from the urban fringes (asphalt, bus stops, diesel); there was also a small mastic tree, an exotic southern species crowned with light-colored leaves—hard to understand how it had managed to germinate in this sunless spot.

"I will tear down this hovel," I said with a determination that surprised me. "The first thing I will do is tear down this annex, nothing good ever comes of an annex." "You must do what you have to do, sir," said the notary with dignity.

The chilly air seized hold of our breath; our words drifted in front of our mouths, thin clouds dissolving into the ruinous silence; we wandered through the garden, looking around; a drop of water drummed into the zinc tub. The door to the hallway, which we tried to open next, was stuck so tight that Mr. De Potter had to ram it open with his shoulder. The pressure made it give way unexpectedly; the plump notary lost his balance, his distinguished head almost smacking into the doorframe. He waved away the damp spiderweb from his sleeves, gave a slight cough, and said, as if making a solemn pronouncement, "Well, my good man, now we've done the whole *rez-de-chaussée*. The stairs beckon us, come along now." "The reddish what?" I asked sheepishly, but my guide headed off to the stairwell with a shrug, no longer looking back at the young fool who would be taking this accursed house off his hands at last.

14

Herr Steffens, the German stationmaster at Sint-Pieters in Ghent, is a middle-aged man, polite and reserved, who obviously feels more than sympathy for Mientje. He sometimes joins them at the table in the annex, pitying the children as they nibble at the sticky ration bread and reluctantly slurp at their cabbage soup. He knows the *Verwaltung* has ordered Willem to use part of his handsome salary to cover the incidental expenses of his growing staff and ever-larger bureaucracy, but still . . . One day he brings German army bread and sausage for the children. Willem feels humiliated; I have to feed my family with Belgian ration coupons, he says, my commanders won't let me do much more for them, I often bring the children treats saved from lunch at work. I understand, Steffens says, but your children look a little pale, spending all their time in this dark house, and then the city air, maybe this summer you can send them along with the KLV, the *Kinderlandverschickung*. A few months in Germany will do them good. Mientje stiffens; she's heard that Baldur von Schirach was appointed by Hitler himself to evacuate German children to the countryside so that, as the newsreader put it, they would be sheltered from "anti-German war violence"—the Allied bombings in the cities.

Since 1942 the occupying regime has been trying, for propaganda purposes, to send collaborators' children to Germany for a restorative trip to the country. But perhaps because the German term *Kinderlandverschickung* ("relocation of children to the countryside") is too redolent of collaboration, the same initials have been given a Flemish meaning: *Kracht, Leven, Vreugde*, or Power, Life, Virtue. Fighters on the Eastern

Front and actively pro-German families received brochures in the post, urging them to think of the Thousand-Year Reich's future generations. Mientje once looked at one such brochure, on a visit to an acquaintance of Willem's. She hissed to her husband then: I would never allow such a thing, and don't you forget it. Now she gives her head a slow shake and shuts her eyes.

It would be good for the children's health, Steffens repeats; we Germans have a centuries-old *Kultur* of summer camps, out in the fresh air, and the *Hajot* has given that fine old tradition a grand, national character. What is the *Hajot*, sir? Letta asks. That's the club you'd have to join first, Steffens says, our famous *Hitlerjugend*, Hitler Youth. The next time he visits, he brings KLV folders, along with a few articles from the fascist newspaper in Flanders, *Volk en Staat*, applauding the solidarity shown by young Germans with the "West Germanic" children in Belgium and the Netherlands. One article quotes Himmler as saying that any Flemish children who visit Germany will love the country for ever afterward. Mientje turns a fiery red and glares at Willem, who avoids eye contact. Silence at the table; Steffens says it's time for him to go. Once the door has shut behind him, Mientje sends the children to bed. Even before they reach the first landing, they hear the latest of countless arguments break out in the kitchen.

Not long afterward, Willem springs into action after all, perhaps in an attempt to keep his marriage from running completely off the rails. By "pulling a few strings," as he puts it, he arranges for the children and their mother to travel to Oud-Zevenaar—an exception to the usual rules. There they receive an emotional welcome; even the old gentleman farmer wipes away a tear when he sees how much the children have grown, and he gives each of them, especially Adri, a surprisingly hearty squeeze. The children take possession of their rooms; for several minutes, Mientje stands staring in the yard in front of the farmhouse.

She comes inside, still wide-eyed, and wraps her arms around her father's shoulders; the children have never seen their mother like this. The table is set, and to their astonishment they are served sausage, ham and cheese in generous portion; there is fresh bread and more milk than they can drink. Later, when they go down in the cellars, they see large stocks of ham, cheese, potatoes and flour. Can we stay here forever? Suzy asks. Her mother brushes a lock of hair from the girl's forehead and says nothing.

The next day, Mientje takes Adri to see the Wartenas, leaving the girls behind on the farm. She tells the pastor she needs his advice—Willem wants to send the children to Germany, she says. She bites her lower lip. Oh, dear girl, says the pastor's wife, and she lays her hand on Mientje's arm. The look in Adriaan Wartena's eyes is as dark as a thundercloud; he stares out ahead with pursed lips. What should I do? asks Mientje. I can't stay here in Oud-Zevenaar with the children, can I? After a long silence, the pastor says, Mien, listen to me now, and his stern voice startles her. Those Germans may act friendly, but it's all an act. Didn't Goethe say, "In German, to be courteous is a lie?" In the ensuing conversation, the pastor does not hide his bitterness, sorrow and dismay; he has not one good thing to say about Willem. You don't have to get your hands dirty to commit crimes, he growls. The words make Adri cringe. He keeps a stealthy eye on how his mother reacts; the German and Flemish officers who visit their home always seem friendly enough, don't they? All this is hard for him to follow. Mien chokes back her tears and stares out of the window at the fields and pastures of her youth. The pastor's wife breaks the silence: But just suppose a summer in Germany is the best thing for the health of those poor children? What could you have against that? I'm sure their father knows just how to organize the whole thing in an orderly fashion. Or are they supposed to spend yet another summer in that rat-infested backyard, in a city full of drunk soldiers and other scum?

—

Two of the children, Adri and Letta—Suzy was still too young for a summer camp abroad—describe the experience, which has stayed with them all their lives, in their respective memoirs. The son remembers more—he was thirteen years old, after all. Letta keeps her account of that summer much shorter, partly because her slender book is a reply to her brother's memoir; while he concentrates on dredging up their father's painful past, she tries to write an ode to her mother. Her only comment on this episode is that Mientje was utterly opposed to the plan.

"My sister and I," Adri writes, "two young people without uniforms, just leaving the nest for the first time, felt like fish out of water on the train to Germany." They were intimidated by the other children, who sang nationalist battle songs the whole time, engaged in "heavy petting" and acted as if their uniforms made them strong. Their mother wouldn't allow the two of them to wear uniforms, even though Willem had pleaded with her again and again—the children of his fellow officials wore the Flemish nationalist costume of the political youth movements affiliated with collaborationist parties like the Flemish National Union and Flemish Rexists; they filled the railway cars with shouting and laughter, sang themselves hoarse—martial tunes like "The Blauwvoet, Song of Flemish Sons" and "As Long as the Lion Can Claw"—and had a barrel of fun. But Mientje had put her foot down. Wim, she said, this is as far as I go; the children are going to summer camp in Germany, I won't complain, they need it, mainly because you're the kind of stickler who won't even bring home a few extra ration coupons for fear of compromising your

Germanic honor. But they're *my* children too, I'm responsible for their upbringing, you can do as you please, but *my* children do *not* wear uniforms, not now, not ever, and that's the end of it. To which Willem said, a little sheepishly, All right, Mien, it's all right, don't get yourself so worked up about it. The next day Mr. De Pestel, who by this stage was Willem's personal assistant, took the children to the railway station.

It was a long journey.

We took a special train by way of St. Vith, Letta later recalls when I speak to her. It followed the Vennbahn, the line to Aachen that the Germans had built and then lost after the First World War, when they had to give up the area around St. Vith to Belgium as war reparations. During the second occupation, they had triumphantly brought it back into service as a German line. It was a large railway complex. These days it has fallen into disuse; the old tunnels in Lommersweiler have been bricked up, the dark passageways are home to countless bats, and the route has become a bicycle path for tourists. Sometimes people still go there to gape at the old complex.

The train stops in Aachen all night because of the risk of bombing. A group leader in lederhosen tells Adri and Letta that they will spend the night in two different towns, so they have to be separated now. Hungry, timid and confused, they beg to be allowed to stay together. Eventually, the two of them are sent to Neuenstein, a town in the Baden-Württemberg region, some four hundred miles from Ghent, where a bed has already been found for Letta—but not yet for Adri. As they travel the last few miles, they are tense and frightened.

The train stops at the small station; men open the doors, shout to each other, and order them off with about ten other children. A shrill whistle, the doors close, the train jolts into motion. A moment later, the silence on the platform is deafening; you can hear birds chirp, a few civilians wait at the far end, saying nothing; the children are shy and nervous; one starts to cry. A list of names is read. Letta is to stay with the mayor, a notary whose name she doesn't catch. A chaperone takes her by the hand and leads her off. Adri still has to find a place to sleep; the bashful boy is inspected by a couple of curious townspeople; a farmer picks him as a field hand, because he looks strong for his age.

"The farm was average in size and in the center of the village, at the end of a little *Gasse* not far from the station," Adri recalls. He learned all sorts of things from the family there, he writes: how to yoke the oxen, and drive an empty cart to the field a few miles outside the village and help to fill it with wheat or clover.

He finds out the farmer is no friend of the National Socialists; he responds to the mayor's *Heil Hitler*, when their paths cross on the streets, with a grumbled *Grüß Gott*. Adri and his sister exchange shy smiles as they pass hand in hand with their respective host parents. They see little of each other; it's quite a distance between the farm and the mayor's house.

A visiting aunt from nearby Karlsruhe asks the Flemish boy where he comes from. His stammered reply provokes an astonished response: *Aber dann sind Sie Feinde Deutschlands!* But then you're enemies of Germany! Dutiful Adri, the adolescent son of a Nazi collaborator, as helpful as ever, feels obliged to make a drawing of the Flemish IJzertoren monument in Diksmuide, to make it clear to this iron lady "why the supporters of the Flemish Movement don't feel we are enemies of Germany." In his memoir, he adds a surprising remark: "Yet I have never forgotten that once I met someone who did not assume that the people of the occupied territories harbored warm feelings toward the Germans."

The more I leaf through Adri's memoir, the more I notice what he was unable or unwilling to think through completely. As if sin could be passed down from generation to generation, and his own inheritance was too heavy a burden—a son with his father's dead weight on his shoulders. Pain lay in the silence between the words of his testimony.

On Sundays, Adri accompanies his host family to the evangelical church. It's close to the mayor's house, where Letta is staying, just opposite Neuenstein's impressive castle. In the evening, he is sometimes allowed to go out with the boys in the local division of the Hitler Youth. They generally march to the forests outside town, where one of them plays the *Hajot* song on a trumpet while the others sing and shout along, making the forest echo. "*Vorwärts, Vorwärts, schmettern die hellen Fanfaren! Unsere Fahne flattert uns voran!*"

"Politics was never part of any of this," Adri writes, absurdly. It seems the whole thing was merely a colorful experience to him—"Beyond that, I delighted in the large portions of good food I was given that summer, the delicious chilled cider we were allowed to drink cold on the hottest days, and the *Zwiebelkuchen*, savory onion cakes the grandmother brought to the fields, where my host father, my host mother and I would work until the sweat ran down our backs."

That's all we know; the archives of the Berliner Reichsdienststelle KLV, which organized the summer trips, were obliterated in the final days of the war.

15

It is the spring of 2019 when I finally find a few days to visit Neuenstein—almost forty years after my first visit to the house in Drongenhof and seventy-six years after Adri and Letta spent a summer there that they would remember for the rest of their lives. At first, I see nothing but a German provincial town like so many others, with a *Volksbank* at the roundabout. Just off the slip road to the center I notice the splendid castle, home to the princely House of Hohenlohe—a sight made more exceptional by the partial Allied destruction of many German towns in acts of retribution. I park under one of the old trees along the moat and amble down the quiet streets to my hotel. The manager is a Thai woman married to a jocular German man; they draw me into a long conversation about recent elections all over Europe—they're deeply concerned about the xenophobic trend. Later that evening, I see a few young black men in the near-deserted streets, a little later a couple of Indian boys, and then a few girls with Eastern European features, Romanian or Bulgarian. There's a Turkish kebab shop displaying advertisements for German sausage and German beer. The city seems peaceful, even charming, despite the pinched expressions of the passersby, who avoid a stranger's eyes. The most noteworthy recent events are a racist attack on an asylum seekers' center in early 2017, and an armed robbery at the Volksbank Hohenlohe in the spring of 2018, committed by a man from local neo-Nazi circles, which are rabidly opposed to immigrants and to the general humanitarian tendency in German politics.

The castle, the tower, the church, the timber-framed houses, the geese

in the moat, the swallows in the warm dusk, the park and the gardens—
everything is so flawless and manicured that it suggests an obsession
with purity more than a desire for happiness. I enter the hotel; the multicultural family are enjoying a meal together. I have an excellent red-hot
Thai curry and go to bed early.

The next morning, I step into the courtyard of the old castle. Against
one wall is a large, imposing gravestone. The centuries have left it deeply
worn; the letters are faded, but the date is legible: *MDCXXIX, 3 Juli, Mor-
gen zwischen 8 und 9.* Two coats of arms: Mühlen on the left, Merlau on
the right. What happened on that morning of July 3, 1629? A wedding?
A funeral? I run my fingertips over an inscription that has barely survived the erosion:

WER DA LEBT UND GLEUBT

AN MICH DER WIRT NIMMER

MEHR STERBEN

The words Jesus spoke after raising Lazarus from the grave. Words of
hope for the resurrection of the dead.

In the *Zentralarchiv* of the House of Hohenlohe, on the second floor of the great stone castle, I am presented with a few books and documents from which I learn that Hohenlohes moved back into the castle in 1946, after Russian troops captured their estate in Upper Silesia. It's an odd feeling, in the middle of my search for traces of two Flemish children, to be sitting in the home of one of Germany's most illustrious families, who can trace their ancestry back to the fourteenth century. The region is dotted with their country estates, all equally prosperous and impressive. Goethe's grandfather, Johann Wolfgang Textor, a member of the Hohenlohe dynasty, lived here in Neuenstein in a house in Schloßgasse, the Textorsches Haus; I pass it several times during my stay.

In the archive's quiet reading room, learning about the town's history from its *Heimatbuch*, I discover that in the late years of the war Neuenstein experienced an influx of refugees from all over the world. Some were returning Germans who had fled the Russian advance or the Allied bombings; other townspeople came back after years of absence to find their homes occupied by foreigners. But still other groups also settled in Neuenstein after the war: German speakers from Silesia, Romania and the Czech lands, who had faced the vengefulness of their neighbors after the fall of the Third Reich. Many were desperate and had lost all faith in the future. They had no idea how to go about building a new life for themselves. Senior civil servants, skilled tradespeople, professionals, administrators, judges and teachers who had belonged to the Nazi Party were expelled from their positions, and many of the people who replaced them had no relevant experience whatsoever. The results were friction, general incompetence and deep dissatisfaction. The town chronicler even ventures to say that Neuenstein was *occupied* by the Americans; nowhere does he use the word "liberation."

After an hour of searching and thumbing through pages, I find a document that mentions a Nazi Party attempt to requisition the castle as a storage place for valuable artworks, under the cover of an "Adolf Hitler Art School." But the town employee working at the archive assures me that the Hitler School never became a reality, and that the *Schloß* was never really taken over by the SS.

—

At *Stunde Null*, midnight on May 8, 1945, Neuenstein had the same desolate appearance as many other places in Germany; all the shutters were still closed before dusk. There was a strict curfew, many staples were in short supply, and a rigorous system of rationing was enforced. After large parts of Germany had been bombed into ruins, the chaos must have been overwhelming. The sadistic Nazi administration was followed by an equally rigid, moralistic regime. New regulations and ordinances were issued daily. Everything had to be shared to stave off utter destitution. Townspeople who owned two or three pieces of underwear or more than two shirts or jumpers were required to turn over their extra garments. Wearing a Nazi uniform was strictly forbidden, but this prohibition had to be lifted a week later because of an acute clothing shortage. Even in the 1950s, some older men still used their threadbare uniforms, with the insignia removed, when they worked in the garden. The city library had to be purged, *denazifiziert*; the piles of books published during the Third Reich had to be handed over. It is not clear what happened to all of them; mayors were not inclined to organize a second book burning. In contrast, those who had hidden away books banned by the Nazis were invited to dig them up again and donate them to the half-emptied libraries. With an eye to the winter ahead, messages to the public were posted on walls: conserve firewood, heat only the kitchen and the library, and seal the chinks around windows and doors with daub for the coldest nights. The list of recommendations concluded with this clarion call: *Warmth before beauty.*

In the winter famine of 1946–47—two years after the wartime famine that the Germans caused in Arnhem and much of the rest of the Netherlands—an adult received a monthly ration of eight pounds of bread, two pounds of miscellaneous foodstuffs, four hundred grams of lard, two hundred and fifty grams of cheese, and five litres of milk. Meat scraps were used to prepare a thin soup, which was crawling with maggots the next day—We ate them, an old man sitting on his couch later told me, it was nutritious, you closed your eyes and gulped them down, we would have eaten anything. Mayors were once again asked to be *unempathisch*, this time in cracking down on black marketers and beggars.

Warmth before beauty. This is the sentence that echoes through my mind a few days later, as I sit in the small office of the district archives, where I discover the name of Letta's host: Arthur Zeilein, civil-law notary and wartime mayor from 1940 to 1942. An hour later, I am standing in front of the gloomy, impressive house, where the word "Notariat" is still on a plate by the entrance. The moment makes a deep impression. I picture eleven-year-old Letta, who was required to close her letters to her mother with *Heil Hitler!*, skipping up the stairs here—homesick for the first few days, but soon enough happy and relieved, and gradually becoming healthier and enjoying the abundance, the country air, the castle gardens, the rural setting. I send Letta an email with a photograph of the stately entrance; she is moved and excited by the memory.

By a marvelous coincidence, I also find the former location of the farm where Adri must have stayed. As I wander around the area near the station, it soon becomes clear that there is no longer any farm to be found there. I stop a few passersby, but no one can help me, until I reach a flower shop on the square and see a woman at work in her shop window; I walk into her shop and ask if she can remember a nearby farm from her childhood. I certainly can, she says, the Scheuermann family lived close by, in the Bahnhofstraße, they cultivated a large plot of land there. The farm was demolished in the 1970s; now there are two apartment buildings in the style of old-fashioned German barns. But you should pay a visit to Eugen Vogg, she says, the old *Gärtner* just outside the village; he can tell you much more.

An hour later, I am on the sprawling plantation of a man who seems more than happy to answer my questions. The Scheuermanns had three sons, Vogg says: Fritz, in the year 1930; Ernst in 1932; and Walter in 1933. I tell him Adri was born in 1929—he must have felt a little like a brother to the boys. Adri's host mother, the elderly Mrs. Scheuermann, took her own life after the war. When I ask Vogg why, he stares at the ground, shrugs and says, *Melancholie*. It ran in the family. She took a powerful poison she'd made herself from a hemlock plant in her garden. A few years later, Walter hanged himself. I don't know, he says, it was something in their heads. He falls silent again, watching me with good-natured eyes as if to say, Now you know as much as I do. I realize I cannot ask him straight out whether their tragic ends had anything to do with their wartime sympathies; in any case, Mr. Scheuermann was a fierce anti-Nazi, Adri's book makes that clear.

I walk back along Bahnhofstraße. What have I learned? Why was I so determined to see this for myself? Maybe visiting a site of memory, even if the memories are other people's, is a way of giving history a chance to settle. Back in my hotel room, it occurs to me that both the buildings targeted in the recent attacks—the asylum seekers' center and the bank— are close to the presumed location of the old Scheuermann farm. I wish I could tell old Professor Verhulst.

—

As I'm about to step into the car the next morning, I find myself hesitating. I change my mind, walk all the way back across town to *Gärtner* Vogg's place, and ask if he has a wisteria plant for me; the children who spent one summer here during the war lived in a house in Antwerp with a wisteria on the fence around their small backyard, I tell him, feeling foolish for volunteering so much information. He picks out one of the best for me and charges next to nothing; I head back to my car with it. I told the enthusiastic family at the hotel I'd be back, but I know it's an empty promise; I have found what I was looking for. Yet I've come no closer to what Letta and Adri saw, to Germany as it was then: a landscape much the same, perhaps, as the one Hölderlin had loved a century and a half earlier, but cluttered, in their day, with swastikas, shouting mobs, and drummers, with jackboots and processions, with blaring radios and frenzied tirades at every turn—the clamor of war, the incessant buzz of aircraft, the dark victory in the summer of 1942, a triumphal advance

140

that in no time became a headlong plunge into hell. But that meant nothing to the children at play.

16

I ask Letta what it was like for her to have a one-eyed father; did it make any discernible difference in everyday life, by daylight? Did he ever miss a step on the stairs, trip over a doorstep, or reach for his knife in the wrong place? Hmm, she says, what I remember most clearly is the thick window glass on one side of his spectacles, as if that lens was fogged up. I never saw him wear a black patch over his eye, like a Nazi stereotype from a Hollywood film; when he took off his glasses, we saw a clouded eye, matte and gray, a dead fish in the ice. And yes, every so often he would drive his car into a post, or get into a minor accident and dent the car, no more than that, because he was under orders not to drive too fast. His eye was also the reason he was too clumsy to use his gun properly; I think it had something to do with that, the time he shot the bust of Hitler in the front room. He only saw half the picture, even after he'd been trained to use his weapon to defend his unit from attack. It was after Willem was rejected for the *Waffen-SS* that he became a *V-Mann*, a spy for the Nazi intelligence agency; only later, in 1943, was he awarded a military rank, maybe in gratitude for services rendered, despite his lack of training—since he'd never made much progress with that. Whatever he was up to during the war, he never spilled his secrets to us. He kept gaining weight and had a slow, heavy way of walking. Sometimes he had to go along "on a march," as he put it. The day before one exhausting all-night march, he left the house in his slippers, laughing, in the firm belief that he'd found the perfect pretext for staying behind. The next morning, he sat groaning with his feet in a tub as we looked on and made fun of him; his commander had ordered him to walk the whole way in his slippers. He would have been just young enough to qualify for Himmler's *Volkssturm* of 1944, along with all the teenagers and grizzled old warriors who were mobilized in the last year of the war, in the hopeless tragedies of the *Totaler Krieg*, Letta says with a sigh, but maybe the new fatherland of which he dreamed would have declined his service.

Yet his clumsiness with weapons was matched by his cunning with the pen. For instance, he took an active part in preparations for the large roundup of February 28, 1942, a reprisal following an attack by resistance members. An unknown number of people were arrested and sent to Fort Breendonk, a Nazi prison camp that would become notorious for the horrors that took place there, and may have been tortured. Willem sat calmly at his table, making lists, nothing but lists. His counterespionage service was discreet and efficient; he had his closest associates checked by outside agents—you never know.

One day at dusk, Mientje climbs to the second floor. Her legs tend to swell up and bother her, and the cold and damp are hard on her lungs. From the first landing, she has a view of the flat roof of the annex. A few lead pipes are lying there; dry leaves whirl about in the wind and then fall motionless. Winter is coming; she goes to the library to light the small stove. Willem has had a bookcase placed there, with glass doors and a lock. The chairs and sofas from the salon downstairs have been moved up to the room, along with a conference table that seats eight; a few matted carpets cover the wood floor, and in the fireplace is a small stove—a Godin model from France, called "the little devil" because you can see the glow of the hot coals through the mica windows. The small cylinder can hardly warm up the big room; it gobbles up coal, nearly burns off your face if you stand too close, and makes no perceptible difference just

143

six feet away. To make matters worse, the windows don't shut properly; in the blink of an eye, the heat has seeped away again. The master bedroom on the third floor is no different. The bed sheets stay clammy for months; you have to crawl into bed shivering and warm up the linen with your body heat. In the morning the windows are feathered with frost. Now that the first really cold nights are on the way, Mientje has laid three fireproof bricks on the large stove in the annex; once they've heated up thoroughly, she wraps them in brown paper. When Letta and Suzy say good night, they take a warm brick upstairs for their shared bed—they now sleep in the attic under the tiled roof, safe from the sounds of even their parents' most heated discussions. Adri also takes a brick up to his bed, which is still in the back room on the third floor. Late in the evening, the last brick is laid in the conjugal bed. As they drift off to sleep, they can warm their feet against the hot lump; it's a safe, almost comforting feeling, and when you wake up for a moment in the middle of the night, your toes automatically reach out for the brown paper, lukewarm by now, which makes a slight crackle.

Long before she finds out about the true state of affairs, Mientje spends many nights alone in bed in the cavernous bedroom. More and more often, Willem is away in the evening and returns late, or not at all. When he does come home, he parks his car on the Tichelrei, some distance away, and walks home in the dark. He seems increasingly guarded; she can't ask him about it; he reacts with irritation or dismissal; he shakes his head and always says there's nothing for her to worry about. In moments of anxiety, she suspects there's someone else, that her husband is with another woman, as she lies awake, tossing and turning. The coal-guzzler in the library went out long ago; it's early in the morning, the temperature has sunk just below freezing, she pulls the coarse sheets over her cold shoulder and drifts off again for a while, dreaming of fields of wheat in Oud-Zevenaar and of "gleaning." Everything is bright and summery;

144

soon she'll wake up in the wintry dark and trudge up the many stairs to the attic, still half-asleep, time to get up, girls, then back down to the third floor, wake up, Adri, my boy, it's time; shivering in her threadbare dressing gown, she goes downstairs to light the stove. In the morning silence she hears the tram rattle past, down Lange Steenstraat, through Grauwpoort, as the daily hubbub of life begins in Sluizeken Square; why did Pappie stay out all night again, oh well, as long as nothing happens to him, it's in the hands of the all-knowing Lord, the master of our fate.

17

It must have been sometime in the mid-1930s that Willem Verhulst met Greta (Griet) Latomme, nine years younger, who would become his mistress. It probably happened in the days when he was on the road in his car as a "traveling light salesman" for MEGA, during his unpredictable wanderings past houses and farms across the Flemish countryside. Griet Latomme was a girl from a poor farm family in the north of the province of East Flanders. In her memoir, written on an old-fashioned typewriter and now in the collection of the Archives and Documentation Center for Flemish Nationalism in Antwerp—filed, tellingly, under "Willem Verhulst"—she sketches the hardscrabble setting of her childhood: "I was the thirteenth addition to our family. We lived in a whitewashed cottage with a thatched roof in Kaprijke, in the north of Meetjesland." Today, Kaprijke still has a *dries*—a village green—of unusual size, surrounded by trees and houses, an enduring reminder of its late medieval period.

She describes her childhood years as a familiar tale of small farmers struggling to get by, a hard life that nonetheless had its idyllic scenes: rollicking in the orchard, picking fruit, scutching flax, her mother sitting out in front of the low farmhouse in the spring sunshine, doing her mending. But they worked hard and worried about money. "I became a pretty little blonde with bright blue peepers," she writes coyly.

In those days, her mattress was filled with chaff given to her father for nothing by a local farmer; the down from the chickens was used to fill the pillows. Her parents, despite being "none too Catholic" themselves, decided to send their daughter to a convent school, where she showed off a stone figurine that someone had given her to a nun, who snatched it out of her hand in horror because it was naked. Her toy was returned days later, in an elaborate costume; the girl had no idea what to make of it. "I became stubborn and unruly—even a little cheeky sometimes," she notes.

Griet Latomme portrays her young self as an enterprising nonconformist who showed a healthy measure of rebelliousness and independent mindedness in her clashes with the nuns and priests. She complains that every aspect of her life was controlled by the church and the prioresses. As a young girl, she slipped off with her friends one day at lunchtime to see boys swim naked in the nearby pond. "Gratified, we hurried back to school." From that moment on, her words crackle with barely concealed erotic energy: "We were all teenage girls and could feel the swelling of our pretty little breasts. And of course we were proud . . . Some would show the others quick flashes of their bounty."

She went on to a well-known Catholic teacher training institute for girls in Eeklo, then known by the French name of Notre-Dame aux Épines, but later by the no less prickly Dutch equivalent, Onze-Lieve-Vrouw-ten-Doorn. She complained about the French lessons, and about the nuns forbidding the girls to speak Dutch to one another, but she was absorbed by her history and Dutch classes. "In a fransquillon environment like that, anyone would become a flamingant!"

Again and again, she was the first to provoke the conservative nuns, and the other students followed her lead. They were strolling down a narrow street one day when they ran into a group of male students going in the opposite direction; she describes how nervous the nuns were as the young men came closer, the tension in the air; there was no side street, no escaping the encounter; as the two rows of students passed each other, the nuns became nearly apoplectic. Griet made a bet with a friend that she had the guts to speak to one of the boys. She stepped out of the line to tell a joke to a boy with a shy grin. A nun screeched, grabbed her by the hair, pulled her back into place, and shoved her hard. Griet's punishment was three days' expulsion from classes, and she accepted it with a self-satisfied smirk.

Later, when the class sang the Belgian national anthem, she baited the nuns by singing her own parody of the lyrics. Even though she merely murmured it into the ear of the girl in front of her, a monitor overheard, and the rebellious young woman was summoned to the office of Mère Chantal to account for her unpatriotic act. The elderly Griet set down these stories of banal acts of youthful defiance with a naive boastfulness, perhaps inspired by her conduct later in life; as she wrote, she was obviously still basking in the imagined attention, or even admiration, of her lover Willem Verhulst.

Young Griet was also proud to be chosen, not long afterward, to sing in church because of her "*gentille petite voix.*" The entire memoir is suggestive of a vain, flirtatious young woman who did whatever she could to attract attention, to step out of line, a woman who longed for something more adventurous than the tepid future laid out for her. When required to wear an unflattering black hat in church while working as a trainee teacher, she made sure that her two long Nele braids poked out from underneath it, looking so out of place that all the pious souls in the congregation burst into laughter. "That was how I turned that ordeal into a barrel of laughs." "Nele braids" refers to the hairstyle of the legendary Tijl Uilenspiegel's girlfriend Nele; in the pre-war Flemish imagination, Tijl and Nele stood for romance, rebellion and a spark of anarchistic freedom.

Once she had her diploma, she returned to Kaprijke, where she spent her days taking long bicycle rides along the edges of the small ponds that dotted the region, singing in a choir and attending talks by flamingant speakers. She acted in a theater group for young women, in a play about the life of "our great idealist Dr. August Borms." She became friends with Raf Van Hulse, later an infamous SS man, who was then a teacher in a nearby village. She took unskilled work because it was "hopeless to look for a job in the educational field." Even so, she was eventually offered a job as a teacher in the West Flemish village of Langemark, near Ypres, more than forty-four miles from her parents' house—almost five hours by bicycle. So, she moved to Langemark. There, too, she became involved in amateur theater and was even given roles in a few operettas. "I adored it. That liberated way of being filled my whole life with delight." In Ypres and Roselaere, she attended all the performances of the Vlaamsche Volkstooneel, a groundbreaking theater ensemble affiliated with the Flemish Movement. She writes in suggestive terms of visiting her boyfriend one day, "to give him a little treat. The boy, astounded by the wonderful surprise, rose in a flash and, standing erect, kissed me as he never had before." The boy in question is ill and dies soon afterward. "I had a lot of grief to go through, all by my lonesome . . ."

And then, without fanfare, it happens, without any hint of how it came about: "I became acquainted with the Verhulst family and the poet Richard De Cneudt." This is all the explanation the fiery young woman from Kaprijke gives of how she met our traveling salesman Willem and his cousin and faithful friend from his days in The Hague, the poet whose collections littered the house in Drongenhof. It wasn't long before Griet took a trip to Ghent. "In this way, I gradually became a family friend of Wim's and made many other noteworthy friends. I spent marvelous days there: Christmas parties, walks, visits to the opera, and so much more . . . Now and then I was invited along to the Netherlands."

Her parents' farm in Kaprijke burned down, and her father died, but by then she was an independent young woman with a life of her own in Langemark, where Willem was a frequent visitor. In other words, Griet gradually became "Auntie Griet" to the children, and Mientje had to suffer in silence as Wim's "good friend from Langemark" wormed her way deep into their lives. She was reassigned to Maria-Aalter a while later, when "that terrible war" broke out and Willem began his work for the occupying regime. "That spelled the end of the visits from Wim, Mr. De Cneudt, and others with whom I had passed many an interesting day. We called them our *Kultuurdagen*." The term means nothing more than "cultural days," but has a vaguely German look with that capital "K."

The reader learns that she was well liked by many farmers and poachers and had ways of obtaining all sorts of food; Wim may sometimes have picked up provisions from her in his car. During the war, Wim asked her if his family could use her house over summer vacation. She was happy to oblige: "Then I went to Ghent to take care of Willem, who was on his own."

I sit and stare at this innocent-looking sentence. So in Drongenhof, in the midst of the war, after installing his devoted wife Mientje in the house in Maria-Aalter, Miss Latomme's secret love nest, Willem would spend summer vacation in that big, lonely house in Ghent with lusty, young, enterprising Flemish Griet—with her irrepressible Nele braids, the hidden "bounty" of her bosom and her Flemish nationalist passion. The young lady doesn't waste a lot of words on the story, but it's easy enough to fill in the blanks.

I am struck by the nonchalance with which Wim's mistress, who was fast becoming indispensable, describes her secret life with him as an innocent family matter; she enjoys "everyday life in the city" and takes "great pleasure in the opera, the cinema, and visits to friends." I slowly awaken to the dismaying truth; at some point, Mientje must have found out.

Yes, of course she did, the elderly Suzy tells me later, during an afternoon of copious white wine and chain-smoking. Our mother put up with it, but it caused her a great deal of sorrow. I think she felt guilty because she herself had met our father at the deathbed of his first wife, Elsa; I don't know. With a shake of her head, Letta adds, Whenever the subject came up, Mama would give me a wistful look and say, I hope it never happens to you, dear.

In a photograph from around the same time, taken on a trip to the Nijmegen area, Griet stands beside a sullen-looking Mientje and the children like some kind of governess. The photo was taken in August 1938; the Waalbrug, a bridge that was later destroyed, is visible in the background. There is also a third woman with them, on the left. Who's that? I ask. Oh, yes, that's Aurélie Willaert from Ertvelde, Suzy says, another teacher. Oh my, was she another . . . ? I have no idea, says Suzy; she was Griet's close friend, that's all I know. I don't know how she wound up in this picture; apparently she was invited along to Oud-Zevenaar. And Letta says, His harem. The sheer gall of that man.

Griet, I love you.

Sighs. Turns once again to face the beaming blonde against whose belly he has nestled his rear for the length of their catnap. Puts his arms around her again. Now it's her turn to sigh, as she traces a circle in his chest hair.

You have to go home, Willem.

He grunts. Her hair makes his nose itch. He lays his hand on her small breasts and slowly caresses her nipples. His hand wanders down to her flushed belly; he feels how moist and warm she is there. Desire returns, she can feel it; she takes hold of him there, guides him between her legs, kisses him full on the mouth. They make love again. Lie in each other's arms afterward and doze.

Willem, it's already after midnight. You promised Mien you'd go home before the weekend.

A growling noise. A nudge against her underbelly.

I want to stay here.

Willem, you have to go home.

I don't want to. It's such a long drive, on wet roads in the rain and the dark. You don't want me dead, now, do you?

He tries to tickle her under her arms. Squealing with laughter, she pushes him away.

You know Mien will be worried, Wim . . .

He kisses her again, intoxicated by the scent of their bodies together, burning, full of a lambent bliss that warms the depths of him. He falls into a dreamless sleep.

He arrives home on Saturday, just before noon. Mientje is chopping vegetables she bought from a farmer outside of town. The house in Drongenhof is filled with children's voices; there's a party for Letta, he had forgotten, he has no gift.

I had to drive someone home, Mammie, and then there was a major operation last night, and I couldn't get away. I had to spend the night somewhere.

152

Sit down, Willem. It's almost time to eat.

Something deep inside him is making him desperate. The sense that nothing can be mended. At the same time, he's so much in love he could burst into tears; he's afraid the smell of his mistress is still on his skin.

He takes little Suzy onto his lap and says, I'll tell you a funny story.

And the girl asks him, Not the one about the three little lambs in the cave again, Papa?

⸻

Got it for Christmas from the *Hauptsturmführer*, he says with a grin to Mientje, who is staring in astonishment at the Kodak Duex camera in his hands. What . . . Willem, what's the use of that thing? What are you planning to do with it?

Take pretty pictures, he says, as excited as a child.

Oh, Wim. Well, at least remember not to close one eye while you're using it.

His expression is blank for a moment, then he bursts into laughter.

He carefully sets down the camera on the top shelf of the bookcase in the front room.

Years later, when her husband is in prison, she finds the note that he slipped into a book behind the camera.

For you, my Wimpieman, take lots of pretty pictures of us.
Much love, your playmate Nele

Below that, two hearts and a swastika.

She tucks the note back into the book; by then it has been so quiet in the house for weeks that she can hear herself breathing.

18

Almost forty years later, the library on the second floor exudes a calm vacuity, an indifference to the passage of the years. The floorboards look bare, the door no longer closes all the way, the black Ardennes stone of the hearth is covered in a thin layer of dust, a few delicate spiderwebs are hanging against the thin windows of flecked wartime glass; somewhere a clump of hardened putty dangles from a slender nail, tapping against the window like Robin Redbreast in a children's song: *let me in, tin tin tin*. I hesitate, see the notary musing by the window, and then walk over to look outside with him. My esteemed guide turns his broad torso toward me, lays his Statement of Condition down on the dusty sill for a moment, and clasps his hands behind his back. A modest neighborhood, but quite peaceful, wouldn't you say? he asks me. On the floor I see some old newspapers and a few yellowed photos, damaged by moisture; at that moment, I give them no thought whatsoever.

There we linger, side by side, looking out of the window. The silence is cradled in the soft hum of the city, a slight vibration in the brickwork, in the bleak sky over the roofs.

What is that old vacant building across the street? I ask.

Ah ça, he says, startled out of his reverie, that's the old *biseautage*, Mr. Hertmans—which is to say, a beveled glass workshop.

I see a sign with flaking letters, "Glacegand," against a waterlogged wall in the subtlest shades of decay.

Biseauter, says De Potter, is a process of grinding and polishing that creates an angled surface, or bevel, around the edge of a mirror or pane of glass, such as those used in the interior doors and decorative windows of the better houses in the old days. It is a noble craft and art, demanding great patience and precision. That workshop was always there, as far back as I can remember; it produced the beveled glass for our office doors. Now it has gone out of fashion, dear sir, but it was fine work. Opaline glass was also ground and polished to order here: granite gray, milky white, robin red and cobalt blue, some pieces shot through with thin flames of a lighter blue tone, others like clouds solidified in glass.

The long workshop protrudes about three feet beyond the line of the other buildings, making that stretch of the sidewalk darker and narrower. On one side it abuts Drongenhof Chapel; on the other it extends to the end of the small street. It is a vast ruin. From this room, you look out onto a maze of low roofs and open courtyards. Through the broken windows, you can see shards of glass everywhere: bright blue, coral red, yellow swirled with green, transparent emerald.

Later, I often roamed this labyrinth; the iron and wood, and even the brick, were decaying, but when a little sunlight hit the glass, it sparkled as if newly blown. The better-preserved offices were still fully furnished, left behind as if the company had been forced to close without a day's warning, as if the workers had fled while the city was bombed: files, invoices, letters, ledgers with stained pigeon-gray cardboard covers—all this lay undisturbed there for years after I moved in across the street. The building was a complex of hallways, workrooms, side rooms, studios and old offices; it had intermediate floors connected by small wrought iron spiral staircases, and openings onto a surprisingly vast hall with a large skylight, where broken panes of glass shook high above in the wind, capable of cleaving your skull at any instant. Below that, among layers of glass that crunched underfoot, were the cutting tables, scored deeply from years of use; there was something touching about the tidy rows, with the old-fashioned cutters still in their places on the damaged tabletops; not far away were the sanitary facilities for the workers, encrusted in calcium and rust, where I found a few brown dustcoats and, in one of the pockets, a scrawled note, "Roger, bring along 20 fr's worth of putty, please, merci, Jeanne"; large cellars lined with Balegem sandstone, smelling like engine oil, where homeless visitors had left behind their stashes of rags and foam rubber after spending the night; the archaeology of collapsed industries.

Willem, Mientje and the children had a view of this workshop for decades, and when I ask Letta about that, she says, Yes, of course, we would wake up at seven a.m. to the sound of the day's work beginning. Our morning started with the high whine of the grinding, followed by the tinkle of falling crystal edges; through the glass roof of the studio, we saw the men standing at the cutting tables, vague silhouettes in yellowed light, and then the glittering clouds of tiny splinters that rose from the glass like snow. An hour later, on the rare working days when we didn't have school, the carts would arrive, and after a little while we would hear them leaving again, the clatter of horses' hooves on the paving stones, the rattle of the wooden wheels, the coachman shouting, the men loading and unloading the large plates of glass—some polished, others rough, all wrapped in horse blankets like fragile invalids who must be transported with care.

The building was razed to the ground in the mid-1980s; when the innermost rooms became overgrown with grass and moss, and ferns and nettles began shooting up between the shards of glass, the local authorities decided to demolish the building and build apartments there. As the demolition date approached, I removed old company records, some white opaline tiles for my bathroom, ledgers, small supplies of glass in phantasmagorical polychrome patterns, and some old cutters with diamond tips. In one of the books, I found a note I understood only later: a brief announcement to the employees about their working hours, signed by someone named W. Verhulst. Just above the signature were the neatly typed words "Heil Hitler!"

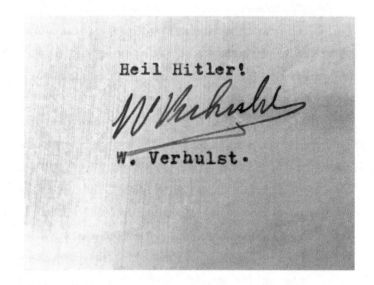

19

Heinz Flügel is in town; Mien is delighted, even a little worked up. She flits through the house in her best dress and an old pearl necklace; soon, she will have the privilege of helping Pastor Pichal prepare for this evening's talk. The German poet and public intellectual Heinz Flügel has accepted the position of lecturer at the Deutsche Akademie established in Ghent by the occupying regime. In this cultural role, he will need to strike a careful balance between his humanistic values and the stringent demands of the National Socialists. To Mientje, he nonetheless represents the very highest ideals; Flügel is the cosmopolitan son of Brazilian diplomats, a socially engaged playwright, the author of a poetry collection she much admires, *Mythen und Mysterien*, and a university lecturer with a slight activist bent, who has remained critical of the Nazis but, faithful to his deep-seated Protestant values, has never become a militant or a fanatic. That is why the Nazis have offered him a good deal of latitude at Ghent's Deutsche Akademie; they see him as the ideal figure to appease the Flemish intellectuals.

In 1987, the elderly Flügel published a memoir entitled *Zwischen den Linien* (Between the Lines). The book provides a fascinating window onto his time in Ghent. He describes his love for the city, his summer strolls along the Leie; he confesses to an affair with a married woman, referred to affectionately as Pau-Pau, who taught him "love in the French style" but also revealed the secrets of "the Flemish soul" under the cover of flowering bushes or in a little riverside grotto. He relishes the memories of his promenades through the city streets and calls Gravensteen a "ghost castle" watching over the merchants, fishmongers and conjurers; he makes a naive, romantic comparison between the bustling crowds there and the enchanted world of Tijl Uilenspiegel. He reports that he heard a great deal about Cyriel Verschaeve and praises the poet's "mystical soul" but holds his Nazi sentiments against him, preferring Ernst Jünger's more refined style. Patriotic Flemings found themselves on the horns of a dilemma, he writes. Flügel stayed on the most diplomatic terms possible with the German authorities, but he feared the Gestapo, which used *"flämischen Agenten und Spitzel"*—Flemish agents and spies—and *"die fanatischen DeVlag-Leute"*—the fanatical members of the *DeVlag* organization to which Willem Verhulst belonged. At the start of his assignment, he had complained to Oberfeldkommandant General Bruhns, a cultivated man, that these Flemish spies turned up to his lectures and opened his letters. If it's any comfort to you, Bruhns replied, they are keeping an eye on me too. *"Jeder misstraute jedem"*—everyone distrusted everyone.

That evening, Heinz Flügel speaks in a small lecture hall in Ghent to a select audience: the few humanists and pacifists who still have the courage to stand behind their opinions in public, as well as a few silent intellectuals, a group of Pietistic Germans who read Hölderlin's poems to each other at private gatherings, a couple of broad-minded officers, and some cultivated people who are fond of Goethe and Schiller. Mien's heart trembles in anticipation; she recalls the evenings at Pastor Wartena's home in Oud-Zevenaar—inspiring lectures as twilight gathered outside; psalms and poems, one after another; the light that seemed to spontaneously enter her heart; the sound of divine inspiration in the voices. Her old shoes are worn out, but so are everyone else's in the war years; she is wearing the hat with the little black veil, which she hasn't worn in years. Willem is still at the office; the children can look after themselves, she made their dinner before she left.

She is walking along Groot Kanon, across the deserted Vrijdagmarkt, down Serpentstraat and Schepenhuisstraat, past the checkpoint in front of the blacked-out city hall, the belfry, the cathedral, and the Duivelsteen building by the city gate, and onto Vlaanderenstraat; she has permission to return home after dark, in the form of a document from the Deutsche Akademie. By the time she enters the hall, there's already quite a crowd, a quiet, well-behaved crowd, talking softly among themselves. A few men linger by the entrance, smoking third-rate tobacco; she tries to ignore the two soldiers keeping watch across the street. Here comes Pastor Pichal with Heinz Flügel, who cuts an elegant figure in his long coat; at the age of thirty-five, the man still has a youthful air, like a boy in a man's body, Mientje thinks to herself; she finds it endearing. She shuffles past a few people to a vacant seat in the third row, her favorite: you can see the reactions of the distinguished guests in the first row, and you're close to the speaker but not out in front where everyone can see you. Flügel is in good spirits; he seems full of self-confidence, yet understanding, approachable and at ease. He looks the audience members straight in the eyes, takes a deep breath, leaves ten seconds of silence, in which everyone holds their breath and the last of the mumbling stops, and begins his talk with a few lines by the poet Hölderlin, at the request of the small reading group: *O komm,* he solemnly declaims. *Komm! ins Offene, Freund! zwar glänzt ein Weniges heute / Nur herunter und eng schließet der Himmel uns ein . . .* Oh, come, come out into the open, friend! Though today little sunlight reaches here below and the skies close in tightly around us . . .

She misses some of his lecture because her thoughts are flying in all directions in pure joy; she can hardly contain her tears, what is wrong with her? Sometimes she has to dry the corners of her eyes on the sleeve of her coat. The lines about peace and European culture make her heart sing; she feels like a young girl again, oh so foolish, here in this lecture

160

hall among all these well-meaning people of faith. About ten minutes into Flügel's talk, she hears the door of the lecture hall opening, a few steps, people muttering; she turns around, irritated, who could be disrupting this wonderful person's lecture, just as he's citing Rilke and Stefan George, isn't it sublime; but when she turns her head, a little too sharply, she sees two figures in black leather jackets entering, she recognizes the hated uniform underneath, the caps with the death's head under their arms, at least they had the manners to take them off when they entered, maybe they've just come to hear the lecture . . . with a shock she recognizes Willem, half in the gloom between the two SS men, looking a little out of place. He is holding the Kodak Duex, to take pictures, that must be it, pretty pictures of the great man and his fine words up there in front. She breaks into a heavy sweat, it dizzies her, him, here, now, in this place, not to listen but to monitor . . . she feels herself grow nauseous, acid glugs into her throat, she tries to get a hold of herself. Flügel, too, has noticed the men. He is daring enough to interrupt his own talk. "*Gnädige Herren*," he says with elegant irony, "there are still a few seats here in front, be my guests . . ." At those words, the three forms, like ravens in an old children's book, turn and make a silent exit. From that moment on, Mien no longer hears a word of the event she had so looked forward to; images fly back and forth in her head, and everything is sucked into a shadowy whirlpool, as if life could swirl away into a dark, stinking drain; after the lecture, she wants to stay and talk, but her mind is like a bubble that has burst; all the deep questions she'd hoped to ask Flügel in eloquent words are gone now, and all that remains is a kind of wet clay, something crude and heavy and stupid, wet clay and three black leather ravens turning to the wall, the crazed mental failure born of misery and panic. She'd intended to ask an insightful question about the book he'd published the year before, *Tragik und Christentum*, but instead she merely stands there, numb and dumb, even though the charming Heinz throws more than one look in her direction, friendly and curious, because he's heard so many good things about her from Pichal. But there is only thick saliva like glue around her tongue. Self-pity consumes her; she curses the humiliating feeling.

In defeat, she makes her way back through the pitch-black city to her house in Drongenhof, where the children are in their rooms. She hears Adri playing his violin and her well-behaved girls, seated side by side, singing; the old walls close in on her; in her bedroom, she stands by the window in the darkness. Across the street, she sees a vague light wandering, the nightwatchman patrolling the old glass workshop, she perches on the edge of the bed, she takes up her psalter, the Lord is my salvation, the Lord is near. She tries to hum a melody, and that is what makes her burst into tears after all.

Willem never kisses me anymore.

She reaches for her diary and jots down, without corrections and with a swell of relief in her heart, a psalm version she will later read aloud at a service in Brabantdam.

She lies down to sleep; hours later, she is woken by the bang of the front door.

After some clattering downstairs, Willem comes up to bed; he lies down next to her, his back to her, in a fug of sweat, cigars and wine. She is relieved and infinitely sad; she lays her hand on his back.

⁓

"I have to take my lists to Brussels, see you tomorrow."

"I have to attend a meeting of the *Feldgendarmerie* in Brussels, I won't be done until late so I'll spend the night there, see you in two days."

"The *Stadtkommandant* wants me to go to a conference in Hanover, see you next week. Be good now, children!"

"Don't forget your sandwiches and your thermos, Pappie."

"Thank you, Mammie, how kind of you."

20

Night is falling, it's a chilly evening in March 1943, he walks home from the office, past Gravensteen Castle and through the narrow streets of Patershol. A few men are clustered together talking at the corner of Ballenstraat and Haringsteeg. He walks on without looking at them, tired and irritable; a couple of steps past the men, he hears hissing: *Bastard.*

He whirls around as if stung by a wasp and asks the men who they are.

That's no business of yours, fascist pig, the oldest one says, his stare so intent that it's Willem who lowers his eyes. His emotions are whirling; he tries to stay calm.

Where do you live, he says in the flattest possible tone. Tell me, or I'll take you in right now.

How do you intend to do that, take us in, all by yourself? the man asks with a grin.

The look in his eyes is so stony that Willem begins to feel unsure of himself; he wishes he could add all the names of the conspiratorial scum to his lists for the *Sicherheitspolizei.*

I will track you down, he growls.

I don't give a rat's arse about that, the man says. Bring your black-shirted ravens with you, my rifle's ready and waiting.

The other men smirk provocatively. One runs his finger across his throat.

On an upper floor of one of the rundown buildings, someone opens a window.

Salaud. Fasciste.

A woman's voice. A melodious voice. The voice of a young woman. He

164

looks up; it's a lovely, attractive woman he's seen on the street before; he once gave her the eye as she passed. She's clenching her fist.

Willem's world goes black; in an instant, he is transported to the schoolyard of his childhood, and the memory of humiliation sinks its teeth in, like a treacherous animal that for years has bided its time and now leaps for his throat. He sees the little bourgeois boys who taunted him; to be called names again now, in French no less, by a young woman—him, a personal friend of Jungclaus . . . oh God, the French-speaking girls of his youth, the sweet lightning under their skirts, what a cruel sting he feels, a flame of hate, but this hate feels like sorrow, sorrow so immense it's hate, he wishes he could round them all up now, throw them into a cell, fucking vermin, every last one of them.

Belgicist filth, he snarls, and is about to walk on, but in front of him in the dark stands another man, a man he knows and fears and hates.

Well, well, the man says, who have we here, our mighty hunter.

Hey, Omer De Ras, what are you doing here in this nest of serpents, stirring up trouble, no doubt.

De Ras spits on the cobblestones. So, you little fascist, you think you decide what I can and can't do? You don't have such a big mouth now, out in the streets without your trained rats, do you?

Willem steps to one side to pass De Ras, who steps aside with him.

What do you say, De Ras, shall I send you down to the cellar sometime for a quiet conversation with Gaston Delbeke?

Suddenly he feels an iron fist clutching his collar.

Listen up, Verhulst. I don't know if you've seen the news in your German gazettes, but the wind is changing. Better pack your bags or we'll be the ones looking you up after the war, d'you get my meaning, cockroach?

De Ras relaxes his grip; Willem steps to one side and walks on, his hand on his bruised larynx.

Back in his house in Drongenhof, he thinks, Suppose they break in when Mientje is alone with the children . . . He is flooded with tender concern for his family. They need a chain on the front door. I'll take care of it tomorrow, someone from the office can come and install it. He drinks another glass of water in the annex, takes a pill, goes up to the second-floor library, and sees, to his left, the roof of the chapel, grave and steep in the night. *Those communists have a hideout there, they tell me. Just underneath the trusses. I should have it checked out.*

The next day, gnashing his teeth and wielding a sharpened pencil, he will add Omer De Ras to his list; less than a year later, on May 20, 1944, De Ras will be arrested in a pub by members of the *Außenstelle*, betrayed by a woman who recognized the names on the list. Along with a number of friends from the resistance, he will be subjected to brutal beatings and interrogation and sent to Buchenwald, later returning alive. During the interrogation, Willem will be sitting upstairs in his office, only vaguely aware of the screams from the cellars, ignorant of the details, that's none of his business, he has work of his own. Whether their paths ever crossed again after the war in the narrow alleys of Patershol is anybody's guess.

From that time on, Willem Verhulst will always carry a gun under his coat, in a leather holster under his arm; when he arrives home and takes off his uniform, the children will sometimes see that dark instrument resting against his shirt—the way he undoes the leather strap, as cautious as a Jew with his phylacteries, the way he puts the pistol in a drawer, which he carefully locks with a key always in his pocket, except when he sleeps, when, as the children know, he tucks it under his pillow. He no longer parks his German luxury car around the corner in Tempelhof but leaves it in front of the requisitioned École des Hautes Études, home to his Dietsch Action Committee, where guards are on duty day and night. When he goes home in the evening, he sometimes calls Mientje first to ask if one of the children can meet him in front of Gravensteen Castle. A father with his children, he says, they won't trouble me then.

It is a fine September day. Willem is on his way to work. The wispy clouds over the city suddenly growl, everything starts to tremble, the air fills with oncoming motion, everyone looks up in consternation; the first aircraft are approaching, swerving, throwing off black dots that fast grow bigger, everyone runs in a panic in all directions, huge explosions follow, the bombs strike somewhere in the suburbs; Willem runs the quarter of a mile back home, where Mientje and the children have already fled into the cellar; he runs down the stairs to find not only his own household, but also a few neighbors, the Vandermeulens from Grauwpoort, all huddled together in the dark. Then the doorbell rings, long and emphatic, someone knocks on the door, they hear a man's voice, hysterically crying for help. Mientje runs upstairs and out into the hallway, opens the small window in the front door, and sees a man in an SS uniform weeping with fear; she lets him in, they run to the cellar together.

The Allied bombing of Ledeberg, that fifth of September, signals the turnaround. The events of that day fill the resistance with fresh purpose, and the *Deutschfreundlichen*, the German sympathizers, are increasingly hounded. Letta remembers as if it were yesterday: There I sat in our cellar next to that SS man, who was quivering like jelly in his Nazi uniform; we children were just excited. Little did I know one hundred and eleven people would lose their lives that day just outside Ghent.

21

Mientje is down on her knees, scrubbing the tiled floor in the hallway; she still has a little stash of the old-fashioned black floor wax she uses to give the grayish tiles their black gleam again; for the white strips of Carrara along the edges, she has colorless wax, which smells like a mixture of beeswax and turpentine. She rubs and polishes, flushed with effort, making the tiles shine, lending the hallway the elegance of a distinguished bourgeois home. Willem practically commanded her to make sure the whole house is squeaky clean, because he's expecting some very important visitors. The portrait of Kees Boeke has vanished from the hallway; it is now in the back room where Adri sleeps, replaced by the heads of August Borms and Heinrich Himmler, the heroes of the hour, with the Symphonion on proud display beside them.

Only when I had gained access to the archives of the Krijgsauditoraat in Brussels, which oversaw the postwar military tribunals responsible for trying suspected collaborators—would I truly realize how much Willem had to answer for. But how high Willem had climbed in the hierarchy of collaborators became apparent to Mientje that day.

In the late afternoon, a number of official German vehicles drive into Drongenhof, stop at the house, and park half on the sidewalk in a show of authority. Doors slam shut and men leap to rigid attention; fierce shouts of *Heil Hitler* reverberate, and black-clad arms are outstretched in front of the door, which opens slowly, almost ceremoniously; across the street, the workers gather at the open gate to gape at the intimidating spectacle; the engines of the large black cars keep running as Willem, gleaming with pride in his most elaborate uniform, welcomes them all.

The procession marches into the hallway; the boots squeak on the freshly waxed tiles; when Letta tells me about this moment, she recalls "the clicking and clacking of all those heels"; the children are sent to their rooms immediately; Mientje refuses to stay and serve the visitors cookies and weak tea; instead, she goes into self-imposed exile in the annex, where she will spend the whole visit swallowing her ire. The door is shut, the chain attached; the men sit down in the front room, where the beautiful Comblanchien mantelpiece now boasts a new bust of Hitler, because the *Verwaltung* still provides speedy delivery to Flemish brothers who have demonstrated their goodwill. Taking their places in the salon are the wheezy Jef van de Wiele of the *Waffen-SS*, leader of the *De Vlag* movement and editor-in-chief of its magazine, a notorious antisemite and author of inflammatory pamphlets, known as Jef Cognac because of his alcohol addiction; Jef François, leader of the SS in Flanders and *Obersturmführer* in the *Langemarck* division, the Flemish SS force on the Eastern Front; and Raf Van Hulse, a good friend of Griet Latomme, a *Kriegsberichter* (war correspondent) from the Eastern Front and the future chief inspector of the Flemish Hitler Youth, who is a frequent guest in Willem's home; as well as an *Obersturmführer* whose name has been lost to history, *Oberfeldkommandant* Bruhns and a few senior officers from the *Verwaltung*. They all make themselves comfortable in their overstuffed chairs; four bottles of excellent brandy have been delivered for them; Mientje left them out on the polished coffee table with the borrowed glasses. There are cigars—Willem II brand, of course, that tickles Herr Verhulst's funny bone. A fire is blazing in the hearth; Adri brought in plenty of wood at Pappie's request. The tall double doors to the modest middle room are shut.

Through the large gaps around the old doors comes the smell of cigars, of leather jackets and of the cozy, crackling fire; the men's voices sound warm, occasionally breaking into polite laughter, or chuckling. After a few glasses, the voices grow shriller. Flemish and German mingle like the musical rivulets in Beethoven's *Pastoral* Symphony; now and then, when one glass taps another, you can hear a cheerful *Heil!* Mientje goes slowly up the stairs; her daughters are obediently reading in their rooms; Adri is standing at the window looking down at the cars on the street, their engines still running; the employees at the glass workshop have gone back inside, and the rasping whine of the machines and jingle of excess glass have resumed. Mientje lays her hand on Suzy's head; the girl says nothing, just picks her nose as she reads. She can hear the powerful engines of oncoming aircraft in the distance and see pennants flying over the castle; it's a day in wartime, nothing worth mentioning, a friendly get-together in the front room. Later, when they've all gone home and Willem has retired to his study, she will burn the German newspapers in the fireplace.

22

Willem has become more and more obsessive about his lists of names. He's surrounded himself with a whole staff of petty officials, who fear him and are only too eager to betray their neighbors. He receives compliments from the *Verwaltung*, as well as occasional torrents of abuse, for reasons he doesn't understand, but they incite him to do his best, as if he's become addicted to pats on the back from his superiors.

He collected absolutely everything, Letta recalls: He took great pleasure in making those lists and worked until late in the evening at the large table in the second-floor library.

The more worrying the international situation becomes, the more doggedly he works, as if it is his only source of hope. He entrusts his buddy Frits Sabbe with the task of sniffing out art "with Jewish influences." A member of his staff, Joannes De Boevé, helps him to compile a long list of the city's Anglophiles; some will be arrested and deported. He asks De Boevé to find him the names of leading Freemasons, even though Ghent's lodges have suspended all their activities; there is even a list of the city's wealthiest industrialists, many of whom have Francophone backgrounds. But the textile barons are mostly exempt; they supply large quantities of textiles to the Germans.

When a number of British prisoners of war escape from the jail on Ekkergemstraat, Verhulst goes after the people who helped them, without mercy. He arranges for the training of *Wachtmänner* (watchmen), who first have to sign a declaration that they are not Jewish, and he establishes secret contacts with the infamous I-Netz, a network of informers behind enemy lines, as well as with the counterespionage service.

Following an attack on the headquarters of the Flemish Guard paramilitary group, Verhulst is instrumental in the taking of fifty hostages. Seven people receive the death penalty for acts of violence against the *Deutsche Wehrmacht*.

On January 15, 1943, a group of "Israelites," arrested a few days earlier, are sent to the Mechelen transit camp. Among them is a woman named Martha Geiringer, who was protected by her family doctor but betrayed by one of Verhulst's cronies; the letter denouncing her, filed by Verhulst under the title of "the Martha report," describes her as "a Jewess, a creature of about 28 years of age, with brown eyes, black hair, and the inevitable nose."

In his office at the Dietsch Action Committee, he is the bigwig, but when he walks home in the evening, there are more and more niggling incidents: "You son of a bitch, your time is running out"; "Hey, you uniformed sack of shit, keep your nippers off the street or we'll find 'em"; "Your house will burn, my friend, you'll need more than one jug of German wine to douse it." He walks on with a fixed expression; sometimes he turns to respond but finds no one else in the alley. At home, he is grimmer than ever, with a sour twist of the mouth; he insists they call the newspaper the *Zeitung*—would you pass me the *Beobachter* there on the table, Adri; he gives a Hitler salute when he leaves the house and another when he returns home.

Sometimes Mientje thinks, He is losing his mind.

Wim, no more of this fuss and nonsense here in the house, you're making yourself look ridiculous.

Mammie, if I didn't know you, I'd think you were a resistant.

I damned well am, Willem.

Don't goad me, woman, I have more than enough on my mind.

At the oddest times he will swallow a couple of pills: Pervitin. It helps me concentrate, he says. When he leaves the house, Mientje reads the box: methamphetamine, for fatigue and depression. He has a new pair of glasses, paid for by his employer, hideous frames, she thinks, much too heavy, and then that thick matte lens, perfectly loathsome, if I didn't know him . . . and she says, Nice glasses, Wim, they really suit you.

One Saturday toward noon, he arrives home, dead on his feet, from God knows where, and sits down at the table. The whole time, he seems embroiled in a silent, furious conversation with himself. Mientje serves the thin soup; he takes a piece of bread and bites into it, too nervous, too distracted; it goes down the wrong way, setting off a terrible coughing fit. He leaps up, gulping and panting and coughing so hard that he gags. Mientje takes two quick steps and is by his side, slapping his back, calm down, husband, slow breaths, that's right, sit down, Pappie, take it easy. He sits, recovering, still drawing ragged breaths, rubs his watering eyes, looks around at his startled children and bursts into tears. He stands up again, walks over to Mientje at the stove, and wraps his arms around her, sobbing and hiccuping, an animal whimper rising from his throat. The children look on in bewilderment; Mientje puts her arms around his neck and cradles his head, speaking to him in a soothing tone, Now, now, Pappie, there, there; nothing seems to help, he's bawling even harder. Children, she says, go to your rooms and read for a while. They creep away and stumble up the stairs. The crying goes on for several more minutes; again and again, he runs out of breath and falters, but is overcome by the next long wail; Mientje sits him in a chair again. When he has calmed down a little and the only sound in the annex is his heavy, anxious breathing, she sits next to him, her hand on his knee.

Then he mumbles, I've lost all my eyesight again.

He stays in the chair; outside, pale green leaves are trembling in a rain shower.

Mientje helps him up the fifty stairs to the third floor. He stumbles and lets out an occasional sob; Mien, he says, oh Mien, Mientje, his lips

174

search blindly for hers but she fends him off; cut it out, Wim, let's get you up these stairs first; she helps him into bed, where he starts to wail again. She pulls the covers up over him, closes the door and goes down the stairs; the children come out of their rooms, What's wrong with Pappie? Nothing, my darlings, Papa's so very tired, that's all.

He remains blind until the next day. On Sunday evening, twilight is already descending when he mumbles, almost too softly to hear, I can see you again. He walks over to her once more; the whole scene repeats itself, but in muted silence this time. She feels him shuddering into her chest, against her coarse, soiled apron, and she says, Hush now, says, What's the matter, says nothing in the end and just holds him in her arms, not knowing if she should feel relieved or very, very worried. She thinks of Saul, struck blind by God on the road to Damascus, and still has hope, but says nothing.

~

Willem does not know where it comes from, any more than she does, this demon that torments him night and day.

Nothing destroys a person's joy in life so swiftly as the secret sense of always being accountable to an intimate judge, who remains incognito. He sees everything and disapproves of everything; it is never good enough, you are always the loser, whatever you do; he is nebulous—sometimes he resembles an old lover, sometimes the friend who betrayed you or the woman with piercing eyes who laughed in your face in the half darkness; at one moment the demon is cheerful and ironic, even tolerant of your foibles, but an instant later he piles on the scorn and condescension because the very event you hoped so sincerely to avoid has, in fact, come about, and it's all your fault, your own stupid fault, your

unbelievable, irredeemable fault; the next time he is a well-dressed bourgeois, murderously elegant, who turns his back on you because you've
just been so foolish and he is the sole witness; he is waiting for you when
you open your eyes in the morning, and he lets you drift off to sleep with
a shrug, because you did what you did, that's all there is to it, you don't
know how you could have done otherwise.

You're much too nice, Wim, says Griet, as she serves him a cup of
chestnut coffee. You shouldn't always try to be so nice to everyone. He
sighs. His superiors are haranguing him, it's as if nothing is ever good
enough, they're getting more antsy and aggressive by the day, fulminating that the *Flamen* will never make good Germans, that he's too slow,
that he has too few names on his lists. Over the fields in Maria-Aalter, a
low, pale sun shines through the morning mist; it is March 1944. The
Langemarck division, he says, should I join or shouldn't I, I'm not sure
anymore. Mm, Langemark, says Griet, shall we drive over there sometime,
Wim? The place holds such good memories for us, after all . . . She winks
and kisses him on his unshaven cheek, leaning over the narrow table.

23

Division Langemarck? My father? Get out of here Letta says with a laugh, he could hardly keep his shooter straight. What I do remember, she tells me, is that he locked the door with that heavy chain every night, and even in the daytime, if someone rang the doorbell when he was at home, we first had to open the little window in the door, just a crack, and ask, What is it regarding, please; we had to get his permission to unhook the chain. Sometimes timid locals came to plead for help in obtaining a passport or some other favor, but what scared him most was the hostility in the streets. I have always fought for the right cause, he sometimes said; then our mother would snort and look away, out of the window.

The "filth," the "vermin," as he tended to call his neighbors in Patershol, are less and less inclined to disguise their hostility. Willem is in growing danger; more and more often, Mientje lies alone in their bed in the large front bedroom on the third floor of the tall, quiet house in Drongenhof, where she sees the first glow of morning through the thin curtains as the pigeons roo-coo on the tiled roof of the glass workshop and she hears the high, thin grinding of the opaline plates, an early start to the working day.

One day, Suzy recalls, there was suddenly a black truncheon hanging from a leather strap to the right of the door; the children were scared to go near it. What's that for, Papa? Go to sleep, children.

⌣

Mammie, will you come and help me?

There is panic in his voice.

Together, husband and wife, they walk in the early morning to the *DeVlag* headquarters.

Just before leaving the house, they threw the last incriminating documents into a burlap bag, which they have with them; it also contains the large photograph of the Führer that Willem put up in the hallway a few months ago. They have to watch out; they are being hunted.

The building is guarded by two SS men, who snap to attention for Willem, extending their arms, but without the familiar cry; upstairs, two soldiers have already started clearing out his office. One of them is tearing up papers by the ream; Mientje throws the photo on the pile, along with the books and a few documents and letters that Willem had kept in the second-floor library at home. She feels a mixture of relief and nausea; she is helping her husband escape his just deserts, but he is her husband; she spends hours on end clearing out the office with the others; she sees documents that make her head spin; is this what Willem . . .

She throws them into the big barrel; how many times have they filled and emptied it already? When they finally stop for breath, in a building stripped almost bare, Willem produces a brown envelope from under his coat and hands it to her.

Here, Mien, you'll need this.

A thick wad of cash.

She nods and slips the money into her purse.

What will you do now, Willem?

I don't know. I'll take care of us. It will be all right.

Mientje shakes her head with a bitter sniff.

They walk back home.

Somewhere, they hear a few men singing the national anthem, "La Brabançonne."

But it's a parody, only too familiar to them.

Beloved Belgium,
the donkey's constipated.
Because its bum
Is plugged with chewing gum.

The donkey said,
It might help if you ate it.
Don't be half-hearted!
Father bit . . .
The donkey farted.
Ta-ra-ra-ra, ta-ra, ta-ra, ta-ra-ra-ra . . .

Willem doubles over with laughter that racks his body, beyond his control, a giggling sickness, not a pretty sight, a man in an SS uniform slapping his thighs with hysterical laughter; Mientje watches her husband in horror as he writhes and hiccups, turns purple; a tear runs from his good eye, and dear Lord above, is she going crazy, how can this be, now a tear drips out of the clouded eye, under his glasses, and runs down his cheek. The next moment Mientje finds herself running, racing as fast as she can; she arrives at the house in Drongenhof alone, slams the door behind her, puts it on the chain, Willem has to ring the doorbell for several minutes before she will open it.

24

In her memoir, Griet describes the mood among collaborators in those days. "The German soldiers were withdrawing, and the *Deutschfreund-lichen* faced severe reprisals, even though nearly everyone had cheered on the soldiers when they arrived. It goes to show how people change!" she writes, full of disdain.

While his family waits in dread, scared to imagine what their future might hold, Willem contemplates fleeing. He discusses it with Mientje, asking if she will go with him to Arnhem and from there to Germany. Mientje refuses; she intends to stay with her children in the house in Drongenhof. It is July of '44; the headlines are screeching about the attempt to assassinate Hitler; confusion and panic are rife; the torture chambers throughout Europe are operating at full capacity. A detention camp in a former barracks in Mechelen, the Kazerne Dossin, is the point of departure for one of the final transports to Auschwitz. Among the deportees is the German painter Felix Nussbaum, who lived in hiding in Brussels for years. The Flemish SS men still dream of sharing a Greater Germanic Reich with their brother people, even as the Americans are liberating Le Mans. Soon afterward, the Allies also take Alençon and Orléans. Willem's beloved *Zeitungen* may not have printed the news yet, but danger is closing in from all sides as long-suppressed atrocities come drifting to the surface. On the Rieme-Oostakker execution site to the north of Ghent, resistance members are still being shot dead by the Nazis and buried in secret. Were they the men on the lists made by hardworking Mr. Verhulst? Day by day, panic tightens its grip on his heart. In the cool, high-ceilinged entryway to the house in Drongenhof, husband and wife are at daggers drawn.

One Sunday morning, early, Adri looks through the window of his back room and sees smoke swirling in the first light. When he opens the window and looks down, he finds his father at work in the narrow backyard, amid heaps of documents, newspapers, magazines and even a few books, spread out on the ground on all sides; in front of him, a fire is burning, a few logs, onto which he throws the newspapers and magazines one by one, crumpling some at first, or tearing them into strips so that they'll catch fire faster, but soon heaving in whole stacks at a time.

Adri calls down to him, Papa, what are you doing?

His father looks up and puts his finger to his mouth.

Quiet, Adri, for fuck's sake.

The boy goes downstairs in his pajamas, Why are you doing that, Papa, should I help, No, Adri, just go, I . . . just let me take care of it.

The boy goes back upstairs, knocks on the door of his parents' bedroom, and asks his mother why Papa is burning his—

Just leave him to it, my boy, she says, let him clean up his own mess.

That same day, after lunch, they start arguing yet again. The backyard smells of ashes; a few clumped remnants of *Zeitungen* are still smoldering. They have taken a seat in the front room. Mientje asks what he plans to do, now that he hardly dares to leave the house after sunset.

We'll go to Hanover, he says, we'll be safe there.

Mientje stares at him, appalled.

Have you lost your mind? Haven't you read those *Zeitungen* of yours? The people there are going through hell, and it will only get worse.

No. He shakes his head firmly. No, the tide will turn again, you'll see. We have such a glorious future—

Shut your mouth, Willem. And not one word about the children.

Come with me, wife of mine, he insists. Our children will be safer in Germany.

Papa—there's a fire in her eyes that frightens him—Papa, I will not. If you want to go, then you should go.

But . . . you won't have anyone here to protect you, he stammers. And the little ones . . .

Mientje repeats, Willem, you should *go*.

She rises to her feet, turns her back to him, and makes her way down the long hallway to the kitchen in the annex, moaning, God, the whole house stinks of ashes.

*

And Willem goes. Or rather, he runs for his life.

A paragraph from Letta's memoir casts the moment in sharp relief.

Father fled in early September 1944. I still have a vivid memory of
him driving away, toward Lange Steenstraat, alone in his car, heading for the meeting place at *De Vlag* headquarters. That was where
the whole crowd of officials gathered before they left in two cars and
a trailer.

Letta tells me later that he turned around and called out that they
"would be back again." To her astonishment, he said it in German: *Wir
kommen zurück!* He turned from the waist in the open car and tried to
extend his arm in the old salute, almost steering into the corner of the
glass workshop. Then, swerving away just in time, he made a clumsy turn
out of sight, like a character in a silent comedy. The stunned girl went
back up the three steps, shut the door, walked down the cool, high-
ceilinged hallway, and climbed the seventy-two stairs to her treasured
attic room, where she picked up her picture book and tried to go on
reading.

The next morning, when Mientje goes to the École des Hautes Études in
Korenlei, with Letta in tow, to find out whether her husband has
really fled, she hears from Mr. De Pestel, the janitor, that he has.
Thirteen-year-old Letta asks, on impulse, whether a woman named Griet
Latomme was among the fugitives. The old janitor, who remembers
them well from the MEGA days, looks at Letta and Mientje in embarrassment and mutters yes.

Mientje flinches as if struck in the face, blinks her eyes, and then
murmurs—half to Letta, half to herself—So in the end . . .

They walk home in silence. The tragic impact of what they've just heard is not really clear to the girl; only decades later will she fully understand, when her father, on his deathbed, gives her some unusual instructions regarding Griet Latomme. Mientje, whose cheeks are ashen, takes the child by the hand and starts to drag her back to the dark, empty house, but comes to an abrupt halt at the window of an old flower shop; she knows the salesman, they sometimes talk about flowers and plants, there's not much to do in wartime, he always says, and she says, in the dark times, that's when you should plant as much as you can, dear fellow. But now she stands there in indecision, with a lump in her throat and a feeling somewhere between anger and resignation—and fear, too, fear of what's ahead. A car trundles down the street, coughing and honking; it startles her; she steps into the shop and sees, in the back of the greenhouse, a slender vine, all the way in the far corner among cobwebs and clutter, in a weathered old pot, oh, she says, oh, that's a wisteria . . . we had one in Oud-Zevenaar too, growing by the south wall, it smells so bittersweet in spring . . . she sees before her the summer mornings when, as a young girl, she walked past the flowering plant and its fragrance surrounded her like a sheltering dome of joy, while the animals milled around in silence in the stables . . . and, seeing the absent look in her eyes, the gardener, who knows what has happened to her husband and what she must now face alone, says, You oughta take it, madammeke, please, take it home and plant it somewhere where it can grow. She doesn't know how to respond at first, then refuses, half out of politeness and half out of pride, but the man has already fetched the pot and is pressing it into her arms, here it is, you see, that'll brighten up your backyard, he says, *bon courage*, Madame Verhulst, may our dear Lord preserve you, good day to you Letta my girl, good day to you ma'am—and Mientje shuffles home with the wisteria, too fragile to speak, and with a large coal shovel—since she doesn't have gardening tools—she digs in the black earth behind the annex, just inside the fence that separates the garden from the brackish waters of the Lieveke; there she plants the wisteria, waters it carefully, murmurs a prayer, turns to her children and says, The Lord will make it grow until long after our death, amen, and the children—who dislike the word "death" because it reminds them of the weird black-clad men in the death room—the children say nothing and stare at the limp, delicate shoots that Mientje has wound around the fence posts, tying them up with leftover pieces of string.

25

It was there on the third floor, after I had stood for a while with the notary, that the sun broke through the clouds again; in an instant, the grim city transformed into an oasis of pastel hues like an Impressionist painting. Everything lit up, the patch of blue sky grew, and in the distance white billows rolled over Gravensteen Castle, and over the peaked roof of the old chapel. The pantiles on the roof of the glass workshop, row on row of deep curves, blazed up in red ochre and sienna.

The front of the house, I now understood, faced southwest, so on clear days it caught the afternoon sun; the light came slanting in and slid across the floor in long, thin parallelograms, which grew wider as you climbed from story to story. But in the back rooms, which faced northeast, the light stayed blue and cool: complementary colors, more moisture in the air, the smell of old plasterwork and wallpaper. Meanwhile, the small backyard barely felt the sun's touch; only at the height of summer, just before noon, did the sunlight angle in from the southeast for an hour before disappearing behind the tall roof. The house was literally in its own way.

From the stairwell of the house to the left there came a noise like someone drumming a cane on hollow stairs. I listened closer; the notary's eyebrows shot up. Ah, hm, he said, your neighbors . . . the thing is, these four houses next to each other here belong to my family, so your neighbors are my tenants . . . The sound grew louder, I heard a shrill voice say something I couldn't make out, the tapping cane came closer, someone stumbled up the stairs to the level of the floor where we stood, on the other side of the thin dividing wall; a man's voice followed, still more halting speech, like two people arguing—elderly people, that much I could tell, old voices like ghosts in a B movie, echoing in a hollow-sounding room, and then, vaguely audible in West Flemish dialect: *Won't ye leave me be, Arnold, damn it, Arnold, no*, tap tap tap, the cane tapping and thumping farther up the stairs, a clattering, a tumbling, then vague shrieking, *Keep yer paws off me, ye dirty thing, ye filthy pig . . .*

I cocked an eyebrow at Mr. De Potter.

Who . . . what . . .

Ah well, said the real estate expert, don't pay them any mind, I'm sure you'll get used to it, they wouldn't hurt a fly—each other, perhaps, but be that as it may . . .

The fact of the matter, as I came to learn, was that around the same time Willem fled to Germany, new tenants had moved into the house next door. Ada, a nurse with wispy red hair and a beaky face like a plucked vulture, used a cane; she had a club foot and wore one of those thick-soled shoes; her husband turned out not to be her lawfully wedded spouse but a charity case from the nursing home. After the home was bombed, she had taken him in, to her everlasting regret. For the first few months, Arnold was on his best behavior, but the simpleminded man, prey to all the usual urges and desires, gradually began harassing the gaunt Ada—only in the evenings at first, just before bedtime, but later he sometimes stood outside her room at night, swearing and banging his fists on the barricaded door and shouting that he would teach her a lesson if she didn't let him in, that she had to let him in, by golly, that when he got his hands on her . . .

I heard the cursing and banging for years. Sometimes you decided you had to do something, you rang the doorbell, and utter silence followed. They would keep quiet for hours then, sometimes even days, as if in hiding.

187

Sometimes I'd see her on the street; *affernoon, sahr,* she'd say in her dialect, her gaunt neck quivering as she nodded, her cane tapping on the bluish-gray paving stones. Ada always comported herself with dignity; she would limp up the three steps to her front door with a grocery bag made of worn-out carpet, open the door—an arduous process—and vanish into the shadows of her house, where her scarecrow awaited her with screams and curses. Mientje and the children must have had the same experience, at least for a few years; around eleven o'clock, Ada and Arnold would climb the stairs, and you could hear their labored footsteps reverberate through the high walls of the stairwell. Ada's cane made a ticking sound on the hollow steps; the sinister tapping and the clunking of her left shoe were followed by the man's breathless curses, then by mutual recriminations in wavering voices—they were no spring chickens even in those days. Sometimes I would hear her moving a table or a chest of drawers, probably to block the door; the moribund couple played their game of love, always unrequited, for decades, and the tick of her stick went straight through the walls, echoing like a poltergeist that couldn't leave the house, like an ancient demon in a house in Patershol—hadn't I read something like that as a child, some fantastic tale, some horror story set here in Ghent's old city center?

In any case, Ada and Arnold were part of my life for years, and when I asked her in passing about her previous neighbors, she told me she knew nothing about them; *ah may hail from Langemark,* she added, *but ah have nothin' to do with all that, sahr.*

26

September 6, 1944. Griet has found a place to stay in Ghent, so that she can be at the Dietsch Action Committee offices by six-thirty in the morning; she's brought some provisions for the journey, a bundle of clothes and some personal effects. By the time she arrives, the meeting place is abuzz with activity; some of the fugitives seem scared and rushed, others are laughing—Hey, fancy seeing you here. Come on, we're going on tour!—the cars and trucks drive up, the trailers are attached, and the little column of vehicles is rounded off by an open truck that dozens of people crowd into. The entire staff of the radio rediffusion service has also been tipped off; Griet learns that Willem is addressing them inside, on the upper floor. Meanwhile, a large trailer is being attached to his own car, with dozens of jerry cans of fuel loaded onto it. These are covered with a coarse canvas tarpaulin. When the line of cars lurches into motion, shouting is heard from all along the roadside, where the people of Ghent have gathered and are waving their fists; from somewhere among them, a stone is hurled at one of the vehicles; an SS man jumps out, brandishes his pistol, and fires a few shots over the heads of the now-fleeing crowd.

They drive out of Ghent. Griet sits beside Willem, stunned; he says nothing and gazes out ahead, sullen. He looks handsome today in his *feldgrau* coat, his black gloves and his black cap. The car makes a reassuring growl. She rests her hand on his knee.

Now events are taking a radical turn. All over the country, confrontations are flaring up between Belgian patriots and collaborators; both sides carry out attacks, dragging their targets from their beds and shooting them dead on a lonely country road, or in some alley. Vengefulness poisons the minds of people who once, before the war, lived together in peace. Resistance fighters have watched their flamingant compatriots slide into a morass of high treason and self-enrichment, spying on their neighbors and blood relations, betraying their fellow townspeople, all the while proclaiming their Flemish ideals with growing fanaticism. Meanwhile, on the other side, families are in mourning for pro-German uncles who were beaten to death, stabbed in the chest or strangled by resistants. The mutual resentment keeps growing; society is split into two camps, each filled with an implacable hatred for the other. In this period, the collaborators arrive at the position that some of their children and grandchildren will go on defending in our own time: the guilt belongs not to those who betrayed their country, but to the Belgian patriots who remained loyal to it, because that country itself was the cause of all the trouble. The German sympathizers refer to resistants and patriots as snakes in the grass, filth, rabble, un-Flemish types; they consistently call the Belgian flag "that old rag"; and collaborators, camp guards and SS men pose as victims while fleeing like thieves in the night for their beloved Germany, leaving behind the country they hated—along with everything dear to them.

From every direction, masses of refugees are on the move, running into each other along the roads, in remote barns, under lean-tos in the rain, in half-bombed-out village schools, wanting to go somewhere but not knowing exactly where or how; there are so many contradictory reports, and they have to make sure they aren't recognized en route. The world is turning upside down; knives are being sharpened; those who were scared are becoming overconfident, while those who terrorized their neighbors are now on the run; regardless of loyalties and ideology, no one has forgotten who went hungry and who filled their bellies. The roads are crowded and busy, and almost every day brings a new flare-up of bitter violence between Belgians.

Willem is at the head of the small column; in the vehicle behind him are a few men with their rifles at the ready. During a brief stop just before they reach the Dutch border, he checks the papers of a few refugees in the truck and stumbles upon the scared, jittery Heinz Flügel, who has fled his grand house in Grote Huidevettershoek in Ghent. Flügel first spent a few days in hiding in the home of Edmond Vandermeulen, the president of the German Chamber of Commerce, near Drongenhof. Willem knows he has to treat this man with special consideration. On the bench next to Flügel, he notices a copy of Goethe's *Faust*. They look at each other for a moment in silence. Willem lowers his eyes and returns the identity papers to the trembling man. For the next few hours, he is gruff and short with Griet.

They avoid the towns and village centers as much as they can, sometimes reaching a barricade and taking the long way around. Griet is responsible for tracing their route on a military map; Willem sometimes grumbles at her to pay closer attention. Past Eindhoven, somewhere between Veghel and Uden, they take a wrong turn and hit a dead end; the whole column has to turn around on a narrow country road, a slow, uncertain maneuver; the truck drives one wheel into a canal and almost tips over; everyone has to get out. Willem shouts, his voice cracking, that the refugees must stay together; the two official cars are roped to the truck; their engines growl for minutes before it's back on the road. In the late afternoon, they finally pass through Nijmegen on their way to Arnhem, which they do not reach until the end of the afternoon. The group finds accommodation in a country inn, but there aren't enough rooms for everyone. A few men say they can sleep outside in the garden; a local member of the Dutch Nazi Party helps find additional lodgings at a farm down the road. Willem secures a large room for himself and

Griet and says to her, You get settled in, I'm going for a quick drive to Oud-Zevenaar.

It is seven o'clock in the evening when he parks the car there. The farmstead is a quiet, peaceful sight; he hears the animals in their stalls and thinks back to the old days; he pauses beside the millstone into which he slipped his love letters to Mientje. He loiters by the door for a while, hearing the rumbling voice of Mientje's younger brother Gerbrand. When he knocks, his mother-in-law opens the door; she doesn't recognize him right away, with the death's head grinning down from his hat. Then she says, quietly, Come in, Willem. His brother-in-law turns from the stove to look at him without a word, steps outside, and slams the door behind him.

The woman does the talking; her husband, old Wijers, has recently died.

What do you hope to find here, Willem.

How is my daughter.

Are the children really safe there.

Are you sure.

What do you have on your conscience.

What will you do now.

Where is your sense of responsibility.

Don't let the neighbors see you here in that dreadful outfit.

I'm dying of shame, just as you should be.

You'd better leave now.

Outside, Mientje's brother is standing next to the barn.

He glares with his head lowered as Willem passes, mumbles goodnight, steps into his car.

Gives a parting wave.

The farmer holds up his fist and shouts something Willem cannot make out.

*

192

Later on, Letta, in one of our conversations: To Oud-Zevenaar, in uniform, no less. That takes some nerve!

In the hotel, his mistress is waiting for him in bed, wearing a black negligee and glowing with energy.

Oh, Wimpie, it's not all bad—it's quite an adventure, isn't it? We're finally going to Germany, after all! *Allez*, get that uniform off. Come lie here next to me and let me spoil you.

—

The refugees reached the Arnhem area just as the Allies were in the midst of their secret preparations for what was known as Operation Market Garden, one of the greatest miscalculations of the war, which would reduce the whole city and region to ash and rubble. But Griet's sole comment in her memoir is that the refugees there were fortunate enough to "be allowed to pick out a few Hitler Youth uniforms from a whole heap of clothing—the trousers and jackets came in handy."

Thanks to Willem's German papers, they cross the German border with ease. "I don't know what documents Wim showed them, but the officers gave us priority. What a feeling of liberation. Full of sympathy for our tragic flight, the German people greeted us, bearing pies and cakes and all sorts of foods . . . Wim, our leader, was ingenious."

Letta's recollection is somewhat different. She tells me the two official cars were soon confiscated, and Willem narrowly escaped a dark fate; he had turned tail like a hound and—as she will later repeatedly insist, after learning for herself what he'd hidden from them all his life—he was "a pathetic excuse for a hero, a gutless bastard."

27

Drongenhof, two days later, September 10, around eleven a.m.

This is when, as Adri and Letta will later describe it, the "rabble" that Willem has feared for so long come pounding at the door; they hear screaming and ranting, this is where he lives, this is it, the bastard, here, the coward, we'll smash in his windows, I'll cut his throat—so that Mientje, shooting out of the kitchen in the back like an animal defending her young, wiping her wet hands dry on her apron, as the shrill, relentless sound of the doorbell goes off like a red alert in every corner of the house, now strides toward the booming front door, takes the chain off the hook, sweeps the door open, and says, in a cutting tone, What is this regarding, if I may ask?

The two men at the front shrink back with a gulp; they hold sticks in their hands and wear the armbands of the Independence Front. Their contorted, unwashed faces search for an expression, until one of them says, Well, my dear little bitch, where's your crafty husband now? The game is up, tell him to come outside, he knows what's waiting for him, and Mientje replies, He's not here, upon which she notices to her distress that Adri is now at her side. She pushes him back behind her with one hand as she tries to shut the door, but it's too late. One of the men in black adjusts his cap and says, Then we'll take it out on his whelps, the fucking bastard. Someone raises a stick to beat Mientje out of the doorway; another heads for the windows; and there, wonder of wonders, comes Mr. Wellens, Willem Verhulst's former shop assistant, strolling down the street, a man who worked with him at the MEGA in Oudburg and later joined the resistance. Mientje fears the worst, but Wellens approaches, surveys the scene, joins her in the doorway and says to the crowd, Leave this woman alone, she and her children have nothing to do with it. Verhulst has already fled.

Crestfallen, the men remain clustered there for a moment, not daring to contradict the resistance leader; the silence is broken by a shot in some nearby alley; they disperse like leaves in the wind, search the area, come back and gather outside the door again. Now Adri recognizes among them a boy who only a week ago dived into a drainage ditch with him for safety during an aerial bombing; at the boy's request, Adri delivered a closed envelope to an address in Ghent, Belgradostraat, it comes back to him in a flash, and there's the boy in front of him; I helped a resistance member without realizing, he thinks. Rotsaert, he says, you're Rotsaert who was with me in the ditch and gave me that letter . . . you know you did . . . The boy returns his gaze in fright and then lowers his eyes. A man with a gun steps forward, clearly in charge. It's Jean Daskalidès, already well known in Ghent, Greek by birth, a sophisticated charmer, jazz trumpeter and Anglophile, later not only a gynecologist and film buff, but also the manufacturer of the world-famous Leonidas bonbons. But now Jean-the-resistant is just a young man of twenty-one, angry and determined, and he says with a growl, Well then, we'll search the house ourselves, come on, and he pushes Mientje aside, leaps through the doorway, grabs the paralyzed Adri by the throat, and says, You're coming along, don't even think of giving us the old runaround, and don't leave anything out, or this stick of mine will give you a headache you won't forget, and Adri limps on his clumsy foot from room to room with three men on his tail, smelling the sweat and grease and iron filings in their overalls; they slam open cabinet doors, sweep aside dishes, but by some miracle they break nothing, not one porcelain saucer, they leave everything whole, as if Mientje's wide-eyed, dignified silence has put them on guard, for she shows no fear, her eyes reveal nothing but focused attention. Don't you hurt my boy or I'll gouge your eyes out of their sockets, she warns them; and Adri, with Daskalidès's great paw on the nape of his neck, bowed like an animal under a yoke, stumbles and struggles his way up the stairs, and it is here, on the way to the third floor, that one of the men sees a black-and-yellow portrait of that blackshirt August Borms on the wall; he dashes it to pieces on the floor, the glass breaks, there is momentary confusion, because everyone is on edge, and because it's hard for Adri to walk with that clumsy foot, and the men give him another rough shove and are getting ever angrier about not finding anything when Adri simply slips and falls, the man behind him trips and falls too, panic breaks out, Daskalidès's rifle clicks behind them, Jean is on edge, his trigger finger itching, and Adri shouts, *No!* His mother tries to calm the men down, the girls at the top of the stairs start screaming, the men are jumpy and worked up, what is this fucking mess here, one of them says. Adri scrambles to his feet, blinks, pulls himself together and leads them upstairs. In the back room on the third floor, they find a little stack of poetry collections by the Flemish bard Richard De Cneudt, the popular poet of Adri's early childhood, but apparently, in the recent days when their father took all those burlap bags out of the house, he did a meticulous job of removing all incriminating documents; relief washes over Adri as he remembers his father's fire in the backyard, the full day he spent burning mountains of paper—the *Brüsseler Zeitung* and *Völkischer Beobachter, Arbeit und Freude, De SS-Man, Volk en Staat,* and much more in that inspiring vein—his heated face lit by the glow; the men are now searching even the tiny attic room, where Letta's little table for doing her homework stands beside a child-sized bed and a disused cradle; the floor is littered with some of little Suzy's wooden toys, a doll with one eye missing; under the high ceiling of the dark attic, pale daylight seeps in along a few loose roof tiles. Fine silver dust swirls down from the ridge, a few pigeons are cooing in the gutter, the bust of Hitler is hidden under a pile of rags, my God, why didn't he destroy that, did he forget or did he lack the courage, the fool, the goddamn fool—Mientje's heart skips a beat, now we're in for it, she thinks, but the men have no interest in the pile of dusty rags in the corner with the plaster Führer slumbering underneath it. The resistants turn to the panting Adri and say, We will find your pa, that son of a bitch, tell the scared little bunny we have a snare ready and waiting for his juicy neck. They thump their way out of the house, the door slams shut, Mientje secures it with the chain. The girls are sniveling quietly. Come on, their mother says, there's beet and turnip soup, it's all right, we will thank and praise the Lord, for He has protected us.

The next morning, they find a large black swastika painted on their house front; yes, we had it removed as fast as we could, of course, the elderly Mr. De Potter told me many years later when I ran into him somewhere in town, we're a good Belgian family, after all, and then that disgraceful thing on one of our houses, all because of that charming Mr. Verhulst, you see, life is never as simple as we make it out to be, n'est-ce pas?

Mientje goes up all the flights of stairs. She digs out the bust of Hitler from under the rags, takes a long look at the clumsily molded head, and then smashes it with the hammer she brought with her, until nothing remains but plaster of Paris and dust. She sweeps the white rubble into a heap, scoops it into the coal scuttle, takes it down to the backyard, opens the gate and heaves it into the black mire of the Lieveke, where it turns to pulp immediately and sinks.

28

And we climbed higher, gaining a sweeping view of the small backyards, the bumpy paving stones of Lange Steenstraat and the Grauwpoort gate, shabby little Sluizeken Park, and the pockmarked front of the café called Roosje, where the sidewalk was being scrubbed with a thin solution of soft green soap and water; the gangly birches brushed their meandering shoots along the rain gutters of the old houses; blackbirds and thrushes picked through dog poop in search of worms, in the black soil of the filled-in canal, which did not really hold the German boat sometimes said to lie there, sunk by the hard-drinking elders at Café Roosje; it is almost noon, silence falls for a beat or two between one thundering truck and the next at the Grauwpoort city gate, and below, across the thin grass of the small park, comes a feeble little woman with a cane, and a man behind her muttering in protest, and Ada, the little lady in the worn astrakhan coat, turns around, comes to a halt, waves her cane threateningly at the grimacing fellow and shouts, *Arnold, one more word outer you and ah'll slap yer mouth shut, d'y'unnerstand me?*

Griet Latomme and Willem Verhulst are now on their way to Hanover. Griet is wearing a *Hajot* jacket, which looks fabulous on her; she tries on Wim's hat. It makes him laugh; you look just like a movie star, he tells her. To save fuel, the second car is hitched to the first; the passengers laugh and curse at the primitive convoy's bumpy ride through Germany. Somewhere near the edge of a forest, they stop to rest. There are two large blocks of blue limestone along the road. Because the second car is well equipped with tools—hammers and chisels of all sizes—someone comes up with the idea of chiseling a few words into one of the blocks of stone. They opt for the first line of the song "To Eastland we'll go a-riding"—the lyrics originate from an old love song in the sixteenth-century *Antwerp Songbook*, but of course our fugitives prefer the adaptation for fighters on the Eastern Front by the Dutch collaborator Piet Heins: "To arms! To arms! We're helping to liberate Germania!"

"Wim chiselled the first word," Griet writes in her memoir; he was followed by a man named Fons; she herself came third, and since Wim had carved the word "To" and Fons the word "Eastland," and it therefore fell to her to carve "we'll," she hesitated; the men were having a smoke a little way off while she wielded the chisel. Instead of "we'll," she carved into the stone "we must," because by that stage, as she admits herself, she "was very pessimistic about their predicament." The identity of the person who carved the rest of the line has been lost to history, but we do know that the group, with their united strength, shoved the stone with the line of Flemish verse to the side of the road, where it would remain as a sign of Flemish loyalty to Germany—*Heil.*

I have pored over maps, but of course their route can no longer be reconstructed. From Arnhem they probably went by way of Hengelo and Osnabrück—"Osnabrück," the word on the manhole covers in Ghent. I should really look up which roads had been built there by order of the Führer, but everything had been blown to bits by then anyway; it's just as likely they took local roads, going by way of Bocholt, Münster and Minden. And as absurd as it may sound, I wonder if somewhere along their route—stones are slow to crumble—or somewhere in the German forests, who knows where, along a walking path or behind a snack bar or something, one might not find a stone behind a few spruce or beech trees, a stone with words carved into it, perhaps in crooked script by clumsy hands, maybe covered with moss or overgrown with brambles or nettles, but nonetheless still present, because words in stone can, as we know, defy the centuries, while the messenger's bones decompose beneath the soil.

⁓

The influx of Belgian collaborators into Germany was substantial: an estimated fifteen thousand Flemish *Deutschfreundlichen* and six thousand Walloon supporters of Léon Degrelle's Rexist Party. Most of these refugees ended up somewhere to the north of Hanover, in rural towns like Verden an der Aller and Soltau. The Nazi social welfare organization *Nationalsozialistische Volkswohlfahrt*, which had organized the KLV summer stays for Flemish children a few years earlier, could hardly handle such numbers. Despite tales of atrocities in the East, a number of escaped collaborators joined the illustrious *Langemarck* division almost immediately.

Jef Van de Wiele, alias Jef Cognac, who had always received a warm welcome at the house in Drongenhof, played an indispensable part in accommodating the refugees. Jef was a friend of Hartmann Lauterbacher, a fanatical Nazi and antisemite, who personally went to Himmler to arrange housing and funding for some eight thousand Flemish refugees in the Hanover area. Lauterbacher, that friend of the Flemish collaborators, has gone down in infamy for saying that after the destruction of the Jews, even the memory of their existence would have to be wiped out completely. Later, as the Allies approached, this fine man distributed pamphlets warning that the American soldiers would abduct German women for "Negro brothels."

Willem and Griet—she sometimes went by Titi in Germany, Titi

Latomme, it sounds like the name of the singer she'd once hoped to become—Wim and Titi were swept up in the fleeing mass of terrified exiles, indignant bourgeois, deserters, forced laborers, widows with toddlers, young hotheads, desperate elderly people who had fled for fear of reprisals, leaving everything behind. Sometimes the Flemish were welcomed as Germanic brothers; other times, doors were slammed in their faces because they were Belgians. Panic, and resentment of the Belgian nation said to be "retching out its own people"; makeshift accommodations with distant relatives or acquaintances; hope, fear, betrayal and dirty tricks, and sometimes outright absurdities: later, some Flemish refugees went on insisting—under questioning in military tribunals, for instance—that they had merely been biding their time in Germany until they could return to their Flemish fatherland, which they had believed would be absorbed into the triumphant German Reich in a matter of days. In other words, they claimed that their faith in a German victory had remained strong even after the Allied advance became unstoppable and the Germans were suffering massive losses on every front. The SS panicked and improvised; the militias, while in rapid retreat, inflicted many sadistic reprisals; the concentration camp ovens were emptied out in haste and the hellish death marches began; the massacres in the East went on unabated; the German economy collapsed completely; and the German cities, bombed into ruins, were ravaged by famine, chaos, and violence. Soon the 27th *SS-Division Langemarck* was almost annihilated in combat on the Eastern Front.

It must have been strange to arrive in Germany with naive ideas like Griet's about the promised land, and instead find apocalyptic scenes of chaos and destruction. Hanover had practically been wiped off the map by the British air raids of October 9, 1943. Although Griet could have provided an eyewitness account of the aftermath, her memoir says nothing about what went on in those months; the raw reality was too jarring a contrast with her brittle ideology.

———

In rural Soltau, fifty miles north of Hanover, Griet and Willem are put up in classrooms, where they apparently have a few run-ins with "Dutch people who are very unfriendly and full of themselves." The former sweetheart of a high-ranking German officer, a girl from Eeklo, discovers that she has been robbed; her bathing suit and jewelry have disappeared. The commanding officer places Willem in charge of the investigation: "He was outraged and did not take half measures. Everyone there was searched down to their underclothes (if they had any)." The thief is found—Griet's memoir does not give details of Willem's approach to the investigation, and she certainly doesn't say how the perpetrator was punished. But one way or another, the group of refugees falls apart. The local authorities send them to Hanover city center, where Willem gets in touch with the military authorities; he is invited to resume his espionage work among his peers and returns to making lists of names and reporting "suspicious elements" to Nazi intelligence. Griet helps him, becoming his hardworking secretary; her memoir proudly notes that she corrected his language errors, that her work was *ehrenamtlich* (honorary and unsalaried) and that she received a commendation from the military administration.

Verhulst the *V-Mann* is assigned a beautifully furnished apartment. "The former residents had moved to safer climes," Griet writes. I am drawn up short by this sentence, so innocent on the face of it; what it really tells us is that they laid claim to the home of people who had fled persecution, or else had been sent to a camp and perhaps had even already been murdered. Or was it the home of German civilians who had fled the Allied bombing?

They go through air raid after air raid—fifty-three, if Griet Latomme's account is to be believed. By night, they hear the dreaded RAF bombers flying overhead, setting the cities of Germany aflame; by day, they go on excursions to Hildesheim, Dresden and Berlin. When their new apartment in Hanover is damaged in a bombing, they are offered luxurious new accommodation, this time in a sprawling country house outside the city. Griet's stories verge on the idyllic: "We are learning to hunt for edible mushrooms in the woods . . . under a weeping willow, we ate with gusto." She describes Wim's addiction to tobacco and constant search for it; he sometimes has to settle for dried willow leaves. They distrust their compatriots and keep them at a distance, as if they have a contagious disease, because "according to Wim they were real Belgians." Not a word about the horrors, not a single war scene, no names of victims, or battles, or looted or shattered streets littered with corpses; not a hint of what must have been omnipresent; no, Titi and Wim munched porcini with gusto in an Arcadian setting, after he met his deadline for reporting the latest results of his espionage to the *Sicherheitspolizei*. Her account reads like postcards from a happy holiday.

In the serene reading room of the Antwerp documentation center, I look up from Griet's memoir in a kind of bafflement and stare out into the quiet courtyard.

One early morning in the autumn of 1945, a commando unit from the Belgian White Brigade comes knocking. They ask for *Sturmbannführer* Raf Van Hulse. The German woman who answers the door doesn't quite catch the name; oh, yes, she says, there's a Hülst here, up on the second floor, in the right-hand bedroom.

So while Willem's family in Drongenhof is struggling through the months after liberation without any news of him, he is arrested after all and sent to the *Polizeipräsidium* in Hanover. Griet remains loyal, supporting him even under the most trying circumstances; she finds out where he is being held, talks to his jailers, scours the surrounding area for tobacco, buys eggs and bread, and has food packages delivered to him by a guard she bribes with sweet words, smiles and cigarettes.

She is eventually interrogated and imprisoned too. A "uniformed Belgian" tells her he will release her if she sleeps with him; she proudly refuses and says she's never heard the names he's asking her about. In prison, she meets a different class of people: Do you have syph too? she hears one ask, and the answer is: No, I have the drip. Revolted, she reports that the German girls "whored themselves out to the British occupiers"— though she will not hear a word said against the Flemish girlfriends of German officers.

Cold, deprivation, pride, stubbornness, rashes, hunger, despair, poor hygiene, suppurating wounds—the obstinate Titi remains provocative and gutsy. The coffee is so terrible she morbidly calls it "Jew sweat." Eventually, the two of them are sent to Brussels in separate convoys; just before departure, on a teeming railway platform, she has a chance to attract her lover's attention with "fond winks and waving" as he is led off in chains with other men. She is first held in Forest, a suburb of Brussels, then transferred to Begijnenstraat in Antwerp, and she ends up in a former factory on Wollestraat in Ghent, converted into a prison. He is first sent to Saint-Gilles in the Brussels region, then moved to Ghent, sometimes to Wollestraat and sometimes to the prison known as Nieuwe-Wandeling, or to the internment camp for suspected collaborators in Lokeren—places where his children, on their infrequent visits, will find him much thinner and helpless.

Griet even has the audacity to describe her prison on Wollestraat as a "concentration camp."

The End of their adventure in Eastland.

29

It must have seemed strange to Griet Latomme that Langemark, that familiar place where she'd first been exposed to Flemish nationalism, became such an important symbol for the collaborators who fled to Germany. The town had been on the front line in the First World War and was catapulted into history when German propaganda bulletins reported a crushing defeat in the nearby villages of Bikschote and Noordschote as having taken place in "Langemarck." That had a Greater Germanic ring to it, much more so than those other, foreign-sounding names. In Nazi lore the *Sturmbrigade Langemarck*, spelled with the German "c," was stripped of its associations to the small Flemish town, instead becoming emblematic of Germanic military heroism. Adolf Hitler, who had been stationed in Wervik on the Flemish front, only twelve miles away, was one of the many soldiers for whom the name had an almost sacred ring, because of the tens of thousands of German infantrymen who had died in battle there. On his fifty-third birthday, April 20, 1942, he decided to dub the 4th *SS Totenkopf* regiment the "Langemarck" and amalgamate it with the volunteer Flemish Legion. *Reichsführer-SS* Himmler described this strange new brigade as an enduring tribute to the blood sacrificed by the Germanic people on Flemish soil. The tribute was not as glorious as he had hoped; the brigade was decimated in the final stage of the war by Soviet troops.

In May 1944, when Nazi Germany's chances on the battlefield had become almost nil, the *Langemarck* volunteers were mostly withdrawn and sent to Lüneberg Heath in Lower Saxony, "because most of the Flemish refugees were accommodated in the Gau of Eastern Hanover," as Himmler said. There, in the rural town of Soltau, Griet and Wim were witness to the arrival of these troops in Flemish colors and made contact with fellow Flemings in the SS division. As we now know, some of those soldiers from the Eastern Front had even worked as camp guards in smaller concentration camps in the East or led the infernal death marches, which meant committing acts of heinous violence against the half-dead refugees in the snow. Langemark!—the romantic couple's first love nest, now immortalized in a heroic saga, which collapsed as swiftly as their pan-Germanic dream and their refugee existence in their bombed-out, exhausted dreamland.

And here an excruciating memory comes back to me.

I was just seventeen years old and lorded it over the rest of my class; it was May 1968, and we were swept up by all the rumors around us; the evening before, I had seen the scenes on TV from the streets of Paris—and Flemish cities too, Leuven and Ghent. It looked like one big celebration of rebelliousness and energy, effervescent joy, adventurousness, and we—who took orders delivered in fretful whispers by the priests who taught us, all the while brimming with an undirected vitality that we could barely keep under control—we had speculated, during the lunch break, about how we could take part in the huge demonstrations planned for the next day in Ghent and Leuven. We had talked each other into a fervor; the newspapers, radio and television told of nothing but revolution in the streets, a new young generation; some condemned and others encouraged them, society was divided, and our seventeen-year-old brains seemed under the influence of a dizzying drug. The university students were going out into the streets; could we, in high school, do any less? We had to take a stand, participate, whatever it took to escape those stuffy classrooms.

The streets of Ghent were teeming with noisy students, floods of young people with signs and banners, some shouting about a common front with the working people, others chanting slogans like "Flanders the Lion!" "Away with the Walloons!" and more in that rich vein. Could this be the same liberation struggle that was sweeping Paris, in the name of proletarians everywhere? Hadn't we heard that the students were showing their solidarity with the working class? Or had we been too carried away to listen properly? Oh well, what did it matter—"Flanders the Lion!" In any case, I and a few other mischief-makers managed to whip the whole class into a frenzy, and the next morning a squadron of adolescents cycled out of the schoolyard, heads high with pride like medieval knights—we were on strike, right? The energy was dizzying on that spring morning as we whooshed through the streets to the city center, where we left our bicycles heaped at the door of the notorious Café Schippershuis, a cellar near one of the city's broad avenues that reeked of stale beer, where we raised glass after glass to our newfound freedom, which we knew would cost us dearly. Sometime after noon—we were already dazed and delirious—a scruffy collection of students went by, conducting an actual protest; we stormed out of the café and walked alongside them, there was screaming and shouting—it was a party, right?—a revolution, something happening for once, at long last, God yes, but we hadn't paid close attention to the caps and badges the students were wearing, and before we knew it we were in the midst of a group of men with medieval-looking headwear and spiked clubs, shouting along with them at the top of our lungs, half-baked revolutionaries with reeling heads, because Flanders was for the Flemish! Away with the Walloons! Left-Wing Rats, Roll Up Your Mats! And that was the revolution, all the way from Paris, right? One of them even shouted *Sieg Heil*, which didn't sound French either, come to think of it, but it must have been quite a joke, because everyone burst into laughter, and as we made our way down Langemunt, somewhere on a second floor an old window opened and a woman's face popped out, a lovely face, an elegant woman of about sixty, and she cried, she screeched, *Fascistes! Bande de Nazis!* Off to Langemark with you, you bunch of idiots! You heard the lady, Langemark, that's what she said, God knows why. In fact her meaning was as plain as day, but we didn't know the first thing about anything, we were revolutionaries and the energy felt so good coursing through our veins. A while later we passed through Patershol with a bunch of drunken rowdies, and then through Drongenhof, and somewhere along the way an old woman was looking out of her door, wistful fear in her eyes, and—yes, of course, obviously—I may have imagined it later, but even if I did, that imagined scene is the essence of what torments me; for wasn't that the only time I ever saw her, in the open door of the house where I would later live: the elderly Mientje, who must have thought all her old nightmares were coming back to life and marching down the street again, past the old chapel and the glass workshop and past her door, old, lonely Mientje, a couple of months before her silent death in the shadowy middle room of the house, where I would later have such a wild time with my hip friends and girlfriends? Yes, there she stood at that open door, that large door I would paint black some fifteen years later, knocking the can of paint from the ladder, clumsy me, sending the black stuff splashing in all directions, covering the whole sidewalk and half the street with that anthracite glimmer, one huge black stain, you dig, you rebel, you?

That evening you asked your father what "Langemark" meant, and that law-abiding citizen bowed his head and said it was a question for your grandfather, but your grandfather stood up, shook his head and went out into the garden for a breath of fresh air. The next day your father was summoned to the principal's office and informed that you were no longer welcome—your son is a rotten apple in our barrel, the priest told him, he will end up behind bars, mark my words. And your father, that

hardworking man, came home red-faced and tried to tell you something but wasn't able, because something made him swallow and his eyes
teared up and you laughed, remember, big man? You laughed.

―――

It doesn't help an awful lot that decades later you stood in the meadows
of Langemark on one of those rare mild days in February and saw the
countless flat stones with their numberless German names flattened into
the soggy soil of the polder, and not far away the monument marked
"Flandern" and the three grim dark crosses of rough granite arranged
side by side. It doesn't help that you saw the children's memorial, with the
innumerable black metal poppies—nothing will help at this stage. You
drive into the center of the once-ravaged town, there is roadwork in progress, you have to take a detour. Sleek modern apartment buildings are
rising from the ground, with home automation for today's discerning
buyers, and a fresh coat of asphalt will be laid on the churned-up road,
where do you think Griet might have lived, where did she roll in the hay
with her sweet Wim, no idea. The church smells of lye soap and echoes
with Flemish pop songs, caramel lyrics about love and peace; the surrounding building site is strewn with concrete pipes, plastic-wrapped
towers of blocks, wire mesh for pouring concrete, workers' materials,
torn plastic tarps, and garbage—the town must be spending money like
water.

You drive back through the flat landscape, a dried-up sea floor that
smells of soil and manure in the late winter sun; just outside Langemark
you come to a halt at a sign along the roadside and take a picture; you'll
later learn it's the name of a hamlet.

The sign says, "DE NIEUWE WERELD." THE NEW WORLD. "After a
former inn of that name."

210

30

The raid on the house in Drongenhof is so upsetting for Adri that he decides to leave the neighborhood. "My father had terrified me," he will later write in his memoir. "He claimed they would hold me hostage to trade for him." Even though he didn't witness his father flee, the images he did see jumble together in his mind: Daskalidès poking him with the gun barrel, the unfortunate fall on the stairs that nearly cost him his life, the ache in his feet from pounding the pedals of his bicycle; in his mind's eye, he sees the men leering suspiciously at his mother; sees Mientje, quiet and dignified, running her fingers through his sisters' hair; sees the fear in little Suzy's eyes. Yesterday, he rode to Korenmarkt Square, which had seen heavy combat the night before; there were dark spots on the paving stones that made him gag; he bought an issue of the resistance newspaper *Bevrijding* (Liberation) from a vendor and brought it home for his mother to read.

He cycles to Deurle, where he knows he can stay with his friend Willy Welvaert. He sweats and snorts and pedals, he sees the peaceful woods rise up on the horizon, he inhales the smell of grass and forest soil and can't help thinking of that long, happy summer with the Scheuermann family in the peaceful town of Neuenstein; he wonders how Fritz and Ernst and Walter are doing these days; now he's winded, having cycled the seven miles from Patershol to Deurle in half an hour; here and there he saw bullet holes in a house front, the charred remains of a barn, a swastika daubed on a front door, patches of scorched earth, warped iron, a house with empty windows and soot-stained walls. Here in the woods, he needs to get some rest, wait and see what will happen; the war appears to be over but he distrusts all the evidence of his eyes. Here and there armed men are walking in and out of houses shot halfway to rubble. There is his friend's large garden, and look, it's Adri's neighbor Oswald and his sister Lieve, Lieve from Grauwpoort, the girl he's had a secret crush on for so long, Lieve with her braids. Now he needs to calm down and not let anyone notice his feelings for her; he smells spruce and white ferns, his sweat-soaked shirt clings to his back. Willy comes out to greet him; Adri steps off his bicycle; his friend says, *Bienvenue*, Adrien, and throws his arms around him. Adri bursts into sobs.

The prosperous Welvaert family, who owned a large property in the rustic village of Deurle, were people of their time, well educated and proud of their Flemish identity but at home in the bilingual cultural milieu of the *haute bourgeoisie*. They approved of the cultural side of collaboration with the Germans and held annual meetings of Flemish poets in their garden. Anton van Wilderode, a poet who would be ordained as a priest in the last year of the war, was another regular guest. It was partly thanks to his friend Willy that Adri had pieced together, bit by bit, what was going on with his father; it shocked him and tore at him; he learned to distance himself, on the inside, from everything his father stood for, even as he could not stop thinking about him. What is Pappie doing now, ran the endless refrain in his head in sleepless hours. At the same time, he had his reservations about his friends' religious views; his mother had warned him about their conservatism and misguided Catholic dogmas.

In his memoir he notes, "I had my mother at home, keeping a discreet and anxious eye on my spiritual development. She made sure I wasn't drawn into right-wing Catholic circles by my friendships with boys like Willy and Oswald . . . even though they remained my best friends. The time I spent with them, our long walks in the woods, and especially our outings to Sint-Martens-Latem and Deurle are among my finest memories from the war years."

With Oswald, he learned how to put together a radio transmitter; they still had enough parts lying around from the old MEGA warehouse to experiment with. The two boys launched their own program, Radio Dietsland, in which they commented on the latest developments in the German occupation. "What exactly our message was," Adri writes, "I cannot recall, but I do know that we always began and ended our broadcasts—which, I might add, were fairly brief—with the Dutch national anthem, the Wilhelmus. I owned a record of the song, which we played on my hand-cranked gramophone."

The two friends had last seen each other a week earlier, just before the resistants had barged into the house. Adri had been in a panic. His father was no longer sleeping at home; he had turned up a day earlier, in the early afternoon, gathered up a few belongings in haste, said to the children, God bless and keep you, and told Adri, Take good care of my books, before heading out of the front door again. Yes, part of the French collection in the second-floor library was still there; where could they take the stolen books from the École des Hautes Études? The Allies were nearing the city, the resistance was growing bolder every day, their house could be torched at any moment—they had to work fast. Mientje had already hidden their few valuables under the roof of the coal shed by the back fence, beneath rags and blocks of wood: a beautiful antique candlestick from her parents, some lace, an old clock from her grandfather, and some copper pots and pans.

They asked a couple of Oudburg neighbors with unsoiled reputations to keep as many books for them as possible. Adri cycled back and forth, lugging heavy cardboard boxes; he brought other books to the family Welvaert in Deurle. When the bookshelves in the library were empty, he stood in front of his father's large collection of gramophone records—popular classical music that he and Oswald had often played on their program—and felt his heart sink; the shellac was as heavy as lead, there was no way he could move them on his bicycle; then Willy reminded him that behind the garage at the radio rediffusion service there was still a canoe tied up, which his father had built a few years earlier for fair-weather excursions on the Leie.

The boys piled the records into the canoe and threw some blankets over them; Adri added his impressive stamp collection. They rowed down the Leie to Sint-Martens-Latem, a journey of several hours, paddling themselves into a sweat. The next day they had to transport another load—a risky venture that could have had fatal consequences.

Only one record went overboard: the "Horst-Wessel-Lied." His friend Willy saw it and said, Oh, no, Adri, this has to go, right now. With a sweep of his arm he cast it away; the record skipped over the water, was tipped on its edge by a slight swell, and sank.

But now Adri is safe in the home of the Welvaerts in Deurle. The young people there spend their days in alternating fear and relief; sometimes they hear gunfire, confused sounds, shouting and scraping, or the roaring engine of an all-terrain vehicle racing down a forest path. On the trees along the road there are warnings in English; Adri doesn't understand, since the only languages he's learned at school are French and German; Willy has to translate. They walk through the woods and go for long rambles along the Leie. Lieve Vandermeulen, who wrote her own memoir of those years, remembers that Adri, with his deformed foot, could not keep up, and that she always waited for him, but he never had much to say.

When I visit Lieve and let slip, in the course of our conversation, that Adri was in love with her for years, the refined old woman is astonished: I never realized, she says, where did you hear that. Letta, I tell her, Letta told me. Now that you've said that, I can see the forests of Latem and Deurle before me again, she muses, her eyes wandering to the window. There was an old ice cellar there . . . a dark underground vault in the castle garden . . . the only way to find it was through a narrow corridor under a hill . . . some boys took girls there to . . . you know . . . I was still a child then, a girl with blonde braids coiled into buns and pinned next to my ears . . . that ice cellar, the smell of cool earth in the darkness, I can't forget it . . . there was also a Marian grotto somewhere around there, the kind you found all across Flanders in those days . . . that time is shrouded in mist for me . . . the constant fear of everything to do with sexuality whirled over my childhood like a cloud of bats . . .

31

Less than two weeks after Willem fled, all hell broke loose around Arnhem. Mientje had not heard from her parents in weeks, and the telephone hadn't been working since Willem had left. Market Garden began; this massive invasion by air and by land, aimed at forcing the Germans out of the Rhine area from Nijmegen to Arnhem, was one of the most formidable coordinated Allied operations. The military might that was exerted in this apocalyptic offensive was unprecedented. In his book about the Battle of Arnhem, Antony Beevor mentions 872 Flying Fortresses loaded with fragmentation bombs, a total of 84 Mosquito fighter-bombers and Boston and Mitchell medium bombers, and 147 P-51 Mustangs. The operation was a hopeless failure, mainly because the British field marshal Bernard Montgomery had grossly underestimated how hard the Germans would fight back; many paratroopers were shot dead even before reaching the ground. It became a tragic debacle for the Allies, utter hell for the civilian population because of the horrific German reprisals, and the last major victory for Hitler.

Mientje is glued to the radio, listening with pounding temples to the latest reports until late in the night. There is no way on earth to contact her family in the middle of that disaster area; all she can do is pray and wait. Adri is with Oswald and Willy in Deurle, listening to British radio; his chest tightens as he hears Churchill's speeches, followed by snatches of the enraged Führer screeching hysterically; meanwhile, Mientje sits in the middle room in Drongenhof in the twilight, staring into the half darkness. British and Polish fighter-bombers sometimes swoop low over

Ghent; now and then, she can hear intense bursts of rifle fire. During the day, she sees jumpy, ragged soldiers shooting wildly in all directions before stealing bicycles and rushing off like mad dogs. She thinks of her husband, passing his days God knows where in Germany, if he hasn't already died in combat or an air raid. She will remain in the dark about his fate until well after the German capitulation; from day to day, she lives in fear. In the afternoon, she often goes to the church in Brabantdam to keep herself occupied with straightforward tasks, as she listens to the wailed complaints of the people who have sought refuge in that peaceful place. She hurries home again just before evening falls, aware of the danger if she is not safe at home in Drongenhof by dusk.

⁓

They are difficult months. There is almost no coal to be had, and the farmers Mientje goes to for food are stingier with their wares every time. Her bicycle is in need of repair; the front wheel was caught in a tram rail one misty morning and bent completely out of shape; the long-haired bicycle repairman in Patershol has absconded; public transport is unreliable; and when she does take the tram, there are still people who hiss that she's a kraut-loving whore, the wife of the hated Verhulst. She hears more and more news of famine in the Netherlands and hopes her brother has kept the cellar well stocked and is taking good care of their elderly mother; she burns with longing to see them both, but it would be madness to attempt the journey with all the trigger-happy Germans at the checkpoints; she reads in the newspaper that there is heavy fighting around Arnhem. Letta and Suzy can return to school safely; Adri comes home from Deurle once the situation in the city has calmed down a little; but not until January 1945 does he dare to show his face on the street again, usually camouflaged with a thick scarf and winter hat. Early that

218

year, they are surprised to see some familiar faces pop up in Ghent, back from Germany—forced laborers, volunteers, and even a few of the less prominent collaborators. Whenever she runs into one of them, Mientje begs for news: What can you tell me about my husband? The answer is always shrugged shoulders and silence.

"One day in the course of May 1945," Adri writes, "a man rang our door-bell: the brother of Aurélie Willaert, a teacher from Ertvelde and a close acquaintance of my parents. He had been a baker in Germany and met my father near Hanover or Hildesheim. My father had dictated a few messages: he was doing well and told us not to worry about him." After relaying this information, the man produced a brown envelope from a jacket pocket and handed it to Mientje. It contained a thick stack of Belgian thousand-franc notes. She stood holding it in shock: how had Willem gotten his hands on this money, what was she supposed to do with it?

To address the financial chaos that had come in the wake of the occu-pation, the finance minister, Camille Gutt, had announced a massive operation to fight inflation by withdrawing all existing cash; the old cur-rency would soon become worthless. Citizens could exchange their masses of devalued money for a few of the new bills; when larger sums were involved, the money was deposited in an account monitored by the authorities. Gutt's initiative was a radical new departure, bringing to light all the currency that had changed hands under wartime conditions or in shady transactions, unless it was thrown away or incinerated. Entire fortunes were frozen, bank deposits and bonds had to be submitted for revaluation. Mientje had nowhere to go with Willem's cash. The only way she could recover a small fraction of the money was by giving a few trusted friends who were not as well off a few bills each, which they could deposit in their own accounts and later pay back to Mientje in cash—a humiliating necessity. The rest of it had to be thrown away; Mientje never saw the documents from the tribunal, so she never knew that Willem had raided the accounts of his own Dietsch Action Committee the day before he fled. If she had known, she would have hurled the envelope into the fire at once.

—

Because the family no longer had money coming in, Mientje decided to let out the unoccupied rooms and the attic. The girls moved to the back room on the second floor; she kept the front room on the third floor as her bedroom but also set up a little office there, because for many years she would rent out both the middle room on the ground floor and the large front room on the second floor. The attic room was still furnished with an old iron bed, which she made up with pillows and a simple mattress she borrowed from the neighbors. She had Adri tell his friends and acquaintances that his mother was taking in boarders. It wasn't long before people were coming to the door, more and more of them, begging Mientje for a room, because the housing shortage was dire after the bombings. And of course, a few collaborators, friends of Willem, asked her if they could go into hiding there. Soon, a number of unconventional guests had taken up residence in the house. Meanwhile, Willem was behind bars for months, awaiting trial; during that time, it seems he was unable to send any sign of life to his despairing family.

32

Mientje's diaries of those years were later carefully photocopied by Letta and made available to researchers. The first notebook I saw runs from August 29, 1944, to June 26, 1946. Her recollections are vivid and elaborate, offering the reader a detailed account of the days surrounding Willem's flight, but she does not say a word about the flight itself, or about the scene that Letta described. She does evoke the fear they feel during the last heavy fighting in Ghent, the destruction of houses along Ottogracht, Dampoort and Lange Steenstraat, the violent combat around the tollhouse bridge and Sleepstraat: "Hell is just around the corner, but the weather is lovely; we're sitting upstairs in the sun." At night, she hears still more "terrible screeching and grenade explosions." Again and again, she writes that she and her children have been spared, that her life is firmly in God's hands. She copies Psalm 91 into the notebook in its entirety to give herself courage: "There shall no evil befall thee, neither shall any plague come nigh thy dwelling. For He shall give His angels charge over thee, to keep thee in all thy ways . . ."

She reports on the constant difficulty of finding food after rationing begins, but also on her almost-daily efforts to ease the suffering of refugees and the wounded, including a few old acquaintances. She introduces a whole series of friends and associates; sometimes she lends a hand at Bijloke Hospital, which at one point takes in wounded Dutch patients from Hoofdplaat, Biervliet and Breskens, coastal villages that have mostly been obliterated. Many families have nothing left; there are refugees with ugly injuries; some were forced to help Germans flee and thus became targets for the British. She visits the infirmary daily, listens to victims and speaks comforting words to them. She offers solace to bed-ridden patients, sometimes holding a weeping woman's hands for a full hour. The "Hollanders" are being robbed by heartless locals, she writes; their last scraps of food are snatched away, and as if that weren't bad enough, they're also taunted: "Thanks, cheesehead, we enjoyed that." She never becomes bitter. Nor does she take sides; when she hears about fugitive collaborators whose families have suffered reprisals, it makes her no less emotional than does a Christian service celebrating the liberation of Ghent and recalling the horrors perpetrated there by the Germans. One day, on the way to someplace or other where she hopes to be able to buy food, she suddenly finds herself staring into heavy artillery; the rain falls, the wind blows, the dark clouds race over the half-destroyed houses. The war machines, in a gust of late sunlight, glow harshly against the ashen sky as if she is witness to something apocalyptic.

> The muzzles of the tanks, fiery mouths that would soon kill thou-sands more people. The harsh wind matches the harshness of the scene, and I think of the prophet Elijah in the mists of antiquity, how alone he is, and the great wind passes, and he hears the Word, but the Lord is not in the wind. And after the wind, the rustling of a gentle silence, and it came to pass that Elijah heard it, that he stood before the Lord again and cried out, Leave me, Lord, for I am a sin-ful man . . .

Here comes the tram at last, her story continues. It's already some forty-five minutes late; she lugs the food home and then rushes to the hospital with Letta to tend to a Dutch girl disfigured by a grenade. The treadmill of her days. No news of her captured husband—but she's grate-ful that Adri will be admitted to university. She describes the repeated raids of her home by resistance fighters; one time they search the house, another time they come to ask what happened to the receiver at the radio rediffusion service. Some men are surprised to find Adri playing the violin when they enter the house and become much friendlier to her, but there are also official searches by order of the "Commissioner-Inspector for State Security," like the one that takes place on February 11, 1946. According to the document, the purpose is to find "all writings, personal effects, photographs and miscellaneous objects that may relate to charges of membership in a pro-German organization or any other offense against the Security of the State"; it also states that the officers should proceed "as appropriate" to "*interrogation* regarding the discovery." After one of the searches, which seem largely unsuccessful, the policemen decide to seize a few photographs of August Borms and Kees Boeke, at least. Mientje reports with pride in her diary how stoic she always remains: "because my conscience is clear."

"Meanwhile, the number of martyrs to the Flemish cause keeps growing; Watervliet is in ruins, and terrible things are happening in Ertvelde," Mientje writes in a diary from the final months of the occupation. There is more heavy fighting nearby, around the tollhouse bridge. Houses in Krommewal and Speldenstraat are ravaged by bombing; on Sleepstraat, grenades swoosh through the air. "We are sleeping well," she writes; "Adri even missed all the noise. We realized only the next day how close we had come to death and destruction; all our neighbors spent the night in air-raid shelters. O how miraculous is God's grace, we join in thanks to Him for preserving us" . . . A picturesque scene in one room: the children with their hands folded and their eyes shut as their mother leads them in prayer.

In those months, amid the noise of war, she thinks back to Luther, "how he posted his 95 theses against the sale of indulgences on the castle church in Wittenberg and thus taught us that we are justified by faith alone... While swarms of bombers hover over the city, we enjoy a peaceful lunch in the sunshine with the window open, read from John 17, and sing 'I hear in the air, 'neath the canopy blue' and 'Safe in the Arms of Jesus.'"

She carries full baskets to the nearby laundry, and when she returns, she sits in the sun for a while in the front room on the third floor—the master bedroom—and then, at the end of the afternoon, visits a few neighbors in need of some assistance. Later she walks down the ugly remains of Ottogracht: "Is that war? Terrible destruction... It's as if we've awoken from a dream or gone outside for a look around after a terrible earthquake; we didn't know it had been so bad ..."

September 20: "We can hear a terrifying number of planes, and the paratroopers have reached the Arnhem-Nijmegen area ..."

September 23: "The fighting is dreadful around Arnhem ..."

"I am in the Lord's hands," she writes, and to give herself courage, she rereads a booklet by her beloved Reverend Wartena, *Apostle of the Victorious Faith*—"What riches of the Spirit reveal themselves to me; what a blessing to lead a life of Faith ..." "Drongenhof is our refuge," she writes; "as long as we remain here, nothing can harm us."

Adri begins his university studies, Letta has a painful ear infection, it's Suzy's birthday. Mientje sees elderly people stumbling down the streets, wounded people with crutches, desperate people digging through the rubble with scarred hands because they've lost everything. In Zeeland, she writes, the battle rages on; the seawall has been bombed to bits and all of Walcheren is underwater; the railway employees are on strike, so it's harder and harder to travel anywhere. There is fierce combat near Maldegem and Eeklo; the fighting in Breskens is ghastly too, then the conflict moves to Breda, Venray and Nijmegen, "but to my delight, I found sugar today for the children, and plenty of fruit, oh may peace come quickly."

She hears that some of the prisoners in Lokeren have been charged with war crimes, but says nothing of her fears that the same fate awaits her husband. The suffering of the blackshirts is terrible, she writes, but "the Father always remains the Father, full of compassion for his prodigal Son . . . the wisteria in our garden is in beautiful bloom."

Adri and Letta run into trouble in the classroom; Letta, who must have been briefly signed up for the Hitler Youth by her father—there is a letter signed "Heil Hitler" in her file—is summoned to the "Bureau of Education"; Mientje refuses to bring her there and gives Letta a note declaring that children should not be dragged into politics. Thanks to her mother's assertiveness, Letta is left alone from then on.

"Today is Sunday. How I sometimes long for this day of rest, when silence falls, and the travails of earthly life are put aside awhile for the things of the Spirit . . . I observe it more and more over time, this longing for the King, the Savior—but today people long for an earthly king, when only Jesus Christ is the Fulfilment of the human heart . . . and when I rose before dawn, I saw the Morning Star, and I thought of God's Word in Revelation: 'I am the bright Morning Star that comes before the Light of the Sun.'"

*

June 24, 1945: "The summer is excessive in its fruitfulness, lots of fruit, but still expensive—we hear from all sorts of people how the Flemish are faring in Germany; Cyriel Verschaeve has been dragged off with all his trappings; when a priest and shepherd recruits for the Eastern Front, there must be consequences . . . Each day it becomes clearer to me how the poor Flemish people were led on . . . that's how the deceivers of the people go about their work—now everything is growing more intense in this political chaos, and sharp dichotomies are gradually emerging . . . Distressing news is still reaching us; we are told the SS men wear the insignia—the mark of the Beast from Revelation, I thought when I heard it . . . AND THE BEAST WAS TAKEN AND WITH HIM THE FALSE PROPHET THAT WROUGHT MIRACLES BEFORE HIM, WITH WHICH HE DECEIVED THEM THAT HAD RECEIVED THE MARK OF THE BEAST AND THEM THAT WORSHIPPED HIS IMAGE. THESE BOTH WERE CAST ALIVE INTO A LAKE OF FIRE BURNING WITH BRIM-STONE . . . Sometimes worldly cares force themselves on me; I've spent my last franc and now have to borrow—but He who has called me is steadfast."

She prays in a mood of despair, but that very day she finally receives permission to sell Willem's personal car, which he left behind when he fled. The money will tide her over for a few more months. "Bless the Lord, O my soul, and forget not all His benefits."

July 10, 1945: "Today is Pappie's birthday. We think of him, and we faithfully leave everything in the hands of Him who shall unfold His plan for our lives."

That same evening, she attends a lecture in a house in Kasteellaan: a priest who was a prisoner in Dachau describes his experiences in the camps: "He talks about his life as a prisoner, about the many who died in defeat there by tying themselves to the barbed wire, which is fatal because the fence is electrified, and in the mornings he would find whole rows of them dead . . ." Afterward she writes in horror, "What is national socialism, what is the SS man?"

The next day, July 11, when the Battle of the Golden Spurs of 1302 is commemorated, she attends another lecture, this one arguing for the "rehabilitation of the Lion of Flanders, which has been so abused." On July 21 she jots down a few sentences about the debate surrounding the king, which is dividing Flemish politicians; the Catholics demand the return of Leopold III, who was imprisoned in Germany during the war, but the socialists, liberals and communists are vehemently opposed; on July 22 she recalls her wedding day "in silence, alone with the children—but our housemates did bring flowers."

A new boarder arrives; she doesn't give his name, but she's happy that he can help the children with their lessons. "I'm very busy," she says, "always so many people in my life, it's wearing me out, I was nearing the point of breakdown. I feel that if I pay attention to the waves, I will be lost . . . My children, if you read this later, please know that your mother has only one prayer—Lord God, preserve them from Evil."

She runs out of money again and has to sell a gold necklace. "Deliver me from my possessions, Lord, as long as I can follow You and walk my path in Your light."

It is January 23, 1946 when she finally receives a letter from the lawyer Henri De Potter, her landlord, informing her that her husband was arrested the year before in Germany and taken to Saint-Gilles prison in Brussels. On January 26, there is a letter from Willem himself. A few days later, he is apparently being held in Nieuwe Wandeling in Ghent; then he is transferred to the prison in Lokeren. They speak to each other through bars and wire mesh; he's in good condition, Mientje notes, even though he did go hungry in Germany; she has brought him food—"a prisoner, yes, now I know what that word really means."

In April she visits her childhood home in Oud-Zevenaar. As she travels through the war-torn landscape, she cannot maintain her usual stoic reserve. Her diary sketches her profound emotion: "The Westervoort bridge has been destroyed, and everything from Nijmegen to Arnhem is one vast wasteland . . . but how beautiful the forests of the Veluwe are! The journey from Beekbergen to Silvolde is breathtaking! . . . It's the same landscape I saw yesterday evening in the dark, but it was like a labyrinth then, because the light had gone, and because—how is it possible—I had lost my way so completely . . . yet the Father's Hand leads us through even that labyrinth to safety . . ."

It seems almost certain that all the clamor of battle around Arnhem must often have made Mientje homesick for the landscape of her childhood, the wide-open spaces, the fields and pastures stretching to the horizon, the peaceful rural life she'd brought to a sudden end with her foolhardy choice to follow that Flemish ding-a-ling to Belgium, darn it all to darnation, and whittle away her years on a shadowy street where little sunlight entered, amid a turbulent troupe of boarders she could never have dreamed would surround her one day—and, most of all, that she would look after them, serve them all dinner every day, wash their dirty underclothes, iron their shirts, that all that life would run up and down her stairs and eat at her table from her plates, while her husband was in a bleak prison cell, consumed with resentment.

For her daughters, she sewed colorful dresses from a piece of Dutch fabric that she must have gone to great trouble to obtain.

33

One day I decide to try my luck after all.

I submit an application to the National Archives in Brussels, where the records are kept of the proceedings of the Krijgsauditoraat, the postwar tribunal for suspected collaborators. Letta gives me written permission to consult the documents in question; a few remarkably helpful scholars support my application. After a few weeks, the letter of permission arrives from the public prosecutors' office.

Then I make my way to the back street where the archives reside, in a building with high windows reminiscent of a factory, tucked into the armpit of the narrow street, with old-fashioned cut glass in the door. Up the bluestone steps to another double door, a reading room, silence under large yellow lamps. A metal trolley that was put aside for me is rolled out to my table: seven large cardboard boxes piled high with half-decayed paper, dog-eared manuscripts, flimsy carbon copies, penciled notes, lists marked up in pen, petitions, depositions, confessions, declarations, psychologists' reports, requests to view the records (denied), applications for clemency (refused), and yet another request for early release, dismissed by the court with a snort. The documents in the case, the stamps, the initials, the signatures, the scribbles, the strikethroughs, the second tries—stacks of papers bound together with cord and bearing in large letters the word SECRET; the cord is woven from black, yellow and red thread, the Belgian national tricolor.

The present falls away; the sounds in the Brussels street are muted, the documents crackle, the pages of officialese fan out before me, and on the far side, as if through the dust clouds of history, a man approaches me, wearing glasses with a matte lens in front of the left eye, you can't see that so clearly in the darkness but you know it, and he's also wearing a black uniform under a long black leather jacket, it's two-thirty a.m. and with a dozen soldiers behind him, armed and ready, he bangs on the front door of a large building in Korenlei, a French language institute, an enclave for a disappearing caste, but it's night, no one sees, mist billows from the waterway alongside the building. Isn't everyone sleeping, and didn't the porter go home hours ago? A young man, the nightwatchman's son, is roused from sleep by the pounding at the entrance and the piercing cries of *Mach sofort auf*—Open up at once! More banging and shouting, a lot of fuss and noise in the street now, searchlights slide across the building, the boy hurries to open the door, as elsewhere, in a room on the upper floor, his father wakes up and hastily pulls on his clothes. The entrance is opened; the watchman stares into the aggressive light, half blinded, what could be so urgent in the middle of the night? Then he sees the menacing clutch of SS men in front of him; they push him aside and march in their glossy black boots to the administrator's desk; a man named Verhulst utters threatening words, grinning and saying, You hadn't expected this, had you? A little present in honor of everything you've done to us since 1918.

Ah. This figure bears not the faintest resemblance to the sweet Pappie without whom Mientje now sleeps in her lonesome bed, unsuspecting and cold around the shoulders, in the large front bedroom in Drongen-hof; she would swear to her sacred Protestant Dutch God it couldn't be him. But it is him, exuding grim determination, the electric light making the soldiers' silhouettes ghostly and ominous as they roam the defense-less, rudely awakened building.

Here is where all the puzzle pieces and scattered stories fall into place for me, with this proof in black and white on paper. Yes, that show of brute force was the actual way that the École des Hautes Études was commandeered by the Nazis. In recognition of his bravura performance, Verhulst—the *V-Mann*, the "confidential agent"—was appointed the spanking new director, alongside his position as the radio rediffusion director. I learn that he led the institute for four years; one day in 1943 he registered his entire staff, without asking, as members of the SS organization *DeVlag*, but after some of them protested, he rescinded the measure the next day, while reprimanding them for being such ungrateful sheep, unaware of how much they owed to that great Flemish-German organization—their jobs, for example. In late August 1944, seeing the writing on the wall, he paid his staff two months' wages in advance (some, in their testimony, say three months; others claim that it was promised but never paid, that this was exactly the half-million Belgian francs he snatched before he fled). He also demanded 36,000 francs' worth of petrol before he took off. The petrol was not for his personal use, he would later declare under interrogation; furthermore, he was swindled out of it, and he'd planned to use the money to pay those wages when he returned . . .

From statements by other collaborators, I have learned how thoroughly and systematically they lied under questioning in hope of minimizing their role. Verhulst is no exception to the rule; he has pat answers to every question, answers contradicted by eyewitnesses. In any case, he felt certain, right up to his arrest in 1945, that he would return one way or another to "clean up the mess." According to one witness, Verhulst never waved a pistol at his staff, all he did was use a threatening tone of voice; this is an old crony providing cover. All the voices in these awkwardly written testimonies, contradicting or complementing each other, whispering, arguing, screeching or shamelessly denying; they form a strange choir that rages on in the quiet reading room.

Now I open the file about a raid on a textile factory belonging to Mr. Raymond Goethals in Eeklo. The building was apparently requisitioned in the same crude manner, a mini-blitzkrieg, unexpected and unrelenting, but in this case some witnesses speak of a full squadron of black-booted men in the small country town, just a stone's throw away from quiet Kaprijke, the childhood home of a certain Greta Latomme, the woman who so admired her lover's energy and determination, although that day she was teaching at a school in another part of the country; but be that as it may, it happened right there in Eeklo; the name means "woods of the oak"—the Führer's favorite tree, the sacred German tree—yet it has a gentle Flemish sound: Eeklo. The town is home to a vast military site, later reinvented as a peaceful natural park, but on that day in wartime, factory director Raymond Goethals is the object of snarls and threats; the trembling man confesses that, yes, he did have large quantities of soap stashed away, oh yes, with all these shortages, it's only sensible to stockpile, don't you see, Mr. Verhulst? That shivering sissy could not count on any sympathy. A few resolute kicks with those glossy boots, followed by the joyous mayhem of knocking down piles of covered-up goods, revealed a great number of other undeclared items under the burlap bag and canopies: sacks of flour, potatoes, salt pork, even coffee and canned food. Well, well, a smoking gun, a grave offense, my dear man—one German soldier is already grinning broadly—you were asking for it. Oh, yes, Director Goethals says, I know, forgive me! Forgive me! He stammers and stutters, and *jawohl*, Herr Verhulst is apparently privy to outstanding intelligence about the little director's every move, thanks to his agents, who never sleep; he is surrounded by German men in leather jackets and those jackboots and those caps with skull-and-crossbones insignia; Mr. Goethals trembles and confesses, under these intimidating circumstances, that yes, of course he does keep two sets of books. Well, now, that's high treason, that means you're off to Deutschland, if you don't cooperate fully we can put you on the train right away, and, and, and . . . Oh God, all those smirking SS men, so intimidating, stomping all over his beloved factory, and all his workers removing their caps and mumbling good day, a Walloon worker even saying *bonjour* to those SS men, imagine that if you can, in *French*, what an affront, just look at the soldier raise his eyebrows menacingly, don't play with fire, fellows . . . Goethals, on the verge of tears, is ordered to go home and fetch the secret accounts. Verhulst, as vigilant as ever, does not trust him and insists on accompanying him, so they pass through the streets of Eeklo together; a few bystanders make the sign of the cross as Mr. Goethals goes by, Verhulst behind him, holding a gun and giving an occasional push. When they arrive at the director's fine house, Goethals stammers that he has to go down to the cellar to open the safe and wants to do it alone; the talented Flemish SS intelligence officer snaps that Goethals will most certainly *not* go down there alone, and when the factory director has the impertinence to say that after all he has the r— the r— the right, Mr. Verhulst of Drongenhof snarls the biblical words: What right? There are no more rights here! Open it! Now!

Willem himself took charge of interrogating the good Mr. Goethals. It was not a pleasant chat. Oh, if you want the gruesome details, you can find them in the typed transcripts, or in the prosecutor's statement, in which Verhulst is called "a real gangster" . . . or in the testimony that refers to "gangster methods" . . . I can see now why Adri never wanted to read this . . . And what is still more difficult to read is how the press sided with the occupiers in the war years—the Flemish Nazi press absolutely ate up the heroic story. What a skunk that Goethals turned out to be, one inkslinger writes in the service of the occupying regime, what a ballsy bastard, what a Belgicist piece of shit, hiding petrol and soap underneath the coal, one of those "fat-bellied rich men who rest their feet in embroidered slippers or patent leather shoes under a table laden with good food, giving no thought to the hunger of their workers," and what good news that this factory in rural Eeklo is now the first National Socialist factory in the racially pure Meetjesland region; we should be proud, Flemish readers, that our German brothers wish to do us such an honor, and what did that little soap baron think would happen? Those betrayers of the Flemish people, that elitist clique, will receive their just deserts; long live the State and the *Volk* that it serves! "Finally, the Augean stables will be swept clean. Again, all thanks to the German Wehrmacht." The collaborationist press had plenty of fun in those days.

In well-deserved recognition of his heroic exploits, Verhulst was appointed the new factory director, a position he had to relinquish to a real German SS man a week later, because a Fleming, even if he does his damnedest, can only ever be an ersatz German, a "Western Germanic" type, *Division Langemarck* and all that, if you know what I mean.

A long list of witnesses turned up to testify. The documents seem endless; I fumble and fidget my way through the sheaves of duplicates bound together tightly and sometimes only half-legible because of the primitive binding; the red-yellow-and-black string sometimes passes through the middle of a page instead of the margin; to make photocopies, I have to remove the binding, but I can't, the knots are too small, everything has been bound together much too tightly by the stern hand of Justice, it would tear and be destroyed, it would fade and vanish like hieroglyphs in a newly opened tomb exposed to the harsh light of day, so I read what I can where I can in the bundles of flimsy carbon copies, in which the firm strokes of the typewriter left the occasional hole. Workers, engineers, technicians and Mr. Goethals himself all had to appear before the tribunal and provide details, which combine to paint a fairly grim picture. I take cardboard box number such-and-such off the rack—a person wonders, there in the serene reading room by the warm glow of the yellow lamps, how a man like that could sit down to soup and potatoes at home every evening in the rear of the house in Drongenhof, perhaps even in excellent spirits—after all, he earned the princely sum of 15,000 francs a month—while his patriotic neighbors were slaving away to make ends meet and trying to ignore their rumbling stomachs, at a time when the average unemployment benefits for a family with three children was about 400 francs. Not that he felt entirely secure in his position; there were frequent objections by the German authorities to Verhulst's salary and the prodigious expense claims from his organization, which formed a serious drain on financial resources—a complaint voiced more and more often as Germany's losses mounted, the tribunal records show.

The God-fearing Mientje can see that Pappie is a little tense; it's nothing, dear, he says, everything's fine, he takes another little Pervitin pill, he asks if the children are doing well at school, and what a good clever boy Adri is to play the violin so well already, don't you think, Mammie, he does such a beautiful job and what a treat to hear you sing with him, how about Handel's "Largo" one more time for Papa, it always gives me a lump in my throat.

In the photograph, taken in front of the door of the radio rediffusion service, Verhulst is the third from the right.

34

Defendant Willem Verhulst. Please rise.

Yes, Your Honor.

You are familiar with the accusations against you.

Yes I am, Your Honor.

We will now proceed to the prosecutor's statement.

Yes, but, Your Hon—

Be quiet, Verhulst, it's not your turn. Sit down.

Mr. Beyer. You have the floor.

Thank you, Your Honor.

We shall now proceed to set out the case.

Verhulst is only half listening.

Member of the Front Party and later of the Nazist Party known as the Flemish National Union . . . spy for the Sicherheitsdienst, *"high-level operator" for the Dietsch Action Committee . . . violent seizure of the Ghent Radio Rediffusion Service, the École des Hautes Études, and the Goethals & Goethals factories in Eeklo . . . leader and founder of the Dietsch Action Committee . . . spy for the* Propagandastaffel *and the entire German military command . . . leader and chief propagandist of* DeVlag *Security Corps . . . recruited for* Abteilung VI *of the* Sicherheitspolizei . . . *member of the* Allgemeine SS, *founder of the Flemish Film Initiative . . . theft of more than a million from the Ghent Radio Rediffusion Service . . . betrayal of countless fellow Belgians . . .*

Willem fidgets in his chair, sometimes lifting his eyes to the ceiling with a sigh of contempt, sometimes shaking his head; once he taps his index finger meaningfully against his forehead, as if to say, Have they lost their minds?

The statement continues.

Your Honor,

I shall now read aloud a highly incriminating document: the minutes of the founding meeting of the Dietsch Action Committee, also known as the Verhulst initiative, as drawn up by the defendant.

. . . radical extermination of all centers of degeneracy and bastardization in Flanders . . . ruthless opposition to all counter-revolutionary institutions . . . Belgian plutocratic regime . . . "Knock it down and run it over" . . . Heil Hitler!

In closing, Your Honor, we quote these words from a memorandum to his staff.

"It is our opinion that the restored Low Countries should be incorporated as an independent entity into the Greater Germanic National Socialist Community of Peoples, under the leadership of the Germanic core country, the German Reich."

Very well.

Defendant Willem Verhulst.

Stand when addressed by the tribunal.

Do you admit that you wrote that your nation had to be "knocked down" and that you and the SS would "run it over"?

Your Honor, I would like to ask my lawyer to have Mr. Beyer removed from the case for his lies. He is a Belgic—

Verhulst, you are in no position to demand anything.

He sinks back onto the bench.

Defendant Verhulst, do you admit that you unlawfully seized the Ghent Radio Rediffusion Service by force, with the assistance of six armed SS men, at three o'clock in the morning?

Willem is sweating and shaking his head insistently.
   He leaps up.

Your Honor, I did my duty for Flanders! My only motive was the love of humanity! I was simply an idealist serving his people. And now see what thanks I get. What kind of circus is this!?

Verhulst, spare us your commentary. Just answer the questions.

Do you, Defendant Willem Verhulst, admit that you threatened Mr. Vinck, director of the Ghent Radio Rediffusion Service, just prior to his forced departure, and expelled him from his rightful position?

But Your Honor, I never laid eyes on that Vinck character . . .

Anything for Flanders! I do not acknowledge Mr. Beyer as my legitimate represen—

Behave yourself, Verhulst.

Do you admit your responsibility for the deportation of an unknown
number of Ghent residents?

Belgicist buggers! Flanders the Lion!

Laughter and whistling in the hearing room.

Verhulst, one more time and I will have you escorted back to your cell.

The witnesses take the stand one by one.

Some of his former acquaintances avoid his eyes; while one is in the
middle of testifying, Willem hisses *traitor*. Others, especially resistance
members, shoot triumphant looks at Willem as they give their incriminating testimony.

Witness N, janitor at the École des Hautes Études.

It's the truth, Your Honor, he put his pistol to my chest and shouted, Stupid fransquillons, this is what you owe us for Versailles!

Witness X, secretary.

I swear, on the sixth of September, with his gun aimed at us, he shouted
that he and the *Sicherheitspolizei* would come back in a couple of weeks
to take vengeance on anyone who tried to report him . . .

*

241

Witness Y, worker.

. . . he held that piece right up to Mr. Goethals's head and said he would have him dragged off and locked up, and our Mr. Director was shaking in his shoes and crying . . .

Witness Z, guard.

Yeah, sure, he made me pump all that fuel into cans, those big ones, then they loaded them onto a big trailer and drove off to Germany with them . . .

Verhulst?

But Your Honor, do we really have to rehash all of this, after all, they took that petrol from me later . . . and that Jewish bandit Gutt cut our people's economic balls off, but I don't hear you talking about that, now, do I? French-speaking Jews still have a leg up here in Belgium. I was stupid enough myself to save a Hungarian Jew and his missus. Could have cost me my head. Some thanks I get!

Your opinion of the Jewish citizens of our nation is well known to this tribunal, Verhulst.

Willem is now in a state of severe agitation. He undoes a couple of buttons on his dark gray shirt and uses the fabric to clean his glasses.

The session is briefly adjourned.

Willem feels unwell; his intestines are grumbling and churning. And then that prison food—they're wearing him down here. He wants to

242

protest, everything goes hazy before his eye, he feels queasy and is escorted to the toilet where the swill spurts out of his innards. Haven't I been through enough yet, sadists? He wipes his rear with a section of a Belgian daily and pulls up his dark gray trousers again.

He is led to his place and shoved down onto the bench.

Owww, not so rough, Mr. Officer, come on, I'm not an animal.

Do you, Willem Verhulst, admit that you participated in the violent seizure of the venue known as Vooruit so that you could install the so-called *Wehrmachtskino*, where you were in charge of screening propaganda films in support of the Third Reich?

Those were terribly beautiful films, Your Honor, films that lifted the heart and made people happy.

Well, well. You are speaking of films such as . . . *Jud Süß*?

Well, a dodo is no eagle, Your Honor, you mustn't be naive.

Let us now hear from the defense.

Mr. De Potter?

Many thanks to the Honorable Judge of the Tribunal.

I do in part acknowledge the crimes committed by the defendant and shall return to this point shortly, but first wish to remark that the defendant committed many of these crimes to support his family under difficult circumstances. Let it be noted that the defendant acted in part out of misguided idealism and that his wife, Mrs. Harmina Wijers from 'Olland, known to the Tribunal Registry as Mrs. Verhulst, a resident of Drongenhof, house number X, and the mother of three

243

children from her marriage to the defendant, has informed us of his solicitude as a husband and father, always prepared to take responsibility for his aforementioned family, and in the process losing sight of the ideological incompatibility between his fatherly care and his administrative affiliation with the enemy nation. Furthermore, we call attention to his wife's pacifist convictions and her well-known efforts on behalf of the Belgium-loving congregation of the Protestant church in Brabantdam in Ghent, where she strove to promote understanding between peoples in general and those of the Greater Netherlands in particular . . . *Cough.*

In view of the defendant's cooperative attitude in pre-trial detention, where he showed goodwill and intelligent insight into his responsibilities . . .

In view of the good upbringing his children have received from their father . . .

The room is swelteringly hot and stuffy.

Verhulst nods off, overwhelmed by fatigue, a sleepless night behind him. His head drops to his chest and he lets out a deep snore that startles even him. Mr. De Potter has just completed his defense.

Our thanks to Mr. De Potter.

Verhulst, do you have anything to add?

Willem leaps up.

Your Honor, I have merely defended my own country, my cherished Flanders, our people who, ever since the founding of the criminal Belgian state, have been persecuted without cease by the degenerate Francophone el—

*

Enough, Verhulst! You offer a demonstration of everything your well-meaning counsel has just urged us to overlook in our sentencing. You are evidently more or less incorrigible.

A buzz of voices in the hearing room. The judge bangs his gavel.

Calm down! Silence!

Then the judge and his team of lawyers withdraw for deliberations. The sentence will be read out that afternoon at three.

⸺

3:12 p.m.

Silence in the room please. We will now read out the sentence.

In consideration of . . . with due attention to . . . having heard the testimony of X, Y, Z and N . . . after ample and thorough deliberation as required by due process of law, we sentence the defendant Willem Verhulst, founder of the Dietsch Action Committee, member of the *Waffen-SS, V-Mann* and spy, active and prominent participant in wartime activities inimical to the people and subversive to the nation, in view of his repeated use of violence and his central role in the violent interrogation of patriots and other citizens, as well as of the unrepentant wickedness expressed in his testimony here, to death.

The crimes of which he is convicted are, in a nutshell: *Taking up arms against Belgium and its allies, political collaboration, acting as an informant, and theft.*

At the urgent request of the defense, the death penalty is commuted to life imprisonment and lifelong deprivation of civil rights.

*

The presiding judge pounds his gavel, and the hearing is closed.

Muttering and the shifting of chairs in the room.

Willem Verhulst is led off in handcuffs.

He does not seem to see a thing and stumbles down the hallway; the officers escorting him have to tug him along a little.

Back in his cell, he's so shaken that the whole world around him seems to be spinning.

He needs to use the toilet.

Vomits until his stomach is empty.

Then lets out a plaintive cry: Mammie, Adri, Lettie, Suzy . . .

And falls back onto his wooden pallet.

—

Adriaan Verhulst, professor emeritus, recalls in his book *Son of a "Bad" Fleming* that the summer of 1947, when Willem's trial took place, was an "excruciating ordeal" for the family. Willem was often taken from one building to the other for interrogation; the prosecutor, Beyer, clung to the case like a pit bull. Adri claims it was because Beyer had once supported the Flemish Movement himself that he wanted others to pay such a high price for choosing the wrong path: "Furthermore, according to my father, Beyer hoped to turn the trial into a high-profile case to enhance his own prestige. That explains why my father was not tried as an individual, but as the leader of a so-called gang, which Beyer thought he could unmask by linking my father to a number of other figures, some of whom he'd had very little to do with . . . That was one reason we didn't attend the proceedings." These are remarkable words, coming from a historian who is otherwise always so meticulous; in legal terms, the Dietsch Action Committee fell squarely under the definition of a

Nazi gang. How much reality can a person bear, when the subject is his own father?

The case went to trial on July 11, 1947, the day after Willem's forty-ninth birthday. Mientje stayed at home with the children and made pancakes. Her trembling hands couldn't mix the batter; Adri took the bowl and whisk and finished for her. They ate in silence; Letta and Suzy did the dishes. None of them said a word about what was going on that day. But when Mientje fell into bed that evening, she was on the brink of despair; she lay awake all night and rose the next day feeling shattered. The lawyer, De Potter, visited her in the late morning, while the children were playing outside, to inform her of the sentence. They spoke in the front room, by the fireplace. She burst into tears and nearly collapsed; the counselor had to catch her as she swooned.

35

After the trial, Mientje was in close communication with their lawyer-landlord, because she hoped at first that Willem could apply for clemency. It is clear that De Potter did everything he could to ease Mientje's suffering. He was an influential man, the head of the bar association in Ghent, and according to Adri "a man whose strict features concealed a warm heart, tolerant and broad-minded." It was Mientje who had persuaded him that Willem was not driven by greed nor any other base motive; it was she who, against her better judgment, painted the portrait of the idealist gone astray—even though she'd spent enough years arguing with the man to know the truth. She chose to protect the father of her children, unconditionally. When Willem was ordered to pay a large financial penalty, De Potter recommended a legal separation between husband and wife. "Thanks to this," Adri writes, "we were no longer in danger of having our furniture seized by the receiver; that would have made it impossible to continue taking in boarders, our sole source of income."

Then unexpected help arrived; during the years of Willem's imprisonment, the Verhulst family in Antwerp paid her a modest monthly allowance, enough for her and the children to keep their heads above water. "We are grateful to the family for that support to this day," Letta writes in one of her messages to me.

—◡

Mientje, who never learned the details of what Willem had really been up to but suspected the worst, was a loyal visitor in those early months, always toting a heavy bag of vegetables, fruit, milk and bread. Her husband complained of a constant stomachache, claimed he had an ulcer and always asked for huge quantities of milk. During visits, he would sit at a table, behind bars, in the light of a bare bulb, staring out at her helplessly through his thick lenses. On either side of her were similar tables with bars in front of them; everyone spoke in loud voices, because the visitors were kept more than five feet away from the prisoners, so that they wouldn't have the chance for even a quick word in private. She would ask him, Pappie, are you all right, and he would say, It's hard to bear, Mien, my stomach is bothering me again, and she would say, Be strong, my husband, I'll see you next time. After he was led off, she would pile the contents of her bag onto her side of the table, knowing the guards would take a large share for themselves before passing the rest on to him; and when one day, sometime in 1948, as she entered her name in the visitors' log, she saw the previous visitor's name there—"Greta Latomme"? what was this? had she already been released? how could that be?— something burst inside her once again, oozing caustic juice like a pressed grape, a rising poison in her stomach, her gullet, her mouth; and with that bitter taste in her body she turned around, left the bag of food and clean underwear behind in the hallway, and walked out of the building. The Lord will stand by me, she mumbled, this is God's will and He is testing me, I have to go to the children, and she scuttled down Nieuwe Wandeling as fast as she could, into town, past the elegant houses along the Coupure canal, toward the poor working-class neighborhood where she made her home: Patershol, "the priests' stinking butthole," as Willem had once scoffed. But first she went into a church, and a Catholic church to boot, Lord-a-mercy, what was she thinking. And it was only then, as she felt the wicker of the prie-dieu pressing into her knees and the flaking paint on the Christ Child filled her with desolation, that she sobbed and swallowed and sniffled and thought: I won't go back, let *her* take care of him then, may the Lord forgive us both for it, amen.

She returns to the house in Drongenhof, her fortress and only refuge, to her children, her boarders, her money troubles, her drudgery and her prayers, in which—against her better judgment—she thanks the Lord. In her diary the only trace of her traumatic discovery in the prison is one heartbreaking sentence:

"Pappie had another visitor."

36

To Eastland

To Eastland we went a-riding
To Eastland, that was our plan
Two Fords with a trailer behind them
A modern-day caravan

We drove across the heath there
In Soltau we stopped for a rest
Our automobiles were seized there
So we put our legs to the test

Weighed down with cumbersome rucksacks
We trekked to the town of our dreams
The bombs rained down every day there
Life's not easy in Eastland, it seems

Then armies came from the Westlands
To search for us there in the East
In time we were found by the Belgians
To Flanders we went in defeat

They said our searching had ended
For a fatherland where we could stay

They had our names in their records
In prison they shut us away

So now we sit here and worry:
Which is wrong and which is right?
A Reich that's just for the Germans
Or a Greater Germanic Reich?

As Willem Verhulst, confined to a cell, passes his time penning doggerel, at least he shows some sense of irony in his adaptation of an old Flemish song into an account of his own bathetic flight. Perhaps as he writes this poem he is thinking of the stone along the German highway with the clumsy inscription . . .

His "prison letters," as he calls them, form a strange and colorful miscellany. There are wild-eyed diatribes scribbled in pencil against the Belgian state, "Aphorisms on Nationalism," and laments for the Fleming, whom he describes as a "negro" in his own country of despicable French colonialists; there are drafts full of crossed-out words, illegible corrections, fresh attempts, forceful underlines, and smudges; there is a declaration that the Flemish will take over Belgium and colonize the Walloons for the sake of the Flemish *Lebensraum*; there are plaintive poems, lines inspired by religion, a gloomy piece on his youngest child Suzy's birthday, and a love poem for his "little Rose," whose true identity remains ambiguous; he later makes clean copies of some poems in ink.

In one poem he takes up the defense of the reviled King Leopold III. To Willem and his ilk, Leopold remains the heroic king who defied the Allied countries to display his goodwill to the German *Brudervolk*. Mockery of the British is a staple of Willem's verses. Paying homage to a man who was king of Belgium, the country he so despised, does not seem to trouble him.

Farewell, failure and foolishness,
The King he saw full well
His country's interest was not served
By John the London swell.

Somewhere in his "aphorisms" he calls nationalism a self-evident fact of biology, and refers to priests who call for reconciliation as "hypocritical predators." He writes a large number of polemical poems. Like a Flemish François Villon, he tries to draw courage from his own concoctions, using them partly to kill monotonous time and partly to justify his actions. Pent-up frustrations, vague notions and often-childish outpourings—they offer an embarrassing window into the soul of a man who insists on seeing himself as the victim of a criminal regime. Blindness, cries for freedom, teary-eyed ballads written for his wife and children. But the dominant theme is bitterness at his confinement.

O God, in these dark caves
Allow Your light to find us,
So that the cunning knaves
Will never undermine us . . .

And a few pages later, the closing couplet of a verse appears to be a swipe at his own wife:

Our fatherland's going up in smoke
Soon Belgium will be no more

Flanders will throw off the foreign yoke
Just as it has before.

No begging and pleading; we demand
Real and legal equality
Away with the cowards who claim to stand
For noble sympathy . . .

No, Willem sees little reason, there in his cell, to reconsider his views. The symbolic marriage between the Netherlands and Flanders is a recurring theme, an almost-Freudian allegory of his own guilt-ridden marriage, for which he sometimes seems to yearn intensely; and in the solitude of his imprisonment, his hatred of the state that condemned him swells into an obsession. As so often, confinement is what turns the convict into a true radical. The rabble-rouser August Borms—who paid an official visit to Auschwitz as late as 1943 and returned in good spirits—becomes a kind of Messiah to Willem:

Man of sorrows, O Great Martyr . . .
Man of suffering, O Great man of grief . . .

Then, in a separate section, his actual "prison letters" follow, numbered with Roman numerals, obviously clean copies of earlier drafts that may not have been preserved. These documents are possibly the strangest of all. At first, they mainly describe times when he feels homesick, dreams of encountering a lover "who is not my dear little wife," and his fear that a double entendre will expose his relationship with Griet to several Brueghelesque dream figures who make puns about "pussies" and "holes." Over time these episodes grow more intense—he is arrested in the center of Antwerp while out for a stroll and thrown into the back of a van by a former prison guard who recognizes him as "number 430"; he fights the "thieves and murderers of the resistance" while remaining "proud and un-civic" ("un-civic," *inciviek*, was another term used to describe ex-collaborators), and still another time, he is mauled by "sixteen wrestlers' meaty paws"—but these all turn out to be nothing more than dreams, and he finishes off with the sarcastic remark that meanwhile he is simply lying on his pallet. His cell looms up in the guise of a prehistoric cavern where a huge rat stares up at him from the gutter; the violence in the dream scenes intensifies over the years. Suppressed shame, regret and remorse come out as vengeful nightmares, but his descriptions of the many transfers from one prison to another, the humiliation, the frustration and the pain are only too real: "Peering through the narrow openings in the police van, I beheld the celebrating world with its Christmas lights, as the manacles dug into my wrists and I felt only woe inside—my God, my God, are we really such great criminals in this society?"

At Christmas in 1948, he is stricken with nostalgia: "My fourth Christmas behind bars!" He remembers a joyful Christmas Day in 1944: "We captive Flemings from Hanover will never forget it; we will be eternally grateful to those Germans . . . I lay on my bed of straw in silence and my tears pearled like little stars in that night, away in my own manger, in gratitude for that beautiful night in my bare cell . . . Suddenly I hear Handel's "Largo," which my boy so often used to play for me—before I fled—and I fill with woe inside and sob like a child and can only murmur, Adri, Lettie, Suzy, Mammie . . ."

In the fifth year of his imprisonment, the solitude starts to take its toll on his mind; he describes a dream in which he tries to learn to fly in his cell, rhythmically jumping up and down on his wooden bed, flapping his arms ever harder, ever faster, leaping up, come on, get a move on, faster faster, yes yes, here we go, into the sky, freedom! Freedom! He bangs his head against the ceiling, lands with his feet in the chamber pot, and hurts his knees and his rear. Oh, he's waking up now, it was just another dream, he sees the guard's face staring through the hatch in surprise, bursts out laughing and crows like a cockerel. Cock-a-doodle-oodle-doo!

"'Have you lost your freaking mind?' the guard called out to me. My belly was quaking with laughter under the sheets, because I was lying on my sack of straw, it was the middle of the night, and my noisy crowing had woken the bastards."

The fact that he was invited to be the "fatik"—helper, handyman, cleaner, messenger and toilet scrubber—suggests that he was normally cooperative and well behaved. When I inquire about Willem's penitentiary records at the State Archives in Ghent, a staff member informs me that the Willem Verhulst file is gone without a trace. Maybe, the archivist adds, it was one of the many files gobbled up by rats and mice in the damp cellars of the Saint-Gilles prison in Brussels.

—

In the house in Drongenhof, Letta hears her mother talking in bed one night; she tiptoes down the stairs and puts her ear to the door. O You who know all and understand all, she hears, protect Pappie in his cell, amen.

As Letta tells me this, her eyes fill with tears.

37

In Drongenhof, life follows its fretful course. More and more frightened people come to their door: I hear you rent rooms, ma'am? Some are family members of arrested collaborators whose homes were bombed or seized; others have been shown the door by their landlords or fled their neighborhoods for fear of vengeance. Mientje warily chooses among them, letting the candidates in for a chat, feeling them out and allowing her impressions to guide her to a decision. A young Dutchman moves into the room where Adri slept for years, and promptly puts up a photo of Stalin. Adri gapes at it for a moment and then moves into his mother's bedroom; she, in turn, finds a new place to sleep: the second-floor library, now empty of books.

Mientje cooks for her boarders, washes their clothes, keeps their rooms clean, talks to them about their studies, and reads to them from her well-thumbed Bible. She continues to lend a hand at her Protestant church and makes sure her children are neatly dressed and go off to school every morning. She doesn't have much time to feel the loss of her imprisoned husband.

One of the many who seek refuge in the rooms in Drongenhof is the musicologist André Pols, who was well known at the time. Mientje opens the door to find a rumpled professorial type, hat in hand, who asks if she has a "little nook" for him. He seems scared and shy, clumsy and rushed. Come in, she says with a sigh, because he is the fourth candidate to turn up that day; she did not care one bit for the other three.

Standing in the hallway, she listens to his story: his devotion to Beethoven and Bach, his publications, his Flemish idealism—ah, Goethe, ah, Platen! Such marvelous German music and poetry, ma'am! . . . So many times I visited Germany's magnificent cities, ah Heidelberg ah Dresden ah Tübingen, now everything has been demolished, what a tragedy, the Allies and their massacres in the land of the great geniuses, I made a great analysis of Wagner's *Tristan und Isolde*, I gave lectures in German about the miraculous beauty of *Parsifal*, he who was pure in his foolishness, and now, because I conducted wonderful concerts during the war, I am accused of cultural collaboration, can you imagine, and oh I see you even have a piano here in the front room so that I could . . . His hands are already stretching out hungrily for the instrument.

The man strikes Mientje as something of a wimp, and on top of that he has bad breath, so it's with less than wholehearted enthusiasm that she welcomes him into her household, but ah, well . . . music.

I have only one room available at the moment, she says, and that's the garret under the roof tiles; there's an iron bed and a small table, and I can fetch you a chair from the kitchen, but that's all I can offer you for now. When someone else leaves, I can give you a better room.

Pols clasps her hands in his and stammers *merci, merci,* madame. Don't mention it, Mientje says, turning her head to one side, do you have a suitcase?

No indeed, says Pols, I'll have to pick it up, but I'm scared to go back there.

But . . . he unexpectedly adds, his eyes boring into her. Might I ask you to call me "Mr. Verschuren"? The truth is, I'm sort of on the run . . .

Only then does Mientje realize it will be risky to put up this man.

In recent months, her house has been the target of frequent searches, by order of the tribunal. Because Mr. De Potter is working on an application for clemency, the authorities are asking probing questions and keep visiting the house. If they find this man staying there, she can forget about clemency for Willem.

But then again, music . . .

Very well, Mientje says, pleased to meet you, Mr. Verschuren.

And later that afternoon she tells the children, We have a new guest. This is Mr. Verschuren. He is an excellent pianist.

And Pols takes up residence there just as he arrived: with nothing but the clothes on his back and the modest savings in his breast pocket.

When Mr. Verschuren became emotional, Letta tells me—as he did every time he sat at the piano and lectured to all the students staying in the house—he would scratch his bald head, often so hard that he broke the skin. Sometimes a trickle of blood would run down his forehead, and we children would laugh and shout, Mr. Verschuren! *O Haupt voll Blut und Wunden!* This was the first line of the well-known hymn quoted by Bach in Pols's beloved *St. Matthew Passion*: O head covered with blood and wounds! Afterward Mientje would tend to his scalp: But Mr. Verschuren, how in the world could you do such a thing, come here so I can disinfect that, your fingernails are not always as clean as they ought to be . . . Yes, I know, ma'am, but it's, well, I forget myself . . . To thank her, he plays and sings that beautiful Schubert song, "Ungeduld," and Mientje joins him: "*Dein ist mein Herz / und Soll es ewig bleiben*" . . .

Mama, says Adri, watch yourself with Mr. Verschuren, or he might fall in love with you.

He'd better learn to rinse his mouth out first, his mother replies.

Pols was an inspired, erudite scholar. As a young man, he had published an essay about Modest Mussorgsky; he later translated quite a few libretti and wrote a "trilogy of passion" about *Don Giovanni, Tristan und Isolde* and *Pelléas et Mélisande*, a book about the making of keyboard instruments in Flanders, monographs about composers such as Haydn, Mozart and Beethoven in the ten-part series "Master Composers," and the book that made his reputation, *Het raadsel van de muziek* (The enigma of music), a study whose romantic gushings now seem antiquated, and which you can hence pick up secondhand for next to nothing at the book stalls behind St. James's Church in Ghent, a three-minute walk from Drongenhof.

~

Yes, I knew them, Mr. De Potter tells me one day when I run into him on the well-known Notarisstraat (Notary Street) in Ghent, where he hastily stops, his hand on his hat in the autumn wind, his crocodile-leather briefcase tucked beneath the arm of his loden coat, to say hello to me. There were always people coming and going there, sir, a constant bustle, rush hour, open house, a meeting of the minds. My father often visited while he was working on that clemency application. Sometimes he let me come with him; I was a student then, and he thought I could learn a lot from a delicate case like that one.

I invite the lawyer, who seems to have aged, for coffee. Yes, that would hit the spot in this miserable weather, he says, and my client can wait for five minutes. We stroll past the cathedral and sit in the window of Brasserie 't Vosken. The notary is in the mood—if you have no *objection*, sir—for a little drop of something on the side, just to make the conversation flow.

An impressive series of young men had their "digs" in Mientje's house, De Potter begins—though their names are almost unknown to younger generations: Leon De Meyer, later the rector of the University of Ghent, was studying classical philology at the time. He delivered long lectures to the students in the house, sometimes in French when the subject matter was erotic French poetry or risqué operas such as *Don Giovanni*; that was not for the girls' ears. The future chief inspector of the city schools, Marcel Bots, lived in Drongenhof while writing his dissertation about the nineteenth-century Dutch Jewish poet and Christian convert Isaäc da Costa, a choice of topic undoubtedly inspired by Mientje—he later edited an edition of the classic Dutch novel *Max Havelaar* for Flemish high schools . . . The young poet Lieven Rens stayed in the back room on the third floor for a while . . . I also remember Piet Van Brabant, later a well-known political journalist and lifelong advocate of toleration . . . and just after the First World War, the cultural philosopher Max Lamberty lived there too . . .

As a break from her wearying work for her boarders, Mientje liked to make music with Adri, and André Pols—*du holde Kunst!*—accompanied them on the piano. In the year 1949, they were sometimes joined by the young Jaap Kruithof, the son of Dutch Protestants, who would become a popular eco-philosopher in Flanders in May '68; he is said to have looked up to Mientje in his youth and talked to her about her acquaintance with Pastor Wartena. Not long after it had been defaced with swastikas, the house echoed with conversations, encounters, friendships. The doorbell rang many times a day, and no longer did they ever have to "put the door on the chain."

Now my Scheherazade suddenly remembers his appointment. De Potter springs to his feet, grabs his briefcase and fedora, excuses himself, says goodbye and *au revoir*, makes a little bow in the direction of our waitress, almost bangs into the door because someone else is trying to come in, charges outside, still apologizing to everyone and everything, to the rain clouds speeding overhead and the cathedral, to the dragon atop the bell tower and the passing tram, and flees across the square, disappearing into the milling crowd, a character from a painting by René Magritte.

That was the last time I ever saw him.

—

One early spring day Mr. Verschuren has had enough of being cooped up indoors all the time; the sun is calling out to him. He pushes open the skylight in the garret; he hears the pigeons cooing in the roof gutter, the patter of their spindly feet. Light white clouds drift by, and he feels the temptation of the fresh air. He puts on his coat, dons his hat, and tells the surprised Mientje he is going out for a walk. He takes a deep breath and, in a state of mild euphoria, steps out onto the narrow streets of Patershol. He thinks of Schubert's "Frühlingslied" and flicks away a tear:

> The vale is green, the sky is blue,
> The fragrant May bells are in bloom
> With cowslips strewn among them . . .

He walks into Geldmunt Square, how beautiful Ghent is, he passes the Gravensteen, a young woman is walking a few steps ahead of him, a fair maiden if ever there was one, see the lightness of her springtime step, those shapely calves, the sway of her, it leaves him light in the head; there's a brasserie just over there, a refreshing glass of beer would hit the spot, it's been such a long time . . .

Pols crosses the street, sits down by the window and orders a *gueuze*. He is sipping from his glass in perfect satisfaction when a man comes up to him and says: André Pols? The composer? Gotcha. You're coming with us.

May I finish my beer before—

The policeman flashes his badge.

Come along, Pols. Time to face the music. You're under arrest for collaboration.

Before the inquisitive eyes of the other customers, the absent-minded musicologist is handcuffed; the officer pushes him out of the brasserie.

38

Lieve Vandermeulen, the neighbor from Grauwpoort, now lives in a peaceful green neighborhood of Brasschaat, near Antwerp. Early one beautiful evening in May 2018, I pay her a visit. She invites me into her welcoming home, where the walls are lined with shelves of old books: Novalis, Kleist, Platen, Grillparzer. I have read her memoir and want to talk to her about two women: Aimée Jacobs and Margarethe Fürth.

Lieve, at her advanced age, still remembers the wisteria on the fence beside the muddy waterway, the children dancing with joy when they heard the cries in the streets—"We're at war! We're at war!"—a German soldier standing guard who called her *Liebe*—"I have a *Mädchen* like you back at home"—the black bread made with potato peel, the doses of queasy cod-liver oil she had to swallow, the scanty meals of whatever they could scrape together on the black market, the days when everything was thrown into confusion from one second to the next, the sirens wailing over the city, the children ordered to hurry inside, ducking under the old wine racks in the cellar with nervous giggles and hunkering there as the powerful roar of the bombers passed overhead and faint explosions were heard from the suburbs: Merelbeke, Melle, Ledeberg, Gentbrugge. Throughout those years of want and insecurity, Lieve knew she was welcome in the house just around the corner, in Drongenhof. That house was a palace of mirrors, she says, a great dark edifice where all those unfamiliar boarders going in and out of the rooms made our heads spin . . .

Just a few weeks after Willem fled, Lieve arranged for her aunt Aimée Jacobs to move into the dark middle room downstairs. "Aunt Mée" was a liberated woman. She had studied at one of her era's first educational institutes for social work, had a secret affair with a fugitive German communist that went on for years, and maintained ties with the resistance. She worked as an editor for the pre-war edition of Ghent's socialist newspaper *Vooruit*; in 1940, when the editors fled to London and the Nazis took over the paper, she found herself unemployed. But she soon went to work for an organization that helped to distribute food to Jewish people and find hiding places for them. For the first few years after the war, she drifted from place to place, winding up in Drongenhof. When the socialists regained control of the newspaper, she often ran into Richard Minne and Louis Paul Boon (two of Belgium's best-known writers and outspoken men of the left) in the office. Aunt Mée had a clandestine relationship with the paper's business manager. Whenever he came to call, Mientje would see to it that the children did not barge into the middle room under any circumstances. Aimée was a mistress, a suffragette, a newspaper editor, and a single woman in a dark rented room . . . In 1953, when Willem's application for clemency was approved and he suddenly showed up at the door, Aunt Mée left Drongenhof that very day, unwilling to rub shoulders with a former SS man.

Aunt Mée managed to keep a Jewish woman out of the clutches of the Nazis, more or less under Willem's nose. Margarethe Fürth had fled occupied Austria and happened to end up in Ghent. As a child, she'd been a friend of Gustav Klimt; Lieve tells me Klimt had proposed to paint her, but her strict Jewish upbringing kept her from posing for the notorious seducer. On her peregrinations across the European continent, she had somehow dragged along several cabinets from her distinguished Vienna residence. Those cabinets were the only mementos of her past, Lieve explains; she led a solitary life in Ghent, while hoping for a sign of life from family members who had fled to the United

States. Aimée helped her go into hiding at Avondster, an old-people's home in Ghent. But even there, she was not safe as a Jewish woman. Aunt Mée warned her she had to adopt a new name, fast, because it was looking more and more likely that the *Sicherheitsdienst* would demand Avondster's list of residents—Willem loved to make lists, after all, and the *Sicherheitspolizei* worked hand in glove with the Anti-Jewish Center, which in turn was linked to the notorious *Institut zur Erforschung der Judenfrage*. The elderly lady complains that she is too old for all that fuss; in her mind, she is back in the Josefstadt district of pre-war Vienna, in the grand house in Lange Gasse with the artists she knew there. Tea is served in porcelain cups; there is candy on a tray; the conversation is always hushed, and the woman's silhouette is dimly reflected in the gleaming varnish of the Viennese cabinets. From this moment on, she will go by the name of Marie Fallaert. She is reluctant at first, but Aunt Mée puts her foot down; she must not make the slightest mistake, even under the strain and pressure of telling her name to a visiting SS man. So the distinguished Viennese lady paces her room in her elegant laced boots, her hair in a graceful chignon, chanting in broken Flemish, My name is Marie Fallaert, my name is Marie Fallaert . . . Lieve, who was then a young girl, describes her as "a straight-backed lady, always well dressed, with a white lace collar around her neck, surrounded by magnificent Viennese Art Nouveau furniture."

What I can hardly believe, I tell Lieve, is that the roots of memory run from Drongenhof all the way to the Viennese home of Gustav Klimt, or that Margarethe used to visit Willem's house during his years in prison for a cup of tea and a chat, the same house where leading Flemish SS men had gathered not long before . . .

After the war, Margarethe moved to New York to find a couple of relatives who had escaped the Holocaust. She continued to send cards and letters for Christmas and New Year's. Lieve herself still owns, and displays with emotion, two fine chairs "on which Mrs. Fürth often sat," real Viennese *Jugendstil*, made of applewood; you may have one of them if you finish your book, she tells me. On a genealogy website I find Margarethe Fürth, born in 1866, from Strakonitz in southern Bohemia (now Strakonice in the Czech Republic); in 1899 she and her family arrived in Vienna, where her husband, believe it or not, had a fez factory—a Bohemian Jew making his living as a producer of the well-known hat worn by the Turks who had once made the Viennese tremble. *Alla Turca*, *Mozartkugeln*, the *Wienerwald* and Gustav Klimt—the Central European world of yesteryear.

Margarethe had a son, Otto Fürth, who had emigrated to the United States earlier. During the war, he wrote a book that was published in English translation in 1942 under the pseudonym Owen Elford: *Men in Black*. The subtitle is *Fighting the Nazi Secret Police*. The book describes the exploits of the Czech resistance against the Nazis and the Gestapo and includes the death of Reinhard Heydrich; the notorious sadist's chilling features blight the cover. The story is preceded by a dedication "to the victims of Nazism all over the world."

"Years later," Lieve says, "I was still receiving letters from Margarethe Fürth in America because Aunt Mée, who was already ill and depressed by then, was no longer writing to her . . . She remained eternally grateful to Aimée for saving her life and left her beautiful cabinets to her, but because Aunt Mée moved to a small apartment on the edge of town, they ended up here."

These cabinets, in which Margarethe kept her Jewish paraphernalia, are now in Lieve's daughter's home in Maarn, just a few miles from Austerlitz, where Willem once spent the night with the ailing Elsa. The circles of history.

—

A few months after our conversation, I receive a stack of letters tied with a white silk ribbon: a rediscovered correspondence between Margarethe and her *"liebe Freundin Liebe"*—she fondly translates the Dutch name Lieve, which means "dear," into the German equivalent *Liebe*. A stale scent of violets wafts from the fragile old air-mail envelopes. By this stage, Mrs. Fürth had personalized stationery with a handsome letter-head; her first address seems to have been on Knollwood Road in Norwalk, Connecticut, and later, like so many refugees, she lived in the Big Apple: 5400 Fieldston Road, Riverdale, in the Bronx.

But she went on writing in German, the language of her Hapsburg roots.

Meine kleine Freundin Liebe! Ich fand heute im Briefkasten eine wun-
derschöne Karte mit lieben Weihnachts- und Neujahrsgrüßen in
deutscher Sprache . . .

[My little friend Liebe! Today I found in my mailbox a beautiful card with sweet wishes for Christmas and New Year's in the German language . . .]

268

39

It is March 1951, Palm Sunday; spring is already in the air. The Verhulst children were raised to believe that this day was for public professions of faith, perhaps while holding a palm frond, rather than for foolish Catholic tales of saints or God on earth. Children are being born, people are dying, and the sun is shining on the streets of Patershol. Letta, now a young woman going on twenty, has decided to pay her father another visit at his place of residence in Brussels; she hasn't seen him in a long while.

She gets off the train at Brussels Midi and heads off through the Halle city gate toward the Saint-Gilles prison; the impressive building looms up ahead, looking to her like a castle from the age of the Crusaders. She arrives at the entrance; her identity and bag are checked; she's brought a treat for Pappie to brighten this special Sunday; she feels a little guilty that it's been such a long time. Her father is led out to the visiting area. He is dressed in a brown smock, and to her surprise is not thin but heavier, a little bloated, and his face is flushed. His hair is oiled with Brilliantine and combed straight back. He sits down, sees his daughter come in, oh my girl, oh my girl, he sighs in a smoker's wheezy voice, out of breath because he was brought here in such a hurry; Letta says she has a piece of plum cake for him, a favorite of his, isn't it, and some fruit, you have to eat plenty of fruit, Papa.

Oh, I have so much stomach trouble, Lettie, you have no idea.

They fall silent.

How are things at school, my girl.

Come on, Papa, you know I'm a university student now.

Well, all right, that's what I mean, that's a school too, after all.

How are you, Papa?

I can't complain, I'm the fatik, that gives me a little more freedom here. And how is Mammie? Is she healthy? She doesn't visit anymore.

Mammie's fine, I'm sure she'll visit again sometime. But you have to understand, as long as Griet—

All right, all right, he says, if you've come to scold me—

Papa, I came because I thought you'd like to see me. Have you heard anything about your application for clemency?

Hmph, no, De Potter's working on it.

He lights a cigarette.

They sit together and say nothing.

After a few minutes Letta says, I'll be going now, Papa.

Goodbye, my dear. Study hard, hm?

She walks back down the long hallway with the cold lighting, to the checkpoint. As she is waiting to reclaim her identity card, someone enters behind her.

Hello, Miss Latomme, says the man at the desk. It's Sunday again, isn't it. Willem will be pleased.

Letta whirls around and is eye to eye with Griet.

Hi, Letteke, she says, what a coincidence.

And Letta, swallowing and blinking, says, Hi, Griet.

Not until she is on the train home does the anger wash over her.

I will never go back there again, she growls, I'm done with him.

When Mientje asks, back at the house, whether Pappie was pleased with the plum cake, she says, Oh, yes, very pleased. So pleased he was glowing, or was that the hair oil?

She flings her bag into the corner and curses.

Mientje asks no more questions.

I learn little else about those years; my main source is Mientje's diaries, which display her unfaltering faith and keen social conscience. She follows the news closely and provides anxious commentary. The year 1951 had begun with money troubles; on January 1, the De Potter family had raised the rent by ten percent, "the roof is leaking, and I'll have to pay half the cost of repairs." On March 28, 1951, she visited Zevenaar; she complains of incessant rain. She had corresponded with Pastor Wartena until just before his death in 1948; now she remembers him in her prayers. Willem, she learns, has been moved again; he is now in the prison in Merksplas, where he's permitted to do some gardening.

Letta and Suzy inform me, each separately and telling different anecdotes, that in the 1950s their mother took a qualifying exam to teach religion. According to Suzy, her examiner was her own son, Adri, and she asked him to be strict with her; Letta, however, claims the examiner was a pastor. In any case, Mientje taught religion for years, at a time when she was an avid reader of Christian books like philosopher Bernhard Delfgaauw's *Spiritual Existentialism,* the works of Teilhard de

Chardin, and the poetry of the Catholic convert Pieter van der Meer de Walcheren, a man her journals describe as "magnificent"; she sometimes wrote her own poetry on religious themes.

Mientje heard from Letta that Adri was thinking of becoming Catholic, under the influence of a student of his, a young woman he'd fallen for. "I shudder at the thought," she writes, "because I remember the poet Lieven Rens's Catholic wedding: terrible to witness, the way his parents kissed the Communion wafer." The diary stops abruptly in late 1951, after some notes about the controversy surrounding the Belgian monarchy and the coronation of twenty-year-old Boudewijn: "Unhappy the country whose king is a child."

Adri's flirtation with Catholicism proved fleeting; not long afterward, he played a pivotal role in converting a number of Flemish liberals to Protestantism. They met in the Protestant church in Brabantdam, the same church where Mientje attended weekly sermons by Pastor Van Stipriaan. She reports on his preaching in her diary: "A wonderful sermon today about the human need for Fellowship—which cannot be fulfilled by mere romance, because that always leads to disappointment." Romance that leads to disappointment—sometimes Mientje's understatement is painful to read.

The diaries also reveal that by this stage she had strong political opinions. Under her husband's influence, she had become a supporter of the Flemish Movement; she sympathized with its justifiable demands for Dutch-language education and public administration, which "every right-thinking democrat should support," but strongly objected to all forms of militarism. "No kind of idealism can justify violence; every battle is a cultural battle," she claims. Her hatred of uniforms was so powerful that anyone who showed up at her door in military dress was turned away.

*

Letta also tells one more revealing story about Mientje's pacifism: at regular intervals, she would station herself next to the toy section of one of the department stores on Veldstraat—Grand Bazar or Innovation—to stop the passing mothers and fathers from buying toy weapons, tin soldiers and other military miniatures for their sons. She would try to strike up a conversation, but tempers sometimes ran high: What business is it of yours, you silly bitch, go back to Holland if you don't like it here, out of my way, damn it . . . She kept up her protests until the early 1960s, and was expelled from the stores on several occasions for her one-woman citizen activism.

40

Prison letter XVI
The removal of the un-civic

One night we were roused from our sleep by a terrible clamor: heavy footsteps and loud voices. We were ordered to pack our things right away and line up two by two; we were being transferred!

We were chained together and loaded into large vans surrounded by soldiers armed with submachine guns. Some whispered that the Third World War had broken out—the Russians and General Paulus's troops were advancing westward.

We were taken away from Saint-Gilles in armored vehicles, accompanied by a large motorcycle escort. We heard panic in the streets. At Brussels Midi station we came to a stop and were moved into cattle cars. Once they were crammed with passengers, the doors were shut. There we sat—swearing, grumbling and cursing. It was nearly nightfall by the time our train started to move. We came to a halt once every six miles, sometimes for ten minutes, sometimes for a few hours.

Close to dawn, the doors were opened; we were in Ghent. Each of us was given half a loaf of bread, and they let us scoop water out of a bucket.

Among the soldiers I saw an old acquaintance; I waved him over, and he whispered in my ear: The Russians and General Paulus are already in Belgium . . . half the army doesn't want to fight anymore,

there are mass arrests, and the best of our Volk are being dragged away
like animals. You're probably on your way to Le Havre, and from there
to England . . .

Warn my family not to flee, I asked him . . . and above all, send
word to Greta, let her know where they're taking me!

They made us get back in the cars, which lurched and bumped back
into motion.

After a long journey, which was unspeakably awful in our freight
car, we arrived in a big city that evening, with a grimy platform and
large vessels in the harbor. We stayed put there all night. In our car, our
greatest concern was the men who were unwell—some had fainted, and
one was half-mad. The air was filled with the acrid odor of urine,
which ran back into the car from the crack under the door, and the
smell of the men who'd had no choice but to "empty their bowels" onto a
piece of paper; the stench filled the closed car.

Finally, near morning, the doors were opened. We were put in irons
and had to line up again. We were marched through the city with a
large French escort, as crowds of French people booed and hissed at us.
Some threw stones, horse droppings and trash. We were relieved when
they brought us to a kind of concentration camp, surrounded by barbed
wire. Now we could finally freshen up. On top of that, I ran into my old
buddy Fons among the deportees. He claimed that we would have a
chance to escape and that, if caught, we should use the password
"Skorzeny."

Hearing this made me very nervous. I was scared that someone
would tap me on the shoulder and I could hardly keep myself from
shouting the name at the top of my lungs so I wouldn't forget: Skorzeny!

That evening, a large group of Belgian government officials turned
up, both men and women; we could forget about escaping. But all of a
sudden, from all sides, I heard cries of "Skorzeny!" A woman security

officer grabbed me; I tried to pull free, but she wouldn't let go. I was about to punch her in the face when she latched on to my neck and shouted, Kiss me! Kiss me! Say the password, Wim! It's Griet, hey, Wim, it's me! Then I recognized her and shouted at the top of my lungs, Skorzeny!

At this point we were lifted off the ground, high into the air together, and Griet said, Wrap your arms and legs around me and hold on tight. She didn't have to say that twice; the fit was too perfect. Off we went, whooshing through the air, together with hundreds of others, all shouting, Skorzeny! The bullets were flying on all sides; fighter planes were firing their machine guns at us, but by weaving back and forth we were able to dodge them. As we whooshed through the air, Griet told me that she had thought up the escape plan with other blackshirts, and Skorzeny had guaranteed its success. The plan had to remain top secret, she said, so I'd have to keep quiet about it.

With the two of us clinging to each other like that, I was in for a shock, because my engine, pressed so close to Greta's little machine, was under high voltage . . . We saw white clouds bursting from the anti-aircraft guns; we descended just past Ghent and came zigzagging gently to the ground. Fons, with his girlfriend Mady, had also landed, and we made our way through the city, cheered on by General Paulus's supporters. But the center was occupied by Atlanticists. My children were in the heart of the occupied zone.

Then I remembered an old underground tunnel from St. Peter's Abbey to Gravensteen Castle, near my neighborhood. Somewhere in a cellar I found the entrance; I had a lamp from the MEGA with me and a club in my hand. The rats were leaping away from my feet on all sides; now and then one became aggressive and I had to beat it off me. The hallway slanted downward; I was wading through mud and water that seeped in through the walls. I reached a locked room with a rotting door at the bottom, half eaten away by rats. I knocked the door down with my shoulder and entered a tomb with two coffins. I heard something like music, white powder drifted down. In the coffins were the corpses of two old Belgians, sometimes I heard a rat squeaking, the sound seemed to be coming from those lead coffins, I broke into a sweat.

I waited until evening, wrenched a stone loose from over my head, and ended up in an old chapel. I crept outside, there were armed Atlanticists everywhere. I saw houses shot to rubble, the city seemed deserted. Pulling my hat over my ears and putting away my glasses so I wouldn't be recognized, I made my way down Lange Steenstraat to Drongenhof. When the door opened there was great confusion and great joy. I led the whole family out through the old tomb. At the end of the hallway I shouted the password: Paulus!

We were free! A few days later, the whole city had been liberated.

And Greta showed me her little Skorzeny machine—which I kissed in heartfelt gratitude, and put to grateful use many times afterward . . . Heil Wim, who is no more than Uilenspiegel and will go on playing his role, and to hell with whoever objects!

41

After my first look at this deranged "prison letter," I stared into space for long minutes. I reread it several times—the Freudian dream recounted in this "naive" text is almost stomach-turning. It's a minor tongue-in-cheek masterpiece of *ars combinatoria*: politics and adventure, a woman described as a sex robot, flight and orgasm, the dark fairy tale of "liberation" by General Friedrich Paulus—the commander who took part in Operation Barbarossa against the Russians and after the catastrophic defeat at Stalingrad not only capitulated but also became the leader of an anti-fascist resistance movement—but the most shocking thing of all is the precise description of what happened to the Jews during the Nazi transports in freight cars, the stench and the squalor, the barbed wire and the concentration camp, all this in a distorted mirror-image tale in which heroic "blackshirts" are deported by the Allies ("Atlanticists"). The persecution complex of the Flemish collaborators in a nutshell.

This reversal is fascinating in its obscenity. It raises the question of when and how Willem learned so many details about the death trains. As an SS man, he must have been aware from 1942 onward of the transports, the roundups in Antwerp, and what happened to the Jews he threw onto his lists. The pro-Nazi Antwerp newspaper *Volk en Staat* wrote in breathtakingly direct terms on August 13, 1942: "The measures for purging the Jews are becoming ever more frequent and are enforced more strictly by the day. Bit by bit, we seem to have more breathing room around our editorial offices, and with more houses and apartments in this neighborhood emptying out every week, we can at least go undisturbed from home to the office and back home again." He must also have known about the Kazerne Dossin, where the Jews were gathered together for deportation to Germany; maybe he was even in direct contact with Antwerp's rabidly antisemitic SS division. There is no way of knowing whether he was aware of the atrocities committed in the Breendonk concentration camp, but it seems improbable that a high-ranking SS man like him would not have been; the *Sicherheitspolizei* had their own prison there. This whole embarrassing fantasy crackles with the repressed fear of undergoing what he had inflicted on others. He clearly knew all the dismal details about the packed cattle cars, and he "spills" them here in this torrid dream about his mistress, who shared both that knowledge and Willem's convictions—the heroine who, around the same time, compared a Belgian women's prison to a concentration camp and bad coffee to "Jew sweat," who would keep her cherished photo of the Führer on her mantelpiece until her dying breath. But their dream adventures are frivolous and lighthearted—they soar to orgiastic liberation, climaxing with joy, as it were, because they have escaped the "Atlanticists."

The obligation to keep silent about the gruesome truth of the pogroms and deportations was an intrinsic part of the ethos of the SS man. Himmler, who was in direct contact with the *Sicherheitsdienst* for which Willem worked, had left no room for misunderstanding: it was clear to everyone in the *Sicherheitspolizei* and the *Sicherheitsdienst* what *must* happen, what was involved in the *Endlösung*, the Final Solution, what a "difficult" task the Reich faced if it wished to purge itself of the "Jewish virus," what horrifying things were therefore actually being done to the Jews, and how many soldiers had suffered from mental collapse after following orders to perform mass executions. But the SS "code of honor" required that nothing ever be said about it. The SS man was to remain *unempathisch*, a demand once made of Willem in the front room of his own home in Drongenhof. That was the "sacrifice" made by SS members; they bore this weighty "moral duty," as Himmler had called it with his usual perversity, in silence. That was why, after the war, they *had* to keep insisting they had known nothing; their *Ehre und Traue*, their honor and loyalty, required it—and Willem remained true to this code of omertà during his trial: "I never heard anything about that, Your Honor." And then, as irony would have it, he gave away everything in a dream . . . The most telling detail is perhaps the corpses of the "old Belgians" in the burial chamber, which squeak like rats, filling him with terror.

Then there is the mysterious appearance of the code name "Skorzeny." Otto Skorzeny, who was born in Vienna in 1908 and died in Madrid in 1975, had the status of a mythical hero in SS circles. He advanced through the ranks at high speed, becoming an *SS-Obersturmbannführer*, the equivalent of a lieutenant colonel. Skorzeny was credited with a saga's worth of heroic exploits; his name was associated with stories that could not always be pinned down as myth or reality. He was involved in the sensational liberation of Mussolini in 1943; he is said to have been linked to a conspiracy to murder Stalin, Roosevelt and Churchill; he was part of a secret plan to bump off Tito; and during the Ardennes Offensive, he taught German soldiers English so that they could infiltrate the American lines. It was he who urged Hitler to manufacture a new wonder drug so that soldiers could remain numb even after Pervitin, the brand of crystal meth that Willem had on his nightstand, no longer did the job. He played an active role in the last line of defense around the Berghof, Hitler's residence in Berchtesgaden, and he is regarded as the founder of the infamous ODESSA—the *Organisation der ehemaligen SS-Angehörigen*, which took on the task of conducting the leading SS officers to safety after the war, in part by helping them escape into hiding in Argentina. Skorzeny himself sought refuge under Francisco Franco's dictatorship in Spain, where he became a rich and powerful industrial magnate; he later advised the Egyptian president Gamal Abdel Nasser and the Argentinian president Juan Perón.

The appearance of Skorzeny's name as a secret code in Willem's fantasy makes the mind reel. Consider that Willem was in solitary confinement, with little or no connection to the outside world, and his only source of material was therefore his wartime memories. Skorzeny must have figured regularly in the role of hero in Willem's German newspapers and in other reading for collaborators. In the privacy of his thoughts, Willem must have idolized Skorzeny. The fact that this SS man from Drongenhof inflated Skorzeny, in his dream, into a symbol of spectacular liberation makes it clear how well informed he had been in the war years. A textbook case of the dream as an admission of guilt: Willem's wooden pallet became the psychoanalyst's couch.

Since Willem never sent these letters to anyone, and they were found by his children after his death, the recipient is imaginary; Willem writes them to exonerate himself in his own eyes—his resentful version of a topsy-turvy trial. This prison letter is one of the last he wrote. Mientje may never have read these letters and poems; he must have tucked them away in a drawer somewhere, in the folder in which Letta still preserves them. In the dream scene, Mientje is completely neutered, a mere part of the "whole family," and he is the hero and savior whose reward is the use of Griet's "little machine." His invisible housewife forms a stark contrast with his mistress, who performs aeronautic sex acts and takes on mythical proportions. Yet in fact the dream is an embarrassment to Willem, as it reveals him to be the opposite of heroic: a frivolous schoolboy, a banal scoundrel, a parody of the little rascal who has accidentally made despicable enemies. A scared little man who once dreamed of becoming a

282

Flemish Skorzeny but realized he wasn't cut out to be a hero, the same man who would later note in the endpapers of his memoir:

Selon que vous serez puissant ou misérable,
Les jugements de Cour vous rendront blanc ou noir.

It is worth pausing to reflect on this quotation, which comes from one of La Fontaine's fables. During a plague, the animals must stand in judgment before King Lion, so that he can figure out whose crimes brought this misfortune down on them. One by one, the animals confess their transgressions. The fox admits that he killed and ate little lambs, but argues that this is no crime at all; the king has the same eating habits, and it is an honor for the humble creatures to serve as food for nobler beasts. The tiger and the bear clear themselves of guilt in the same way. The donkey, reassured by all this sophistry, confesses that he recently ate a mouthful of grass in a monastery's meadow, where he was not supposed to be. All the animals cry out that this is a grave offense, so the donkey must be responsible for the plague; he is sentenced to death. The moral of the story:

It is your power, or the lack of same,
That moves the Court to clear or smear your name.

In other words, if you are crafty and have a way with words, you can escape your rightful punishment; only a donkey talks his way to the gallows. I examine the quotation again, in Willem's crabbed hand—in French, no less, the language of those he despised. In view of everything I know about him, Willem's choice of passage seems utterly witless, at least if he meant to protest against his own conviction. But if he truly understood the moral of the fable, then his choice was an act of profound cynicism. Was Willem comparing himself to the sly fox? Was he thinking of the helpless sheep on his lists?

Between utter obliviousness and base cunning: the fable of a life.

Prison letter XVII
Solitude

Just a few more days and my fifth year of imprisonment will begin. For three years now, I have been alone in a cell in silent solitude with no hope that things will change anytime soon. How oppressive it is to be alone like this, behind thick heavy bars in a dimly lit cell measuring 9.1 by 13.1 feet. These few square feet are my whole world, and the provisions made for my needs and necessities are of the most primitive kind—straw, a few buckets, a sort of a chair, and a table propped up against the wall so it won't collapse . . . A stall like this is no place to build better people; on the contrary, you turn into a beast here, unless the spirit is mighty over the self . . . no, we aren't dogs, not yet, we still have manners and feel all too human in the face of God's Creation . . . beyond our own lives everything is dead . . . the few people we see here are mirror images of ourselves, and the guards are their own prisoners of us prisoners, even if they are in uniform . . . my musings go to my family, wife, children, a warm cozy house, happiness and work! Good food and a good bed and everything dear to me. Freedom! Freedom! . . . More later. Time for roll call.

42

Willem no longer has any idea of the weather outside, but through the chinks in the window he can hear the wind, and he knows it's a spring wind. Pan pipes played through a crack, a nefarious god ridiculing him with this shrill, headache-inducing tone. There's banging in the hallway, he's just returned to his cell, his chores as a fatik are becoming tiresome. He's fallen prey to melancholy; yesterday, he paid yet another visit to the prison doctor for his chronic stomach pain. The bitter powders don't help; he feels so down today, maybe he had an upsetting dream and forgot right away when he woke up—it's enough to usher in a whole day of listless moodiness, that sense of something still eating at him because it eludes his grasp.

This time it's the guard coming to hassle him again, he was just resting up on his pallet, he's cold, his shit-bucket stinks, he hears the jangle of the key in the lock of his cell, why can't they all just leave him alone, they can kiss my arse, he doesn't feel like turning over in bed, the guard with the nasal voice is moaning again about Verhulst this and Verhulst that, he also hears the name De Potter—Mr. De Potter! Your lawyer is here, Mr. Verhulst, he has good news.

What do you mean, good news?

Willem forces himself to turn over and sit up on his elbows. And there he is, large as life, Mr. De Potter in his dependable midnight-blue suit.

Eh voilà, bonjour, it's been a while, hasn't it? the man says. And how are you today, Mr. Verhulst, kind regards from your wife and children.

Hey, Mr. De Potter, Willem says with a sigh, and he sits up. Seated on the edge of his pallet, he probes with his feet for his worn-out slippers; it makes him look like a nervous child kicking his legs; what's the news, Mr. De Potter, are you already—

Verhulst, De Potter says, Monsieur Willem Verhulst, you are in luck, you're one of the prisoners selected for clemency next month, so what do you think of that, eh? Your good conduct as fatik worked in your favor, and so did your ambition to make an active contribution as a gardener to forestry in the Ardennes.

This can't be true, can it, Mr. De Potter, says Willem. I must be dreaming again, let me pinch my arm. As if he's Pierke Pierlala, the trickster of Flemish puppet theater, playing the scene for laughs . . .

Yet it *is* true, De Potter replies, you are on the list for conditional release within the framework of the well-known Lejeune Act. You have your *bonne épouse* to thank for that, she's been filing and chiseling away at your application with me for months—believe me, you're getting off easy.

Getting off easy, Willem says, with all due respect, Mr. De Potter, I've been stuck here for years like a caged animal, take a good look at me for once, I'm practically falling to pieces from all my pain and suffering and depression . . .

All right, all right, Mr. De Potter says, but if I were you, my fine fellow, I'd be jumping for joy. This was more than a day's work, as you well know.

It's just that I have to get used to the notion, says Willem, and now a grimace, or grin, begins to form on his face, a blissful, tormented grimace twists his harried features, he removes his crooked glasses with the broken earpiece, wipes the lenses with the hem of his grubby gray smock, surely it can't be true, Mr. De Potter, he is almost pleading now, because he fears this is just another dream come to make a fool of him, but then again, he can almost smell the spring wind as it keens and whistles through that chink in the tall barred window.

And I should add, monsieur, De Potter says, that your son has made a considerable contribution to this unexpected stroke of luck. Adri has now graduated from the Université de Gand and has excellent ties to the Liberal Flemish Student Association; as you may know, he is thinking of becoming a brother—

Becoming a *whaddayasay*? You mean he wants to join a monastery, Mr. De Potter?

No, Verhulst, your son plans to join one of Ghent's Masonic lodges, to become a member of a workshop of the Grand Orient of Belgium, as I am myself, but he has his eye on the William the Silent Lodge, you know he has always adored William the Silent, part of his upbringing by your Dutch wife, which explains why your son–

What?! My son, in a lodge with those Freemason bastards? And how do you know about it?

I would calm down if I were you, Mr. Verhulst. Your son, young though he may be, has friends in high places and arranged through them for your file to land on the desk of Mr. Albert Lilar, the liberal minister, who read it personally and took up your cause. You should be grateful to your son.

But Mr. De Potter, what am I s'pose to—

You're not *s'pose to* anything, Mr. Verhulst, I am simply delivering good news, and you act as if I've come to cut off your leg. I will keep you apprised of the further steps to be taken, but the most important step will be out of this prison, as you might suppose. *Allez*, take your time to recover from the joyful tidings, I'll bring around the official papers early next week.

Papers! I could use some more paper to wipe my arse with! They don't give me nearly enough, as I'm sure you can smell.

Mr. De Potter, shaking his head, raps on the door of the cell, the guard comes to unlock it, the lawyer steps out into the hallway, the door slams shut again, again the key jangles in the lock. Willem sits open-mouthed, his feet are swollen, how's it possible that's the first thing he feels, it's still too soon for all the rest. My belly, he thinks, my belly, will it get better when I'm out, I can't believe how much my belly hurts.

288

On November 13, 1953, he signs the document for his "conditional release under strict supervision by the Rehabilitation Service of the City of Antwerp." The document mentions his sentence: "Life imprisonment, reduced to a term of imprisonment of twenty years by decision of 22/05/1950."

A few weeks later, when he has read the decision, signed at the bottom and picked up his personal effects—which is to say, the nothing he possessed, half-decayed after years in the prison's dank storerooms, all the nothing he had with him when arrested near Hanover—he packs them into his little suitcase: a few sagging pairs of underpants, some shaving equipment, a threadbare shirt or two, stacks of paper covered with his scribblings, his two pencils and his pen; his father's pinky ring with the brilliant-cut diamond no longer fits onto his swollen fingers, so he sticks it in the pocket of his shabby wool jacket.

Not long afterward, they let him leave.

He's heard his early release is dependent on certain conditions; for example, he may not set foot in Ghent for five years. Not set foot in Ghent! Are they completely out of their minds? My wife and children!

Mr. Verhulst, have you perhaps forgotten that you agreed to become separated by law from your wife, to spare her financial ruin after you incurred hefty fines in reparation for stolen property? And your children seem to get by very well without you, as we here at the Court Registry have ascertained.

Grumbling and growling, but as lighthearted as a child sneaking out of school in the middle of the day, he steps out on to the street; in the final week of his imprisonment, he was transferred from Saint-Gilles to the Nieuwe-Wandeling, in his hometown, but now they expect him to leave again right away, what kind of foolishness is that?

He walks by the Coupure canal, saunters down Begijnhoflaan and past the old Rabot with its twin towers; just look at that sheen of rain on the branches of the plane trees! He could practically cry like a baby, it's so lovely. He passes the fire station and the Academy of Fine Arts—almost home! As he reaches Drongenhof, he is so agitated he can hardly get enough air, he turns a little blue around the gills, his one eye feels to him like a camera with a dead zone, he turns onto the street, passes the glass workshop, oh look, he's home! He rings the doorbell with a shaky finger, and Suzy opens the door, my little girl, my Suuzeke, he says, yet standing before him is no little Suuzeke but a young woman of nineteen—I'll be damned, he says, and the girl says, Papa? and now his lips really are starting to tremble, can it be you're growing up into such a fine figure of a woman, might I just pop inside for one quick second—

Suzy calls, Mama . . . ! Mamaaaa . . . !

Mientje comes out of the middle room, sees him there in the open door, her crybaby husband, and feels tears rush to her own eyes.

But Willem, oh . . .

Mien . . . Before he can finish the thought, his own theatrical sniffing and gulping overwhelms him.

I'm not supposed to be here, Mien, I have to go . . .

It's just like always, Wim, Mien says with a pained smile, you always had to go. But even so, she puts her arms around him.

III

Once he had played his dirty trick,
he did not remain in Nuremberg much longer but moved on swiftly,
not wanting the truth to come out about what he had done.

—Tijl Uilenspiegel

1

Yes, the notary said, that first day while showing me around the third floor of the empty house, as he led me to the rickety window in the back room, where some hay and a bag of barley straw pellets suggested that someone had kept gerbils, yes, look down there, at the flat roof of the ground floor, that would easily support a nice patio, that would be something, wouldn't it, dear fellow, slipping out onto the roof whenever you please, to view the world from higher up?

Yes, that view from the heights, the great Dante knew all about it.

We left the room, the notary taking one last appraising look as he shut the creaky old door behind him, and we prepared to climb the third stairway, the stairway to the summit, to all the secrets yet to come, which lay waiting in the fallow field of that deserted attic—waiting for me, the disturber of the peace and the house's future tyrant.

Do you mind if I smoke? I asked the notary, and he, who had just retrieved his cigar box and selected a Corona for himself, waved away my foolish question with a grunt. So I dug a cigarette out of the breast pocket of my peacoat, gave the notary a moment to suck fire into the tip of his cigar, and then inhaled the cigarette smoke into the outermost corners of my lungs; the haze rose bluely up the stairs, swirled in the grayish air and vanished along the steps, which seemed to rise farther than we could yet discern.

And in the determination with which the old fellow placed his right foot on the first step of the stairs to the attic, I saw a sudden hint of an ancient sage, an everyday household shaman, and to my surprise I felt sympathy for him. The stairs he was now steeling himself to climb were less solid than the ones below, and excessive enjoyment of the first few puffs of his newly lit cigar may have left him a little light in the head; in any case, the good *Legum Magister* made a most regrettable misstep, twisting his ankle, losing his balance, snatching for support, spinning halfway around and landing with a thump that thundered up the stairwell; because I reacted too late, the most I could do was cushion his body a bit as it crashed into the steps, just barely preventing my guide from banging his head on the banister; so the honorable Servant of the Laws Regarding the Administrative Procedures Relating to the Study of Real Estate, gasping and swaying and moaning *my goodness my gracious my word,* accepted my help in returning to his feet, though his legs were still trembling. He waved me off with a shaky hand as if to say that he would be just fine, handed me his folder and the half-completed Statement of Condition upon Viewing, produced a lavender-colored handkerchief from his left breast pocket, and dabbed at the pearls of sweat on his ample forehead. Only then did I notice the smelly cigar still smoldering on the wooden floor; I picked it up, with some reluctance because one end was moist, held it between my thumb and index finger until the notary had recovered a little from his fall, and proffered it to him; and the official responsible for property transactions took the Corona from my hand with gratitude, placed the folder (after recovering it from me) on the fifth step of the still-unscaled stairs to the attic, expelled a deep sigh, closed his eyes for a moment, opened them again, forced an indulgent smile, removed his glasses, cleaned them with an unused corner of his hanky, and said, You must ascend this staircase on your own, my friend, I can no longer guide you, you'll find your way, you've come this far already, you can do the rest under your own steam. A little taken aback by this dramatic outpouring from a notary who otherwise seemed so reliable, I nodded to show that I understood, that

I would find my way, and thus wound up unexpectedly climbing the stairs to the attic alone.

On the next landing, I looked up and saw a dingy skylight overhead; through a chink I heard the rustling trees and the roaring cars at the Sluizeken intersection. I continued upward, the stairs creaked, a faintly toxic vapor of dry rot rose from the walls, which offered the ever-industrious dust mite an immense terrain; and the little cornflowers, faded and scarcely visible on the wallpaper, lay waiting in deathly silence for the passerby, for the one who must learn to be a passerby, as Christ says in the apocryphal Gospel of Thomas: *Be passersby!*—for me, who now reached the summit, a little short of breath, leaving the notary behind, out of sight and out of earshot, only his cigar smoke rising to reach me. I turned around and looked down. I saw the ribs and coils of the staircase dwindling into the dark depths, all the way down to the black floor tiles of the hallway. I was overcome by old dust; to my right, a ramshackle door stood ajar, opening onto a garret. There I saw an iron bed with a few protruding springs, a stained mattress lying askew over the bedframe, and a writing desk in the corner under a leaky skylight.

This room, in the final year of the war, while Willem was in an even-smaller cell, was the hiding place of poor "Mr. Verschuren," who once, in his dithyrambic enthusiasm about one composer or another, fell through a decayed floorboard—he was giving one of his secret music lessons, you know what I mean, to that quick young pianist with the blonde ponytail . . . *O Noble Art! O Sacra Halitosis!* . . . but now the room was silent, the little window letting in the muted gray light so typical of this gloomy region, low clouds drifting over the roof, a gust of wind rattling the old carcass of the house. I smelled the musky odor of dead mice, saw bunches of horsehair with chunks of plaster protruding from the ceiling, and heard sparrows chirping and pigeons scrabbling, close by, at the edge of the roof, angels of the gutter.

The dust filled my lungs, making me wheezy and breathless. For a moment, I stood staring in indecision at a worn throw rug, a few old books in a corner, a light bulb hanging from a dusty wire that dangled from a broken beam. I pushed open the stubborn door to the attic room. It was like entering a church: the large, empty cranium of the house, I thought to myself, no wonder people are always so curious about attics, you hope to find secrets there that will tell you everything the house has been through, all the concealed thoughts and affairs of its occupants—the letters, the boxes of postcards and passionate confessions. But I found nothing but dusk, thin air, and space. High above, through a gap in a chipped roof tile, a cooing pigeon wriggled its fat ass.

2

Willem has had a bad night, the bed was much too soft, so he lay on the mat on the ground beside it; to make matters worse, Carlo always gets up much too early, what is it with these females who have more energy than they know what to do with. But when the smell of brewing coffee seeps under the door and into his nostrils, he races downstairs on his shaky legs to pour himself a cup in the kitchen. My goodness, brother of mine, Carlo says, to see you here in your PJs, well, it boggles the mind, I swear, I never dreamed I'd see you walking free again. All the same, the whole thing's ended well . . . Willem grins and nods and sighs. And will you be staying long, she asks, just so's I know, not that you're underfoot but it is one more mouth to feed, I mean till you find a job, *if* you can find one . . .

Now, now, says Wim, hold your horses, I'll have a word with Nuncle Schamp tomorrow, and you'll see, it'll all be right as rain.

That evening, Carlo sets an extra place at the table, but Willem hasn't come back.

She's made beans in tomato sauce, a favorite of his; very well, then, she'll leave a portion on the counter for him, he's a grown man, as long as he's not hanging around De Hand until closing time, like their dear departed father. She goes to bed around ten p.m., by which time she's a little worried.

The next morning, Willem still hasn't returned, should she call the police, fresh out of prison and already up in smoke, that Wim of ours, it's always something.

Around noon he breezes in with a smile on his face, looking a sight better than the day before—he's even wearing a new shirt. Oh, Wim, she says, where've you been hiding yourself?

Went to see an ol' friend just around the corner, Willem says, and my God am I famished.

He lies down for a nap, a prison habit, what else can you do with those long afternoons, well, be that as it may, Willem snores away the day until five or thereabouts.

Then he comes back downstairs; Carlo's still at work in the dance studio, he can hear the music and the shuffling feet, he goes in for a look, recalling the dancing lessons of his childhood. The dance floor has changed, everything has changed, and yet it's just the same as it was then. Mambo, waltz and cha-cha-cha, one, two, three and, whoops, turn—Carlo's as energetic as ever.

Shall we have a bite of supper at De Hand, he asks after the lessons, and Carlo says, Fine by me, my cupboard's bare in any case.

At about half past six, they wander over to the pub.

And would you look at that, if it isn't Griet Latomme at the table by the window. Evening, Madame Latomme, how's life treating you?

Griet bursts into laughter. You idiot, she says with a cackle, and then she asks Carlo, How are you?

Carlo rolls her eyes, always the same old story with you, she says to Willem, does Mientje know about this? Pff, Mientje can look after herself, he says, we're separated by law, you know we are, and besides, I'm starting work for Nuncle Schamp next week.

Griet joins them at their table; Carlo mostly keeps her mouth shut, the dish of the day is lemon sole with fries, Willem orders a German beer, why not.

The lovebirds snigger, clearly rubbing knees under the table.

Sleep wherever you like, Carlo says, it doesn't mean a thing to me, but I don't intend to play housekeeper for you.

298

I'm happy to pay if you like, he says.

Griet's adoring look makes Carlo's stomach churn.

So Willem returns, as if nothing had happened, to his job as a traveling salesman for the Antwerp branches of MEGA; he is invited to pick out a company car, and before long he's driving up to Griet's house to show off his new luxury Mercedes. The two of them go shopping for a suit, she picks out a few good shirts and two shirt fronts, now all he needs are two pairs of shoes, no, no Wim, you can pay me back, try on those moccasins there, they'll be more comfortable for your swollen feet.

And so, Letta tells me, to make a long story short, they knew nothing in Antwerp about his high jinks in Ghent. Mr. Verhulst won everyone over yet again with his infectious smile, his charming little ways, his goofy jokes and his friendly features—all in spite of his one blind, cloudy eye and his corpulence, which by this time was considerable. He smoked too many cigarettes, he drank too much white wine; the doctor warned him about "the disease of French kings," and when he asked, What do you mean by that, Mr. Doctor, the doctor told him that too much white Rhenish wine gives you bladder stones. Perfect, said Willem, then I'll be pissing diamonds, if only I could tell my pa.

Some days he flies off the handle, other days he's melancholy, after a few months he starts to have nightmares. It scares the life out of Griet every time, that bellowing beside her in the middle of the night, enough to stop your heart, then he starts to whimper again, God almighty, just like a drowning rat, come on, Wim, wake up, what's the matter with you . . .

They, they—*nicht . . . einsperren . . .*

Calm down, my boy, calm down, you're dreaming.

Lord, woman, I thought we were in Soltau with that plane swooping down straight at us and I had to go down to that cellar where those two . . .

He gets out of bed, sweating and panting, splashes water on his face, sits in the kitchen until the sky begins to brighten, and doesn't return to bed until daylight has reassured him.

Then he grabs hold of Griet and says with a smirk, Didn't I have some business with you, my dear . . . She slaps playfully at the wandering hands under her nightdress.

3

You'll need regular habits, Wim, says Nuncle Schamp, you mustn't over-sleep, I need to know I can count on you.

Willem is sometimes sentimental and sometimes rebellious.

He tries to please everyone and displeases himself.

Other days, he's full of overconfidence. Hurrah, he's entitled to a German war pension, a stipend from the German state to former collaborators for their services to Nazi Germany, what's the world coming to, Carlo says to Griet, that little bandit of yours is even drawing a pension now for his monkey tricks. What are those Germans thinking? Haven't they learned a thing?

It's my reward after everything I went through, Willem says, but he's looking at them like a toddler who's soiled his pants. And well he should—he hasn't even finished spending the 50,000 francs he received from the Borms Commission during the war, "reparations" paid by the occupying power to Flemish activists and collaborators for the suffering supposedly inflicted on them by the Belgian state. His "friend" August Borms was the initiator and president of the organization.

How can it be you still have money from that commission? Carlo asks him in surprise. How did you slip that past the Gutt operation?

I converted it into marks in Germany in 1944 and gave it to Griet, who hid it in her underwear when she was arrested and gave it to one of her woman friends, who exchanged it without sniffing it first, ha, ha. Not as simple as I look, am I?

He tries to do his job well, but so many things can suddenly get on his nerves that he sometimes feels like puking. The bouts of bitterness and depression take their toll on his body and his mind. He drinks more than is good for him, but as long as he stays a little fogged, he doesn't feel his gnawing stomachache.

Once every few weeks, he drives his sleek Mercedes to Drongenhof; the police never stop you anymore anyway, the few cops along the road are always dozing. One time he brought candy, but he's had to face the fact that his daughters already have boyfriends, and their minds are on treats of a very different kind. He sits in the front room with Mientje, it really is beautiful stone, isn't it, that pink marble mantelpiece, what's the name, Combleu . . .

Yes, Comblanchien, Mientje breaks in, do you know where that is, Comblanchien? And do you know about the horrific events of the war there?

The war—please spare me, says Willem. *Schwamm drüber*, let bygones be bygones. Or else tell me next time, I have to be back home at Carlo's place by dark.

But he doesn't drive home, of course not. He looks in on his old drinking buddies at the Roeland House Café, the social hub of the Flemish nationalist movement, where the former blackshirts are having a pint together and reminiscing, they're good folk, a little rough around the edges but true to themselves, the kind of men that Willem has always looked up to. You don't want to hear the jokes those fellows make, he tells Griet with a laugh, that's one place a man can still speak his mind, unlike everywhere else in today's world of prigs and schoolmarms. I run into old pals there from my year at gardening school. We sing the good old Flemish songs, and when the door is locked up tight, we also sing a certain German song: *Die Fahne hoch! Die Reihen fest geschlossen!* Yes, we've had some great times at the Roeland House.

The police barge in on us regularly, they've even arrested a few men they'd been searching for ever since the war, imagine, it's practically 1960, and those cops keep harping away, they just won't let it drop.

It's a warm evening sometime in early June 1959; at the Roeland House, they're bickering about the dominant role of the Catholic Church in the school system. A year ago, the government finally came up with a fragile compromise, but you can't let those Catholics out of your sight, just like those Walloons; every one of them could use a good fist in the face. And the situation in the Congo is no better: those blacks are getting too big for their britches, and the fransquillons in charge there do nothing but screw over the hardworking Flemish taxpayers—if we tried to get away with that, they'd come down on us in no time.

They should cut the hands off that bastard Lumumba, someone says, and the room bursts into a volley of laughter.

If you have such a problem with blacks in the Congo, says a man at the bar who's been following their conversation, then why is there a black African animal on your flag?

Hold on a sec, Willem says, who does this joker think he is?

One of his burly friends goes up to the man.

He wobbles a little from one foot to the other.

You a communist or what?

The man gives a derisive sniff.

If you people had your way, we'd soon be back to *ein-zwei-drei* and onto the train with you!

The punch in the face sends the man keeling over backward between two tables. His attacker spits on his fist.

All right, another round over here.

But the man stands up, wipes his mouth on his sleeve, walks out, and returns ten minutes later—with four friends.

Just a few minutes later, everyone in the bar is throwing punches, no matter how many times the bartender shouts that they all need to calm down. The mob eventually pours out onto the street, here and there a window opens up, the police arrive and check passports. Seven men are arrested, including Willem, who is plastered enough to put up quite a fight.

Kiss my ass, you Belgicist piece of shit.

He is forced into the van. Officer Van Belle handcuffs him and takes a closer look at his passport.

Well, well, Verhulst, don't I know you from someplace? Aren't you supposed to stay out of Ghent? Weren't you told to behave yourself?

He is taken away and thrown in a cell with three of the others.

I find the detention file in the State Archives in Ghent:

Officer Robert Van Belle, sergeant of the gendarmerie, declares that he arrested the above-mentioned person.

The party in question, Willem Verhulst, spent the night of June 5 to 6, 1959, in the city jail.

The medical file on the prisoner is full of vivid details:

Verhulst, Willem
Occupation: Traveling salesman
Religion: Protestant
Age: 60
Physical description: 1.84 m, 83 kg
Identifying features:
Blind in one eye
False teeth
Suffers from obesity and mild eczema
Bronchial rattling in lungs

Slight varicose veins

Lesser curvature visible because of stomach ulcer operation

Blood pressure: 140/90

Pulse: 80

Medical permission for: Bed rest, partial capacity for work

"Obesity," but his body mass index was in the normal range—it must refer to Willem's distended stomach.

He was held in cell 51. The doctor recommended a quart of fresh milk a day and two pounds of fresh fruit a week for his gastric disorder. When he was placed in detention, the briefcase he had with him was confiscated; it contained "a few textbooks, his wristwatch, a razor with 15 blades, bags of photographs and papers, four keys in a pouch, a pocket knife, a nail file, cigars in a cigar case, his medications and a few letters."

The next day, he filed a request for the return of his razor ("brand: Gillette"), three textbooks, and *Elseviers Weekblad*, a Dutch weekly news magazine—more evidence that he liked to keep up with cultural developments in the Netherlands. A censorship committee approved the request, and later records show that he had long underwear, pajamas, two undershirts, a towel, a pair of trousers, a jacket, three pairs of socks and a spare pair of shoes—the tenderhearted Mientje must have rushed to the aid of her sixty-year-old brawler again, bringing him a few necessities.

The file also includes a handwritten note that his application for clemency was initially rejected.

His loyal son, Adri, who had earned his doctorate with distinction two years earlier with a study of St. Bavo's Abbey in Ghent and embarked on an impressive academic career, had to wield his influence once again to secure his father's release, through his connections in the liberal party and at the lodge.

The aforementioned convict was provisionally released from custody on June 11, 1959, by order of Director D'Ours, delivered by telephone by his staff on June 11, 1959.

According to a handwritten note, this order for immediate, albeit provisional, release came directly from the ministry, upon which Willem—not especially humbled by the experience, still certain the Belgian state was not much more than a gang of thugs—returned to civilian life, after promising to stop antagonizing people.

In an online directory of Belgian Freemasons, I find confirmation that Adri belonged to the Ghent workshop of the Grand Orient of Belgium, a strain of Freemasonry reputed to be undogmatic and liberal. He does not appear to have been a very active member. Since Willem, in his days as an SS spy, must have kept the lodge members under surveillance and perhaps reported some of them to the *Sicherheitspolizei* for arrest by the Nazi intelligence service and possible deportation to a prison camp, he may have found it especially mortifying, or even downright humiliating, to owe his freedom, on two separate occasions, to special favors called in by his son from those same people. But it is equally possible that his characteristic frivolity, which enabled him to laugh off even the most inconvenient of paradoxes, spared him from giving much thought to the matter. *Schwamm drüber!* Belgicist buggers!

Again, he is banished from Ghent for a certain length of time; he doesn't dare continue his secret visits to Mientje, at least not for now, she'd just give him the scolding of his life anyway. He should call his son and thank him, yes, yes, he'll do it next week, he needs to catch his breath first. When he shows up at Griet's place again after his week in detention, all he says is that the soup in jail was much too salty and that one day he'll settle the score with that Officer Van Belle. Too bad there are no longer any lists.

4

Not long after that, Mientje sees an article in the paper about an apparition of the Virgin Mary somewhere in Belgium. As a Protestant, she's
always been a little skeptical of all those Catholic superstitions, but they
also fascinate her, so she asks Willem to drive her to a meeting where the
woman who has seen the apparition will speak. Willem parks the car and
says, You go on without me, still slightly reluctant to make such a public
appearance when he doesn't know who might be there. Mientje rings the
doorbell and is shown inside, where an audience of about thirty is
crammed into a small parlor. The atmosphere is electric, little is said, and
as the mystic begins her story, you could hear a pin drop.

I beheld the Most Sacred Virgin there, lit from behind, she murmurs . . . it was around three o'clock in the afternoon . . . suddenly, the
sun blazed through the clouds and in its transcendent rays I saw the Holy
Mother slowly feeling Her way along the wall . . . yes, that wall there to
my left, that one with the ivy that you can see through the window . . .
She wore a white slip and a sky-blue cloak adorned with golden stars, oh,
She shot me a piercing look and yes . . . She nodded to me, slowly,
slowly . . . my heart pounded, out of control, I could barely breathe . . . I
whispered a quick prayer and wanted to ask Her something, I fell to my
knees and cried out, Oh, Virgin Mother, what do You wish to tell me? . . .
but by then She had already disappeared . . .

The woman sits back, panting, and lays one hand on her bosom. Her
eyes have been shut the whole time.

A few people are staring openmouthed.

Mientje raises her hand, Excuse me, ma'am, may I ask you something?

What did you actually see? How should we picture it—the physical apparition of a divine body?

She doesn't mean to be aggressive; in fact, she's fascinated by Catholics and all the colorful trappings of their faith, but the woman looks at her in astonishment. What right does this cheesehead have to question my vision?

She points a finger in Mientje's direction and stammers, with rising indignation, There sits a heretic . . . there sits an unbeliever . . . sent to lure us astray . . . sent by the Devil! As she speaks these final words, she covers her eyes and her voice rises to a shriek, pandemonium breaks loose, a man jumps up and gives Mientje a shove, Out with that witch, he says, go on, get out of here, you, and a woman shouts, Throw her out, that Dutch bitch, what does she think she's doing here.

Rough hands push and crowd Mientje down the hallway to the front door; someone grabs her by the collar and kicks her out onto the street, where she almost falls to the ground.

The door slams shut; Mientje walks to the car, which is parked nearby. Her husband, smoking, sees how upset she is, she tells him what happened to her and, oh, Willem, she says, as if that weren't enough, now I've left my purse in there, would you please go get it for me, I can't go back inside. No, Willem snaps, I'm not doing that, you can do it yourself.

She stares at him for a moment, openmouthed, gasps for breath, glances over her shoulder, seems to clutch at the air to keep herself upright, and then retraces her steps, rings the doorbell, and is just preparing to ask for her purse when it hits her in the face.

During the drive home she doesn't say a word; Willem drops her off at home in Drongenhof and says he has to go, she knows where he's going, back to Griet, same as ever, why does she see so little of him, I'll be alone again tonight, she thinks, I'll sleep on the sofa in the middle room, all those stairs, it won't be easy. But it's all right, the children are healthy, goodbye, Willem, see you next time, the Lord's ways are inscrutable, whom He loveth He chasteneth.

This is the period when she makes a habit of reading *The Imitation of Christ* by Thomas à Kempis. The meditations and arguments in the third book, about the forms of peace one can learn to find within oneself, are especially dear to her. Sometimes she reads them half aloud, it calms and comforts her. That evening she can't get to sleep, there on the sofa in the middle room. After tossing and turning for a while, she gets up, throws on her dressing gown and sits down at the lion's-paw table. That night she writes a prayer. She types it up the next morning, pecking at her little typewriter with two fingers, and gives it to Letta not long before her death.

PRAYER

Lord, you know I am getting older and will be old one day.

Don't let me become too fond of the sound of my own voice, or fall into the deadly habit of thinking I have something to say about every subject on every occasion.

Protect my spirit from the temptation to go into endless detail; give me the joy to go straight to the heart of the matter.

Lend me enough manners to listen to other people's troubles.

Seal my lips when it comes to my own troubles; I seem to take growing pleasure in recounting them.

Let me remain friendly; an embittered old woman is one of the greatest achievements of the Evil One.

Let me be thoughtful and helpful but not bossy.

When I think of all the wisdom I have gathered, it seems a shame not to put it all to use.

You know, Lord, that as I near the end of my path, I will need many
   friends.

Oh, that mother of ours, Letta sighs. Ever the idealist, always so
self-effacing . . .

She hands me the thin carbon copy and tells me that Mientje made
several copies of her prayer and read it aloud in the church in Brabantdam. In the late 1960s, she handed out copies of *The Imitation of Christ*
at the entrance to St. Stephen's Church in Patershol; she may well have
paid for the booklets herself.

Now maybe you understand, Letta says, why, after my brother published *Son of a "Bad" Fleming*, I published my own little booklet, *Daughters
of a Fantastic Mother*. Here, I have still have a spare copy for you.

A few months later, Suzy places her mother's wallet in my hands. I open
it and see a small edition of the Sermon on the Mount.

5

The sixties are coming, Willem often shakes his head, the world is going crazy, they should all just . . .

Everything should just go back to . . .

Turn off that American hullabaloo! It's like negroes from Africa! . . .

If only Germany had . . .

And what is that racket? The Rolling *what*?

It's all right, Willem, don't get so worked up, it's not good for your heart.

His health is not especially good; he still "hits the road" as a salesman at regular intervals, but it's wearing him down. He loves a good meal, eats too much fatty food, eats too much, period—we've known such hardship, he'll say, before plunging his knife into a T-bone steak. Many evenings, he drinks more than one glass too many of Rhenish wine; he climbs a couple of steps and he's out of breath; he smokes his Willem II cigars; his airways are clogging up; his own wheezing keeps him awake at night. He often gets irritable, or overwrought, or sentimental. More and more often, he complains of a "terrible bellyache." After repeated urging, he gives in and consults a doctor, who suspects that he has Crohn's disease or worse. He is subjected to unpleasant tests; the gastroscopy in particular is a nightmare. A tube is inserted into his throat until he starts gagging and heaving; he later has a colonoscopy, lying with his poor ass bared on the doctor's iron table and feeling the endoscope poking around inside him, ah well, a person's no more than a sack of bones and shit, getting older, how do you do it? He complains about it to Mientje: Woman, you

wouldn't believe it, they make you drink liquid plaster so they can photograph slices of your guts—Oh, you mean they took X-rays of your
stomach, Willem? The burning acid sloshing up into his throat keeps
him awake at night; he has cramps; give me another glass of that Antwerp liqueur, Elixir d'Anvers, that's what they give colicky horses. You
have to take your pills, Mr. Verhulst, the doctor admonishes him, seeing
no improvement, and no alcohol for you, you heard what I said, but oh
well, one little pint of ale or glass of wine, that's not going to kill anyone,
now is it, Doctor? If you get old enough, you're not allowed to do anything, so pour us another one, we all end up six feet under anyway. His
belly is like a barrel now; just lugging it around is hard for him. Some
days, he goes about looking almost as if he's just soiled his pants.

The children see less of their father now; he's usually at Griet's place, but
on paper he still lives with his family. He's started coming to Ghent more
often again; after a management dispute at MEGA, he and a partner
have started up their own business, where I bought my own first
do-it-yourself kit in late 1968, for an amplifier. I remember the taciturn
man with glasses in the back of the shop; I could be wrong, but it's certainly possible that my feeble imitations of Jimi Hendrix, Jimmy Page
and Eric Clapton were backed by a stereo system, parts of which had
been handed to me by Willem Verhulst.

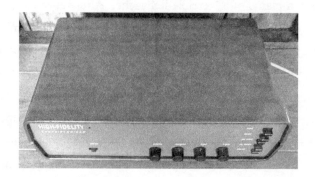

Adri has now become well known as Professor Adriaan Verhulst of Ghent University, an expert in the evolution of cities, historical geography and the critical analysis of documents; he publishes influential articles on agriculture in the days of Charlemagne, the agrarian archeology of the Middle Ages and the earliest history of Bruges. He is the first in Flanders to lecture on the shared history of the Southern and Northern Netherlands, thus uniting the cultural heritage of his two parents. He becomes an advocate for the rights of progressive, free-thinking people in a political landscape still dominated by Catholicism. He is married, and he and his wife stop by now and then at the house in Drongenhof, where Mientje now lives alone.

Suzy marries a lawyer from the Antwerp area, and the two of them build a spacious modern house in a green setting. Suzy is a liberated woman who regards herself as the heir to her aunt Suzanne's feminism; she condemns her father's role in the war in sharper terms than her brother and sister do. She bears a striking resemblance to Mientje but has inherited her father's weak eyes. She is clear-minded, full of fight, and blessed with a keen sense of irony. When her eyesight goes into rapid decline, she signs up for the library's talking book service. She buys an old jukebox and, at the age of eighty-five, blasts 1960s hits through her large house. She sips white wine and smokes as if she has lungs of steel. Her laugh is as gravely and infectious as an aging blues singer's.

Back in the early 1950s, Letta became involved with Rudi, a scion of Ghent's well-known Mahy family. He had been a classmate of Adri's in high school, at the Koninklijk Atheneum, and a frequent visitor to the house in Drongenhof; Letta was smitten with him, to Adri's annoyance, and they became engaged. After marrying in late July 1955, they lived for a short time in a small apartment in the well-known Wintercircus, a former event hall and hippodrome near the center of Ghent. That's a story in itself. After the war, Rudi's great-uncle, Ghislain Mahy, had bought the spectacular old wreck of a building and converted it into a large parking garage. Rudi was then working for him as a mechanic. The original Wintercircus dated from 1894, but it had burned down in 1920. Its huge dome completely collapsed: "it looked almost like the Frauenkirche in Dresden falling down," I read somewhere. It was rebuilt to seat more than three thousand. Even during the war, there were events there; the last was in the spring of 1944.

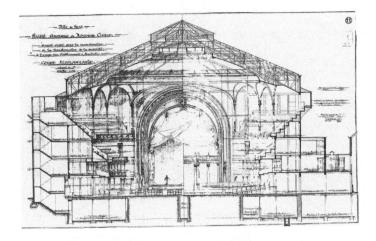

Ghislain had all the old infrastructure dismantled, but around the time of Letta and Rudi's engagement, he converted some of the enormous space into an apartment. The rest of the building housed his collection of rare vintage cars, which grew systematically and became so well known that the Wintercircus was renamed Circus Mahy; in Ghent, it was known simply as the Cirque. It was in this apartment, this storied building, that Letta and her husband Rudi lived for a while. Most of the fabulous car collection was later moved to a museum dubbed Mahymobiles, in the Hainaut region of Wallonia; the Flemish television producer Paul Jambers made two colorful special reports about the family and their exceptional passion for legendary cars. To this day, the Mahys have a large parking garage in the Ekkergem district on the edge of town. In the years when I was taught by the strict Professor Adriaan Verhulst, the Wintercircus went mostly unused. On the steep slope of Lammerstraat, I would often pass the plaque commemorating the glory days of the Wintercircus. Once, I broke into the building with a friend, just to have a look around. Back then, I could never have suspected the symbolic link between this peculiar structure and the house where I would one day live.

6

It's February 1963, an unusually harsh winter, the coldest in the meteorological records, which go back to 1815. January was exceptionally snowy; week after week, it stayed below freezing. The North Sea was covered with ice, the waves froze, and there were icebergs in the Wadden Sea; February brought more of the same, with morning temperatures sometimes plunging to –20°C (–4°F). From about five to six a.m., Mientje would lie in bed with chattering teeth, her toes pressed to the lukewarm hot-water bottle. She avoided the annex, where icicles hung outside the windows; she went back and forth with newspapers, kindling and coal. Today she is taking the bus to Antwerp to visit Letta and her husband. Several times on the way there, she feels a kind of nausea well up inside, making her dizzy. She walks the quarter of a mile to Letta's house, slips on a patch of ice and almost falls, feels her legs wobbling, the icy air taking her breath away. I'm growing old, she thinks, I don't feel good. She stops for a moment to rest her weight against a house front; under her hand, she feels the chill of the plate with the house number. She recalls a Ghent saying, often said to her in the years when Willem was behind bars: "Hold on to the house numbers"—a strange way of wishing her well in difficult times—and she can't help laughing, despite the pain in her chest.

She waits there until she catches her breath again and then goes on to Letta's house; the warm living room feels unbearably stuffy, the room reels around her, she stumbles to the toilet and has to throw up. Then she sinks to the floor.

Letta's husband hears the thud, and they lift the unconscious woman to her feet; with a cry of pain, she wakes. It's her heart, Letta says, she needs help, fast. They lead the gasping woman to the sofa and prop her up.

In the ambulance on the way to the emergency room, she starts to come back to her senses a little. At the clinic in Mortsel they tell her that after such a severe heart attack, she'll need a month to recover. She sleeps and has intense dreams, day after day; severe sleep apnea wakes her with a jolt as if she's drowning; through the window she sees construction cranes and treetops. In mid-March, she comes home to a house like a palace of ice; the winter light sparkles, cruel and bright, in the glass workshop's broken windows.

⁓

These days, she is usually alone in the big, gloomy house, which is gradually being left to decay. The many rooms she used to rent out now seem deserted, full of furniture, junk and forgotten souvenirs; the roofing felt is blistering and cracking; when there's heavy rain it leaks onto the porch, and she can hear the furious drumming in the zinc tub from the middle room where she sits by the stove and reads her Bible; moss is growing along the edges of the dingy skylight; and condensation on cold mornings is damaging the kitchen. Neglect and vacancy are taking their toll on Patershol; the large former monastery is deserted, the glass workshop is slowly caving in. In the bars, the locals drink hard and fight hard. In the narrow side streets, more and more houses are unoccupied; the working-class district has acquired a bad reputation. During the many weeks that Willem is away "for business" in Antwerp or abroad—who does he think he's fooling, she knows who he's with—she sometimes wanders through the upper rooms, her heavy footsteps thudding on the floor of the stairwell because she's tired; then she looks around, picks up one thing or another—a book of poems by Richard De Cneudt, oh Richard, dear boy, where does the time go, what a lovely party that was in the old Sint-Jorishof guildhall . . . She lays the thin volume back down where she found it, rummages around a little longer, opens the old dresser in her bedroom and smells the penetrating odor of mothballs; she looks at her clothes, picks up a garment, examines its condition, shakes her head and hangs it up again. Is there still a forgotten suit of Pappie's in this wardrobe? She looks at the unused marital bed, much too large for a person on her own. How might Pappie be doing these days? It's God's will, it's the Lord testing and refining her. Anyway, doesn't she sleep comfortably enough in the middle room, you don't even need curtains there, and she sometimes naps in the front room in the afternoon, when the sun enters through the tall windows for a few hours. During the day, she does her shopping at the markets in the squares, Bij Sint-Jacobs and Vrijdagmarkt, you can find all sorts of things there, and a Turkish greengrocer has opened a little shop in Oudburg, what's becoming of the world, but never mind, all people are creations of the Almighty, there's a West Flemish butcher shop in Sluizeken Square and a bakery along the Leie. Sometimes she can be spotted with a kerchief on her head, wrapped up in a gray jacket and wearing sturdy shoes, still the dignified daughter of a Dutch gentleman farmer, strolling through the park with a large bag in her hand. Soon Adri will visit with his wife, she'll enjoy that, they'll talk about music and the university. She is proud of him; her son is now the general secretary of the Willemsfonds, the cultural association of liberals who support the Flemish Movement. He is also a member of the Royal Flemish Academy of Belgium for the Arts and Sciences, she thinks that's just wonderful, and at the university he is considered the new authority whose work on urban archaeology has called into question the earlier theories of the renowned historian Henri Pirenne. He's

318

amassed an impressive list of publications; Adri is a hard, dogged worker.

⁓

It's Sunday afternoon, Adri and his wife are visiting, they've brought a bombe au chocolat from the Jewish bakery Bloch, and now they're all sitting in the front room, with photographs of her children and parents on proud display on the mantelpiece. Adri asks if she remembers the time she sang the "Largo" and the plaster Hitler was blown to smithereens; they laugh nostalgically as they sip their weak coffee.

How are you, Mother, with the pain in your legs and all.

Getting by, son, getting by. Tell me *your* news, I'd rather talk about that. People in the streets keep asking the same question, in a pitying tone: How are you, Mrs. Verhulst, and how are the children? As long as we have our health, isn't that right?

Just as you say, Mr. De Pestel.

In the lonely evening hours—she doesn't watch television—she hears the noise of the neighbors in their own big, empty house: *Arnold, where'd ye put the brush, allus the same ol' story.*

She dips into her Bible—Proverbs 31, in praise of the virtuous housewife:

She layeth her hands to the spindle, and her hands hold the distaff.
She stretcheth out her hand to the poor; yea, she reacheth forth her
    hands to the needy.
She is not afraid of the snow for her household: for all her household
    are clothed with double garments.

⁓

She has a second heart attack in 1965, while staying with her daughter Letta. Her grandson Jan, then six years old, is woken by her raspy, labored breath. His parents call an ambulance. Mientje recovers, but her heart is seriously weakened. She continues to get herself too worked up about social and political developments.

In autumn 1966 she starts keeping a journal again, filled with commentary on the collapsing negotiations between the Flemish and the Walloons. She remarks that "the country is now becoming irreversibly divided." In October 1966 she notes that her former lodger Marcel Bots has left for Elisabethstad in the Congo and that Pastor Van Stipriaan has been transferred to Eindhoven. She provides a "brief overview" of events since her previous journal, which makes it clear that Van Stipriaan played a crucial role in lifting the order that had prevented Willem from visiting Ghent.

December 1966: "Terrible floods are ravaging Belgium—hundreds of hectares of farmland are under water. The Leie is running high—our own cellar has flooded, even worse than last year around Christmas. Our neighbor has been so kind as to scoop out the water for us."

March 1968: "The political situation: elections on March 31. Of course, every party is doing its best to push its own point of view. It's unfortunate that so many young people haven't formed their own opinions yet, don't yet follow all the theatrics on the political stage—so the outcome of the voting is unforeseeable. Before the government fell, they rushed to buy tanks, aircraft and all sorts of devilish military equipment—apparently there's plenty of money for that, but none for sports fields, schools, etc. Lots of tax increases, little care for the elderly. With America still spending a fortune on its war in Vietnam, of course there is a so-called gold rush in progress. The British pound has already fallen, and the dollar is weak. Wealthy people are exchanging their pounds and dollars for gold. On Saturday and Sunday, the directors of the banks in the gold pool countries met in Washington—there are two gold markets now, one fixed at 35 dollars an ounce and one free one—and of course there will be lots of speculation. What will the consequences be?"

In the last years of her life, Mientje paid regular visits to Letta in Edegem to see her grandchildren Jan and Lina. The family didn't want Mientje to be by herself in Drongenhof for too long, especially in periods when Willem was off with Griet, "painting the town red." She had severe arthritis, and stumbling around that empty house on her own had become seriously risky. She would take the regular bus from Ghent to Astridplein in Antwerp, where she would wait with a cup of tea in Brasserie Le Paon Royal until Letta arrived in her car to pick her up. In the park was a lane of beautiful old beech trees, one of which had a small pool by its roots, where rainwater collected over rotting leaves. Her granddaughter Lina asked Omoe Mientje to stir the dark water with her cane, which she obediently did. A little further down the path, she scattered white snow-berries out ahead of her, so that the children could crush them under their feet for the satisfaction of hearing them burst. "Omoe had a special cane that supported her elbow. She limped slightly, swaying from side to side," Lina writes.

Mientje struggled with her fast-deteriorating health; she had a hereditary genetic mutation that kept her blood cholesterol at a constant high level. Her troubles included coronary artery constriction, calcification, and fluid accumulating in her lungs; more and more often, she panted her way through her difficult days. She did a lot of knitting for her grandchildren in those lonely months, soothed by the ticking of the needles in the silent house, and on her Sunday visits, when Letta asked if she was making progress, she said with a wistful smile, I still haven't reached the end of my yarn.

She didn't hold on quite long enough to see Adri become chairman of the board of the Dutch-language Belgian broadcasting company, BRT, but his illustrious career as a champion of cultural policy for the Flemish cause had always been a comfort to her; she had so many anxieties about the political situation that they almost brought on yet another heart attack, so she retreated into her prayers and her Bible reading. That was in 1968, sometime in the politically turbulent spring. One day in May she watched through her open door as a mob of shouting students marched past, chanting dubious slogans, some carrying sticks. The sight gave her a sharp, constricted feeling, her heart pounded, she shut the door and went to read in the half-light of the middle room.

On November 11, 1968, two days before her death, she wrote about the commemoration of the First World War, which had ended exactly half a century earlier. But even the war in Vietnam occupied her thoughts right up to the end; she never ceased to be horrified by the violence in the world and the misery it created. "That's still painful for me to think about," Jan writes, "and I know it's hard for my mother Letta, too, to talk or write about it."

—

From a letter from her grandson Jan:

"I did not witness Mientje's death. A few weeks earlier, she had paid us a visit and spent the night . . . She must have had another heart attack in the early morning of Wednesday, November 13, 1968. By then she had been sleeping, alone, in the dark middle room on the ground floor for several years. When Opa was home, he would sleep in the third-floor bedroom. Willem had left a bell next to the sofa where she slept so that she could get his attention if something went wrong. Although she tried to call out to him or wake him up, it didn't work, and that was the cause of her death. You know from your own experience how big the house is, how distant two people can be from each other . . ."

Letta remembers that Mientje lived on for a few hours after the attack; Adri rushed over and sat by her bedside until she let out her last breath. The Dutch relatives in Zevenaar were informed; Mientje was "laid out tastefully in the middle room, she had just had her hair cut the day before, it wasn't an unpleasant sight, we were grateful." On Saturday, November 16, Mientje was laid to rest following a ceremony in the church in Brabantdam, led by the pastor dearest to her heart, Van Stipriaan, who had come from the Netherlands just for that purpose. He delivered the sermon and directed the choir. Griet was absent. Willem arranged for coffee and a lavish buffet in the fabled Restaurant Du Progrès in Korenmarkt Square; you can't let your family go back to Holland on an empty stomach, he said. But the meal did little to bring them closer together.

Oh yes, Letta adds, at the funeral I couldn't stop thinking of that story about the early years of their marriage. As you know, when my parents were newlyweds, before 1930, so before Adri was born, Willem rented an apartment in Grotesteenweg in Berchem, across the street from the brewery, for Mientje to stay in whenever he was in Ghent, or "on the road" for work, doing God knows what with God knows who . . . When my father told me that, not much more than a year before he died, I said to him, Oh, you filthy swine, treating a devout religious woman from the Dutch countryside that way . . . and he replied, It showed her from the very start what it meant to live in the city. My mouth dropped open, Letta tells me; my mother had always said, with every new trouble or sorrow, I hope this will never happen to you, my girl. She once pointed out to me the apartment he'd banished her to. Look, over there, she said, I lived there for a few months. And it suddenly comes back to me now, Letta adds, that I saw a violin on the windowsill there, and it made me think of Handel's "Largo," strange how clearly I can picture it. She swallows and is silent.

———

On May 25, 1984, almost sixteen years after Mientje's death, an event was held to mark Adriaan's departure from the Willemsfonds, the independent liberal organization where he had served as president for twenty years. A farewell speech was delivered by Michel Oukhow, a well-known cultural figure in Antwerp and a good friend of the leading Flemish poet Maurice Gilliams. Oukhow was of Belarusian ancestry, had grown up in a Protestant environment, and later became an energetic advocate of secularism in Flanders. His speech attributed Adriaan's broad cultural interests and lifetime of service to Mientje's influence:

That intellectual interest has another source: there was a house in Drongenhof in Ghent, and that was your house. I know of no other house frequented by so many students, not because of your sisters—though they were friends of ours—but because of your mother, that wonderfully sweet woman your mother was. Generations of university students, now professors or scholars, or politicians, whatever measure of success they have had in their lives, look back in gratitude on her warmth and hospitality, her calm, quiet conviction . . . At difficult times she offered support, much more so than advice. She could listen. The joy she radiated was all the greater because she herself had known her share of trouble . . . Behind the heated debates was that strong and resolute woman . . . we didn't have to ask any questions, because she saw with a glance what answers we needed . . .

7

It is June 1971; I am sitting in the hallway with a couple of my fellow students, waiting to take an oral exam for my introductory survey of the history of the Low Countries. Every time someone comes out of the professor's office, we all leap up and pelt them with questions—What did he ask? Is he in a good mood?—which meet with a hesitant frown and a mumbled reply: I'm not sure, hard to tell what he's thinking.

I leaf through the textbook one last time; I can't clear my head, confusion takes hold.

Finally it's my turn; I've tied my long hair into a ponytail and put on a formal shirt that makes me feel ridiculous. Entering the room, I half stumble over the thick coconut mat.

Have a seat, my friend. Your name? All right.

What can you tell me about . . .

The mustached professor's eyes bore into me. He asks his questions in a tone of grim perseverance, as if to say, I hope you're the one who will finally give me a decent answer. Sitting closer to him than ever before, I see for the first time that his hair, always combed in just the same way, is actually a wig, clinging ungracefully to his head.

He clasps his hands together and looks me straight in the eye, awaiting my response.

I gulp, there's a ringing in my ears, I can't think of anything else but that hairpiece, in my mind's eye it is sliding off his head, I have to suppress a foolish giggle. Darkness comes over me like a warm blanket in which I am wrapped up, engulfed, *verhulst* . . . I can't think anymore. But I seem to be talking.

When I stop, it feels like coming up for air, and I notice the professor's astonished face.

No, Mr. Hertmans, he says in a slightly pinched voice, you are mistaken, that was a hundred years earlier. Come back sometime in September, after you've cleared a little more space for studying in your calendar.

Next.

I stumble outside.

And . . . ?

Repulsed by Verhulst, I stammer.

Now, so many years later, I can picture him at his lectern, already in place before we began our usual disorderly surge into the lecture hall. And strangely enough, he would remain there until the last of us had left. None of us wondered why; it was just the way Verhulst was.

Until one day I left behind my textbook on the folding desk and had to go back for it.

In the deserted, neon-lit auditorium, I saw Professor Verhulst walking from his lectern to the upholstered door beside the large blackboards. His misshapen foot caused him to limp, an invisible ball and chain.

In September I breezed through the re-examination, for which, if memory serves, he gave me a passable but ungenerous 12 out of 20. Even so, I couldn't shake the feeling that I owed him.

—

In those years, the ambitious professor had something other than stammering students on his mind; in fact, he was fighting for the very thing they were shouting about in the streets. His stature was such that Godfried Bomans included him in his renowned series of television interviews *Een Hollander ontdekt Vlaanderen* (A Dutchman discovers Flanders). Bomans also spoke to philosopher Jaap Kruithof, but could never have guessed that two of his guests had been shaped in part by their experiences in the house in Drongenhof. Adri was uncomfortable with Bomans's jocular tone as he inquired about the professor's many activities, and his answers were curt. He wasn't in any mood for lighthearted banter, and later felt offended and ridiculed when Bomans described him in a book as having a "Burgundian" outlook and belonging in a painting by Brueghel. This description played into Dutch stereotypes about those hedonistic Roman Catholics down south, when in fact Adri Verhulst was the Protestant son of a Dutch mother, while Bomans himself, ironically, was Catholic. Verhulst had fought for a Flemish Cultural Pact designed to guarantee religious freedom and pluralism. He was the architect of radical reform in the liberal culture fund, he supported abortion rights, mutual toleration between religious and ideological groups, and public media that truly sought to educate the people. He opposed the subdivision of the public broadcasting system by religion, advocated splitting the university in Brussels into Dutch-language and French-language institutions and ensuring equal cultural rights for the Flemish minority in the capital, and condemned the Flemish Movement's ties to

the South African apartheid regime. Thanks to his Protestant background he stood, to some extent, above the fray, but he had strong
principles. For example, he barred an extreme right-wing splinter group
from protesting with shovels over their shoulders, because that stirred
up memories for him that were dark indeed. He was a feared and
respected opponent in all public debates about culture or equal rights
for the Flemish. Soon afterward, the media fell under the spell of neo-
liberal free-market ideology; for him, with his humanist convictions,
that was a huge disappointment.

Adri made his last public statement in September 1999, when a legislative amendment providing financial support to surviving collaborators
was declared void by the Court of Arbitration. This legislative proposal
had been intended to make life easier for the surviving collaborators,
who were quite elderly by this time, and for their families. Among the
Flemish, there was a widespread feeling that the court's decision was just
the latest in a long series of vengeful acts orchestrated by French-speaking

groups. Yet the proposal had been controversial in the Flemish parliament, adopted only because of support from the far-right party Vlaams Blok, which was deeply rooted in collaborationist circles; in other words, the members of parliament who had supported the proposal had dirtied their hands. Adri's open letter was a kind of request for political clemency, and it spoke volumes. Adri began by acknowledging that the Flemish cause had been thoroughly discredited by large-scale collaboration with Nazism, but he went on to argue that many of the punitive postwar measures had been unjust, a vengeful form of "repression based on Belgian nationalism." The letter can be read as a personal confession of Adri's beliefs about the life of his father, who by then, in 1999, had been dead for almost a quarter-century; it shows that some wounds stay fresh. Yet at the same time, he was writing his book *Son of a "Bad" Fleming*, which would be published a few months later, and in which he mentioned in passing that his former student Stefan Hertmans was living in the house in Drongenhof where he himself had spent his difficult childhood.

8

Now that Mientje is gone and Willem returns regularly to the near-empty house in Drongenhof after work, he is struck by one memory after another. He's parked his Mercedes in front of the house, but before entering he goes for a stroll through the narrow alleyways of Patershol. Could Omer De Ras still be alive? . . . He looks up at the window from which long ago an attractive young woman once stuck out her head and shouted to him, *Salaud!* The window is cracked and dusty. On his way back, he passes the old chapel. As he is groping for his key, he runs into Ada—Ada with her ever-present cane and her clubfoot. *G'day, Mr. Verhulst, how are ye?* Fine, Madame Ada, how is Arnold? *Still the same ol' guffernothin,' Mr. Verhulst.*

He opens the door, smells the familiar damp odor in the high-ceilinged entryway, and walks through to the deserted annex. In the backyard, he sees the wisteria clutching the fence in its skinny black tendrils. He closes the back door with the rusty key, puffs his way up the stairs to the third floor, and stands there peering out of the window for a while; a clump of putty has come loose and is tapping against the window in the breeze, *tin tin tin, let me in.* On the ridge of the partly collapsed roof of the glass workshop, pigeons are walking back and forth, their heads bobbing like mad, looks like they're walking along the horizon, he thinks to himself. He finds the photo of Kees Boeke, holds it in his hands for a while, and puts it back on the dusty mantelpiece. What a hollow sound his heavy shoes make on the floorboards in the big, empty room. On the drive back to Antwerp, he is troubled by stomach acid and melancholy. He drives straight to Griet's apartment, goes inside, and says, Titi, will you marry me? A strange, dry cough escapes him.

One day at breakfast with her husband, Letta opens the paper and scans the headlines with half an eye. On the last page she sees the marriage announcements: without telling anyone a thing about it, her father has gone and married Greta Latomme. Rudi, she shouts, guess what he's done *now*? They've heard nothing about a wedding or even a reception; maybe they had a quick ceremony at city hall and then shared a pot of mussels with fries at their favorite restaurant, just across the Dutch border in Philippine.

He's considering moving back to Drongenhof, but the idea doesn't sit well with Griet. The rent was paid up until sometime after Mientje's death; he doesn't know what he's thinking, why can't he free himself from that house now that Mientje is gone? All right, Wim, if that's really what you want, let's go. So they pack up all their things and move to Drongenhof. Griet doesn't care for memories; as she always says, she lives completely in the now. After just a few months, she is tired of going up and down those stairs all day long, and of the rickety old furniture—all that bric-a-brac, she says, it's not her style. She returns to her apartment, and for more than a year they split their time between the two addresses; sometimes he spends the day alone by the hearth in the front room, gazing into the fine Comblanchien fireplace, smoking and woolgathering. What could have happened to that impressive bust of Hitler? What were they up to behind his back when he was in the clink? It's late; he looks up from his book; he slips the bookmark between the pages, shuts it and yawns. From past the harbor, the big, strong east wind brings the sound of rattling freight trains, an interminable string of containers, tank cars, auto carriers and closed cars, no one knows what's inside them, they rattle on minute after minute, trains without end, a clatter that spreads through the night like a cloud; the sound reminds him, just as he falls asleep, of large switchyards, night trains, war years, empty platforms. The trains rattle and rumble and finally silence falls, night gathers the house in its folds, amplifying its faint hints of life, from the creak of the smallest floorboard to the whisper of sandy dust beneath old wallpaper.

A photograph has been preserved of Willem in the backyard in Drongenhof, possibly from the last year that he lived there; it shows a Flemish statuette of Mary between two decorative Dutch clogs on a whitewashed wall. On the left, a tendril of Mientje's wisteria seems almost to be groping its way toward Willem. He wears a slight grimace, but it may also be the smoke from his cigarette end. "Smoke gets in your eyes . . ." Could that milky eye still feel the sting of smoke?

It is the autumn of 1970. In Drongenhof, Griet is cold. The chill in the high stairwell depresses her. The whole neighborhood does, really, the ragged people with their twisted faces. The smell of the sewers fills the streets and sickens her. The glass workshop straight across from their door is a ruin, with rats running in and out in the dusk. She hates it here, she longs for her imperial city.

But then something happens that knocks her socks off; she is walking home from Vrijdagmarkt with her shopping bags and there, in one of the alleys, she runs into a man whose face she recognizes, but from where, from where? It's . . . who is it? Let me think . . . By the time she reaches Drongenhof she knows for certain; she rushes into the hallway and shouts, Wim! Wim! That actor from *Citizen Kane*, what's his name, Orson . . . Orson Welles is here, walking around Patershol! Wim shoots her a skeptical look and asks if she treated herself to sherry at the market, but she says no, come with me, you'll see. And seeing as it's almost noon and he could use a little glass of something himself, he puts on his coat—a little drop at Vrijdagmarkt can't do any harm. They have just passed Drongenhof Chapel when Willem cries out, There! There! That French snotnose! Johnny Hallyday! And yes, it really is the young rock singer rushing by in a white suit, pursued by a film crew with cameras and microphones at the ready. And around the corner, in an alleyway, they find no less than child star Sylvie Vartan in a fur coat with only a skimpy sequined dress underneath. What in God's name is going on here? Then a man comes up to them and tells them the street is closed off and they have to take a detour through Oudburg.

Once they're finally seated and sipping their drinks, they find out what's going on: someone's shooting a movie here, what's the name, based on that book about the haunted house here in Ghent, *allez*, it's on the tip of my tongue . . . that house named after the fox's hole . . . Malpertuis, right! Willem considers this big news; he's just read the book, the leading Flemish author Hubert Lampo translated it from the French, he explains to Griet, it's by Raymond de Kremer, a Ghent writer who publishes under the pseudonym of John Flanders, he writes in French sometimes, the fransquillons call him Jean Ray . . .

It's conceivable that Willem knew about *Malpertuis* even before that peculiar book was published in Dutch translation; the title would have caught his eye right away. Malpertuis is the name of the fox's lair in the well-known medieval saga of Reynard the Fox—and as we know, Willem had an enduring fascination with tales of vulpine cunning. But it had also been the name of the Antwerp headquarters of the Flemish National Union, the wartime pro-Nazi organization in which he had been exceedingly active.

Jean Ray, aka John Flanders, had originally published the book in the war years. The story is drenched in a dark atmosphere of magical realism. An elderly gentleman, Cassavius, finds a collection of ancient creatures, gone into decline, on a Greek island, and loads them onto his ship; when he arrives back at his large, gloomy house in Ghent, he stores the creepy things away in the attic. He hires a taxidermist, no less sinister, to craft new human skins for the formless human clods, and in this garb, like a pack of poltergeists ceaselessly pestering each other, they keep turning the house upside down.

Little by little, the reader learns what is going on in the nightmarish attic of the lunatic-infested house: the nocturnal rustling and whispering, the turmoil, the surreal characters . . . All this is placed in the light of a breathtaking discovery, which gleams in the dark like a gruesome suspicion: dwelling in that haunted house in Ghent are the ancient, ragtag remnants of the Greek gods. Cassavius's mission was to save the dying gods of Olympus, as if they were refugees washed up on an island. But they have become mere shades of themselves, human, all too human—peevish squabblers who have lost most of their memories. They rummage around and lament and hate and desire and live out their tenebrous days in the surreal limbo of that grand old bourgeois house, remembering only vaguely who they once were, kept in line by Lampernisse, a strange ghost who proves to be what remains of Prometheus ...

Time and the powers here are subject to strange whims that impose on one, by turns, forgetfulness and memory ...

Malpertuis was adapted into a movie by the Belgian director Harry Kümel. His chosen locations included the rundown neighborhood of Patershol, the deserted monastery, the alleys and the former Drongenhof Chapel ... The closing credits were impressive: Orson Welles, Mathieu Carrière and Susan Hampshire in the leading roles, French nymphet Sylvie Vartan in her debut, as a singer in a brothel, and yes, Johnny Hallyday making an appearance as the sailor who gets to kiss her. At the end of the trailer, which is on YouTube, a series of tasteless horror images are followed by the word "Malpertuis," dripping with blood, and for a few seconds, believe it or not, you can see Mathieu Carrière crossing the little square next to Drongenhof Chapel, turning the corner and heading toward the glass workshop ...

I later rewatched the entire movie; various locations were spliced into the chase scene in Patershol to spice up the atmosphere, but even so, it shows beyond doubt how neglected and seedy the area was in 1970. The interior shots are partly from the old, dilapidated monastery, the same building where, a few years later, we oblivious students would organize an occupation with our guitars and our joints; by then, the picturesque district faced the threat of complete demolition, because the city council had hatched an insane plan to replace it with a gigantic parking lot. The student protests put a stop to that.

But now Willem, corpulent and short of breath, and Titi Latomme, her arm in his and a lovely new goose-quilled hat on her bleached ash-blonde locks, are staring openmouthed at the goings-on inside four temporary fences; Susan Hampshire is wearing such a beautiful dress, thinks Griet, and oh that look in Orson Welles's eyes, my God, the sight chills you to the marrow . . .

That night Griet dreams that the Olympian creepy-crawlies from *Malpertuis* are haunting the house in Drongenhof; she wakes with a start and says, Wim, I think I had too much vol-au-vent. She gets out of bed and opens the curtain a little, revealing the pale night sky and the tall slanted roof of the old chapel; no, she still doesn't feel at ease here. She lets out a burp or two, feels better, creeps back into bed, curls up against the snoring man, wakes him and says, Wimmeke, what do you say we go and live in Antwerp again?

9

So Willem, confronted with Griet's increasing sulkiness, decides to give up the house. He returns the key to the son of the lawyer Henri De Potter, to whom he owes so much. The notary accepts the key from him. Farewell, Mr. Verhulst, and *bonne chance*. We may sell the house, we'll have to see, he adds, and Willem wonders, what kind of gullible fool do you imagine would buy that waterlogged hovel? But he keeps his mouth shut.

Not long afterwards, Adri, Letta and Suzy go to pick up the few antiques that Willem left behind. An attractive old pew is taken home by Suzy and her husband; the Symphonion accompanies Letta to her house in Edegem. She hangs it in the entrance hall, winds up the old wonder box for her children, lifts a finger in the air, and says, Now you will hear the music of a vanished world.

Willem and his Titi now live in Hove, not too far from Letta, who comes by to look after them. In the summer of 1972, his grandchildren invite him and Griet to join them on a trip in Anhausen, an idyllic Bavarian village near Augsburg. Willem has a new ice-blue luxury Mercedes and insists on driving all the way there without stopping. He zooms down the road, the German landscape makes him cheerful, he sings at the wheel. In Anhausen, to his surprise, he runs into a few like-minded people: a former *Obersturmführer* with whom he gets along like a house on fire, and an ethnic German from Silesia who worked for the *Sicherheitspolizei*. Golden memories, happy days—enough to make you practically yodel with contentment. Together, they admire the onion dome of the local church, the work of a great-great-uncle of Mozart's. They go for a brief walk in the mountains; it suddenly starts to pour; the rain is ice-cold. Willem can't see a thing through his fogged lens; he's too winded to walk on. His two friends support his considerable weight on their interlaced hands and help him to a nearby cabin. No sooner have they arrived than he lights a cigar and downs a few glasses of schnapps. Well, he says, panting and cheerful, the sun's already breaking through the clouds.

But he's going downhill fast now; from 1974 onward he is often bed-ridden, and his condition deteriorates. His stomachaches are growing worse and worse; after a bout of severe vomiting, he sometimes spends the whole day on Griet's sofa, depleted; she helps him into the car, the doctor's diagnosis is late-stage stomach cancer. His dreams are restless and tortured; he wakes gasping for air. But when Griet asks what happened, he says with a crooked grin, As soon as I wake up I forget the whole thing. He refuses to change his diet; the doctor tells him to limit himself to one small glass of red wine a day, but he drinks almost a bottle of white every evening at dinner, and sometimes a little drop of something afterward; he is often grouchy, fulminating against Belgian politicians and the half-assed ways of the traitors to the Flemish cause; he calls Brussels a cancer, the Belgian tricolor an old rag, and his fatherland the sick man of Europe; he declares that they should have been more radical during The War, that the Germans should have rid themselves right away of those arrogant fransquillons in Brussels, that Flanders would be better off attached to the Netherlands, but now things are just as much of a mess up north in Amsterdam, where long-haired bolsheviks roam the streets like savages, smoking drugs and screwing around with each other; the whole of Europe is one huge mattress, as one of those beatniks had the nerve to write. What's become of the world?

In early March 1975, Letta sits at his bedside, holding his hand. His breathing is labored; he keeps nodding off, flinching awake and staring at her in shock; at one point he tries to sit up, mumbling something she can't make out. What is it, Papa, she says, and he says, Tit . . . Titi . . . You have to take care of Griet after I'm gone, will you promise me? Letta grits her teeth, it's the last thing she wants to do, she knows it will lead to arguments with her sister, Suzy, and with her husband, but she promises she will. As she later tells me, You can't say no to your dying father, no matter how outrageous his request is.

But that isn't the end of it. Two days later—looking sallow and wasted, only his swollen belly still bulging grotesquely under the white hospital sheet—he asks her to pour him a glass of wine. But there's no wine here, Papa, she says, what are you thinking? He becomes weepy, saying, You'd refuse me even that, on the last day of my life? So Letta walks to the corner store, buys a bottle of white wine, doesn't tell him it's French Sauvignon, and says, Here, Papa, a nice glass of Riesling for you, and he pecks at it like an old bird, his neck so thin you could almost wrap one hand around it; and he swallows and collapses onto the pillow and says, staring at her with his single eye, My last will and testament, Letta. Listen carefully. He takes one shaky hand in the other and twists off the two wedding rings on his right ring finger. I want to be buried with Elsa. Not a word about this to Griet.

What the . . . ? Papa, she says, what do you mean?

Well, as I said, you should put . . . you should . . . me on top of Elsa. I want to lie on top of Elsa. *With violets on my belly.*

A quiver speeds through him, a laugh that never reaches the surface.

He closes his eyes; Letta sits and stares in astonishment at the wheezing man. He wakes up once more, that evening, but not for long. Griet watches over him from his bedside. Before dawn—the date is March 11, 1975—Willem Verhulst dies. He is buried as he had requested, the SS man above the Jewish woman he loved; they scatter violets on his grave.

*

The death announcement, which it goes without saying is a bright yellow card with black lettering and a lion showing its claws on the envelope, includes a few provocative lines that he had dictated and the children, with more than a hint of fatalism, had agreed to use. They say, in so many words, that he always remained "proud and incorrigible" and express, one last time, his fervent wish for Belgium's downfall.

Letta, holding the card in her hands, shakes her head: "In other words, he had learned nothing."

In 1986, "when Griet took a turn for the worse," the grave, in Berchem Cemetery on the outskirts of Antwerp, was emptied out. Although emptying out graves is standard practice in the crowded Low Countries, it's not often done after only eleven years. Maybe the lease was allowed to expire in order to spare Griet's feelings. She felt cheated; Wim had married *her*, but now he was "lying on top of that Jewish lady." I wandered around the cemetery myself, but of course there was little point. I wondered if Adri had gone there with his children, if Letta had gone to see her father there, and if anyone had put flowers on the grave. Letta's children, Jan and Lina, told me they had visited a few times over the years.

Here come the gravediggers to empty out a row of old graves; the soil is churned up, the shovels flash in the morning sun, and the smell of rotten wood rises with the chill of the earth. They are simple graves; the name Meissner has already faded on the weather-worn cross that the workers throw into a hole in the ground. The remains are bundled together and dumped into the old charnel pit, a mass grave where nameless bones await the Resurrection—and a more capacious bed in the clouds, as the author of "Todesfuge" tells us.

10

There is one last anecdote from Willem's life, which says a great deal, if not everything, about him. After seeking refuge in the Netherlands after the First World War, he had to find work, and at one stage he wrote to Wilhelm II, the German emperor, who by then had abdicated and withdrawn to the rural Dutch village of Doorn. It must have been the autumn of 1919 when Willem applied—as surely as I sit here—to become *gardener to the emperor*. But he didn't get the job; the emperor already had a gardener.

I try to imagine the situation. Willem is still young; he is living in The Hague, with Elsa, as a political refugee; he often goes on at great length about the injustice done to the Flemish activists after the war. At this stage in his life, he describes himself as a "crypto-communist-Christian anarchist" and takes great pride in his friendship with the pacifist Kees Boeke—he appears to be a devoted seeker, confused by the complex political situation and the many opinions booming all around him; he is uprooted, searching for support and clarity. So without hesitation, he does the most absurd thing imaginable: he applies to the fugitive emperor for work. After all, didn't he learn a thing or two at the gardening school in Vilvoorde, near Brussels, where he seduced Elsa and eloped with her? He must feel the time is ripe to give something back to the ruler-in-exile, whose estate in Doorn is not so far away—well, all right, it's a long journey, perhaps more than two hours on the train from The Hague, with a change in Utrecht, but Willem is young and energetic. He receives a courteous reply: a handwritten postcard from the "Grand

Chamberlain to His Imperial and Royal Majesty," bearing a message in elegant Fraktur calligraphy:

> Amerongen, the 26th of November, 1919. In reply to your application addressed to His Majesty the Emperor and King, I have been instructed by His Imperial Highness to inform you that all the positions in question have already been filled and that, sadly, this makes it impossible to grant your request.

The original card, signed and stamped by the grand marshal of the imperial household, is still in the possession of Jan Mahy. It came into his hands sometime in 1972, when Jan was thirteen years old. Opa Willem handed him—"in such a solemn manner that I still remember the moment and the setting"—Wilhelm II's memoir *Ereignisse und Gestalten 1878–1918*, which Willem had cherished all his life. "It was in the middle room in Drongenhof." Tucked into the book was the card from the grand marshal.

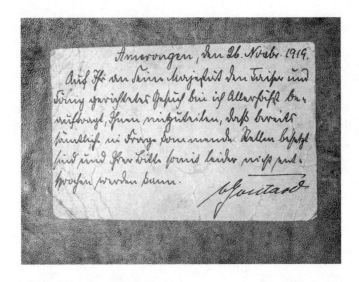

On the envelope was the address where Willem then lived with Elsa in The Hague: Weimarstraat 348.

I blink.

Weimar. Goethe and Schiller.

The republic brought down by the Nazis.

Buchenwald.

I look it up right away; it turns out to be a large corner house with an attractive bay window on the second floor and a small balcony on the third. It now houses an embroidery shop called Personality. Next door is a barber's.

⁓

Still, I can't get the image out of my mind. Amid all the misery the twentieth century ushered into the world, amid all the chaos and hairpin turns in Willem's own messy life, an improbable interlude almost took place: this man of confused ideals, the future SS man who would seize control of his own city's institutions by force with the assistance of armed Gestapo men, and would help to send an unknown number of people to their deaths, raking the serene garden paths of a Dutch country estate under the benevolent eye of the German emperor. They could have exchanged a few words about the weather as the ex-monarch ambled around his park, his hands clasped behind him, gazing with pleasure at the neatly trimmed ornamental bushes. The emperor might have called out to him in the rising morning mist, as the dew evaporated from the roses, *Ha der Wilhelm*, cheered by the sight of his one-eyed, slightly bumbling Flemish namesake spreading compost with an old-fashioned pitchfork. Wilhelm the emperor and Willem Verhulst—a peculiar thought, an imaginary snapshot. Herr Kaiser, Willem says, may I offer you *eine gute Zigarre*? It's a Willem *Zwei*. First-class tobacco from Brabant, *Majestät*. The monarch cannot suppress a hearty laugh. The Emperor and the Gardener—a gripping title for this book, it seemed to me, but I settled on something closer to home, to the house in Drongenhof; I found all the space I needed in those rooms where the walls breathed out stories that settled on the floor like a thick layer of dust, where the pale garlands on the musty wallpaper inspired me, that first day as Mr. De Potter led me on my ascent through the house.

—

Von Gimborn, the ink manufacturer from Zevenaar for whom Willem worked for a short time, planted an arboretum in Doorn. The National Tree Museum, also known as the Von Gimborn Arboretum, is still there; its collection is said to be like no other in the world. There is also a park in Zevenaar named after him: Gimbornhof. There, deep in the Dutch countryside, you enter the park from the Guido Gezellestraat, named after the famous Flemish bard of old. Gezelle, all the way up north there, between the rivers Rhine and IJssel? Could Willem have had anything to do with that? By then his wife Elsa was ill; he had already run into the farm girl Harmina a few times beside his wife's sickbed, never suspecting what their future would bring. He thinks of the revered German emperor he'd hoped to serve; he carries bundles of wood to a barn under the leafy treetops, which are still dripping after a light shower. Hello, Willem. I suddenly wish I'd known you, because then I might have understood more about what went on inside you. I might have smoked a cigar with you; we might have admired the trees together. Then, who knows, maybe I'd have found the stammering start of an explanation.

11

In the ADVN, the Archive and Documentation Center for Flemish Nationalism in Antwerp, I consult Griet's diaries, in which she describes her final years in detail. She kept a thorough record of when Letta called her, when she invited her to lunch or dinner in her home, and when they did groceries together. In her old age she lived alone in a retirement home, receiving regular visits from leading Flemish right-wing extremists and ex-collaborators. Yes, Letta will later say to me, what can you do, I had promised my pa I would look after Griet, I kept my word, we sometimes got along well, other times I enjoyed it less.

Griet's ninetieth birthday was celebrated with a big party in Wijnegem, near Antwerp, on November 16, 1997. Willem's grandson Jan still remembers it well; he refused to attend the event, because the entire Vlaams Blok Party and a few collaborators were expected to show up with their families. The ADVN file includes a booklet printed to commemorate the occasion. I open the book and do a double take: the essay in honor of Griet is by Bart De Wever, now the mayor of Antwerp and leader of the largest Flemish nationalist party, the N-VA. De Wever, who came from a far-right background, must have written it when he was a district councillor for the N-VA's more centrist forerunner, the Volksunie. The third and final "Mrs. Verhulst" was, of course, more popular in Flemish nationalist circles than her Dutch predecessor ever had been.

The young politician calls Griet a "feisty lady who dedicated her life to the cause of Flemish emancipation" and makes an unblushing reference to Griet's membership in *DeVlag*. He mentions a number of former SS men, her good friends and acquaintances; her marriage to "Wim"; her flight with him to Hanover, her arrest, and her refusal to apply for the restoration of her civil rights after her release; her unceasing engagement with the Flemish nationalist cause; some deceased friends who'd risen to the top of that far-right movement; her political work for the Volksunie in the town of Hove; and—a vivid detail—Willem's car, decorated with a Flemish lion flag, which De Wever says was always parked in front of the door to their home. "Prison life was not easy, but Griet never let her spirits sink," De Wever writes with youthful enthusiasm, and he adds, "She meant so much to so many; we hope to enjoy her friendship for many years more."

I stare through the window at the courtyard of the tranquil ADVN building, where I am leafing through Griet's memoir; everything around me is quiet and calming, people talk in soft voices and everyone is friendly and helpful. The booklet for Griet's ninetieth birthday—which, as you might expect, has a black-and-yellow cover—describes the menu in an overabundance of savory detail: cream of North Sea shrimp, a salmon tartlet with green herbs, pork tenderloin in cognac sauce, almond croquettes, and for dessert, a cake decorated for the occasion. But did they drink German or French wine? On that point, alas, the historical record is silent.

Every year, Griet had faithfully taken part in the Yser pilgrimage, an event commemorating the Flemish soldiers who died in the First World War, which became a kind of political rally for the Flemish nationalist movement. She continued to attend even as more and more neo-Nazis showed up to hijack what had once been intended as an assertion of humanist values. She admired Leni Riefenstahl, who would die in the same year that she did; she could grumble on and on about the Egmont pact that reorganized Belgium into a federal state, saying the Flemish had "taken it on the chin" when the "cowardly Belgian politicians" had given French-speaking citizens in the Flemish communities around

Brussels the right to government services in their own language; she complained that it was a disgrace that the lion on the Flemish flag had red claws and a red tongue after the war, a symbolic concession to the Belgian tricolor flag that she despised. But most of all, she went on hating "sanctimonious phonies," as she had ever since her years with the nuns in Eeklo; although she remained a member of the Christian teachers' union, she went on taunting and provoking the credulous and the devout until her final months. In the retirement home where she lived, she still had a framed photo of her Führer on her dresser. She could sometimes stare at the portrait for hours, as if witnessing an apparition—like Flaubert's character Félicité, a humble working-class woman who confuses her parrot with the Holy Spirit. One warm July day, Griet became unwell, lost consciousness, fell into a coma, and drifted out of this world without realizing. Some girls have all the luck.

12

It took me a while before I learned who had made the bust of Hitler displayed in the front room of the house in Drongenhof, and I was surprised when the trail led to a friend of mine.

Koenraad Tinel is one of the best-known contemporary sculptors in Flanders; one day I visit him in the charming country manor where he has his workshop. In the courtyard, a vegetable garden and a bed of flowers have burst into the abundance of early summer. To my left, I see the workshop's entrance. I approach the open gate, keeping as quiet as I can; he has his back to me and is hammering away. Inside are unearthly sculptures in mixed media—rusting steel, rough wood, crumpled balls of indefinable fabric soaked in plaster and wrapped around strange figures. In their midst, the sculptor—a stocky, balding, well-muscled man in his eighties—is hammering with the intensity of Hephaestus at his volcanic forge. With unfailing intuition, he turns brusquely and spots me there.

Hey there, buddy, he says, putting down his sledgehammer, wiping his hands on his leather apron, coming over and throwing his arms around me. Then he smiles at me, his blue eyes sparkling as no one else's can, looking me up and down with an approving nod; the collarless shirt under his thick apron is a pristine white; his hands, gnarled with labor, grab me by the shoulders again.

Shall we have a drink? he says with a smile. We go into the large, cool house and drink white wine.

This compact, powerful man—who had just barely turned five when he sat in the half-ruined Ekkergem church and drew the broken slate roof tiles on the floor, which had fallen and shattered in an earthquake—goes through life with a deep scar. In the Second World War, his father and brothers were fanatical Nazis. He tells me the story with a bitter expression, shows me photos of his brothers in gray uniforms and one of the whole family: his father's cold stare in the background, the foolish arrogance on his adult brothers' faces. He himself is a small boy, next to his mother on the sofa, his arm around his little sister's shoulders. He ends with the resentful obituary published in a right-wing flamingant newspaper after his father's death; from the brittle, yellowing paper, words leap out at me: son of the Golden Spurs, indignities, idealist, punished, man of the people, disgraceful injustice—the familiar clichés with which, for decades, a whole generation of Flemish nationalists refused all moral responsibility for collaborating with the Nazis.

Koen, I said, what do you know about that bust of Hitler in Drongenhof, the one that must have been on the mantelpiece? He sighs. My father, Frans Tinel, was a sculptor, as you know. He had a workshop in Ekkergem, near the German military hospital, and paid regular visits to the *Verwaltung*. Every right-thinking Belgian shook like a leaf when they had to go there, but my father played the friendly local artist. He made plaster-of-Paris busts of the Führer and brought a few of them to the headquarters there. He produced dozens of them, all from the same mold—they must have sold well. I once heard him say that the busts he had made were all over Ghent. He once carved a huge head of Hitler out of wood; he wanted to have it delivered to his beloved Führer. What a fool . . .

His lips curl into a grimace.

My father had a soft spot for all that propaganda rubbish the Nazis came up with—*Jud Süß* and all that drivel . . . he'd been friends with the elegant fascist aristocrat Joris Van Severen, who liked to speak French, often visited us, and used to flirt with my mother, who was a real beauty . . . I should mention that we had a huge house, with twenty-seven

351

rooms . . . there were photos of Van Severen hanging all over the house, next to posters that said, *Juden Raus!* . . . yes, August Borms used to visit too, my father called him a saint, and the young poet Lieven Rens, a famous name back then, have you heard of him? . . . that big-mouthed pip-squeak used to come by with that Verhulst fellow of yours—they were personal friends. Ah, well. We were actually a very cultured family—my father, Frans, was the nephew of Edgar Tinel, the celebrated Flemish composer who became the royal family's *maître de chapelle* and lived in the fashionable Zavel district of Brussels . . . but it's all tainted now . . . my brother wasn't much better; he joined the *Sicherheitspolizei*, the kind of people who chased the arrested Jewish families onto the trains at the Kazerne Dossin transit camp in Mechelen, kicking those terrified people up onto the straw and tossing a bucket in after them before slamming the doors, with moronic grins on their faces . . . a textbook example of cruelty, so proud of their German slogans and their swastikas, all lining up and sticking their arms out in front of them . . . my brother admired all that, the stupid ass, and my father was even a camp commander somewhere . . . my other brother came back from the Eastern Front seriously wounded, maimed for life . . . he was in the SS-Panzer-Division Wiking, he helped to defend Hitler's bunker to the last . . . after the war, people spat on the sidewalk when a Tinel passed . . .

The old sculptor swears under his breath and sinks into his memories.

After a long silence, he goes on: I don't hate them, they're my family, after all, but it still makes me furious when I think about it. Not a day goes by that I don't have a mental argument with my father . . . but there was never any hope for reconciliation, his resentment outlasted everything . . . if my father had shown some insight or regret, even just for a second, I would have grabbed him and said, Come here, you're my pa . . . but no, he remained embittered until his last gasp, gray with hate and misplaced pride . . .

He falls silent again, we stand and wander back to the large, open gate; in the countryside around us, animals are grazing. In a barn by the entrance, he shows me the old tractor, which he preserves like a precious jewel. His timeworn hands stroke the hood. Now you know where the bust of Hitler in your house came from, he says. Another hug, in the quiet of the late afternoon, and he whirls around and heads back toward the house.

13

A Friday, June 2019.

It's market day in Ghent—a market that for several years now has been as colorful and multicultural as its counterparts all over Western Europe. The statue of the local hero Jacob van Artevelde stands over the stalls with one arm outstretched, gazing valiantly into the distance. It's supposed to be an awe-inspiring gesture, and it dates from long before the twelve dark years of the Reich, but with just a little bad will, you might imagine that the "Wise Man of Ghent," a fourteenth-century Flemish leader, is giving what amounts to the well-known German salute. History is a prankster with no sense of propriety. *Gestapo*, we would shout at the statue when I was a student, the same term we used to taunt the Ghent City Police. We loved to snatch the officers' caps off their heads and run off with them—a memorable act of heroism, performed in the name of global revolution.

I have an appointment with Roger, the elderly dean of the Patershol parish. I've known Roger for decades; you couldn't walk the narrow streets of Patershol without running into him. An energetic man with a long career on the Belgian railway behind him, he is now ninety-five years old. He came to live in Drongenhof in 1949, when Mientje was raising her children on her own and the house was buzzing with lodgers.

When I ask him about the SS man who lived on his street, he doesn't remember right away, but he tells me an astonishing tale about Drongenhof Chapel, where a group of resistance workers went into hiding during the war. In the attic! he says, opening his eyes wide and lifting a didactic finger high in the air. There, under the huge peaked roof, they'd set up a

354

whole hideout up there, with weapons and everything. I stare at him in surprise. You mean around a hundred feet from Willem's bedroom as the crow flies, under that tall pitched roof, the one he could see if he lay down in bed?

That's right, Roger says, and one day when the SS caught wind of the rumors that something was going on there, they sent two men to inspect the place. The chapel had been deserted for years by then; it was covered in pigeon shit, the floor was ruined and they found nothing. Then they climbed the stone steps to the rood loft, went on to the next narrow wooden staircase and ascended it carefully, because they thought they could hear the sound of feet shuffling above them. And just as they were about to kick down the door, they were pulled inside and had their throats cut. Of course, the resistants had no idea what to do with the two half-beheaded SS men; if they were found, the Germans would take revenge by razing all of Patershol to the ground and murdering half the people who lived there. So what did they end up doing? They chucked the bodies down the stairs and pulled a couple of old gravestones loose from the church floor; as you know, there were a few seventeenth-century abbots buried there, and even an organist and his wife. They dumped the two SS men into the old graves there and pushed the stones back into place. No one's figured out exactly where the bodies are yet; you can't go lifting up the whole chapel floor for a couple of Nazis. I think the SS believed they had deserted, and no one ever looked into it. By now, years of neglect have taken their toll on the chapel; everything is smashed up, and even the old graves are buried in sand.

I stare at him, astounded; it's unthinkable that anyone but Willem could have sent those SS men to the chapel; who else could have come up with the improbable idea that resistants might be hiding under the roof, except for the man who stared at that roof every night as he lay in bed? Had he just been chewed out for losing those two SS men, that time when he sat with Mientje and bawled like a baby?

That is not the only story Roger has for me.

One day—the lively old man tells me, speaking the most colorful Ghent dialect I've heard in years—one day, in the town of Menton in southern France, a fellow strikes up a conversation with me because he's heard me talking and can tell I'm from Ghent; he tells me he made a fortune soon after the war collecting waste and filling canals and waterways, the Lieveke for instance. Ah yes, I say, the old waterway that used to run alongside Drongenhof, that's where I live; I'm sure you didn't have to look far to find material for filling it, the streets were strewn with shattered bricks in those days. Get out of here, the man says, I didn't use rubble from the streets, I filled the Lieveke with fly ash. With fly ash, beg your pardon, what do you mean? You heard me right, he says with a nod, just after the war the Ghent power plant installed two big new Cockerill ovens, and I collected all the fly ash, the ash left over after you burn coal; it's filthy stuff, I'll tell you, gets into your lungs, sometimes I didn't know where to put it all, truckload after truckload of the stuff, so when I heard the Lieveke had to be filled, I didn't think twice, I had my boys dump the whole mess in there.

Roger looks at me with a twinkle in his eye, as if he's just told a hilarious joke. So the filled Lieveke, my dear friend, is full of heavy metals, the most hazardous oxides and other muck. Fly ash is normally used to make paving stones and asphalt, but in this case it was just chucked into the water along a row of houses. You needn't wonder, Roger goes on with a grin, why the gardens would hardly grow around here back then; things have already improved, I think the poor trees must transform the poison through their roots, but then again I'm not trained as a gardener like your Mr. Verhulst, couldn't tell you for sure.

But in Mientje's diaries, I protest, she writes that the city gardeners did their level best to plant flowers here. I read to him from the diaries I have with me:

September . . . Even our little park here looks very pretty—the city parks department keeps it in good shape. But the public has to learn to pitch in and keep it clean.

Yes, the gardeners did their best, Roger says, but after a few weeks the new plants would start to droop. It's the fly ash, we would tell each other back then, those plants have been *gassed* . . . er, that is . . . Anyway, you've seen for yourself how unstable it still is here, and how black the soil is in the neighborhood parks, and how hard it is to grow anything . . . And what about that boat, I ask, is there really a sunken boat in the Lieveke or not? Course there is, he says, but it's not German—just an old tug that got stuck in the mud and couldn't get free, so Mr. Garbage Man filled it with rubble to make it sink as deep as possible into the silt, that was a big job in its own right, and then they just dumped the fly ash on top of it . . . I saw for myself when they sank it, I still remember the boat cracking open in the middle and the onlookers shouting, *Drown it! Drown it!*

As for turning it into a German boat after the war . . . well, everyone loves a good story.

I step outside, stroll through Oudburg, and stand still for a moment in the walkway to the old MEGA courtyard. Unrecognizable. Nothing anyone might remember, not a trace of the past. Only the sound of someone practicing clumsy drum rolls. The Turkish restaurants are still empty at this hour, the streetlamps shed patches of pallid light on the pavement; I wander the alleys of the old working-class district, assailed by memories. I find myself looping back to the same little square, Kaatsspelplein; night has fallen now, and I see in the glow of a streetlamp—clearer than ever before after a dusting of rain—the glazed bricks light up on the chapel's right wall, forming patterns. There's the first figure: a Star of David, unmistakable, and a big one at that. I stare at it, taken aback; in all the years I've lived here, I've never seen the star shine so bright. Why was the chapel decorated with a Star of David in 1607, when it was built? Did Willem ever see it?

Oh—I picture him skating with the beautiful, graceful Madame Hevesy in the water-meadows. Later, she must have had a star just like this one on her coat.

⁓

Then I stop in front of the house again. The black paint I used on the door decades ago is still flaking off. I walk to the end of the street, turn the corner and see the back of the house, the garden and the old gate. As I approach, a bright spotlight flashes on. But the light only makes it clearer: around one of the rails there is still one last tendril, a fragment, like a scrawny black arm clutching in a void, without a root, without a trunk, the last remnant of Mientje's wisteria. I lift my arm and place my hand on the brittle wood. Then more lights wink on in the house I know so well; a figure comes to the window of the porch, peers outside, sees me there in the spotlight; a woman opens the door and asks in a loud voice if she can help me. I tell her I wanted to touch that black branch. She shuts the door fast and locks it, convinced there is a lunatic at her back fence.

A few days later I return to take a picture of the vine. In the drab light of day it looks even leaner and blacker, a kind of snake clinging to emptiness. It won't be long before it loses its grip, lands in the dusty earth of the little park and vanishes there without a sound; not a soul will know what it once meant.

Epilogue

In the end, perhaps driven by some kind of fetishism, I visited Comblanchien. The name of the brown and pink marble of the fireplace kept going through my head. It wasn't even an especially interesting fetish: I just wanted to see the source of the marble that decorated the front room of the house in Ghent and had supported the vulgar plaster bust of Hitler. My thoughts kept returning to the contrast between those two forms of calcium: the polished French stone and the plaster-of-Paris head.

Only then did I learn of Comblanchien's night of horrors, August 21, 1944. Because the Germans knew they had lost the war, their reprisals against the locals grew more senseless and sadistic with each passing day. Rural Comblanchien had resistance fighters hiding out in the solitary woods around the vineyards, so the Germans regarded the village as a den of terrorism whose unyielding winegrowers and stonecutters undermined their authority by remaining loyal to the French tricolor and to their age-old *terroir*, a word that bears an unfortunate resemblance to "terror" if you don't speak much French. It could have been a beautiful night, one chronicler writes; the evening was mild, a few German sentries were sauntering through the streets, and despite their drowsiness after swilling exquisite wine looted from local taverns and chateaus, there was tension in the air.

Just after curfew, two young men come cycling from the nearby wine village of Nuits-Saint-Georges and notice a couple of empty German trucks blocking the entrance to Comblanchien; a little later, they observe that the road from Corgoloin, at the other end of the village, has also been blockaded by German vehicles. Just after nine-thirty, a few barns are put to the torch. Several SS men fire into the air to simulate an attack by the resistance; multiple witnesses will later say there was no trace of any resistance fighter for miles around. Stormtroopers race over from the city of Beaune; thirty shouting MPs and eighty soldiers form a cordon around the village, their guns at the ready, as if responding to the threat of an attack. Five machine guns are installed in the village center. Three collaborators speak in whispers to the Germans, pointing toward particular streets; most of the villagers have no idea what's happening. Without warning, a couple of doors are battered in; the occupants are thrashed, kicked and beaten in the hallways of their houses. Amid shouts of "*Terror!*" "*Terrorismus!*" "*Terroristen!*" ten houses are torched with flamethrowers, with their occupants inside. When the soldiers notice that some villagers have escaped through the fields and vineyards, they set more houses on fire, and pillage, pummel, shout. Not all the houses are attacked; the operation has the hallmarks of a blind reprisal. Several women come out onto the streets in their nightgowns, shivering in the summer night. Because battering the church door with rifle butts is not enough to break it down, the SS men drive the villagers in the streets into a group near the town hall; twenty-three men are taken to a train waiting at the station. It is midnight; a few more violent attacks and identity checks follow. The air is filled with screams, wails and gunfire. Later that night, fusillades are heard in the nearby quarry; the shots echo against the high rock face, grotesquely loud. Then silence creeps over the village; the only sound is the crackle of the houses burning down. Around four-thirty in the morning, it is over; the trucks depart. In the half-light before dawn, heaps of rubble still smolder, sending sparks drifting over the valley to vineyards covered with dew in that hour before sunrise. The train full of hostages leaves the station, heading for nearby Dijon. On the

362

way there, a young man is foolhardy enough to ask a German soldier what the point is of all this senseless violence. "The good must pay for the wicked," a *Feldgendarm* replies.

In front of the church in the village square, the list of executed victims shows the arbitrary nature of the reprisal. Their names are carved into a monumental stone from a local quarry. Comblanchien came within a hair's breadth of complete obliteration, like the much better-known village of Oradour-sur-Glane.

I drive through the vineyards to the quarries I have seen so often from the highway. When I finally reach the enormous *carrière*—a vast, unfathomable, cruel basin, a wound in the landscape that goes on for miles, a gigantic trap, a mountainous void where distant bulldozers crawl along the walls like peculiar insects. From closer by comes the crunch and whine of enormous crushers, a sorting belt, a couple of large cranes—the sheer desolation leaves me breathless. Dust clouds rise to towering heights in the gray air. After my trip through the fresh green April woods, I seem to have arrived in a lunar landscape. So this is the source of the fireplace in the front room, I think to myself. This is the story Mientje wanted to tell Willem the time he couldn't think of the name Comblanchien, but he wouldn't listen, he didn't have time, his friends were waiting in the bar.

I stand and gawk like a child.

I drive the circuitous route up to the edge of the ravine and walk from there to the entrance to the stoneyard. A young woman with a yellow helmet drives up to me right away in a small off-road vehicle and asks me gruffly what I'm looking for; nothing, I say, I'm not looking for anything, I just wanted to take a few pictures of the quarry, that's all. You'll have to sign in at the shed over there, she tells me, and get written permission from the management. All I want is a couple of pictures, I tell her, and I show her my mobile phone with an innocent smile. Be quick about it, then, she replies, it's not really allowed here. Why not? I ask, but she's already rolled up her window. Spraying gravel behind her, she speeds down the rough path to the rocky hell below. The huge blocks of stone that protect the quarry from prying eyes like mine look almost prehistoric, resembling primitive tombs.

Not until I'm back on the highway does it occur to me that the night of horrors in Comblanchien took place just a few weeks before Willem Verhulst fled Drongenhof.

Wir kommen niemals zurück.

Bibliography

The Ascent is based on historical facts and extensive documentary research, supplemented with the author's imagination. I made grateful use of the following sources:

De Wever, Bart. *Feestrede ter ere van Griet Verhulst en Mia Brans*, Antwerp: Archief voor Nationale Bewegingen (ADVN), November 16, 1997.

Latomme, Greta. *Memoires*. Antwerp: Archief voor Nationale Bewegingen, n.d.

Vandermeulen, Lieve. *Van vingerhoed tot voorzittershamer, Georgine Blanchaert 1883–1965*, scholarly paper, Utrecht University, 1996.

———. "Kroniek van een leven," manuscript, 2010.

Verhulst, Adriaan. *Zoon van een »foute« Vlaming*. Antwerp: Pelckmans, 2000.

Verhulst, Aletta, with Suzanne Verhulst. *Dochters van een fantastische moeder*. Edegem: self-published, 2013.

Verhulst, Willem. "Wils jeugd," manuscript, Verhulst family archives, n.d.

———. prison letters and poems, Verhulst family archives, n.d.

Wijers, Harmina. *Dagboeken*, August 29, 1944–June 26, 1946.

———. *Dagboeken*, August 11, 1946–March 6, 1947 / May 31, 1967–March 18, 1968.

———. *Dagboeken*, October 25, 1947–June 10, 1951 / October 24, 1966–May 17, 1967.

The following publications were also very helpful:

Aerts, Koen. *Kinderen van de repressie: Hoe Vlaanderen worstelt met de bestraffing van de collaboratie.* Antwerp: Polis, 2018.

Aerts, Koen, et al. *Was opa een nazi? Speuren naar het oorlogsverleden.* Tielt: Lannoo, 2017.

Boeckmans, Louis. *Hoe ik Breendonk en Buchenwald overleefde,* with Pieter Serrien. Antwerp: Horizon, 2019.

Claeys, Wim. *Mijn papa was bij de SS.* Ghent: Borgerhoff & Lamberigts, 2018.

De Dijn, Rosita. *Gasten van de Führer: De vlucht van Vlaamse collabora-teurs naar nazi-Duitsland tijdens de bevrijding in september 1944.* Antwerp: Manteau, 2014.

De Wever, Bruno, Martine van Asch, and Rudi van Doorslaer. *Gekleurd verleden: Familie in oorlog.* Tielt: Lannoo, 2010.

Flügel, Heinz. *Zwischen den Linien: Autobiographische Aufzeichnungen.* Munich: Christian Kaiser Verlag, 1987.

Gobyn, Winne. "De Sicherheitspolizei und Sicherheitsdienst: Een case-study aan de Gentse Aussenstelle 1940–1945." Master's thesis, Ghent University, 2002.

Ponteur, Leo, et al. *Liber Amicorum Adriaan Verhulst.* Ghent: Willems-fonds, 1995.

Rauser, Jürgen Hermann. *Neuensteiner Heimatbuch.* Neuenstein: Heim-Verlag, 1981.

Saerens, Lieven. *De jodenjagers van de Vlaamse SS.* Tielt: Lannoo, 2007.

Seberechts, Frank. *Drang naar het oosten. Vlaamse soldaten en kolonisten aan het oostfront.* Antwerp: Polis, 2019.

Vandeweyer, Luc. "Etnische zuivering als politiek project in België," *Belgisch Tijdschrift voor Nieuwste Geschiedenis,* no. 5 (1999), 43–71.

Van Eetvelde, Robby. *De Sicherheitspolizei und Sicherheitsdienst (sipo-sd) Aussendienststelle Antwerpen: Het politionele repertoire van een lokale Duitse politiedienst in bezet België—Bijdragen tot de eigentijdse geschiedenis.* Ghent University, 2008.

Van Goethem, Herman. *Het jaar van de stilte.* Antwerp: Polis, 2019.

Verschooris, Marc. *Hoe zwart in het donker gedijt: De Sicherheitsdienst en de Sicherheitspolizei Gent-Leeuwarden, 1940–1945.* Leuven: Davidsfonds, 2016.

Acknowledgments

This book would never have been written without the active and unflagging support of Aletta Verhulst and Suzanne Verhulst, who offered me an abundance of information, documents, recollections and hospitality, and encouraged me to see the project through to completion.

I would also like to thank Jan and Lina Mahy, Aletta Verhulst's children, for their generous support and assistance, their careful reading of the manuscript, and their suggestions.

My thanks to Professor Bruno De Wever and Professor Koen Aerts for their help in obtaining access to the court documents, their collegial support, their critical reading, and their comments.

My thanks to the staff of the State Archives branch office in Ghent and the National Archives in Brussels, especially Mr. Luc Vandeweyer.

My thanks to Laurent Stevens for the photograph of the knobs for the Ghent Radio Rediffusion Service, and Benjamin Praet for the issues of the *Brüsseler Zeitung*.

I owe a debt of gratitude to Koenraad Tinel, Lieve Vandermeulen and Roger Van Bockstaele for my discussions with them and the information they provided.

My profound gratitude goes to my editor Suzanne Holtzer, my diligent guide throughout the years that I spent on this project, and to Nienke Beeking, for her assiduous copyediting.

I remember a series of crucial conversations with my publisher Francien Schuursma, in Montpellier, Frankfurt, Amsterdam, and Beersel, which decisively influenced the shape of this book. Her continuing support has been vital as well.

I also thank Wil Hansen, Herman Balthazar, Chantal De Smet, Marc Reugebrink and Jan Vanriet for their critical readings of successive versions of this story.

Finally, my thanks to my wife, Sigrid, who has not only been by my side, with patience and understanding, for all the ups and downs of the complex journey that led to this book, but has also been my devoted and incisive reader.

A Note About the Author

Stefan Hertmans is the prize-winning author of many literary works, including poetry, novels, essays, plays, short stories and a handbook on the history of art. He has taught at the Royal Academy of Fine Arts in Ghent and at the Sorbonne, and lectured at the Universities of Vienna and Berlin. His first novel to be translated into English, *War and Turpentine*, was longlisted for the Man Booker International Prize, and was chosen as a book of the year in *The Times*, *Sunday Times*, and *The Economist*, and as one of the ten best books of the year in *The New York Times*.

A Note About the Translator

David McKay is a translator of Dutch literature living in The Hague. He received the 2017 Vondel Prize for his translation of Hertmans's *War and Turpentine*.